Seeking Scandal

by

Nadine Millard

BLUE TULIP
PUBLISHING

Seeking Scandal
by Nadine Millard
Published by Blue Tulip Publishing
www.bluetulippub.com

To my husband, children, family and friends for your continued support.
To the Ging Gang Girlies for tea, scones and brainstorming galore!

PROLOGUE

LADY CAROLINE CARRINGTON smiled as she watched her sister Rebecca dance a beautiful waltz with her newly acquired fiancé, Edward Duke of Hartridge.

They looked so wonderful together and so very in love that it almost brought a tear to Caroline's eye. Almost. One did not cry in public.

Her sister had never looked happier and who could blame her? Never in Caroline's life had she seen a man so desperately in love as the duke was with Rebecca. It was a joy to watch and if Caroline felt a little pang of envy well then, that was to be expected. After all, the duke had been intended for Caroline herself!

The marriage contract made between Edward's late father and Caroline's father, The Earl of Ranford, stated that the eldest daughter of Ranford would marry the eldest son of Hartridge. Caroline had been made aware of the contract the day she left the schoolroom, and so her formative years had been spent learning to be the perfect duchess, the very epitome of a lady.

Ironic then, that Edward would travel to their estate in

Ireland having no clue that such a contract even existed, and fall head over heels in love with the scandalous force of nature that was Caroline's younger sister.

Caroline held no ill will toward either of them however. It had been clear to her from the beginning that she and Edward would not suit. The problem was now she felt... lost. She had been raised to be a duchess. She had been raised to stifle silly things like emotions and romantic notions.

Seeing Rebecca and Edward fall in love had made her yearn for the same thing. Was it so wrong for her to want love instead of wealth? Romance instead of a title? How she wished that she could have had both like Rebecca!

She had hoped that seeing Rebecca become a duchess would take some of the pressure off her own shoulders. It appeared however that it had just spurred her father on.

Edward had arranged for her parents and older brother Charles to attend this evening. Caroline had been thrilled to see them since her father had suffered ill health and had been separated from them while the girls had their Season. But once her Father had been settled in their Mayfair townhouse, he had summoned Caroline to his study and sat her down with a smile and a pat to her hand.

"Well Caroline dearest, has any young earl, or dare I hope duke, caught your eye this Season?"

Caroline's mind immediately flashed to Mr. Crawdon, the Duke's extremely wealthy but untitled cousin.

"I cannot say that any has father," she answered truthfully. The truth was, she hadn't even looked at another man since she'd met Tom Crawdon.

If only her father could be persuaded to be satisfied with one titled lady in the family...

"Papa," she began, "surely you are well satisfied with a duchess amongst your daughters, regardless of which of us it is! I am sure I could marry a squire now and you would not object." She said the last with a little laugh so her father would not suspect that she had an ulterior motive to the seemingly innocent statement. She could feel the tension in her shoulders as she awaited his response.

If only he did not care. If only he wanted her to be happy, regardless of who it was with.

Her father peered at her for a moment as if trying to gauge her seriousness before he laughed and patted her hand affectionately.

"My dear girl," he said, "you know I only want what is best for you. But a squire? You are the eldest daughter of an earl, bred to be a titled lady. I would not be happy to see you with anyone less than you."

Once again, Caroline's mind flashed to Tom. Successful, wealthy, more handsome than any man had the right to be. Less than her? He was so much more than she could handle she literally struggled to breathe around him.

Schooling her features to the nonchalance she had practised since her childhood, she smiled serenely and tried again.

"But a title does not make a man, Papa. Why, look at all the wealthy gentlemen from excellent families who do not possess a title, but certainly possess everything else you would look for in a son-in-law."

Her father studied her once again, much more intently this time, making Caroline feel like he could guess what was going on in her head.

His voice was sterner now as he reiterated his refusal to settle for anything less than a peer for his eldest girl.

"My dear I am not getting any younger. And I think we can all agree that my health scare this summer has made it necessary to plan for the future." He held up his hand when she would have objected, and she was struck by how frail it appeared. "I have great hopes that your brother Charles will do a good job as Earl and look after you and your mother. But he is young and somewhat foolish right now. It will put my mind at ease to know that you are settled with someone who deserves you, someone from your own sphere, someone who can give you the lifestyle that you have been raised to."

Her father talking in such a way made her feel guilty and went a long way towards quieting her objections. Perhaps he was right. She had been raised to achieve the highest pinnacle of success. Or at least the highest pinnacle available to a lady, which was an excellent marriage. The problem was, and it was a fairly big problem, she had gone and fallen in love with her future brother-in-law's cousin!

Caroline glanced at her father and was shocked once again to see how haggard he looked. How pale and worn and... old. Perhaps the conversation had been too much for him. Had worried him. Feeling suddenly ashamed of how selfish she was being, she resolved to do anything she could to make life easier for him. And if that included marrying a peer? Well, so be it.

She had smiled reassuringly at her father then and had taken her leave to return to the dowager house that she and Rebecca had spent their summer in, lest she ruin the surprise of her family's arrival for Rebecca.

And so here she stood, surrounded by music, flowers, and love and her heart was breaking every second of it. Not that you would be able to tell by her demeanour. A lady did not show emotion in public, she reminded herself, as her icy blue eyes scanned the room. She remained poised, aloof, and...

Her heart stopped. Actually stood still. She had not thought that really happened though she had read of it in the gothic novels Rebecca was so fond of and that she, Caroline, pretended not to read.

For making his way toward her was Tom, Mr. Crawdon, she corrected herself. It was time to break the tenuous connection that was forming between them. She must. For the sake of her family, for her father. She must. She could not think of him as Tom, her Tom.

She watched as he sauntered in her direction, his deep blue eyes intent on her face. Caroline briefly considered looking away so as not to encourage him, but he was so breathtakingly handsome, and she was a woman after all. With eyes no less. It was only natural for her to look!

Tom stopped in front of Caroline and she felt the all too familiar hitch in her breath and slam of her heart. Really, she would require the help of a doctor if she spent much longer around him!

"What you do to a man with your beauty, Lady Caroline," he spoke quietly, his smooth voice causing her heart to gallop even more.

Caroline was not sure how she should respond. She knew what she *wanted* to do of course. But one did not throw oneself at a man in the middle of a crowded ballroom. So she stayed quiet.

"Shall we dance?" he asked, extending his large hands towards her.

Caroline stared at the hand as her mind conjured up an image of the last time they had danced...

Vauxhall Gardens, the awful night Rebecca had been kidnapped and Edward had been nearly driven mad trying to find her. The night had not started out as terrible. It had been, in fact, quite spectacularly wonderful. Caroline had become caught up in the excitement of the evening, the feeling of the rules not being quite so important. She had spent the night dancing with Tom. Talking, laughing, falling more and more in love with him...

He'd kissed her for the first time that night. An utterly life-changing kiss that had shattered all of Caroline's carefully constructed plans to marry a peer and be a leading lady of the *ton* within a few years. His kiss had awoken a side to Caroline that she had begun to suspect lurked beneath her poised and polished outward shell from the first time she'd met Tom.

That was the night she'd stupidly begun to think that perhaps she would be free to marry whomever she liked. Not that Tom had offered, but a girl could always dream…

Yet now, here she stood. Making every effort in the world to look as though she were enjoying her sister's engagement night when all the while she wanted to cry for what she was about to lose.

She would not refuse him this dance, would take every opportunity to be in his arms. It would be strange anyway if she did not dance with the cousin of her future brother-in-law. People would notice. And talk. And nothing scared Caroline more than having people talk about her in a negative fashion.

After this, she would begin to distance herself. She would stop talking quietly with him in corners, stop looking forward to snatched moments alone. She would not encourage him to be anything more than a polite acquaintance, though the thought caused her nothing but pain.

For now, they would dance. Caroline shivered slightly as her hand touched his. It was a dance, just a dance.

Tom could see the play of emotions, usually so well hidden, flicker across Caroline's beautiful face and he had to force himself not to ask what was going on in her head.

He had decided, having spoken to Edward at length about it, that he would make an offer for Lady Caroline tonight.

The truth was he had fallen irrevocably in love with the beautiful, proud Caroline and had been driving himself mad wondering whether it was selfish of him to pay his addresses knowing that he would never be good enough for her.

But then, what man ever would be? She was, quite simply, perfect.

The dance ended and Tom led her to the veranda outside.

He knew that the right thing to do would be to approach her father first. And he had fully intended to do so. And then he'd seen her.

She took his breath away. Her beauty was such that it almost frightened him. She stood at the edge of the dance floor; her blue eyes pierced him every time she looked in his direction as she scanned the room lazily. The sea green colour of her dress made her golden hair gleam even more and her peaches-and-cream complexion seemed all the more fair. He could have wept. How did she get to be so damned beautiful and not even realise it? For she certainly did not realise it, so sure was she that her sister was the beauty of the family. Lady Rebecca's beauty was enough to send men to war, Tom could admit. But Caroline — Caroline was the only woman in the world for whom he would fight a war single-handed. And he who had never been shy with the ladies, who had the success that other men merely dreamt of when it came to the fairer sex, was as nervous as a lad on the cusp of manhood.

She was too good. That was the problem. Too beautiful. Too refined. Too much better than him in every conceivable way. And yet he loved her. So, although it may be selfish to ask her to tie her life to a man who, although very well off and successful in his various business endeavours would never be more than just a man, he was going to ask her to be his wife.

He felt sure she was beginning to feel the same way as he. The night they'd kissed had affected Tom more than any other experience in his life so far. Such a feeling could not be one sided. Could it?

Tom thought back to his final talk with Edward that morning as he guided Caroline silently toward the steps leading to the dimly lit garden. A fat lot of good that talk had done him!

As soon as Tom had asked Edward about the first time he'd realised that he'd fallen in love with Rebecca, Edward's eyes had glazed over and the look on his face had become altogether seductive. Tom felt certain he could go his entire life without ever seeing that particular expression on his cousin's face again.

Shortly after, Edward had excused himself to find Rebecca. And judging by the sounds coming from the closed library door that Tom passed on his way out, he could only assume that find her he had.

One piece of advice that Edward had given him, which struck Tom as being very sensible, had been to take any opportunity he could to tell Caroline how he felt.

"I almost lost Rebecca, Tom," Edward had said, the fear and pain of that night still evident in Edward's expression and desolate voice. "My life would have ended that day had I been too late to reach her. I could never have lived with the knowledge that she did not know how I loved her. Do not make the mistake of waiting until it's too late."

Caroline's shiver brought Tom back to the present. The evenings were getting decidedly cooler now that the summer months were drawing to a close. And she did not even have a wrap to protect her from the chill. Wordlessly he shrugged off his jacket and placed it over her shoulders. She was taller than her sister, yet his jacket still dwarfed her.

He wondered if he should be concerned at her silence. But he was too nervous to think on it overly much. Besides, he realised he hadn't actually spoken a word.

"Caroline," he squeaked. Marvellous, he had just sounded as if his voice were breaking. He tried again. Clearing his throat he stuttered, "Caroline, there is something I must speak with you about."

Caroline gazed at him expectantly. Damn but she was beautiful. He felt the now familiar pull of attraction that had given him constant sleepless nights and uncomfortable breeches.

He must not get distracted. There would be plenty of time for that sort of thinking after they were married...

The moment had come. Here it was. Right here. He should speak. Any moment now he would. *Speak*, he told himself.

He felt his throat close up as he became unable to talk. At all. He could not utter a word.

Caroline's face changed from expectant to confused. She was going to think him insane.

In his head, he could hear exactly what he wanted to say. It was beautiful! Romantic, poetic. But his mouth was refusing to cooperate. And so they just stood, staring at each other. It was excruciating. Tom could feel a cold sweat break out on his brow.

"For God's sake man," he told himself, *"get a hold of yourself and tell her that you love her, you want to be with her, that nothing makes you happier than the thought of her being your—*

"Wife!" he shouted. One word? One word came out in that entire spiel? Heaven help him.

"I beg your pardon?"

Tom froze up again. Surely she would give up and walk away soon.

In desperation, he did the only thing he could think of to try to rectify the situation.

He reached out and grasped her shoulders, pulling her toward him and bending his head toward hers. He could hear her breath hitch, feel her galloping heart and he smiled, suddenly realising that this was the easiest thing in the world to do. Propose to the woman he loved.

Just before his lips touched hers, before he took them both on a journey of pure sensation, he whispered, "Marry me."

Her heart stopped. For a moment it actually stopped. He felt it. He also felt when she stiffened in his arms. He looked up in surprise and was confused and more than a little scared by the look of despair on her face.

She pulled away from him and turned her back, her head bowed. It was a testament to how much he'd lost his mind because of her that even in his concerned state he could not help but notice the smooth arch of her neck.

But now was not the time.

"Caroline, I—"

"Don't!" She whipped round and he noticed that her eyes were filled with tears.

"Don't what? Tell you that I love you? That I *have* loved you almost from the second I've known you?"

"Tom, please," she sobbed as tears began to fall freely down her pale cheeks.

Tom felt as though he'd been punched in the gut. An overriding sense of fear came upon him. He'd been sure, so sure, that she loved him too. What if he were wrong?

"I had expected a rather more joyful reaction," he quipped, falling back on his failsafe of humour that he used to cover any strong emotion he might have.

The joke failed to raise a smile in either of them.

Taking a deep breath, he asked the questions that he dreaded hearing the answer to.

"Do you not love me? Do you not want me?"

Caroline's heart constricted painfully at the vulnerability Tom tried to cover with bravado. Her entire being ached with sadness. This moment should have been the happiest of her life. He loved her! Oh, and how she loved him. How she longed to be his wife.

For a moment she was tempted to throw caution to the wind and accept. She was sure that her father would not cut her off. And even if he did, Tom was one of the wealthiest men she had ever met. Surely he would not care if she had no dowry.

Here was her chance at the type of happiness she secretly dreamed of. She could have a love to rival Rebecca's and Edward's. It was tempting, oh so tempting to accept.

But her mind threw up the image of her father, frail and old before his time, sitting in his study and spelling out his plans for her. His wishes. She thought of the years of schooling in the art of being a perfect society lady. A perfect wife to a perfect peer.

She thought of her family's plans for her, and of the hope in her father's eyes as he dismissed any notion of her being anything less than a countess, a duchess, a marchioness, anything other than a woman happily in love.

Could she really do it? Could she disappoint her family? She who had never, ever put a foot wrong? Who did not know *how* to be anything other than the perfect lady, the perfect daughter.

How was she to face her parents, the *ton*, after doing anything other than what was expected of her?

Heaven help her, she was too weak, too concerned with the opinions of others; she knew that. She could not break the habit of a lifetime no matter how much her heart cried out for it.

Taking a steadying breath, she dredged up every ounce of that iron self-control that had earned her the title of Ice Queen amongst the crueller villagers back home and schooled her features to an emotionless mask.

"Tom, I have never asked for your love. Never sought it."

She saw the exact moment that her words registered. His face disclosed first his shock, next his anger and worst of all, his despair.

"That does not mean that I did not give it. Caroline, please — I know you must feel something for me."

He gripped her shoulders, his hands biting painfully into

her flesh.

Caroline could feel tears pool in her eyes and willed herself not to cry again. This was too difficult. She needed to get rid of him before she gave way, before she changed her mind.

But she could not stand the look on his face. The doubt and sadness.

So she smiled weakly, it was the best she could do.

"I do, Tom."

"Then marry me, dammit."

"I cannot."

"Why the hell not?"

It struck Tom at that moment that he was probably the only love-struck potential groom in the history of society to shout and swear at his potential wife. But he cared not. He was scared. Terrified, in fact. Although he had always known he was not good enough for her, he had been convinced that she loved him enough to flout the rules.

He should have known better. She was the very epitome of the rules. And being a slave to propriety, she was about to ruin all his chances of happiness.

Caroline bit her lip in a valiant effort to stay composed. She knew she was about to throw away her only chance of real happiness. She could very well go on to marry a peer and live in the style that her parents expected, nay demanded for her. But her heart would be forever torn from her chest.

Her next words were designed to hurt and anger him enough that he would leave without a fight. She would not be strong enough to say 'no' if he should fight for her.

And she was far from strong enough to live with the disappointment of her parents and society. She was weak. So weak, in fact, that she didn't deserve him.

"I am the daughter of an earl," she began in a flat, emotionless tone. She removed his coat that smelled so like him it hurt to let it go, and held it out for him to take. "It behooves me to marry someone within my circle, someone my father considers an equal."

She almost wept as his face took on the expression of someone who had been utterly crushed. As soon as he turned his back, her own face, she knew, would look the same.

"You cannot mean that. Caroline, I love you. Does that not mean anything to you?"

Caroline weakened a little.

"It does," she whispered and her voice cracked alarmingly. Her control was slipping. "Just not enough."

He stared at her for what seemed like an age.

And then, she felt it. The moment he broke away from her. The moment that her arrow hit home. The atmosphere changed between them and all at once he was a stranger. And she, the worst sort of snob.

"Then this is it."

Suddenly panicked at the thought that she would never see him again, selfishly wanting to still be able to look on his face, she answered, "Not really. We shall see each other at the wedding."

Tom grimaced as he took a step away from her.

"I think not."

"You will not miss it, surely."

"You think I would stay? That I would want to be around you and the family so desperate for you to have a title over love?"

He shook his head and turned away. Before taking his leave altogether, he turned back.

"I envy Edward. It seems he took care to fall in love with the sister who possessed a spine."

Then he strode off, returning to the ballroom, no doubt taking his leave for good.

Caroline felt the huge, gaping hole in her chest where her heart had once resided. She wanted to throw herself to her knees and sob for her lost love, for Tom's hurt, for her own damnable weakness and inability to fight for what she wanted.

But she would not. A lady did not show vulgar displays of emotion. She had let him go because she was not willing to give up the person she was. So she wiped her eyes and straightened her shoulders. Then she made her way back into the ballroom, determined to start the future she had mapped out for herself. And if it felt right now as if she had mapped her own path to Hades, well, that was a decision she must live with.

CHAPTER ONE

Two Years Later

CAROLINE CARRINGTON BREATHED deeply as she once again took in the sights of London's busy streets. Her heart fluttered as it remembered the sounds, the smells, the buildings surrounding her.

She could not believe that she was finally back here, ready once again to embark on a Season. This Season, however, held far more import than her first, two years ago. For this time, Caroline would not leave without a husband or, at the very least, a fiancé.

Her ice-blue gaze took in the enormity of the house before her. Edward, Duke of Hartridge and her brother-in-law of almost two years, obviously did not believe in doing things by halves. The splendour of the house took Caroline's breath away, and she had been living amongst splendour her whole life.

As she stepped out of the carriage the huge black door opened and a little army of footmen began to descend on the coach assisting with bags and giving the coachmen instructions for where to stable the horses.

Caroline's excitement mounted as she climbed the steps and entered the spacious entrance hall of Rebecca and Edward's London home.

She had spent two whole years away from the hustle and bustle of London and although she had only spent one brief Season here, it had been the happiest time of her life. Her smile faded and her heart contracted painfully at the memory of her loss as her mind once again conjured up the image of Tom Crawdon walking away from her.

Caroline was surprised and a little worried that the memory still had the power to affect her so. But she had promised herself she would put the heartache behind her and do her best to find a suitable match, appease her parents, and start to live her life. Her father was growing weaker, and the weaker his body got, the stronger his demands for Caroline to marry became. In fact, he was so adamant that she marry he had given her one chance, one Season to find a suitable match. If she didn't, he would do it for her.

And she knew whom he had in mind. Lord Doncastle, a significantly older earl who lived on a crumbling old estate in Cork, miles from her family seat, her friends, and anyone she knew. Caroline had met the earl only a handful of times when he had travelled to Offaly to visit her father. He was boring, arrogant, and entirely inappropriate whenever he had the opportunity. She shivered in disgust as she thought of him. She would not marry him. She could not! So she was determined to find a husband for herself this Season — at the *end* of this Season to be specific. For her plans were twofold. Yes, she would hunt down a suitably staid and titled gentleman. But first...

Her thoughts were interrupted by the appearance of the butler.

"My lady," the tall and rather stiff butler greeted her with a deep bow. His grey hair indicated an advanced age but his face seemed relatively line free. Probably because he'd never expressed an emotion in his life, she thought wickedly. "My name is Jenson. Please do let me know if you require any assistance during your stay. If you will follow me, I shall direct you to the drawing room to await—"

Jenson's ever so proper speech was cut short by an unholy screech from the top of the stairs as Rebecca came into view and saw her older sister.

"Caro!" she yelled, loudly enough to make Caroline wince. Jenson remained impressively unaffected. He was obviously used to the mistress of the house by now.

Caroline's face split into a wide grin as she watched her sister race down the stairs and skid to a halt in front of her.

"Oh it is so good to see you," said Rebecca breathlessly.

Caroline pulled her younger sister into a tight hug and said, "And you, dearest."

Rebecca pulled back slightly and looked at Caroline in shock. Caroline did not blame her. She had never been one for public displays of emotion. In truth, she was rather surprised at herself. When had she last hugged anyone so enthusiastically? *Had* she ever hugged anyone so enthusiastically? But the fact that a hug should cause such a reaction made her feel strangely sad.

Caroline wasn't sure what had come over her. But it had been so long since she'd seen her sister, almost six months. Edward and Rebecca's first born, Henry, was just about to have his first birthday. Rebecca looked as deliriously happy as the last time they'd met, at Ranford Hall for Christmas. And now Caroline felt suddenly overwhelmed by those terribly unladylike things, emotions.

Rebecca recovered soon enough and gave Caroline a huge grin as she linked their arms and set off, not to the drawing room as Caroline expected, but to the stairs.

"Jenson, have Lady Caroline's things brought up to her room please," she called over her shoulder as they made their way up the grand staircase. "I shall show you where to freshen up shortly," Rebecca chattered, "but first you simply must see Henry before he goes down for his afternoon nap. You will not believe your eyes when you see how big he's gotten. And he is so like his father, truly a mirror image…"

Caroline smiled with pleasure as her sister rambled on proudly about the young marquess. Then laughed a little at the thought that she was outranked by her one-year-old nephew, she being a mere daughter of an earl.

When had her thoughts become so fanciful? Probably around the time she had decided to finally take her life into her own hands. The thought caused her skin to prickle in a mixture of excitement and nervousness.

Caroline allowed Rebecca's conversation to wash over her as she thought of her plan. She must inform Rebecca immediately of her intentions. She was, after all, to stay here for the duration since her brother Charles had chosen to forego the Season in order to learn the family business, and she would therefore be unable to stay at the Ranford townhouse.

Besides, nobody could scheme better than Rebecca Carrington! Or rather, the Duchess of Hartridge, as she was now known. If anyone knew how to be scandalous without creating her own ruination, it was Rebecca. And Caroline would make sure she made full use of her sister's talents before this Season was through.

"Caroline, are you even listening?" Rebecca scolded good-naturedly, bringing Caroline's mind back to the present.

"I am sorry, I was wool-gathering," responded Caroline apologetically.

"No apology necessary, I know the journey is tiring. I shall leave you to rest. You can see Henry later if you wish."

"Oh no," answered Caroline immediately, "I cannot wait

to see my darling nephew again. I shall nap when he does," she quipped.

They arrived at the nursery door and Rebecca swept in and scooped Henry from the nursemaid.

Caroline felt her heart squeeze as she looked at her adorable baby nephew. His face broke into a wide grin at the sight of his mama and his chubby hands grasped Rebecca's face before he leaned in and planted a loud kiss on her cheek.

"Oh, what a clever boy you are!" crooned Rebecca before turning to Caroline, her face a picture of maternal pride.

Caroline rushed forward and grabbed Henry from Rebecca's arms, spinning him round to his obvious delight.

"Oh, you beautiful boy, how big you have gotten!" she said as she settled him against her shoulder. She had to agree with Rebecca, he was the very image of his father but his big brown eyes definitely came from his mother.

He blinked curiously at her a couple of times before clearly deciding that she would do as a comfortable spot to stay and settling his head on her shoulder.

Caroline inhaled sharply at the deep pang of — well, she didn't quite know what to call it — shot through her. Longing, she supposed? Envy? How she would love a child of her own. The thought took her surprise. It seemed her thoughts were doing a lot of that lately. Caroline had never considered herself the maternal type.

Caroline had known, of course, that she would need to provide an heir for her husband, whomever that may be. But she'd always thought of children in an abstract way. Another task to be completed in the quest to be the perfect society wife. But now, holding her nephew who was snuggled so securely into her, inhaling his sweet baby scent and stroking the riot of jet black curls, she felt quite desperately that she wanted this for herself.

She experienced emotions that she rarely allowed herself to feel well up inside her. Perhaps she was just more tired than she'd thought.

It wasn't long before Henry gave in to tiredness, and was soon sleeping peacefully in the arms of his aunt. Reluctant to let him go, Caroline settled herself into one of the nursery chairs and rocked him gently before her own fatigue began to get the better of her.

The handover from Caroline to Rebecca was done with military precision. Swift changeovers and no noise. Henry stirred a little as he was placed in his cot, but soon settled and the sisters tiptoed quietly from the room.

They wandered down the corridor to Caroline's room so that she could freshen up and wash the carriage dust from her face and hands. Caroline's abigail, Sally, entered the room not long after Caroline and helped her change into a freshly pressed afternoon dress.

Rebecca had offered Caroline the chance to rest first before taking tea and catching up properly, but Caroline was anxious to talk to her sister about her plans for the Season so they agreed to meet in Rebecca's drawing room in thirty minutes.

Caroline entered the room and found Rebecca waiting with the tea things. The room was quite small, but was very beautiful and very feminine. It had been decorated in a pale lemon with accents of floral prints dotted around in the curtains and some of the cushions on the plush sofas.

"Rebecca, this is lovely," said Caroline in admiration as she took in her surroundings then sat by her sister and took the proffered cup.

"Isn't it? It had been the most jarring shade of red when I moved in. I really wanted somewhere that was just my own. Edward told me to take it in hand, and so I did."

Rebecca sighed contentedly then turned her attention back to Caroline.

"Now—" she started gazing shrewdly at Caroline's face— "I have seen that there is something on your mind from the second you arrived. Pray, what is it?"

"Whatever do you mean?" started Caroline innocently.

"You've either done something wrong or you're about to,"
said Rebecca frankly. "I know because I am extremely familiar
with that expression, though I admit I never thought I'd see
you wearing it."

Caroline smiled. "Someone needed to take over as Queen
of Scandal since you married and settled down to wedded
bliss," she quipped.

"I am glad you at least acknowledge the change in me.
Everyone else refuses to."

Caroline laughed. "Rebecca, I jest. I know as well as
anyone that you haven't changed a jot. Why, did you not write
to me only last month about the unfortunate incident with
Lady Carlton's French windows?"

"I told you that was not my fault," Rebecca objected hotly.
"Who knew the blasted things were so fragile?"

"I believe most people are aware of the fragility of glass,"
answered Caroline.

Rebecca huffed. "Are we to speak of Maria Carlton's
overrated windows, or whatever it is on your mind?"

They had wandered off topic, Caroline thought. But then,
they had a lot to catch up on.

She took a deep breath. This was it.

"Alright. The truth is, I need your help."

"Of course," Rebecca replied immediately. "With what?"

"As you know, Father has demanded I be either married
or engaged by the end of the Season."

"Ridiculous, but yes. I am aware."

"And do you also know that he has decided I will marry
Lord Doncastle if I can't find a groom myself?"

Rebecca stared at Caroline in horror.

"Lord Doncastle?" she gasped. "Is he even still alive?"

"As to that, I cannot be sure," answered Caroline dryly.
"But he is titled and widowed and that is all that interests

Papa."

"But this is outrageous," spluttered Rebecca. "We cannot allow this to happen. The very thought turns my stomach."

"Believe me, I have no intentions of marrying Lord Doncastle."

"So that is what you need my help for. To find you a husband?"

"Not exactly," began Caroline a little hesitantly. She wasn't quite sure how to phrase her request. "I do not wish to sound in any way conceited, but I am not overly concerned about finding a husband."

Here, Caroline blushed a little and continued, "I do not mean that I should have men begging to marry me," she explained hastily, "It is just that, well, my dowry is quite sizeable and—"

"And you are beautiful, kind, clever, and everything else a lady should be," interrupted Rebecca. "Do not worry about sounding immodest, dear sister. You are the least conceited person I know. You are, if anything, completely unaware of what a prize you are."

Caroline blushed at the compliment. But she soldiered on, unwilling to be distracted now that she'd built up the courage to talk to Rebecca about her plan.

"Yes, well thank you. But as I said, I am not concerned about finding a husband. Especially in three months."

"Then what is it?"

Caroline took a big breath. There was no sense dancing around it, she might as well borrow some of Rebecca's famous bluntness and come out with what she wanted.

"I want to have fun."

To be fair, when said out loud it really did not sound overly significant.

Rebecca looked confused. Which was understandable.

"Fun?" she repeated.

Caroline nodded.

"Fun," she reiterated. Just in case there was any confusion.

"Right."

There was a pause while Rebecca waited for Caroline to elaborate. Which she didn't.

"Right," Rebecca said again. "Well, there are a lot of events planned. You know the Smithson ball is this evening and of course I planned to host a dinner to welcome you so that should be… fun."

Caroline smiled. "I should explain."

Rebecca nodded enthusiastically.

"As you are well aware, all my life, or at least since I outgrew the nursery, I have been schooled to act a certain way. Behave a certain way. Be a certain type of lady."

Rebecca merely nodded again and waited for Caroline to continue.

"It has never bothered me, doing what was right, what was expected," Caroline went on. Her mind flashed to Tom Crawdon and the image of him walking away from her when she rejected him. She inhaled swiftly at the sharp pain that cut through her heart.

"Almost never bothered me," she corrected softly. She could see Rebecca's expression and the curiosity stamped on her face but ploughed on before her sister could give voice to the questions she must have about the 'almost.'

"Now I find that being the good one doesn't have as much appeal as it once had. Not that you were bad, just—" Here she coloured a little, not quite knowing how to phrase what she wanted to say.

"Just scandalous, headache-inducing, and altogether troublesome?" Rebecca asked ruefully.

Caroline smiled. "Yes, something like that. But you're also exciting, spontaneous, entertaining and… well… fun! Besides Mama and Papa haven't called you a headache in years."

"Yes well, that's because I give them to Edward now

instead," quipped her sister.

Rebecca leaned forward and grasped Caroline's hand. "I must ask, what has brought all this on?"

Caroline sighed. "I will marry well Rebecca, you know I will. I will do what is expected. Behave as I'm expected. But, for once in my life I would like to be *un*expected! To misbehave a little."

Caroline saw Rebecca's look of surprise and smiled wryly.

"Yes I can see how shocking this must be for you. But that is why it is so important to me. Do you know I almost gave Father another heart attack two weeks ago because I wore blue to a dance? That was it. That was all I did. Wear blue instead of white. Imagine being so good, so utterly, unbearably good that wearing a different colour causes upset!"

Caroline could feel tears beginning to form at the back of her eyes. Tears of frustration, disappointment, embarrassment. She did not know quite what she was feeling. All she knew was that if she were to shackle herself to the 'right' husband for the rest of her life, she wanted to live a little before she did so.

"I want to live, Rebecca," she explained now, her conviction shining in her crystal blue eyes. "I want to be spontaneous. I want to flirt, dance, laugh, and even be a little scandalous. Just once. Just for one Season. Then I will settle down to be a good Society wife as I promised Papa I would."

Rebecca did not answer for some time. When she did, her voice was gentle and, it seemed to Caroline, a little sad.

"I have no doubt that it must have been incredibly difficult for you, Caro. Carrying the burden of responsibility for all of us. We both know our parents never expected much from me and although Charles is now beginning to mature, I don't believe London has seen a rake like him since Tom left for the Americas."

If Rebecca noticed Caroline's reaction to Tom's name, she

did not comment on it.

"I realise now how unfair it was for Papa to pin all of his hopes and expectations on you. But you play the dutiful child so perfectly I suppose I never even thought that you wanted more. And *I* want more for you. But not just for a Season before you marry. Caroline, you are entitled to happiness, not just for a Season, but for always! All your talk of marrying the right person, doing the right thing. It's admirable but sadly lacking the ingredients for a happy marriage. What about love?"

Caroline could not know that her stricken expression spoke more to her sister than the words that left her mouth. She covered it quickly enough but Rebecca had seen it and knew that something or someone was hurting her sister very much.

But rather than confide in her younger sister, Caroline squared her shoulders and answered as flippantly as she could.

"I made the decision a long time ago that I would not hanker after love in a marriage, Rebecca. I have made my peace with that decision. I do not feel that I would miss anything by marrying for less romantic reasons."

Rebecca studied Caroline intently before answering. "And if you should fall in love? What then?"

Caroline took so long to answer that Rebecca thought she must have decided to stay mute for the remainder of the afternoon. Eventually, however, Caroline spoke and Rebecca's heart tore at the bleak tone to her voice, at her valiant effort to act unaffected.

"I shall not fall in love, Becca. Not ever."

"Caro, you cannot know that. Why, it could happen at any moment and I'm—"

"No, Rebecca," Caroline interrupted sharply, "it could not. I am certain, absolutely certain that love is not in my future. A good marriage — respect, support, wealth and a title. Those are what lie ahead for me. Those are the things I decided on. It is what I chose. It is enough."

Rebecca wondered at her sister's cryptic remarks. What she chose? When had she made such a miserable choice? But Rebecca knew Caroline well enough to know that she had pushed her far enough. Caroline would not answer any more probing questions on the subject. So Rebecca would have no choice but to leave it for now.

But something had put that bleak look in her sister's eyes. Rebecca just could not think what.

CHAPTER TWO

CAROLINE LOOKED HERSELF over critically while Sally put the finishing touches to her hair, twining a blue satin ribbon through her carefully constructed curls. The sky blue satin gown showed a larger amount of cleavage than Caroline was used to. It was not vulgar, but it was certainly more daring than anything she'd worn in recent times. She thought back wryly to the pastel blue dress she'd worn at the assembly in Offaly, the one that nearly killed her father.

At home, under the watchful eye of her mother, she had almost entirely worn white. But this was not home! The colour of the gown made her eyes appear vividly blue and one could not help but notice their sparkle. She supposed to others it would seem like excitement. She knew, of course, that they were slightly glazed since she'd been feeling like casting up her accounts for the past hour. Tonight was to be her first foray into Society since her last, two years ago, and she meant to make an impact.

Usually Caroline's aim was to draw as little attention to herself as possible whilst still maintaining a noticeable presence at any event. The trick was to be mentioned in conversation, to be attended to by suitable gentlemen, but not be talked about so much that one became fodder for the gossips. It was a delicate balancing act that Caroline had been perfecting for years.

Tonight though was Caroline's chance to re-launch herself. To loosen up a little and enjoy her freedom, such as it was, being a single young lady on the marriage mart. It would require careful handling of course. She could skirt the line of impropriety, but not cross it. She could allude to being scandalous, but never be fully so.

Caroline was nervous. She could admit that to herself. She was very aware that as much as she chose to enjoy herself, she must still land herself a husband by the end of it. And the type of husband her father deemed respectable would expect a certain standard of behaviour from his potential wife.

She gulped past the sudden lump in her throat.

If all did not go well, she could find herself married to Lord Doncastle and be rusticating in the Irish countryside for the rest of her days. Or his. He didn't appear to have many left, in fairness. But it would be enough for Caroline to have disappeared into obscurity forevermore.

The temptation to revert to being stiflingly, perfectly proper was strong. Why fix what was not broken, after all? She could spend the Season being the perfect lady as always, find herself a nice appropriate man, make her father happy, and continue to live her life exactly as she had been doing.

And never have the chance to experience life the way she wanted to. To experience fun, laughter, adventure! To prove to herself that she was more than a perfect outer shell of manners and poise. To prove that there was more to her than what people thought.

Caroline had done enough sacrificing for her good name and breeding. She'd made the ultimate sacrifice two years ago. She'd given up her only chance of love. And though she had her reasons, she had never recovered from it. Not a day had gone by where she hadn't bitterly regretted doing what was right rather than what her heart had so desperately wanted.

It was too late now for love. Tom Crawdon had taken her heart with him the day he'd walked out of her life. But was it too late for everything else? No. She wouldn't let it be.

Squaring her shoulders, Caroline gave herself another looking over before taking her fan and wrap from Sally.

"Wish me luck, Sally," she said softly.

Apart from Rebecca, Sally was the only other person Caroline had taken into her confidence. The older woman had been Caroline's personal maid from the time Caroline began wearing long skirts. Sally knew Caroline inside and out. Knew the pressures she felt, the hurt she'd felt. Knew about the many, many nights Caroline had cried herself to sleep mourning the loss of her one chance of real happiness, though Sally was not aware of the circumstances. Caroline had kept that from everyone.

"I do, my lady," answered Sally now in her brisk Irish brogue. "Though you'll not need it. The whole of London will be at your feet and 'tis no more than you deserve. Enjoy it."

Caroline smiled gratefully at the older abigail before turning and sweeping from the room. Her nerves threatened to overwhelm her as she made her way down the imposing staircase to where Rebecca and her husband Edward awaited her.

She had not seen Edward since her arrival as he'd been away at one of his estates. Rebecca had assured her however that he would return in time to escort them to the ball this evening and, true to his word, he had arrived in plenty of time.

Caroline had not heard anything of his return, but it must have been some time ago since he appeared as pristine and handsome as ever in his black evening wear.

However, even if he had returned earlier it seemed, based on the display Caroline was currently witnessing, that he hadn't had too much time alone with his wife.

Caroline was torn between retreating to a safe distance and throwing water on the pair of them so they could cool down. Really, it was highly improper to be so wrapped around each other in a hallway. The old Caroline would have turned away then taken the opportunity to lecture Rebecca at another time.

The new Caroline thought she should brazen it out. And while doing so, push the feeling of envy that was threatening to well up inside her back where it belonged.

She did not envy Rebecca her husband. Never had two people been more in love than Rebecca and Edward. She envied the fact that her sister had been brave and lucky enough to embrace her love for Edward and have it returned.

If Caroline had been brave, how different her life would have been...

But no matter. Dwelling on the past wouldn't change it.

Time to separate the pair before she saw far more of the both of them than she ever needed to see.

"Ahem."

At her subtle cough Rebecca and Edward sprang apart guiltily.

Edward had the decency to look abashed. Rebecca grinned unrepentantly.

"Caroline, how good to see you again." Edward issued a perfect bow.

"Good evening Edward." Caroline was amused to see a blush staining the young duke's face. "It is good to see you again, too."

"You look even more beautiful than the last time we met."

Caroline smiled her thanks at the compliment then turned to her sister.

"If you've finished attacking your husband in the hallway, perhaps we can leave," she quipped.

Edward's mouth dropped open in shock. Of course, he

was unaware of the changed Caroline, presuming her to still be as proper as ever, as much a stickler for the rules.

Caroline could not help but laugh at the expression on Edward's face.

"No doubt you are surprised to hear me speak in such a manner dear brother. Perhaps your wife's influence is taking hold of me."

"Yes," agreed Rebecca, "or you've removed the poker from your –"

"Sweetheart," interrupted Edward smoothly, "we shall be late."

Caroline smothered a laugh and winked conspiratorially at her younger sister. Being outrageous would be fun…

The Smithson townhouse blazed brightly in the darkening sky as Edward's ducal carriage made its slow progress to the front steps. Caroline's stomach quivered with a mixture of nerves and excitement.

She so looked forward to an evening where she was more concerned with how much enjoyment was to be had rather than how people perceived her.

Their carriage finally rolled to a stop at the foot of the stairs leading to the imposing black doors of the house. The doors had been thrown open for the stream of guests and Caroline could already glimpse a multitude of people — gentlemen in fine evening coats and ladies sparkling under the lights of the many candles adorning the chandelier.

It was good to be back.

Rebecca came forward and tucked Caroline's arm under her own and together the sisters ascended the steps leaving Edward to trail behind. Of course, Edward should really be escorting them both, but Rebecca had never been one to care for such things and she wasn't about to start now. Luckily, the *ton* found her flouting the rules quite endearing so she got away with it.

Once inside, the noise level increased dramatically so Caroline made no attempt to converse with Rebecca or Edward. There were plenty of recognisable faces in the crowd. Married ladies, made noticeable by the striking colours they wore, who had been debutantes two years ago when Caroline had her first Season. Debutantes, still single, identifiable by the pastels they wore and by the gleam of desperation in their eyes as they surveyed their quarry.

Caroline glanced around the room taking it all in as she awaited her turn to greet the Smithsons. Her eyes took in the variety of faces until suddenly—

No! It could not be, could it?

Caroline shook her head slightly to clear it. She must be seeing things. After all, the last time she had been at an event as grand as this had been Edward and Rebecca's engagement party. So it stood to reason that her mind would conjure up an image of him. And yet...

She was almost sure it was him. In the flesh. Not in America. But here in the hallway of the Smithson townhouse.

Caroline leaned in and whispered frantically to Rebecca, "Rebecca, Mr. Crawdon has not returned to England has he?"

Rebecca looked at her curiously.

"No, of course not. Edward would have known, I'm sure of it."

Caroline felt a rush of emotion at her sister's response. Whether it was relief or disappointment however she could not say.

"It is nothing," she answered, calmer now, "My mind must be playing tricks on me. I thought I had seen him in the crowd."

Rebecca had no time to answer as they had finally reached their hosts and spent several minutes engaging in polite chitchat before moving to enter the ballroom.

The room was resplendent in draped white silks and hundreds of deep red roses. Mrs. Smithson had always had a flair for dramatics and tonight was no exception.

Caroline took in the room with a breath of excitement, and yet her elation was tainted with the feelings her supposed sighting of Tom had stirred up.

She shook her head a little at her own folly. Of course Edward would know if Tom had returned to England. More brothers than cousins, the two were the very best of friends. Caroline and Rebecca had grown excessively close in recent years, but before that there had been an estrangement of sorts, with Caroline so fixated on control and maintaining a stiff upper lip at all times and Rebecca, well, being Rebecca. But no such difference of personality had separated the cousins. Even when Edward left his rakish ways to become the sensible Duke of Hartridge, and Tom continued to be an incorrigible rogue, they had remained as close as ever. It was yet another thing Caroline regretted.

Before her thoughts could turn too maudlin, Caroline shook them off. This Season was about loosening that lip and thoroughly enjoying herself in the process. Harping on about the past, even to herself, was not conducive to mischief making.

They had not been long in the ballroom when they were surrounded by a veritable crowd of people.

Caroline knew that Rebecca always attracted attention, usually from people who wanted to see what delightful scandal she would cause next.

What she didn't realise, however, was that in the two years since her marriage to Edward and since the birth of Henry, Rebecca had become almost respectable. And Town was well used to and rather fond of her mishaps by now, regardless. It would have been a great shock to Caroline to know that it was *she* who caused the sensation, and not her younger sister.

Rebecca turned to Caroline with excited eyes as people, predominantly young and very-much-unattached gentlemen, battled their way over to where they stood.

"Well Caro, you haven't said or done anything even slightly scandalous and here you stand, the talk of the room already!" she whispered as Edward took up the reins of conversation, giving the sisters a small amount of privacy.

Sensing the sisters' want for privacy, Edward had begun to regale the crowd with stories of Parliament. It was long winded and boring and nobody wanted to hear it but they listened regardless. One did not ignore the Duke of Hartridge, after all.

Caroline stared in surprise at Rebecca.

"Whatever do you mean?"

Rebecca glanced at the small army of suitors, interspersed with a few ladies who were probably hoping to achieve notice by association.

"I mean that we're likely to be crushed in the stampede of people hoping to gain your attention."

Caroline frowned in consternation at the sea of faces, now looking decidedly bored. Was that one at the back actually nodding off?

"Surely not, Becca. I am well aware of the stir you cause at these things, having been a reluctant witness to them for years," she answered dryly.

Rebecca merely shook her head.

"Why Caroline, you goose. Don't you know I'm positively respectable now?"

Caroline had to laugh at her sister's obvious disappointment at the fact.

"Believe me, my dear," Rebecca continued, "this is all for you. There's not a debutante in the whole of London who can hold a candle to you this Season. If your fortune, father's and Edward's titles, *and* your impeccable reputation weren't enough to attract them, your looks certainly would be. You are, without a doubt, the most beautiful of them and I do not say that because you are my sister."

Caroline still looked doubtful and more than a little put out about her 'impeccable reputation'. That was no fun.

Rebecca reached up, for Caroline was quite a bit taller, and grasped her older sister's shoulders.

"This is your time to shine, Caro," she said softly, "Enjoy it."

CHAPTER THREE

CAROLINE STARED AT her sister for a moment before bracing her shoulders and smiling mischievously.

"You are right. I will enjoy every moment of it. The sooner I can throw off this mantle of 'impeccable reputations' the sooner I can have some fun."

"Er, yes, well perhaps do not throw it off altogether. Remember you still need someone to marry this Season or you'll end up with Father Time in Cork."

Both sisters laughed at Rebecca's wicked description of Lord Doncastle before Rebecca turned to her husband. "That's quite enough, thank you darling. I believe you've sufficiently bored them to tears."

"Thank God for that," whispered Edward, "I was running out of stories to tell and just started making things up. Thankfully nobody was listening by that time. Though, I wonder if I should warn Lord Woodford, just in case..."

The orchestra signalled the start of the dancing.

"Excellent idea, let us find him at once, since Caroline has already been claimed for this dance."

Edward frowned and his eyes snapped to Caroline's

dance card.

"What? No, I won't allow that. In the absence of your father and brother, I am responsible for you, Caroline, and it should be I who dances with you first."

Caroline looked to Rebecca for assistance. He was right, of course. She really should dance with him first. But how was one to create a stir when dancing with one's brother-in-law? And a duke at that! That was sickeningly proper.

Rebecca just rolled her eyes and winked at Caroline.

"Do not upset yourself, Edward. It is perfectly acceptable for her to dance with Viscount Hadley."

Edward's frown deepened. He remembered how much Hadley had mooned after Rebecca in her first Season. Caroline too, for that matter. He was a determined flirt and was desperate for a woman with a large dowry and small brain to suit his own. The word about Town was that his pockets were well and truly to let, and the longer he remained single and without a rich fiancée, the worse his finances became. Clearly Caroline was far too good for him.

"I do not like him."

"You do not like anyone."

"I like you," he countered and Caroline felt herself blush at the blatantly lustful look he threw to his wife.

Really, these two were uncontrollable. It had been two years, for heaven's sake. Hadn't Caroline heard many a woman bemoan the fact that after a week or two a husband's attentions waned and, with luck, disappeared altogether?

Rebecca appeared as if she was far from minding however and she leaned up to whisper into Edward's ear.

Edward's eyes gleamed and the Viscount in question, who had been making steady progress toward them, had barely bowed to Caroline before Edward grabbed hold of Rebecca's waist and swept her away toward the open doors to the veranda.

"Have fun," Rebecca called to Caroline as she was

whisked away by her enthusiastic husband.

"My lady."

Caroline's attention was brought back to Viscount Hadley by his death grip on her hand. Was he trying to break her fingers?

She tried to remove her hand from his but unbelievably, his grip only tightened.

"I cannot tell you how pleased I am to see you returned to Town. Your beauty, if I may be so bold, has only increased."

Caroline smiled politely, but her teeth were on edge. The odious man was not letting go and was far too loud. Several people were watching his dramatics and the attention was painfully embarrassing.

Caroline tried reminding herself that this was what she had wanted, more attention, more eventful evenings.

However, she had hoped that it would be at least somewhat enjoyable.

After an excruciating few seconds of struggling, she finally managed to free her hand from his. Her face flushed scarlet at the titters surrounding them as they made their way to the dance floor.

Hadley was now staring intently at her, in a way Caroline presumed was meant to show his regard for her, but which in actuality made her feel rather alarmed.

Mercifully, the dance began and Caroline used the opportunity to scan the room. A signal had been previously decided upon that would immediately warn Rebecca that Caroline needed saving.

However, her traitor of a sister appeared to still be missing with her even bigger traitor of a husband, so Caroline would have to endure as best she could.

The couples parted and Caroline's eyes made another tour of the room. Her heart stopped dead and she stumbled forward. There! At the edge of the dance floor, partially hidden by the ostentatious plants Mrs. Smithson had had dotted about the room. It was he. It had to be.

Her heart restarted with a thud and began to gallop frantically as Tom Crawdon looked up and his deep blue eyes met hers. He too was staring intently and unsmilingly at her. But where Hadley's regard made her want to bathe herself or slap his cheek, Tom's reawakened emotions so strong they took Caroline's breath away.

He gave no indication that he recognised her. Made no bow, no gesture. Yet still he stared.

Caroline wasn't sure what she should do. Her first instinct, to run to his arms and throw herself into them, would probably be a little unwelcome.

Hadley had returned to face her and Caroline felt her feet take her through the steps of the dance, though her mind was fixated on the man by the ridiculous plant.

At that moment Rebecca and Edward re-entered the room. Caroline willed Rebecca to look her way, and thankfully she did. Caroline nodded as discreetly as she could toward Tom, widening her eyes to signal to Rebecca to look that way.

Rebecca's head made to turn and look but just then Edward leaned down and whispered to her and Rebecca's gaze was caught by her husband's. For God's sake! Caroline was tempted to remove her shoe and fling it at the pair of them.

Hadley was now at Caroline's side and was mumbling something longwinded to her. She did not even pretend to listen.

Her eyes turned once more toward Tom and she sighed in relief that he was still there. Still watching. Now, however, his mouth was curled up in sardonic amusement. No doubt he found Hadley's efforts to secure Caroline's attentions funny. She remembered his smile, since she saw it almost nightly in her dreams. The cynical slant to it, however, and the ice in his eyes — they were new.

Swallowing hard, Caroline looked back toward Rebecca

who was swatting at Edward's arm playfully with her fan.

The music went on and on and Caroline wondered desperately if the orchestra were deliberately lengthening the song. She had broken from the ridiculously enthusiastic Viscount Hadley again to circle the other dancers and used the opportunity to once again gain Rebecca's attention.

Her cough was about as subtle as screeching Rebecca's name but she was past caring.

This time she caught the attention of both Edward and Rebecca. She subtly nodded her head in Tom's direction once again but could tell immediately from their frowns of confusion that the gesture was not big enough.

Hadley was back by her side and was rambling on in much the same fashion. He sounded rather breathless to her half-listening ear but it wasn't surprising since he'd been jumping about since the beginning of the dance, in between droning on about some matter that she wasn't aware of.

Caroline knew subtle gestures just weren't going to convey her predicament so in desperation, she nodded again, this time making no effort to keep the gesture small.

Unfortunately, at the same moment, Viscount Hadley leaned forward to whisper something in her ear. Their heads met with a sickening crunch. The poor man staggered back from Caroline clutching his head and landed unceremoniously on his backside. Not being privy to the fact that Caroline had been trying to capture Rebecca's attention, he obviously thought that Caroline had gone mad and decided to assault him in the middle of the ballroom.

Caroline had staggered too and clutching her head, she noticed that the room had begun to spin alarmingly.

Rebecca hurried over, followed by Edward who thankfully grabbed hold of Caroline's elbow and steadied her before she fell.

Caroline had once again drawn a crowd.

Hadley was being helped off the floor.

"Good heavens Caro, are you alright?" Rebecca tried to sound concerned but Caroline could tell she was trying desperately not to laugh.

"It's not funny, Rebecca. Everyone is staring!" Caroline admonished with a fierce whisper. Thankfully, the room had stopped spinning but Edward's hand remained fixed on her elbow, ensuring that nobody got too close. Not even Viscount Hadley, who had thankfully given up trying to gain back her attention and wobbled miserably toward the refreshment table.

People were enquiring as to whether or not Caroline was well, all politeness and concern. But Caroline had no time for their pity and brushed it off with as much graciousness as she could muster.

"What are you about anyway?" asked Rebecca, completely unfazed by Caroline's set down and still grinning in obvious amusement.

Caroline pressed a hand to her head and felt, to her dismay, a rather large bump forming on her forehead.

The amusement disappeared at once from Rebecca's expression and she placed a hand on Caroline's arm.

"Are you hurt?"

Caroline smiled weakly.

"Only my pride."

Rebecca smiled. "I must say, it's rather nice not being the one creating a scene."

Caroline stuck her tongue out as Edward led her toward the veranda to get some air. Rebecca kept pace with them and asked again, "So, what *were* you doing? Aside from trying to shut Hadley up, of course."

"I was trying to tell you that Tom *is* here. I saw him again."

Edward stopped and stared at Caroline in disbelief.

"Tom? Here? That's impossible. He's still in America and has no plans to return. I'm sure of it."

Caroline was already shaking her head but stopped immediately as a pain began to form at the back of her eyes.

"He *is* here and I *did* see him."

"Caroline," Rebecca spoke gently now, "do you not think that Edward would know of it? Why on earth would Tom move back to England without informing Edward or the dowager, or anyone?"

Caroline stayed quiet. She had no answer. Of course Tom would not return without informing his family.

Could it be that she was so desperate to see him her mind had conjured him up? That seemed a little far-fetched. And she didn't *feel* insane. But then, how would she know really?

After a tense moment of silence, Caroline shrugged her shoulders as casually as she could.

"I must have been mistaken then. You are right, of course. Why would he come back and not tell anyone?"

"Surely you don't think I would pass up the opportunity to have a little fun with my own family, Edward?"

The deep, masculine voice sounded behind the trio and they all whipped around in amazement.

There he stood, Tom Crawdon. The man who had stolen her heart two years ago.

Caroline's eyes raked greedily over the man of whom she had thought every single day for the past two years.

He was still so handsome he made her knees weak. His dark blond hair was longer than before, a little wilder.

He still towered over her but he was broader now, his shoulders bigger than before.

His eyes were still the same deep, sparkling blue. But they were filled now, not with amusement and joviality, but with an emotion that Caroline could not name. Whatever it was, it made her shiver and an icy feeling of dread filled her stomach.

This was Tom, whom she knew so well and yet, he seemed a stranger. Tom, who before had looked at her like she was a precious jewel and now watched her with disdain.

"Tom!" Rebecca's happy cry awoke Caroline from her intense study of his features.

Caroline watched as Rebecca launched herself at Tom, and was rewarded with a grin so like his old one, and a giant hug that lifted her from her feet.

Caroline felt herself release a sigh of relief. So the old Tom was still there. She had been worried for a moment but that grin — it hadn't changed a bit.

"Good God, man," Edward spoke next, "this is a surprise."

"A pleasant one, I hope," answered Tom.

Edward shook hands with Tom and slapped his back in reply.

"Good to have you home."

Tom smiled again.

"Tis good to be home, cousin."

Caroline willed the pounding of her heart to cease as she waited for Tom to turn his deep blue gaze to her. However, he was studiously ignoring her and Caroline was not the only one to notice.

Rebecca looked between the two, a frown marring her brow.

"Tom," she interrupted the two cousins impolitely but Rebecca had never been one to be overly concerned with politeness when she wanted something. "You remember of course my sister, Caroline?"

Her tone hinted at her unhappiness that Tom had not immediately acknowledged Caroline.

He turned to her now and the warmth in his eyes cooled considerably. Caroline swallowed nervously.

"It is good to see you again, Tom." She did not even notice that her mouth had formed his Christian name of its own accord.

A flash of some undefinable emotion gleamed in Tom's eyes before they returned once again to their cool regard.

Tom stepped forward and made the barest of bows. Caroline heard Rebecca's gasp of indignation but her eyes were locked with Tom's as the iciness in her stomach increased tenfold.

"Lady Caroline," he bit out his tone barely civil.

Caroline could not move. Could not curtsy. Could not speak. Her heart, which was nowhere near healed from two years ago, stuttered painfully in her chest at this most obvious of set downs.

Her eyes began to fill alarmingly. *Do not cry,* she instructed herself severely.

There was another moment of tense silence, this time tinged with Caroline's embarrassment. She glanced quickly at Rebecca and Edward.

Edward was frowning in displeased confusion at his cousin's manner. Rebecca's eyes glinted menacingly and she looked as though she were about to hit Tom squarely in the face.

Tom, too, had sensed the mood and garnered from their expressions that they were less than pleased with him.

His mouth twisted in a cynical smile.

"My cue to leave, I think," he said dryly before turning, and with one final, insolent glance at Caroline, he swept from the veranda without saying goodbye to any of them.

The silence was broken by a string of expletives, issued not from Edward but from Rebecca who looked ready to kill.

"What on earth was that about?" she demanded of nobody in particular.

Edward and Caroline shared a look over Rebecca's head and Caroline knew that Edward must be aware of what had happened between her and Tom.

But he still did not look pleased with Tom's conduct.

Caroline smiled a little wanly, to try to reassure him that she was all right. But she wasn't. And right now, she wanted more than anything to be alone.

"I think perhaps it is time that we took our leave," Edward said softly, his tone hardened by his barely concealed anger towards his cousin.

Caroline nodded mutely and Rebecca looked suspiciously between them both as if realising she was the only one missing something here.

The look on her sister's face however, convinced her that now was not the time to ask questions.

And so it was that barely a word was spoken between the three during the short carriage ride home, each of them locked in their own thoughts.

CHAPTER FOUR

THE NEXT DAY dawned bright and clear. Caroline was awoken by Sally bustling in and throwing back the curtains, allowing the glaring sun to light up the room.

"Top of the mornin', my lady," Sally uttered jovially, retrieving a tray from outside the door and setting it down beside Caroline's bed. "Tis a grand and lovely day. I'm sure you and her grace have plenty you'll want to be doing so I'll take your morning dress off to be pressed now. What were you thinking of for today? Perhaps the sprigged muslin..."

Sally chattered on, either oblivious to or uncaring of the fact that Caroline was yet to respond to any of it.

Caroline groaned and buried her head under the soft, downy pillow. She had no intentions of leaving that bed and facing her family yet. In fact, staying there permanently began to seem hugely appealing.

There was no doubt in Caroline's mind that she would be overwhelmed with a barrage of questions from Rebecca. That, however, she could handle. Sympathy or pity from Edward, she could not.

Her heart stuttered in her chest as she once again recalled

the events of last night.

Her emotions had not been in so much turmoil since she last saw Tom two years ago. And even then, for the most part they'd been good. Until that fateful night at least.

Caroline felt tears spring to her eyes as she remembered Tom's appearance last night.

The love she had felt for him had slammed into her once again and there had been a brief moment of pure, unadulterated joy at seeing him again before the reality of their situation followed swiftly in its trail.

For it had been painfully obvious from his countenance, his flat tone, his sardonic glances that any love Tom Crawdon had felt for her was long since gone. And in its place was a cold, furious hatred.

"My lady?" Sally's voice finally cut through Caroline's maudlin thoughts.

"I'm sorry, Sally. I was wool gathering I'm afraid. I did not sleep overly well last night."

Which was a gross understatement. Every time she had closed her eyes, visions of Tom's disdain for her had burst to the forefront of her mind and consequently she had spent the night tossing, turning, and bemoaning the fact that all of her plans for the Season, for some fun and enjoyment, were reduced to nought.

For the truth of it was that she was still irrevocably in love with Tom Crawdon. And no amount of scandal or mischief was going to make up for the fact that she had had her chance at real happiness, and had turned her back on it.

Any plans or excitement she had for these coming months seemed nothing more than childish games now. Besides, how could she enjoy herself knowing that the man she loved was back in Town and wanted absolutely nothing to do with her?

Sally had known the second Lady Caroline had walked through the door last night that something was very wrong with her mistress.

Although her manner had been slowly softening over the past couple of years, Lady Caroline still tried to conduct herself with the rigidity that the Upper Class were bred for.

The only time Sally had seen it truly shaken had been in the weeks directly following Lady Rebecca's engagement party. And though Lady Caroline had been confiding in Sally since leaving the schoolroom, and had oft said that she considered the abigail more friend than servant, she had never made Sally privy to what exactly had gone on that night.

Sally guessed that it must have had something to do with his grace's handsome cousin. In fact, she had been convinced that there would be an announcement made about Mr. Crawdon and her mistress soon after that of Lady Rebecca and the duke.

But none was forthcoming. Mr. Crawdon had disappeared from London the night of the ball and her mistress had changed that night. First it had been utter misery, the likes of which Sally had never seen from the perfectly controlled Lady Caroline. Then came a sort of depressive acceptance of, rather than interest in, her life. Finally, she had seemed anxious to throw off the somewhat self-imposed shackles of unyielding acceptability. And while Sally was only too happy to see her young mistress soften and have a little fun, she knew that it had all started with whatever had transpired between Lady Caroline and Mr. Crawdon that night.

Even now, although Lady Caroline never spoke of him anymore, Sally knew her mistress had never recovered from whatever had unfolded between them.

Last night, Lady Caroline had returned subdued and pale. Sally had wondered at this behaviour until the servants' gossip this morning had thrown up Mr. Crawdon's name and

Sally had paid attention. It appeared Mr. Crawdon was back, and Sally now understood her mistress's manner.

Caroline could see Sally's shrewd gaze raking over her. She sighed inwardly then heaved herself up into a sitting position. If she did not pretend that all was well then Sally would harangue her to find out what was wrong. And Caroline would get enough of that from Rebecca and Edward.

"My lady—"

"The sprigged muslin sounds perfect, thank you Sally." Caroline spoke brusquely as she lifted her morning cup of chocolate to her lips. The best way to deal with Sally's questions was to stop them before they began.

There was a short, tense standoff between the two women. Would Sally try to pursue the matter, having long since passed the time of unthinking obedience, or would Caroline be able to stare her down in that unique way that she had?

Finally, with a small huff of resignation Sally took the dress and swept from the room.

Caroline smiled a little at her victory. Sally was older than Caroline and sometimes forgot that she was a maid and not a mother. But theirs was a real friendship and Caroline truly appreciated it.

It wasn't long before Sally was back and helping Caroline to prepare for the day.

"Will you be out this afternoon, my lady?" she asked as she dressed Caroline's hair.

"I cannot say. I am not sure what her grace has planned. Though truth be told I would as soon stay at home."

"Well perhaps that is what you will do today. I am sure there are many who would like to reacquaint themselves with you. And that is why you're here, is it not?"

Caroline mumbled something non-committal and then, seeing that Sally had finished her ministrations, quickly left the room.

Yes, that was why she was here. To meet people, socialise, enjoy herself and then, with any luck, settle down with someone of her own choosing and not Papa's.

But since her meeting with Tom last night, none of those things held any appeal anymore and she wanted, more than anything, to go back in time and make the right choice. Living with regret was a painful process at times, but it was nothing compared to the despair of knowing, without doubt, that the man she loved despised her.

Caroline composed herself and straightened her shoulders before entering the breakfast room. She had no idea how much Edward or Rebecca knew of her relationship with Tom, but if they didn't mention it, neither would she.

Taking a fortifying breath, she entered the room. It was empty. Caroline frowned in surprise; she was not very late was she? Sally would have been sure to wake her at the correct hour.

Frowning a little, she sat at the table and accepted the proffered coffee from a waiting footman. Her stomach had been tied in knots since last night so she had no desire to eat any of the delicious food on the sideboard.

Caroline felt a little strange sitting all alone in the huge breakfast room and was contemplating just leaving when the sound of approaching footsteps stopped her. At least now she would not be alone.

The door to the room opened and Jenson entered, bowing formally.

"Mr. Crawdon, my lady."

Caroline froze in horror. Tom was here? Now? But, but she was alone. She could not face him alone. Not after his treatment of her last night.

"I, uh—"

"Really, Jenson," Tom's voice sounded outside the room and Caroline's stomach lurched at the tone of cheeriness which was sure to disappear as soon as he entered the room. He must not have noticed the butler's use of 'my lady' as opposed to 'your grace'. "When will you learn to stop being so formal? Edward does not expect me to be announced. And neither, I'm sure does Rebe—"

Tom's speech cut off abruptly as he finally entered the room and noticed that it was Caroline whom the butler had addressed.

There was a moment of tense silence as Caroline and Tom gazed at each other. Tom's deep blue eyes gleamed with an emotion that Caroline did not recognise, before he schooled his features into a mask of disdainful disinterest.

He did not utter a word, just stared at her rather insolently.

Caroline swallowed compulsively and clasped her hands together as she stood to welcome him.

"Good morning, Tom," she mumbled hesitantly, her nervousness making her voice shakier than she would have liked.

Jenson had taken his leave and apart from the serving footmen, Caroline and Tom were quite alone. Before, Caroline would have balked at the impropriety of the situation. Now, she just despaired of the awkward tension swirling around them.

Rather than reply, Tom's eyes raked her from head to toe with an expression that clearly said he found her wanting.

Caroline forgot her nerves in the face of such rudeness and she raised her chin infinitesimally, her eyes flashing blue fire.

"Is Edward about?" Tom finally drawled, taking a seat at the table.

Caroline almost gasped at his deliberate slight. Tom had long since been an integral member of the *ton*, being both ridiculously wealthy and a Crawdon, and he was well aware that to sit before a lady was a gross misstep. Since he did not make mistakes, Caroline could only assume that the insult had been deliberate.

Caroline did her best to cling to her much lauded self-control, though the temptation to slap him was steadily increasing.

She deliberately stayed standing and gazed down at him imperiously.

"What? Do you think I am hiding him somewhere?"

Tom's eyebrow rose slightly at the sarcastic tone.

"Careful, Lady Caroline, your personality is beginning to show."

That did it. Caroline refused to stand here and be insulted by him.

Without another word, she turned and swept from the room. It took everything in her power not to slam the door behind her.

She was about to make her way back to her room when the sound of Rebecca's cooing voice alerted her to the fact that Rebecca and Henry were on their way down to breakfast. Caroline was in no mood to face her sister who would know immediately that something was wrong.

So she turned instead to the drawing room and closed the door swiftly behind her. Her hackles were well and truly raised.

Tom had every right to be disappointed in her, even angry with her. But that did not mean he had leave to treat her so abominably.

Caroline began to pace in her agitation. This Season was going to be an utter disaster. Tom would be around all the time, treating her badly no doubt. And her heart would break a little more with every jibe.

This Season was her *last chance* to do something for her and her alone. And it was going to be ruined by Tom's anger and her own heartache. Her temper was mounting and she felt less in control of it now than she had in years.

Everyone always assumed her iciness meant her feelings did not blow hot sometimes, but they were wrong. She did not often get in a towering rage but when she did, it was a sight to behold.

She must calm down. Temper tantrums were no good to anybody. But he made her so angry!

Edward stepped through the door of his townhouse feeling thoroughly refreshed from his morning ride. He wondered if Henry were awake yet and decided to make his way to the nursery to check. No doubt he would find Rebecca there too.

He was about to make his way upstairs when he heard the distinctive sound of something smashing. And it was coming from the closed drawing room.

He immediately panicked and cast his mind over the last few hours. Something smashing meant either a clumsy maid, and that was unheard of amongst his impeccable staff, or Rebecca was in a towering rage.

He gulped and made his way toward the room. He was almost sure that he could not be at fault — he had left her more than happy this morning. But then, one could never be entirely sure either.

Taking a calming breath, he pushed open the door.

"Sweetheart what—"

His words were cut short by the sight before him. Not Rebecca, but Caroline. And she looked fit to put a bullet in somebody. Her cheeks were flushed scarlet and her eyes blazed fiercely, like blue fire. She looked terrifying. A family trait, clearly.

"Caroline." He said no more. He was too scared.

Edward's presence jolted Caroline from the fit of temper and her gaze immediately changed from anger to contrition. She felt a wave of shame wash over her at being caught.

"Edward." She sounded a little breathless as she struggled to compose herself. "The vase. I apologise. It was an accident."

Edward did not ask how she had accidentally smashed a vase but Caroline could see from his sceptical expression that he did not believe her.

"Truly, it was. I–I threw a cushion and, well, my aim is not very good."

Edward looked suspiciously like he was trying to contain his laughter and Caroline felt murderous again. If he laughed, she'd smack him. After all there was a vague similarity between Tom and him. A substitute would not feel as good but it was better than hitting nobody.

"May I enquire as to what brought on this fit of temper? I must confess I was rather surprised it was you and not my wife causing such a to-do."

Caroline hesitated as she wondered what to say. She had no wish to cause any problems for Edward, who had welcomed her into his home so graciously. And putting him into the middle of her troubles with Tom would be decidedly awkward. But there was no real way to avoid it, since he would know soon enough that Tom was here. Edward was a smart man; it would not take long to put the pieces together.

Sighing resignedly she answered. "Your cousin has paid a call and we, that is to say I—oh I *hate* him!" she finished fervently.

Edward's eyebrows rose a little at her impassioned outburst but made no comment. He knew that this situation could not be allowed to continue. He was aware of what had transpired between his cousin and sister-in-law. And though he felt nothing but sympathy for Tom, he felt it too for

Caroline, knowing as he did how much pressure was on her shoulders.

Caroline was under his protection for the duration of this Season, and although he loved Tom as a brother, he could not allow him to continue in his disrespectful treatment of her.

Face grim, he held out his arm silently for Caroline to take. She came forward and meekly did as she was bid.

They entered the breakfast room to find Rebecca chatting happily to Tom while he bounced a laughing Henry on his knee. Caroline refused to allow herself to feel anything as she watched Tom doting over his young cousin.

"Hello you two," Rebecca chirped from her seat before her smile slowly faded as she took in Edward's expression. "What—"

"Ladies, please excuse us," Edward interrupted her, "Tom. A word."

Tom looked up and registered Edward's expression with a wry twist of his lips. He glanced toward Caroline.

"Telling tales are we?"

Caroline, who never swore, felt like it was time to break the habit of a lifetime.

"No," she bit back, "I said nothing save that you were here."

"Then what, pray tell, has my cousin in such a fit?"

"Perhaps it is merely your presence," she answered sharply before taking her seat and signalling for some more coffee, meaning to ignore him until he left the room.

"Look at you," Tom retaliated, clearly not meaning to leave her alone, "showing that personality again. Whatever can have gotten into you?"

"Tom." Edward's voice held a world of warning but neither Tom nor Caroline paid any heed.

Caroline refused to answer, refused to take his bait.

But Tom was not done.

"Tell me," he continued, leaning back in his chair as if he

hadn't a care in the world, "if you did not run to my big bad cousin, why is he shooting daggers at me?"

Caroline sighed in exasperation.

"I did not tell him anything. He—I was angry and—" her face flushed scarlet again. She could feel the heat rising in her cheeks. "I broke a vase."

There was a moment's silence as everyone observed this information. This was certainly a shock, coming from Caroline.

Tom chuckled softly, though the sound held no humour and grated on Caroline's overwrought nerves.

"My, my. Showing emotion, my dear? That won't do. I'm sure whatever perfectly staid gentleman you have in your sights would not want a wife with feelings. Best to revert back to normal."

"That's it!" Edward exploded and moved to hand the baby to Rebecca then lifted Tom bodily from the chair. "Out. Now."

Caroline's eyes remained fixed determinedly on her plate while the men left the room. Her anger was on the up again, but so too was her devastation. She had never thought such cruelty would come from Tom's lips. He had changed so very much. No longer the laughing, carefree jester. He was now cold, remote, and cynical. Could she have done that to him? Or perhaps it was something that had happened throughout his stay in America.

"Somebody had better tell me what is going on here." Rebecca's voice cut through Caroline's thoughts.

Caroline glanced up to see Rebecca send a footman for Henry's nurse. Rebecca looked angry and her anger fed Caroline's.

So, he thought her lacking in emotion did he? He thought her incapable of acting like anything other than the unfeeling statue he presumed her to be? Well, she would show him.

"I shall tell you what's going on here," she answered now, injecting her voice with steely determination, "I'm going to prove that odious man wrong once and for all."

CHAPTER FIVE

TOM MADE SURE to keep his expression impassive as he sat back in the seat in front of Edward's desk.

Edward, for his part, remained standing. Prowling, really.

Tom knew that his treatment of Caroline had angered Edward and really, he could not blame him. She was, after all, his sister-in-law now and it would seem that she was staying here for the Season. Of all the rotten luck.

But, there was plenty of time to bemoan that later. Right now he had to put all his effort into making sure his cousin didn't shoot him.

Edward still hadn't spoken so Tom took the opportunity to perfect his appearance of nonchalance. It was harder than he thought. Seeing Caroline last night had brought up a whole host of feelings that he was not ready to address.

He had come this morning to try to explain things to Rebecca and Edward. Edward of course knew the situation, but he was hoping to give Rebecca a passable excuse without having to inform her that her sister had shattered his soul two years ago and seeing her again reminded him why she had the power to do so.

He had been completely unprepared to see Caroline again this morning and his body's immediate reaction to her, just as intense as last night, took him by surprise. Angered him too. He did not want to feel anything for her. Not after what had happened.

But she was still...perfect. And it galled him. So he had been cruel, mean, insulting — anything to hide the fact that she still affected him so, in ways that he did not understand or want to examine.

He no longer loved her. He couldn't. He had no heart left to love with; she had made sure of that. So why then had his first thought been to grab her and kiss her senseless; to see if she still tasted as good as he remembered, as he still dreamed about?

"So," Edward's tone was conversational which immediately put Tom on his guard. He knew the duke far too well to be taken in. "Would you care to explain why you're trying to get yourself killed?"

"What?"

"I can only assume from the way you've been treating Caroline, that you want me to put a bullet in your head."

"A fair assumption, I suppose. But do you not think that I have some right to feel angry?"

Edward looked at him shrewdly for a moment before releasing a sigh and taking his seat behind the desk.

"I don't know, Tom," he answered. "I understand how you must have felt, but—"

Edward's words were cut off by Tom's bark of laughter.

"You understand how I must have felt? And how is it that you would understand, cousin? You, who fell in love with a woman who loved you back. Who accepted your offer for her. Who did not make you feel like the most worthless man in the world."

Tom could hear the bitterness in his tone and he hated it.

He hated that he still felt *anything,* good or bad, about Caroline Carrington.

He stood up from the chair and paced toward the window, gazing unseeingly at the perfectly maintained gardens behind Edward's townhouse.

Dammit! He'd run away for two years to escape the demons of his love for her. Two years of building his empire beyond his wildest imaginations. Of being the most dashing rogue of the New York scene. Womanising, drinking, gambling... until he'd finally felt whole enough to return home. Back where he belonged.

And all it had taken was one damned glimpse of her across a crowded hallway to make him feel broken all over again.

Well, he'd die before he'd admit that to anyone. Especially the man across from him who knew him as well as he knew himself.

Get yourself under control, Tom, he urged himself.

Tom glanced back to find Edward gazing pityingly at him and he swore under his breath. The last thing he wanted was pity.

"Perhaps I do not know exactly how you feel then," Edward conceded, moving to stand beside his cousin at the window.

Strange that two years should make such a difference. Tom had always been as tall as Edward, practically identical in height. But whereas Edward had been broadly muscled, Tom's body had been more streamlined. Now though, he matched Edward in size.

"But I can imagine. When I lost Rebecca, even for that one night, and then when she did not wake for three days, I–I do not know how I got through it. So no, I don't know what it feels like to be rejected, thank God. But I know how it is to feel like your whole world has been lost to you."

Tom swallowed hard as Edward gripped his shoulder.

Yes, that was it. That was what it had felt like. He'd handed her his world, his heart, his soul. And she'd found them wanting.

Tom had thought that he'd come to terms with his feelings. With his loss. He had come to the Smithson ball, knowing that he would not be refused entrance, especially because the hostess would want it to be *her* party that the notorious Tom Crawdon made his return at. He had wanted to surprise his family. Had thought of a fun filled evening, catching up, laughing, planting himself straight back into the world in which he belonged.

His time in America had been more than enjoyable, at least after the first six months or so of doing nothing but drowning his sorrows in brandy and questionable company. For one thing, his businesses had climbed to dizzying heights. For another, the Americans weren't as obsessed with titles and lineage as the British. Yet Tom had still yearned to come home.

He'd sauntered into the Smithson townhouse, aware of and amused by the stares, the gasps, the whispering, the swooning — one unfortunate debutante had actually fainted after he'd winked at her and she had to be carried outside.

And then, he'd seen her. He'd glanced toward the receiving line since somebody seemed to be creating a bit of a sensation, his cobalt blue eyes scanning the new arrivals and then suddenly…

His heart had recognised her seconds before his brain registered that it was she. It had caused him such a fierce slam of pain that he'd almost reeled from it.

Looking more beautiful than ever, her hair like spun gold under the candlelight, her blue satin dress making her eyes appear even more striking than he remembered. His eyes raked greedily over her, taking in every inch, though he willed himself not to care. He felt like a starved man offered a meal. He was horrified by how much she still affected him, he who had been so sure that any and all feelings had been left at the bottom of an empty brandy bottle in New York.

He had felt his hands clench into fists, physically restraining himself from pushing through the crowd and gathering her into his arms.

Dear God, did she have to be here? Now? And did she have to look so damned good?

As if sensing his eyes on her, Caroline had turned in his direction. He had mere seconds to school his features to that of an uncaring stranger.

The truth was, he was shaken by his reaction to her and needed to gather his wits about him.

He'd watched as her cool blue eyes widened in recognition. He could see the second she stopped breathing, but only because of where his eyes had been trained at that moment. Very much south of her face.

But he looked at her face now, determined not to pay heed to the lust roaring through his body.

Her features registered her shock, her disbelief. But had he also seen joy before she turned frantically to her younger sister?

Tom had taken the opportunity of their broken eye contact to slip away. He did not want to see or speak to them yet.

Clearly, Caroline was in Town. Most likely for a Season. Tom knew that this information would change things for him. He just did not know in what way or how much. And until he figured it out, he had no desire to face any of them.

He'd meant to leave. Truly he had. But he was drawn to her, much as he hated to admit it, even to himself. He could not leave. So he watched, careful not to be seen by Edward and Rebecca. It was soon evident however that there was very little chance of him being seen by Edward and Rebecca since they'd taken off somewhere and left Caroline to her own devices. They were terrible chaperones, the pair of them.

He watched as that detestable little runt Hadley tried to

engage her attention by some long-winded ramblings that she was definitely not listening to. He watched as the man leapt about with far more gusto than the dance warranted. She was embarrassed by him but far too well bred to show it.

And he watched as her eyes scanned the crowd frantically, no doubt searching for her missing chaperones, and landed once again on his.

The resultant fiasco still managed to bring a smile to his face this morning. He would always remember with fondness her forehead landing such a blow on Hadley's that she'd near knocked him clean out. He'd had to stop himself from rushing to her side the second they'd collided to make sure she was well, and was once again frustrated with his own folly. Dammit, why should he care if she were well or not? He should not care about her at all. He *did* not care about her.

This frustration kept hold of him all the way out to the balcony where his cousin had steered the two ladies. And it was there that he found Caroline — her voice alone heating his blood as it always had — trying desperately to convince Edward and Rebecca that she had seen him.

He knew that the greeting he'd given her had been unspeakably rude but the second she'd spoken his name, in that breathless whisper, he had realised that he was not strong enough to resist falling under her spell once again. The only way to keep himself safe this time round was to treat her with contempt and aloofness. That was what she deserved.

His mind made up, Tom had come to call this morning knowing that Edward would want to ring a peal over his head for his treatment of Lady Caroline. He hoped to clear the air with his cousin, after all he had returned to be with his family and did not want an estrangement. He had intended to explain to Edward that he would be civil and polite to Lady Caroline and would ensure that his behaviour from now on was above reproach.

And then the damned girl had shown up again! And he

didn't care if it had been he himself who had technically 'shown up'. The point was she was here and he did not want her to be.

It just got worse. Presumably she was staying with Edward as opposed to in her own family's townhouse. That meant he could either avoid Edward like the plague or stop reacting to her every time he set eyes on her.

Tom realised that he'd been silent far too long and Edward was bound to be growing steadily more suspicious. Or steadily more fond of the idea of shooting him. Edward already knew far too much about Tom's heartbreak — the hopes he'd had for a life with Caroline and how they'd been crushed by her rejection. He did not want to appear so vulnerable again.

So with herculean effort, he turned a nonchalant smile on his cousin.

"Nothing so dramatic, cousin. I asked, the lady said no. There really is nothing more to it."

Edward's raised eyebrow was proof enough that he did not believe Tom's assurances.

Not that Tom blamed him, since he didn't believe them himself.

But he could not explain to Edward what he really felt, since he wasn't sure himself.

Edward stayed silent for a few moments then with a look of resignation he moved away from the window and back behind his imposing desk.

"Well, I'm glad to hear it. God knows I'll have enough to deal with without worrying about you too."

"Glad to hear I concern you so," answered Tom dryly. "So what has you up in the boughs then?"

"The same thing as you, I'd warrant. Though I'm man enough to admit it. Caroline."

Tom chose to ignore the jibe.

"And why should you be concerned about Caroline?"

"Is it not obvious? She's staying with me. Her father and brother are both absent from Town. That makes me responsible for her. That means I shall have to put up with the parade of dandies she's sure to bring to my door."

Tom would have laughed at Edward's expression of disgust were he not concentrating all his efforts on not smashing something in a fit of jealousy.

"You think you will have many pups hanging around?" he asked as casually as he could manage.

"You think I won't?" came Edward's reply. "You must have noticed the stir she caused last night and it was our first outing of the Season. She is by far and away the most beautiful debutante on the scene. Her dowry is not to be sniffed at. And her sister is a duchess. *My* duchess," he added with a look that made Tom want to cast up his accounts.

"Well I wouldn't worry overly much. She's never been exactly inclined toward marriage has she?"

"Maybe not up until now. But it seems my dear sister-in-law is on the hunt for a husband. Which means I shall have to keep the gun cabinet well stocked."

Tom knew he had made some sort of non-committal response. But he could no longer concentrate on the conversation. His mind was fully occupied with the knowledge that Caroline was looking for a husband. And wondering why it bothered him so much.

CHAPTER SIX

CAROLINE PLACED A steadying hand to her stomach as their carriage trundled toward the blazing lights of the Hadley Townhouse.

Viscount Hadley had been most insistent that she attend when he personally delivered the invitation some days ago. She had readily accepted. Tonight would be the first night she would see Tom since he had been unspeakably rude four days prior.

Edward had come back to the breakfast room shortly after he'd marched Tom out of it and had returned alone. He did not say where Tom had gone and Caroline did not ask. Rebecca of course had badgered Edward relentlessly about what had transpired between the cousins, but Edward had refused to be drawn and in the end had quieted her with a kiss that had made Caroline leave the room.

Caroline had been so furious with Tom and what he had implied about her. The fact that he had every right to be angry with her no longer mattered. She despised the person he had become. That coupled with her guilty feelings of being responsible for him becoming such a person did little to help

Caroline's peace of mind.

Her emotions had been in such upheaval since she'd first met his deep blue gaze across the crowded room. But enough was enough.

Caroline had first determined that her plans for fun and a little scandal would all be for nought in the face of Tom's return. But his treatment of her since had made her even more firm in her plans to get out into the world and live a little.

His quip about a staid and sensible husband had stung. Mostly because of the truth of it. Well, that may be so, but she was not married yet! And she would show Tom Crawdon that she knew how to be risqué, daring, and even how to be a little scandalous. He may have changed. But so had she.

"Here we are."

Edward's deep voice cut through Caroline's inner monologue and she gave him a grateful smile as he handed her out of the carriage.

Rebecca clutched her arm and leaned in to whisper, "Are you nervous, Caro?"

Rebecca was aware of Caroline's fresh determination to enjoy herself thoroughly and, naturally, thought it was marvellous.

"Not at all," answered Caroline breezily, "why on earth should I be?"

"Well—" Rebecca hesitated a little— "it's just that the last time you decided to live a little you had fisticuffs with Viscount Hadley."

Caroline rolled her eyes. "I certainly did not have 'fisticuffs' with him, Rebecca. Honestly, your exaggerations could get someone hanged."

Rebecca merely grinned and shrugged her shoulders.

"Speak of the devil," Rebecca said in low undertones, nodding her head toward the figure of Viscount Hadley barrelling his way through the crowd gathered in the elaborate hallway.

Caroline didn't swear. Ever. But how tempting it seemed in that moment.

"My lady." Hadley was clearly out of breath. But then, given that his cravat was tied to within an inch of its life, it was no surprise.

"Viscount Hadley, a pleasure." Caroline was all politeness as usual. But she was finding the man's persistence a little wearing. And this was only the start of the Season.

"You are an enchantress, Lady Caroline. If I may be so bold?" the young buck responded with a practised flourish.

"No, you may not." Edward's curt response made the young man's cheeks burn scarlet. But he rallied regrettably quickly.

"Come, I shall introduce you to my parents," he said now taking Caroline's arm and dragging her away.

For heaven's sake! How would she get anything improper done with him following her around all evening, acting as though they were somehow attached to each other?

Inside, Caroline was impatient to get away but outwardly she made polite chitchat with the earl and countess and their young daughter, answered polite questions about her own family, said her polite goodbyes, and politely accepted Hadley's offer to escort her to the ballroom. She was entirely fed up with being polite.

Thankfully, once inside she managed to lose him by requesting a glass of punch then running away.

Caroline's eyes took in several acquaintances but none that she particularly wished to speak to.

She scanned the room for Rebecca and Edward and spotted them perilously close to where Hadley was frowning over the selection of punches. Well, good. It would keep him occupied for some moments with any luck.

Caroline took the opportunity of her time alone to take in her surroundings more fully. The room was packed with people and was still filling up. Lord Hadley was certainly sparing no expense. Expense, it was said, he could ill afford.

The nastier of the *ton* gossips were quick to point out that the young Lady Theodora, the earl's daughter, had been out for three Seasons now and had received no offers. So the earl would practically bankrupt himself this year if it meant he could be rid of her.

Caroline did not know the young lady well. But Theodora had seemed unpleasantly like her brother. She shared her brother's good looks but where the viscount's smile was rather slimy and never really reached his eyes, Theodora's was calculating and cold.

Caroline suspected she would not like the other young lady but knew that they would not be close in any case. For getting close to Lady Theodora meant getting close to her brother and there was no way Caroline was volunteering for that!

She continued to take in the sights and sounds surrounding her when her skin prickled and she knew, without having spotted him yet, that Tom was here. And he was close.

Her eyes darted about until she saw him, off to her right and making his way toward her.

Caroline attempted to still her beating heart. After all, his intention could only be to upset or insult her. And hadn't she decided not to let him affect her anymore?

Tom came to a halt in front of Rebecca. And Caroline, rather than show how nervous she was, raised a questioning eyebrow and waited.

She could have sworn his mouth quirked in amusement before he schooled his features and executed a perfectly polite bow.

"Good evening, Lady Caroline."

What was he up to?

"Good evening, Mr. Crawdon," she answered and waited again.

"You look beautiful." Tom spoke again, this time rather hoarsely.

Caroline was so surprised that he'd offered her a compliment that she blurted out, "Do I?" before she could help it.

"You are surprised?" Tom asked. "Surely not. You have always been the most beautiful woman in the room, Caroline."

Caroline felt her breathing hitch at this murmured statement. She wasn't sure what to say to such a thing, especially in light of how he'd been treating her for the past week.

Tom looked as shocked as she felt at having spoken the words. He did not speak. But neither did he glance away.

Caroline was not sure what was happening and she was afraid to speak or move, lest she break the spell. It felt — it felt like it used to be.

They gazed at each other; Caroline's icy blue eyes warmed by the deepness of his own.

"Tom, I—"

"Ah there you are."

Hadley's booming voice shattered the tenuous spell that had been steadily winding its way around them and just like that, the sardonic glint came back into Tom's eyes.

"Hadley," he greeted the smaller man.

Hadley bowed to Tom and looked between the two. He remembered quite vividly being ousted from a dance with the Duchess of Hartridge once by the duke himself. He had no intentions of losing out on her sister to his cousin! All that money shouldn't be confined to one family.

"Lady Caroline, may I request the honour of the first two dances?"

Swearing became even more attractive to Caroline but she merely smiled, thanked him for the honour, and consented. What else could she do?

"I'll leave you to it."

Tom's voice sounded cold and distant once again, and Caroline could not help but be saddened by it.

Still, she thought as Tom walked away and Hadley led her to the dance floor, it was better this way. If she softened toward him now and he turned insulting again, she did not think she would recover from it.

The festivities wore on and Tom's mood turned sourer with every dance, every bout of raucous laughter, and every glimpse of Caroline in the arms of another man.

He had promised Edward that he would be civil. But civility was difficult when faced with the knowledge that he still craved her as much as ever, and probably more so.

What was she doing, wasting her time with someone as utterly ridiculous as that dandy, Hadley?

Though he had to admit, she had not seemed overly pleased to have been claimed to dance by him.

Tom had been tempted, oh so tempted, to ask her to dance himself. But he held back. For one thing, he did not trust himself not to kiss her senseless the second he laid a finger on her. For another, he still could not work out how he felt about her and would do well to maintain a safe distance until he did.

Edward's assurances that Caroline was in the market for a husband had rankled more than he cared to admit.

Why should he bloody well care if she wanted to marry? He had given up on her the day she refused him and had stopped giving a damn soon after.

He winced as a high-pitched cackle assailed his ears. Dear God, someone needed to put whomever the lady was out of her misery.

He grimaced before swallowing the rest of his brandy in one gulp. Perhaps it was time for him to take his leave.

He had adhered to the obligatory social niceties — flirted

with the married ladies, flirted a little less with the single ones lest they get any ideas, gamed with the gentlemen, and danced with Rebecca, among others. And all the while he'd watched *her*, dammit.

Tom knew that Edward and Rebecca, as well as Caroline herself, would notice that he had not asked her to dance. But a man could only take so much temptation before he did something about it. And since he spent half his time lusting after her and the other half fantasizing about ruining her, crushing her heart as she had his, it was best that he did not ask her. Mercifully nobody questioned or berated him for this minor social faux pas.

For her part, Caroline had stayed as far away from him as possible. Which did not prove too difficult since she'd been drowning in a sea of male humanity all evening.

Tom scowled. Edward was doing a terrible job of chaperoning his beautiful charge. So too was Rebecca, but then she could barely take responsibility for herself so it wasn't terribly fair to expect more from her.

And he was wasting far, far too much time worrying about the lady Caroline, he thought with a frown. It really was time to find Edward and take his leave.

He looked around the crowded ballroom but could see no sign of Edward or Rebecca. What a surprise.

His eyes continued to explore the outskirts of the dancing couples when his attention was caught, as it always was, by the golden bright presence of Caroline. He swore, not very softly, and was rewarded with an affronted glare from the mamma standing beside him, protecting her baby chicks.

Mamma was furious, but her innocent daughters were looking decidedly less than innocent in his direction. He grinned wickedly and favoured the ladies with a rakish wink before the mother hen bundled her charges away with much talk of evil men and the damage they did to impressionable young ladies.

Chuckling softly, Tom turned back to watch Caroline and was confused by her sudden disappearance. Where could she have gone? His frown deepened, she could not have vanished into thin air.

He was about to move off in search of her when he spotted a swirl of sky blue silk a little to his left.

Tom clenched his fists as a barrage of jealousy and rage assaulted him. She was going out into the darkened garden. And she wasn't alone.

CHAPTER SEVEN

WAS BEING FUN and spontaneous supposed to make her feel so uncomfortable?

Caroline felt her companion's hand on the small of her back and she smiled a little nervously before moving slightly away.

Perhaps this had been a mistake.

Caroline had been smarting all evening from Tom's obvious dismissal of her.

Earlier in the evening it had seemed as though he was warming toward her again. Certainly the look in his eyes and his words had made her feel more than a trifle warm.

But since their brief, and strange, conversation he had avoided her completely. At first she had been excruciatingly embarrassed. She knew that people would notice the slight. However, she had reminded herself and Rebecca, who had subtly asked if she was hurt, that she was here to throw off the shackles of society rules and the new, fun loving Caroline would not give a fig that Mr. Crawdon had refused to stand up with her.

Instead she had danced with, flirted with, and been

outrageously complimented by dozens of young men who had been vying entertainingly for her attention.

One in particular had caught her eye from the start. A Lord Stanley, cousin of Hadley. He was tall, dark, and whilst not as handsome as Tom or Edward (which wouldn't be a fair comparison anyway because, really, who *was* as handsome as those two?) he was very attractive. And if his eyes held a predatory gleam that made her feel a little wary, his charm more than compensated.

She was being silly, thinking him anything less than a gentleman. She just wasn't used to such forward behaviour, but perhaps her being more open meant that she was attracting a more open sort of man?

He had been extremely attentive and at first, it had made Caroline extremely uncomfortable and she had been politely but firmly rejecting his offers of air, dancing, and champagne at every turn.

But then she'd caught sight of Tom dancing with that awful Miss Sandson whose dress was astonishingly lower than her intelligence.

Caroline's temper had flared and she'd turned her most dazzling smile on Lord Stanley and accepted his offer of a turn around the gardens. She hadn't felt particularly overheated but anything was better than having to watch Tom fawn over that simpering dolt, Miss Sandson. It was bad enough that he had not asked her to dance, but to see him dance quite happily with such ladies as these made her furious and, quite honestly, desperately sad.

And so it was that she found herself out on a darkened balcony with this strange and slightly frightening man as company.

Caroline felt immediately that she had made a grave error. How could she have been so stupid as to step out alone with a virtual stranger?

She noticed, to her growing horror, that during her

contemplation of Tom, and the extra limb he'd grown in the shape of Miss Sandson, Stanley had managed to manoeuvre her further down the balcony and they had lost what little light from the candlelit ballroom they had, pitching them into virtual darkness.

"Lord Stanley—" Caroline did her utmost not to show her fear— "I think it would be best if we were to return to the ballroom."

"But we only just got out here, my dear. I have been so looking forward to getting you alone."

His words, though dripping with charm, scared the wits out of her.

Caroline flinched as he stepped closer but stood her ground. "I hardly think that is appropriate, my lord."

Stanley merely laughed and before Caroline knew what his intentions were he had grabbed her by the waist and pulled her against his body, his mouth descending toward hers.

Caroline struggled with all her might, pushing against his broad chest and kicking out to the best of her ability. She turned her face away from his kiss but it only made him concentrate his efforts on her neck.

She felt bile rise in her throat as his teeth bit into her soft flesh.

"Let me *go* or I shall scream," she threatened, all the while trying to push him away.

He merely laughed and his mockery made Caroline furious. She redoubled her efforts to push him off but it was no use.

He was too strong and too intent on his purpose.

Caroline was torn between wanting to be discovered and not. She would love nothing more than for someone to come to her aid. She had no idea how far the man meant to go and she was terrified of finding out.

On the other hand, unless by some miracle the only

people to discover her were Rebecca and Edward, she would be ruined. Utterly and completely. For she would never consent to marry such a creature as Stanley and the alternative would be to live in disgrace.

Caroline felt herself grow weary from her struggles. She had managed to move away from him but little and her efforts only seemed to spur him on.

Now he had grabbed her chin painfully and was lowering his mouth once again toward hers.

The resounding slap she delivered to his cheek did not stop him at all, and now he had gripped both of her small hands in one of his, keeping them pinned behind her back.

"I shall scream!" she warned him frantically.

"And draw attention to yourself?" he mocked. "Besides, your brother-in-law seems to have disappeared and who else would come to your rescue?"

"I would."

Before Caroline knew what was happening, Stanley had been dragged away from her. Her eyes widened as Tom turned her attacker to face him before landing a blow on his face that made the smaller man stagger before hitting the ground with a loud *thump*.

Caroline felt a rush of relief so strong that it made her knees buckle. She was rendered completely still while Tom, with a look of fury such as she'd never seen before, bent to drag Lord Stanley to his feet before punching him again.

Caroline had the sudden thought, through the haze of shock, that Tom was very likely to kill the other man.

She rushed forward.

"Tom, please. Please don't."

Tom turned on her so ferociously that she stumbled away from him.

"You mean you *wanted* his attentions?"

"What? Of course not. Don't be so stupid." Her anger flared at his accusation. "Did I look as though I wanted them?"

Tom looked mildly appeased as he turned back to the man who was still flat on the ground and clutching his nose.

"You've broken my bloody nose," he said. The volume of blood trickling through his clasped hands confirmed his claim and Caroline felt her stomach roil at the sight of it.

She had never been very good with the sick or injured.

"I'll break more than that," growled Tom as he once again dragged Stanley to his feet, "if you so much as look in her direction again. Understood?"

Lord Stanley made no reply as Tom shoved him bodily through the doors. Just before letting him go Tom bent to utter menacingly in his ear, "If word of this gets around, I shall know who it has come from. And then I'm coming after you."

Caroline's knees were trembling quite violently by the time Tom returned to her side.

Her hair had come loose and, to her horror, she noticed there was a tear on the sleeve of her gown. She busied herself trying to fix both while she tried to get her breathing under control.

Tom appeared to be waiting for her to speak first, so releasing a calming breath she looked up to thank him.

And was met with that furious look again.

"Are you alright?" he bit out. He sounded furious, too.

"Y-yes. Thank you, Tom. I— that is to say, he—he wouldn't-"

"What in damnation were you thinking, Caroline?" Tom suddenly exploded, interrupting her stammering explanation.

His tone ignited her own temper. Which was odd since she had herculean strength when it came to controlling her emotions. But really, she'd just been attacked for heaven's sake! Why was he shouting at her?

"I beg your pardon?"

"Surely you're not so stupid as to be unaware of what a man like Stanley intended by bringing you onto the darkened veranda?"

"Don't you dare call me stupid. Are you seriously blaming me for being assaulted?"

"Of course not!" Tom shouted before dragging his hand through his hair and blowing out a frustrated breath. "But you're obviously far too innocent to be left to your own devices. Where the hell is Edward?"

"I have no idea. And I am not a child, Tom. I am perfectly capable of looking after myself."

He didn't say anything but the slight raise of a sceptical eyebrow spoke volumes.

"That is to say, usually I am fine in my own company. Granted, coming out here was probably not the best idea but—"

Tom let out a harsh laugh, though he sounded less than amused.

"Not the best idea? You, my dear, are blessed that I saw him drag you out here. What do you think would have happened had I arrived late? Or not arrived at all? Would you have been happy to be leg shackled to a bastard like that?"

He was so angry. Caroline swallowed nervously. She felt shame crawl through her at her own stupidity. She should have known that no respectable gentleman would have lured her away. But she had been so intent on ridding herself of her jealousy that she had thrown caution to the wind and look where she'd ended up.

Opening her mouth to apologise, she was brought up short by his next words.

"Or perhaps that was your intention? Stanley is well known for his predilection for innocent virgins and would be laughably unfaithful. But then, he has a title."

Caroline felt as though he'd slapped her. She felt the colour drain from her face.

"No," she whispered now and was alarmed to feel the tears filling her eyes, "that was not my intention."

Tom stared at her for what felt like forever, but which could not have been more than a moment or two, but Caroline refused to look away. She watched Tom as he watched the first of her tears trickle slowly down her cheek and his face suddenly tightened with some unidentifiable emotion before he swore softly and pulled her into his arms.

And then the tears really came. Because it felt so right that he should be holding her. His scent, the feel of his arms, his heart thudding against her ear; it felt perfect. Caroline wept. She wept for what she had given up. She wept for his pain and for hers. She wept for the choice she'd made two years ago, the biggest mistake she would ever make in her life.

"Caroline," he crooned and Caroline closed her eyes at the exquisite feel of his lips pressed against the top of her head, "please don't cry."

"I'm sorry," she sniffed and pulled away so that she could look at him. "I'm so sorry, Tom." They both knew her apology was for more than her tears.

Tom didn't speak. Slowly, he lifted his hand and gently wiped away a tear.

Caroline shuddered at the crash of desire that coursed through her body. Tom's hold seemed to change from comforting to seductive within the blink of an eye.

Caroline was suddenly desperate for him to kiss her. She wanted him more than she had ever wanted anything. Yearned for him. Needed to see if his kiss was as enchanting as she remembered, as she dreamed about constantly.

She knew the moment he decided he would kiss her. The light in his eyes changed to one of devilish desire and an answering want screamed through Caroline's blood.

He leaned slowly, so slowly toward her but when his mouth was mere inches from hers he stopped.

"Caroline, are you sure? What Stanley did — you must be scared, confused. I—"

Caroline did not give him a chance to finish. Grasping the back of his neck, she pulled his head toward hers and finally closed the distance between them.

As their mouths fused, Caroline knew she'd finally come home.

Tom told himself he was all kinds of idiotic as his mouth found Caroline's in the sweetest kiss he'd ever tasted. He knew he should stop. Knew that nothing had changed, that he still wasn't good enough for her and never would be.

Yet here he stood, kissing her as if his life depended on it. And at that moment, he felt like it did.

He found, to his vast relief, that her kiss was as innocent as ever. Funny then that it should have more power over him than anything else he'd ever experienced.

Never before had Tom felt rage such as he'd felt when he'd walked out here and found that bastard attacking her. Only Caroline's interruption, and the horrifying thought that she wanted Stanley had stopped him from tearing the man limb from limb. He was furious that Stanley could treat Caroline in such a way. Jealous too that she had chosen to spend time alone with the cad.

He had wanted to remain angry with her, too. Of all the foolish things she could have done, coming out into the night alone with one as debauched as Stanley was pretty exceptional.

But she'd cried, for God's sake. And everyone knew Tom did not do well with crying women. At the sight of her first tear he had genuinely considered jumping over the balustrade to escape but had quickly dismissed the notion. One, because he didn't want to break anything and two, because it seemed rather ridiculously dramatic when he could just go back through the doors he'd used mere moments ago.

Then the strangest thing had happened. Her crying, whilst still scaring the wits out of him, had managed to infiltrate its way through the barricade surrounding his heart.

He had felt, to his horror, a stirring of something he'd tried his best to bury. He found that instead of lashing out at her, he was gathering her to him. Fitting her beneath his chin, right where he'd once thought she belonged, he'd tried his hardest to make the tears stop.

So who was the idiot now?

Her scent had surrounded him. She smelled like a meadow in spring. Nobody else had ever smelled like her. Ever. Well, at least no other women. He'd never made a habit of sniffing men.

She'd looked at him then. With those eyes that were dangerously close to piercing his soul once more.

Minutes ago they had blazed with the blue flame of her glorious anger. Now, they were sparkling from the remnants of her tears and gazing at him.

And, dear God, he could not resist them now any more than he'd been able to in the past.

He wanted to kiss her senseless. Remind her of what they'd had. What she'd rejected.

But his conscience pricked him. Hadn't she just been in a frightening tangle with one of the worst rakes of the *ton*? He should not take advantage.

He'd even made a colossal effort to put a stop to it. But then Caroline had pulled his head toward hers and decidedly taken advantage.

Tom had never been able to refuse her anything before, and he was starting to remember why.

CHAPTER EIGHT

CAROLINE FELT THE last vestiges of her control slipping away and she couldn't care less. Her damned control had controlled her for far too long.

Her heart wept with joy. Tom! Tom was back, holding her in his arms and kissing her once again.

His mouth held hers captive and Caroline thought her knees would finally give way she was trembling so much.

Her breathing became ragged but she would rather pass out than pull away from him now. Her predicament was solved however, when Tom removed his mouth from her own and began a slow, gloriously agonizing trail across her jaw and down to her neck.

Caroline felt a surge of something she did not recognize but she very much wanted to explore, settle in the pit of her stomach. She almost sobbed at the sensations Tom was evoking in her.

"Tom," she breathed, her voice hoarse with longing, "I missed you so much."

Caroline stumbled as she was abruptly pushed away from Tom's intoxicating body.

She looked up in confusion, and was filled with an icy dread at the look on Tom's face. He looked angry again. But more than that, he looked disgusted. With her?

Caroline shivered again, but this time in fear of what she was seeing on Tom's face. Oh, she wasn't afraid of him. Just petrified of the hold he still had on her heart. And how much his emotions still affected her.

"Tom, I—"

"Don't." Tom's voice lashed at her overwrought nerves.

"What a fool I am. You missed me?" He laughed but the sound was so bitter it caused her heart to clench. "Who would miss something discarded so easily, my lady?"

My lady?

Caroline swallowed painfully.

"I—"

"I said don't."

He turned his back and Caroline could only stare at his broad shoulders, his slightly long, roguish hair.

Finally, after agonising seconds, he turned back to her.

"I should take you back inside."

"But—"

"No buts, Caroline. It's not safe out here with me."

"I don't feel unsafe," she whispered.

Tom stared intently at her for what seemed like an age, his eyes boring into hers, his face a picture of some emotion that seemed to be causing him acute pain.

Eventually, he reached out and took her hand, tucking it into the crook of his arm and turning her toward the lights and sounds of the packed ballroom.

"Perhaps you don't," he said, his tone gravelly, "but I do."

Tom was furious. Beyond furious. With her, with himself, with Edward and Rebecca for not doing their bloody jobs and watching her.

He had no idea what had gotten into her. Certainly the Caroline he had known would never test the bounds of propriety enough to go, unescorted, outside with a man.

Glowering at would-be conversationalists, Tom battled his way through the crowded ballroom to find his wayward cousin.

She was very quiet.

He glanced at her in consternation. He had expected icy fury or superior distain. Not meek silence.

"Lady Caroline." A red-faced Hadley appeared in front of them, forcing them to come to a stop. He was out of breath and sweating. "I've been searching high and low for you."

Tom was in no mood to entertain the young dandy, particularly since he'd spotted Edward and Rebecca and meant to tell them in no uncertain terms how bad they were at chaperoning people.

"Move."

Hadley's face fell comically at Tom's abrupt tone.

His complexion, though Tom would have thought it impossible, turned even redder. His eyes darted from Caroline, who still hadn't spoken a word, to Tom before he appeared to come to some sort of decision.

"Forgive me Mr. Crawdon, but it was Lady Caroline I sought to speak with."

There was a moment's tense silence as Tom stared down at Hadley and he stared mutinously back. Tom's lips quirked in amusement. The man had guts, apparently.

"Move," Tom repeated, "now".

Hadley swallowed so hard that his Adam's apple disappeared for a moment. His face fell even further and he paled dramatically.

Tom felt rather than heard Caroline's giggle beside him.

Well at least she had reacted to something.

"I—that is to say, excuse me but—but I—" Hadley

stuttered about for a moment before heaving a great sigh of resignation.

Without another word, he stepped aside and watched miserably as Tom marched Caroline once more through the room.

"So you are alive then after all."

"I beg your pardon?"

"Your laughing at that runt Hadley has proven that you are, in fact, alive. I had wondered since you've been mute since we left the balcony."

Caroline glanced up at him, and Tom had to physically restrain himself from grabbing her and kissing her senseless once again, in front of nearly every member of the *ton*.

She gulped before answering in a small voice, "I do not know what to say."

Well, they had that in common. Because Tom didn't have a damn clue either.

Caroline knew she should feel angry or humiliated or something at Tom's heavy handedness. But she could rouse no feeling other than one of melancholy. Being adventurous was all very well. But so far all she had gained from it was a terrifying experience with a horrible man and another nail in the coffin of her relationship with Tom.

Yes, there'd been a glorious kiss, but at what cost? He was furious with her. Still incredibly bitter about what she'd done and still his treatment of her made her want to weep.

She barely noticed when he pulled her to a stop in front of her sister and brother-in-law.

"Well, I didn't expect to see you two together."

Rebecca's voice brought Caroline's head up and as they locked eyes, Caroline could see that Rebecca knew something had happened.

Tom rather rudely ignored her turning to face his cousin instead.

"Edward, much as you seem to enjoy ignoring everything outside of you and your wife lately, you would do well to remember that a chaperone is supposed to, in fact, chaperone his charges."

Caroline felt her mouth drop open at Tom's speech to his cousin. He sounded coldly furious and barely in control of his temper. Little did she know that he was fast losing control of everything and was desperate to get away from her.

It seemed he had been doing nothing since his return to England but run away from her.

Edward seemed as surprised as Caroline but schooled his face to an impassive mask.

"Thank you, Tom. Since you're such a wonderful protector of young ladies' reputations yourself, I feel privileged to have your input."

"Don't try to be clever, Edward. It doesn't suit you."

Caroline and Rebecca shared a look of incredulity. Tom and Edward seemed intent on bickering like old ladies. Thankfully they had not yet resorted to hitting each other with fans so hadn't drawn a crowd.

"Gentlemen, really." Rebecca stepped neatly between the two and turned to Tom with a sweet smile.

"Tom, dearest, thank you for taking care of Caroline in our absence. I confess myself surprised that you bothered. After all, you did not seem overly concerned with her welfare before.

It seemed that under the sweetness, Rebecca had her claws sharpened.

Caroline felt that the time had come to intervene and stop this spectacle before it embarrassed them all.

"Rebecca, Tom was—"

"I was doing your job!" Tom interrupted explosively.

Several heads turned toward them and Caroline groaned

at the avid interest from some of the worst gossips in London.

"Watch yourself, Tom." Edward's voice was furious now too. He obviously did not take kindly to his cousin shouting at his wife.

Tom however seemed to be beyond reason. He swung back toward Edward.

"Watch myself? When I'm wholly occupied with *your* sister? Since you haven't even bothered to ask, I shall tell you why I'm escorting her back to your side, shall I? Not thirty minutes ago she was being attacked on the balcony by Lord Stanley. And where were you?"

Edward's face registered his shock at this piece of news. Rebecca looked horrified, but Tom did not give either of them a chance to speak. His rant continued.

"If you can't do your damned job and look after her, Edward, find somebody who will. Because God only knows what would have happened if I had not seen her leave with him. And if something happens to her because of you, so help me I'll—"

Tom cut off abruptly. Caroline desperately wanted him to finish what he was going to say but he had closed up again.

Without another word Tom turned on his heel and stormed out, leaving a pregnant silence in his wake.

"Caroline, are you alright?"

Caroline dragged her eyes from Tom's retreating form to smile at Rebecca.

"Of course. A little shaken but I am unharmed."

"I am glad to hear it. Who is this Lord Stanley anyway? Why do I not know of him?"

Caroline was spared from having to give an answer by a very angry Edward.

"He was a young pup with no scruples and far too much ego."

"Was? Past tense?"

"Yes, past tense. Because I'm about to kill him."

"Thank you, Edward. But murdering him seems a tad excessive," Caroline commented dryly now, having found her voice. She had a lot to think about and once again found herself rather desperate to leave. "Besides, Tom scared the wits out of him. As well as bloodying his nose. I suspect he shall keep his distance from now on."

"Tom hit him?" Rebecca asked, a calculated gleam in her eye.

"Yes, and probably would have done more had I not stopped him."

"Hmm."

"What?"

"Oh, nothing. It is just, for someone who professes not to care about you he seems terribly interested in what happens to you."

"Believe me, Becca, his feelings towards me have not changed. But I am grateful to him all the same."

"As am I. I cannot believe what happened to you. I am so sorry, Caro, that we didn't know."

"Oh please do not worry yourself. How could you know? I asked for freedom and I got it. I just got more than I bargained for in the process."

Caroline smiled reassuringly, but Rebecca remained unhappy and guilty, and Edward remained silent and brooding so, once again, it was a rather sombre group who returned home that evening.

CHAPTER NINE

TOM WAS FURIOUS as he stormed from the Hadley Townhouse and into his carriage. The damned woman had gotten under his skin again. Had he learned nothing from his time away? From her previous rejection?

Why had he kissed her? Why the hell had he shouted at and practically threatened Edward, his own flesh and blood, over her? How was he still losing control like this? How did his heart still beg him to make her his? How did he still, after all this time, dream only of her face and awake each morning with her name on his lips? And how the hell was he to make it stop?

He was tempted, oh so tempted, to turn tail and head back to America. His life had gone from easy and carefree to, well, to Caroline in the space of two weeks. It was enough to drive a man to drink. Which he intended to do.

Tom sighed and leaned his head back against the plush velvet of his carriage. He couldn't run away, much as he wanted to. He had come back here for a reason. He wanted to settle down. Not necessarily marry — the scars were still too deep for that. The wounds too fresh.

But he belonged here, in England, with the family that he'd just threatened to kill.

He had planned to surprise them all with the news that he was now the proud owner of a sprawling estate in Essex and would live the remainder of his life at it, keeping his business interests going from a distance. Before leaving for America he had lived a leisurely life on a small estate in Surrey. Now, however, his wealth had increased massively and Tom had an estate that actually required his hands-on management.

His plan had been to spend the majority of the season in London, then invite his family and an assortment of friends to a house party on his new estate. He still wanted to do so. Only now, he would have Caroline along too. Bloody hell and damnation, this was not what he had envisioned.

Well, he would just have to be sure to invite plenty of young ladies to keep his mind off Caroline. He smiled to himself as the idea took root. Yes, and it would have the added bonus of seeing Caroline suffer the jealousy that he'd been suffering all evening.

Provided of course that she cared whom he was with.

A frown replaced the smile. Why did he want to make her jealous? He was supposed to be forgetting all about her. Being civil but aloof. Getting on with his life while she got on with hers.

The carriage rolled to a stop outside Tom's newly acquired townhouse not far from Edward's. Ironically enough, it was on the same street as the Ranfords'. Tom's man of business had taken care of the sale whilst Tom was still in America so he had not known of the connection until he'd returned home.

Mercifully, the Ranford house remained closed. He did not think he could have borne living only steps from Caroline and having to watch every available red-blooded male in London falling over themselves for admittance.

The headache increased, as did the desire to drink the entire contents of his cellar.

Tomorrow he would visit Edward and apologise for his behaviour. He seemed to be doing that a lot more often lately.

He headed directly to his study issuing orders for brandy, lots of brandy, and no disturbance.

Some way, somehow, he would rid his mind of the woman. As for his heart? He'd rather not think about it.

"Perhaps threatening to do you harm was a tad out of line. So, I suppose I apologise."

Edward leaned back in his chair studying him as Tom came to the end of his rather grudging apology. Tom leaned back and studied Edward right back. It never crossed either of their minds that they might be being ever so slightly immature.

Finally, Edward relented.

"Apology accepted. Lord knows it was deserved. I realise how remiss I've been with Caroline. Rebecca said she wanted some freedom and, well—"

"And you still haven't grasped the concept of saying 'no' to your wife," Tom finished dryly, "which is all well and good. But not when it puts her in danger."

Tom sat forward as he warmed to his subject.

"I meant what I said last night, Edward. If you do not intend to watch her closely enough, then you need to find someone who will. I do not know what has gone on in the years I've been gone, but the Caroline I knew would never have put herself in such a position."

Edward's face had taken on an expression that Tom knew all too well and never trusted. He looked... scheming. That was it. He'd clearly been spending too long in Rebecca's company.

"I'm a worse chaperone than I thought I would be, I grant you. And Caroline is not as proper as she once was. I do not know what has changed either. All I know is that I thought this Season would be like having a saint living in the house, but she has most definitely been plotting something." He sighed and squeezed the bridge of his nose.

"So then, what do you intend to do about it?"

"Take you up on your offer, of course."

Tom stared at him. What offer? Was he more addled from a night of brandy drinking than he thought?

"What offer?"

"The offer to act as a chaperone for my errant sister, of course."

Tom gaped at Edward wondering if he had run mad. He? Chaperone Caroline? Of all the ridiculous notions.

"That isn't funny, Edward."

"Good. It wasn't intended to be."

Tom jumped up from his seat, suddenly feeling too agitated to remain sitting.

"For God's sake. I can't chaperone her."

"Why not? Because of how you feel about her?"

Tom didn't know whether to punch Edward or — well, no he just wanted to punch Edward.

"I do not feel anything for her."

Edward raised a sceptical eyebrow.

Now Tom really wanted to punch him.

"I don't. And even if I did, which I don't, it would hardly be proper, would it? To be chaperoned by a single man who is unrelated? Do you have no care at all for her reputation?"

"Do calm down Tom. Of course I do. And I'm not asking you to attach yourself to her side for God's sake. Just to do what you've clearly already been doing. Watch out for her and if you see anything amiss — punch it."

Tom dragged his hands through his hair. The headache from his previous night's overindulgence was not being helped by this frankly ridiculous conversation.

"Why? Why ask me to do this?"

Edward's expression lost the faint humour and he was suddenly all seriousness.

"I don't pretend to know what is going on in your head when it comes to Caroline. I have no idea what is going on in hers. But regardless of whether you are ready to admit it or not, the truth is that you care about her. A lot. And she needs people who care about her to look after her. She is fast becoming the shining light of the Season and I don't need to tell you what sort of man shining lights attract since you nearly killed one of them last night."

"I did what any gentleman of honour would have done," Tom protested.

"Yes, you did. But it wasn't a gentleman of honour who rescued her, it was you."

Tom didn't have time to wonder if he'd been complimented or insulted since Edward was still talking.

"Hadley's already been sniffing around again this morning. And you know that his debts are mounting by the day. He is positively desperate for a wealthy wife, so he's trying to land her, and if I end up with him as a brother-in-law I'm liable to shoot you. Or him. Or both."

"Me? How would I be at fault?"

"Because the only way that Caroline would end up leg shackled to him would be if she were caught in a compromising position with him. And that would mean that neither of us were doing our jobs. And, well, I'm hardly going to shoot myself am I?"

This was fast becoming a completely surreal conversation.

Tom's head was fuzzy and the headache was now of gargantuan proportions. But he still picked up on one salient point in Edward's speech.

"What do you mean *our* job? I agreed to nothing."

"But you will."

"Indeed? And what makes you so sure?"

Edward shrugged as if it were the most obvious thing in the world.

"I know you. And I know what you are not ready to admit to. You wouldn't see a hair on her head harmed. So you will help me."

Tom swore profusely and at great length but in the end, he agreed. How could he do otherwise?

He'd be watching her anyway. So he might as well have an excuse to.

Caroline almost let out a yelp of fright as she heard Edward and Tom move towards the door. Perhaps eavesdropping was beneath her but she didn't care. What she cared about was Tom arriving here this afternoon and instead of visiting with them all, immediately requesting a private conversation with Edward in his study.

Rebecca had gone off to the nursery with Henry so Caroline had taken the opportunity to sneak after them.

Unfortunately, the study door was so thick that she heard nothing but muffled sounds.

At one stage she had heard Tom shout something about reputations and her heart had sunk. Was he berating her for her mistake last night?

The thought made her miserable but it was probably no more than she deserved. After all, no self-respecting lady eavesdropped on her brother-in-law and his cousin, who happened to be the man she was in love with, and who was once in love with her but now hated her.

She was starting to get a headache.

However, there was no time to wallow in self-pity since Edward and Tom were clearly finished and moving toward the door.

Caroline panicked. They would see her in the hallway if she didn't move fast. Hastily she turned, intending to dart into the library or drawing room or anywhere but the hallway.

Unfortunately, in her haste she managed to tread on her dress and stumbled head first into an occasional table across from the study door. More unfortunate still, the table was host to a very large, very breakable vase.

Caroline could not break another of Edward's vases. She would never live it down. Her hip hit the table with an almighty crash and the vase wobbled precariously. As if time had slowed, Caroline watched the monstrosity, for it really was rather ugly, wobble to and fro before it finally tipped over.

She dived for it and, thankfully, caught it at the last second. Breathing a sigh of relief, she moved to lift it back into place.

Blast! It was heavier than she thought. Realising that she was emitting very unladylike snorts in her efforts to replace it, Caroline finally managed, with much sweating and grunting, to replace the vase on its table.

Sighing in relief, she turned back to find both Tom and Edward watching her with no small amount of amusement.

"Everything alright, Caroline?" asked Edward, sounding suspiciously like he was trying to hold back a laugh.

Caroline felt her cheeks flame. Rebecca would have brazened it out or laughed, but Caroline was not used to being the subject of ridicule. And she was quite sure they would know she'd only been battling with the vase because she'd been listening in on their conversation.

She felt her cheeks grow warmer still and risked a quick glance at Tom who was not even trying to hide his chuckles.

Gathering the tattered shreds of her dignity, Caroline executed a perfect curtsey to them both.

"If you'll excuse me," she muttered before turning and

running as fast as she could away from them both.

The sounds of their raucous laughter followed her to her room. For goodness sake. They were so childish it beggared belief!

CHAPTER TEN

"OH, MY LADY, how could anyone resist you looking as you do?"

Caroline smiled gratefully at Sally's compliments, taking her wrap from the abigail and giving herself a final inspection in the looking glass.

A visit to Madame Barrousse, the famously blunt modiste, who remembered Caroline fondly from a previous visit thank heavens, had produced several gowns with more promised.

The large and loud Frenchwoman had taken great delight in dressing Caroline again.

"These young girls who have begged me to dress them. *Mon dieu!* I felt like I was being asked to dress a farmyard. But you, you are a rare jewel, fit to wear my creations."

Madame was not the most humble of mantua makers. But she was the best. And Caroline knew how lucky she was that the eccentric woman had taken a shine to her.

Tonight's creation was amongst Caroline's favourite. It was a deep silver satin that trailed behind her with a short train. The bodice was shot through with silver threaded embroidery, the same design skirting the hem. A silver ribbon tied on the empire waistline before falling to the end of the dress. The short sleeves were capped, with the same ribbon. It was simple yet striking and the colour was a perfect complement to Caroline's bright blue eyes and golden hair.

"Thank you, Sally," Caroline responded. "I am rather fond of this dress."

"Tis not the dress, my lady, but what fills it," answered Sally stoutly.

Caroline watched as Sally placed the final crystal pin in Caroline's hair then stood back to admire her handiwork. The hair had been gathered at the nape of her neck, making it long and elegant, and Sally had taken great pains to dot the carefully constructed curls with the glittering crystals Caroline had purchased just this week.

The clock chimed the hour and Caroline moved to collect her fan and gloves from the dressing table.

"I shall not shame you then, Sally?" she quipped.

"As if you ever could. Mr. Crawdon's eyes will likely bulge from his head when he sees you."

Caroline whipped around in shock at her maid's words. For her part, Sally looked as shocked that the words had actually popped out.

"Oh, beg pardon my lady."

Caroline burst into a fit of giggles. Sally's horrified expression coupled with the outrageousness of the comment had sparked her amusement. She also secretly prayed that Sally was right.

For the past two weeks Tom had acted like an overbearing brother, watching her every move. Glowering at the gentlemen who asked her to dance.

But she had a brother. And an overbearing brother-in-law and she didn't need another one!

Besides, Tom acting like her brother meant he was decidedly *not* thinking about kissing her again, which was heart-breaking since she had thought of little else.

Casting her mind back over balls, routs, soirees and dinners, there were moments when she caught Tom looking at her and the expression in his eyes made her heart gallop and that peculiar feeling take up residence in her abdomen with increasing urgency.

But then he would catch her eye and immediately a mask would drop over his features and he would become cool, detached, and unbearably protective once again.

And he had never asked her to dance. Not once.

Well, perhaps tonight that would all change. She could make no better effort with her appearance. In fact, she had experienced a moment's panic when first putting the dress on for the cut was far less modest than she was used to.

But if one wanted to make an impact, one had to take risks. So she squared her shoulders and looked forward to the evening.

Caroline made her way downstairs and found Rebecca and Edward awaiting her arrival.

"Caro! You look breath taking!" Rebecca exclaimed, coming forward to embrace her older sister.

"Truly, you look very beautiful," Edward agreed, bowing over her hand.

"Flatterers, both of you," Caroline quipped as they made their way into the warm summer's evening.

"I cannot wait to see Tom's reaction," Rebecca said wickedly.

"Becca!" Caroline darted a glance at Edward. It felt too strange discussing Tom with Edward sitting across from them.

"Don't worry about me, Caroline. I fully expect Tom to have an apoplexy when he sees you. He is only human after all."

Caroline felt her cheeks flush but she thrilled at his words. If even Edward thought he would not remain unmoved, there was hope for her yet.

"Do we know for sure that he will be here? He arrived back from his trip to Essex only today, did he not?" Though at the time she had tried to pretend that she was barely interested, she had listened keenly as Edward had explained that Tom was going to take care of some business in Essex, a few hours' ride from London.

"I saw him at my club this afternoon. He will be here."

Caroline tried not to look as pleased by the news as she felt.

Turning to look out the window, she was surprised to catch Rebecca looking worriedly in her direction. Lifting a questioning brow she felt even more confused by Rebecca's quick shake of her head and quick glance at Edward.

How strange. Something was bothering Rebecca, but something she did not want to discuss in front of Edward.

The carriage made slow progress through the busy London streets but eventually arrived outside the ball.

Before the ladies disembarked however, Rebecca clutched Caroline's arm to stop her.

"Edward, please do go ahead and wait for us inside. I should like to speak to my sister for a moment."

Edward looked as confused as Caroline felt but conceded without comment.

Caroline watched him mount the steps, the crowds parting as he went. She smiled a little at this. It was easy to forget sometimes how formidable he was since he acted so soft-hearted around her sister.

Rebecca reached out and suddenly grasped Caroline's hand, bringing her attention back to Rebecca.

"Caro, I—" here she hesitated, biting her lip as if unsure as to how to proceed.

"Becca, what is it?"

"Nothing. Nothing, I just — well, I want to make sure that you know what you are doing."

"Whatever do you mean?"

Rebecca sighed and leaned back, casting a watchful look at her older sister.

"When you first came here, we had planned on you having fun, being a little mischievous, a little less proper, and finding you a husband."

Caroline wasn't sure what Rebecca wanted her to say so she merely nodded and waited for Rebecca to continue.

"Whilst you have definitely loosened up a little, it seems to me that you are more concerned with what Tom thinks and does than with finding a potential husband. And as for enjoyment, well, it doesn't seem as though he's letting you have any."

Caroline stared at Rebecca, stunned into silence. What? How could she think that? It wasn't true. Of course she was still looking for potential husbands, or at least not snubbing any gentleman who showed an interest, and she had been *trying* to enjoy herself. It was hardly her fault that Tom seemed to have taken on the role of guard dog. She had never asked him to do so. And certainly didn't want him to.

"Rebecca, you were the one who mentioned Tom's name just now, not me."

She thought guiltily of the fact that even her maid seemed to know Caroline's sole focus had been on garnering a reaction from Tom but pushed the thought aside.

"Yes, I know. And it was thoughtless. It was once my dearest wish that you and he would marry. And I've seen the way he looks at you. But I did not realise how much your feelings were involved until I saw your expression at the mere mention of him."

Caroline wanted to deny it but found that she couldn't.

"I realise now that I was foolish to think of him as a match for you. Father would never permit it."

The truth of her words slashed painfully at Caroline's heart. Somehow, she had forgotten her father's demands for a titled son-in-law.

"And Tom is dead set against marriage in any case."

"What? How do you know that?"

"He said as much to Edward. A shame really. He is quite a catch."

Caroline didn't answer. She suspected Rebecca was trying to bait her. The calculated gleam in Rebecca's eyes as she watched Caroline's reaction confirmed as much. So Caroline stayed mutinously quiet.

"My point, dearest, is that I do not want you to waste your Season so occupied with Tom that you lose the chance to make a happy match for herself. We can't forget what ancient fate awaits you if you leave London still single. And truth be told, you are hardly being scandalous at all. In fact, since your unfortunate run in with that horrid Lord Stanley, you've been positively proper."

Rebecca sounded disgusted by this fact, her face a picture in disappointment.

Caroline felt her temper flare.

"It is not for want of trying, Rebecca. But between your husband and his domineering cousin I haven't had a chance to do anything improper. They watch my every move and scare away anyone who isn't thoroughly boring."

Rebecca sighed in consternation.

"Yes, I've noticed. Well, we shall just have to do something about that shan't we?"

"How?"

"Why, distraction of course. For some reason, Tom is terrified of his attraction to you—"

"Rebecca, I don't think—"

"He is," Rebecca continued stoutly, "so one look at you in that gown and he'll either be completely unable to resist, in which case you shall have your scandal since he's an utter rake, or he'll avoid you like the plague, in which case you shall be free to seek your scandal elsewhere."

Rebecca grinned in triumph and Caroline studiously

ignored the fact that she had no interest in seeking it with anyone else.

"And what of Edward?" she asked now.

Rebecca's smile was enough to put Caroline to blush.

"Leave him to me. I can distract him until his eyes cross."

The sisters shared a conspiratorial wink before joining Edward in the foyer of the large mansion. The poor man had no idea what was in store.

CHAPTER ELEVEN

THE BALLROOM WAS everything it should have been — packed to capacity, well lit, and filled with the sounds of music and laughter.

They had arrived late enough to have missed the first few dances, but not so late that it was rude.

Caroline was once again oblivious to the attention she was receiving.

Much as she wanted to prove Rebecca wrong and show that she was interested in other men her eyes, as if of their own volition, sought Tom out as soon as she entered the room.

Her search appeared to be in vain since she could not see him. Trying to dampen her disappointment, Caroline made to move toward the edge of the dancing, content to watch for a while before her card began to fill.

Then she glanced up and there he was.

Caroline was reminded painfully of Rebecca's engagement ball. He had walked toward her then much as he was doing now.

And her heart called out to him now just as it did then. Probably more so. For now she knew the desolate agony of living without him.

He stopped before her and bowed but did not speak. Caroline curtsied but did not speak. There seemed, once again, to be a bubble around them that nothing could infiltrate. It was just a man and a woman and a little piece of magic.

"Ah, there you are."

Edward's voice sounded behind them causing Caroline to jump and Tom to swear none too gently.

"A pleasure to see you too," Edward said dryly.

Tom ignored him, turning instead to kiss Rebecca's cheek and compliment her on how well she looked. And she did look well. In fact, she looked utterly enchanting as usual.

A fact which had not escaped her husband's notice, judging by the gleam in his eye.

Whilst Tom and Edward began to discuss whatever it was they were wont to talk about, Rebecca pulled Caroline away slightly.

"I shall keep Edward occupied for as long as I can, but standing here with Tom is not going to gain you any chances for mischief is it?"

"I only just got here Becca," Caroline reminded her.

"True. So go and enjoy yourself."

"Lady Caroline."

Tom's voice sent delicious shivers down her spine as it always did.

Caroline turned to look at him.

He was staring at her in that intense way that made her want to do things no lady of breeding should be thinking about.

"Would you care to dance?"

Caroline gaped at him. Had he really just asked her to dance? Her heart was already dancing at the prospect.

Caroline spared a quick glance to Rebecca, who was frowning in disapproval, before turning back to Tom with a smile.

"I would love to."

Tom took Caroline's hand and led her toward the middle of the room. It was either that or drag her outside and ruin her for any other man.

What the hell was Edward doing letting her come out like that? She looked entirely too beautiful for her own good.

He had seen the way the young pups had salivated the second she'd walked in the room. And much as he'd like to, he couldn't beat them all to a pulp. It would be rather frowned upon in good Society to knock half the guests unconscious.

The heat of her skin seared him even through their respective gloves. Her scent overwhelmed him again. And her beauty took his breath away, just as it always did.

He had done his best over the past weeks to remain at a polite distance. Watching that she did not get herself into more trouble. Because Edward was right. He couldn't help himself.

He had, unbeknownst to Caroline, had words with several gentlemen who did not do the term 'gentleman' justice, about their interest in her and had watched with grim satisfaction as they'd scampered off.

And the ones whose reputations were spotless, well, there was nothing he could do about them. Except glare at them. Which he did. A lot.

He had left London three days ago. And not a moment too soon. He was finding it increasingly difficult to keep his distance and he knew that people were noticing the fact that he never asked her to dance. But the truth was, and he would only ever admit this to himself, he was terrified of what he would begin to feel again the second he took her in his arms. So he had stayed away.

Leaving for his estate in Essex had been a blessed relief. While there, he had toured the estate — the farms, the grounds, the orchards. He had walked the halls, ensured that rooms were prepared for guests who would join him in the next week or two. But it was a short-lived relief.

The whole damned time he'd thought of her. How she would look welcoming guests in the hallway. Riding beside him visiting farmers and their wives. Taking tea with the vicar's wife.

It had been enough to drive him mad. So he'd driven back to London. Only to find that while he'd been gone she'd managed to become even more irresistible.

So, he'd asked her to dance. He would feed the addiction enough to satisfy this raging need to hold her in his arms and then he would keep his distance again.

"I'm surprised by your offer to dance, Tom." Caroline's soft voice interrupted his musing and he felt immediately guilty for neglecting her, which was ridiculous.

He looked down into the startling blue of her eyes. He could not believe that he'd once found them cold. Now they burned right into his soul.

"Please do not think I meant any slight to you, my lady," he answered stiffly. He saw her frown at the formality of his tone. In truth, he hated the formality himself, but it was imperative if he was to keep his heart safe.

"I am sure you did not, Mr. Crawdon," she answered equally formally and he found that he hated it all of a sudden — the distance between them.

He turned her to face him and bowed before gathering her into his arms. He had chosen a waltz. He was obviously a glutton for punishment.

Her closeness overwhelmed him. And he found that suddenly he did not want to keep his distance.

"The truth is, when you look like that, I can't resist you. And I'm beginning to feel like I do not want to."

Caroline's breath caught at his statement. How did he expect her to keep her heart intact when he said such things?

She gazed into his too handsome face. Did he have any idea? Any idea at all of what he did to her? How she felt?

She had loved him before and she loved him still. More now than ever.

And when he said those things, her foolish heart thought perhaps she would have the chance to fix the mistake she had made two years ago.

The music began and Tom led Caroline through the first strains of the waltz. Caroline remembered Rebecca's description of her first waltz with Edward.

She had described it as magical. Caroline knew now what she meant.

Tom's gaze never left hers except to briefly glance in the direction of Edward and Rebecca with a knowing smile.

The whole *ton* knew that Edward and Rebecca never missed a waltz together. Caroline began to see why.

Although the dance was no longer scandalous, it was much more intimate than any other. And Caroline knew already that she would never want to dance it with anyone else.

Her heart was galloping at the nearness of Tom, the sight of him looking only at her, the feel of his strong arms holding her gently, the masculine scent that was only his intoxicating her with every breath.

And she allowed herself to hope.

Rebecca was right. Caroline had not spent any time trying to find a gentleman to become her husband. Because she had already found him. And nobody could compare.

So why would she try to capture another when her very soul was so utterly captured by him?

The dance ended all too soon.

Tom led Caroline from the dance floor and bowed over her hand. But instead of releasing it, he suddenly gripped it more tightly. His expression made her heart thump wildly. Whatever he was about to say, it would be momentous, she just knew it.

"Caroline, I—"

"Caro." Rebecca's voice interrupted whatever Tom had been about to say.

Caroline swore under her breath then clapped a hand over her mouth, horrified.

Tom's face dropped in shock before he grinned in amusement.

"How unladylike," he quipped, his eyes taking on a gleam that made her feel far too hot and shivery, all at the same time.

"Excuse us, gentlemen." Without another word, Rebecca practically dragged Caroline to the other side of the room to the ladies' powder room, which was blessedly empty.

"Rebecca, what—"

"Caroline, what on earth are you about? Did we not speak of how your attachment to Tom was doing your campaign no good? Why would you dance the waltz of all things with him?"

Caroline hesitated, unsure of what to say. To confess her true feelings or laugh it off?

Finally, she answered, her voice barely above a whisper.

"Rebecca, I love him."

Rebecca stared in shock for so long that Caroline actually began to worry about her.

"Rebecca?"

Nothing.

Perhaps she should slap her?

When she lifted her hand Rebecca jumped back.

"Were you just going to *slap* me?" she shouted.

"Well," Caroline answered defensively, "I thought you'd gone into shock."

"So you decided to take the opportunity to attack me?"

"Don't be so ridiculous."

They glared at each other for a moment before dissolving into giggles.

Rebecca sobered more quickly than Caroline and turned to grasp her sister's hands.

"You love him? Truly?"

Caroline merely nodded, unsure what Rebecca's reaction would be.

But she needn't have worried. A huge grin split Rebecca's face and she threw her arms around her sister, whooping in joy. Which was terribly unladylike but Caroline let it slide.

"Why this is wonderful. Just wonderful."

"Do you really think so?"

"Of course I think so! Good heavens it was always my fondest wish. I even thought that perhaps you and he would fall in love when Edward and I did."

Rebecca was too distracted to notice the flash of pain on Caroline's face.

"Yes, well things do not always work out as we would wish at first."

Her tone alerted Rebecca to Caroline's turmoil.

"Caro, what are you speaking of?"

Caroline took a calming breath, deciding it was time to tell her sister exactly what had happened between her and Tom the night of the engagement ball.

The door opened and a gaggle of debutantes entered the room, chatting loudly. It seemed someone had arrived and whoever she was, she was creating quite a stir.

Caroline and Rebecca shared a look of frustration.

"Perhaps this is a tale that I should tell at home."

Rebecca frowned in disappointed but agreed and they left arm in arm to see what the fuss was.

CHAPTER TWELVE

LATER THAT EVENING, Caroline would wonder how she had managed to keep her smile in place when she walked into the main ballroom again.

It seemed that whatever had the debutantes excited had infected the rest of the room. It was positively abuzz with talk.

"I wouldn't mind being in his position," came one very slurred, very male voice.

"Well, I cannot say I am surprised. The stories of his time in America were shocking. Utterly shocking." This from a disapproving matron not too far from Caroline and Rebecca.

But the statement that really caught her attention, and filled her with dread, was uttered directly in front of her.

"And after all that attention he paid to Lady Caroline. No wonder he tried to pretend he wasn't interested at first. He must have been expecting her."

Rebecca grabbed Caroline's arm even tighter. Still unaware as to what they were talking about, she knew it could not be good.

They neatly sidestepped the gossipy young chit in front of them and made their way to the front of the gathering crowd.

Caroline had thought she had felt pain before now, but nothing could have prepared her for the spectacle before her.

For there stood Tom, surrounded by an avid audience. And he was locked in a most scandalous embrace with a woman Caroline had never seen before.

She heard Rebecca's hiss of surprise. Heard the mumbling — mostly quite imaginative insults directed at Tom. But she responded to none of it. She couldn't. She was frozen in place.

And much as she implored herself to look away, her gaze remained riveted.

By now Tom had grabbed the stunningly beautiful brunette and was holding her at arms-length, a deep frown marring his brow.

He seemed to become aware of the interest they were gathering and he swiftly glanced around, looking rather displeased.

Caroline knew that he would see her watching in mere seconds. Yet still she could not move.

And then his eyes landed on her face. He mouthed something, Caroline did not know what. But it was the catalyst she needed to turn, and without a word to Rebecca or anyone else, flee from the ballroom.

Tom watched helpless as Caroline, her stricken expression cutting to his core, turned and ran.

"Son of a—"

"Now, now Tommy. That's no way to talk in front of a lady. Or me." Charlotte had always made certain that she said and did things that would draw the most attention.

He turned his attention back to her now.

"What are you doing here, Charlotte? And what the

blazes was that little display about?"

Charlotte's painted lips turned down into a pout which was contrived enough to have been practised.

"Why I missed you, honey. And when daddy said he was coming to oversee his shipyards I took the opportunity to visit. You can't tell me you're not happy to see me?"

Tom bit back the litany of curses he was tempted to spew. It wasn't Charlotte's fault, not really.

The first thing he had to do was escape all of this damned attention they were attracting, then he had to figure out what the hell he was supposed to do next.

"How about some air?" he bit out, conscious of several people listening intently to his every word.

Charlotte's smile was knowing and seductive. And had no impact on him whatsoever. He really had changed.

"Of course, darling. Sounds sublime."

He grabbed her elbow and turned her toward the open balcony doors. His gaze searched the crowd for a glimpse of Caroline, but she was nowhere to be seen.

There was a gnawing worry in the pit of his stomach. She wouldn't be so foolish as to leave altogether would she? No, of course not. But then... he'd never thought her foolish enough to go onto the balcony alone with a rake either.

His mood was turning sourer by the second.

Tom suddenly found the way blocked by Edward and Rebecca. The former looking unhappy, the latter making him want to turn tail and run.

"Why Tommy, are these friends of yours?" Charlotte's eyes gleamed appreciatively as they raked over Edward.

Tom could have sworn he heard an actual growl from Rebecca.

"My cousins, the Duke and Duchess of Hartridge. Your graces." He deliberately used their titles for he wasn't sure that Charlotte would bother to do so and he guessed she was perilously close to injury. "An old acquaintance from America,

Charlotte Noble."

Edward bowed politely, but stiffly, and his face had taken on the expression he favoured when playing the arrogant duke.

Charlotte curtsied prettily. Rebecca barely nodded. *Oh, God.*

"How nice to finally meet you, your grace. Tom talked about you incessantly." Charlotte was completely ignoring Rebecca and it was not going unnoticed.

"How long do you plan to stay in London, Miss Noble?" asked Rebecca sounding so icily cool, Tom was sure she was channelling her sister.

Charlotte, having no choice but to answer, smiled at Rebecca though it did not reach her eyes. Rebecca's eyes flashed fire and both Tom and Edward took a cautionary step back.

"As long as it takes my father to conduct his business, Mrs. Hartridge."

Tom groaned. Mrs. Hartridge? Rebecca was going to claw her eyes out!

"I believe you mean 'your grace'," Rebecca answered now, all pretence of friendliness done with. "If you come out in London Society you will do well to remember that Peers are to be addressed in the correct manner. Further, you'd do well to remember that duchesses, especially this one, do not take kindly to being ignored while their husbands are sized up by little girls that nobody has ever heard of."

Charlotte's cheeks flamed scarlet. Tom did his best to remain impassive but Edward had given up all pretence at cool, calm collectedness and was highly amused at his wife's rant.

The group remained silent, waiting to see who would speak first. It was terribly awkward and Tom wanted a drink. And to find Caroline. Not necessarily in that order.

Finally, Charlotte relented. Which was a first.

"I apologise, your grace," she mumbled though she did not sound happy about it. "I meant no offence."

Rebecca smiled sweetly. A sure sign of danger.

"Well, perhaps it is just in your nature then. If you'll all excuse me, I'm going to find my sister." This was aimed at Tom with a hefty amount of daggers shooting from her eyes.

Rebecca spun away and hurried through the ballroom, her clenched fists the only sign that she still wanted to hurt something or someone.

Edward bowed to Charlotte, for he would always have impeccable manners even in the face of such rudeness, and with a hard look to Tom, turned to find someone else to talk to.

Tom felt like an outcast.

"My, my. Your little duchess has a towering temper for one so tiny." Charlotte had dropped the act of contrition, for an act was all it had been, and scowled up at Tom.

"She is not my duchess, Charlotte. She was the daughter of a very important earl and is now the wife of a ridiculously important duke. She is also an absolute favourite of the *ton*, as well as being my family. Do not cross her."

Charlotte's face took on a look of shock at the scathing set down.

"What on earth has gotten into you?" she asked. "A few weeks back in London and you're stiff as a board."

Tom sighed and ran a hand through his hair.

He didn't want to waste his time doing this. He wanted to find Caroline. He wasn't sure what he wanted to say yet, but finding her was his priority.

"Things are different here in England, Charlotte. The rules of Society are decidedly stricter. For example, coming to a ball uninvited and unescorted is inexcusable."

"Well your Society sounds ridiculously dull. But do not worry yourself. I came with my father who *was* invited, since he has business dealings with Sir—uh—oh, whatever his name is."

Her lack of manners was breath taking. Tom had never noticed before. Caroline wouldn't dream of so disrespecting a host.

"Well then, I suggest you go and find your father. I have pressing business to attend to."

"Would this pressing business be the boring blonde that the little duchess is fawning all over right now?"

Tom's head whipped round and he saw Rebecca looking at Caroline with some concern and Caroline, to his utter shock, downing glass after glass of champagne. This was not going to end well.

"Do not speak of her that way, Charlotte. Not to me. Not to anybody."

Charlotte's cheeks flamed once again.

"I'm starting to think you aren't entirely happy to see me, Tom."

"I am very happy to see any of my acquaintances from New York. But—"

"But not happy enough to take your mind off the blonde?"

Tom gritted his teeth as his temper flared.

"Her name is Lady Caroline."

Charlotte smirked. "I don't care."

That did it.

With a quick bow, Tom turned and walked away.

Why had he never noticed how crass Charlotte was? Had he just not cared?

Tom had always had a bit of a reputation as a rake, though mostly a harmless one. But even those who had known him before would not excuse such a vulgar display as the one Charlotte had just put on — with him as her co-player, unfortunately.

Charlotte had shouted his name loud enough to bring the chandelier down and had run across the ballroom and thrown herself into his arms, planting her mouth firmly against his.

Tom had been so shocked he hadn't been able to move until finally his common sense kicked in and he pushed her away. He was immediately aware of the fascinated crowd, the gleeful gossips. He needed to get away from her and fast before...

His skin had prickled, and he was aware of her, as he always was. He scanned the crowd until he'd seen her. The look of devastation on her beautiful face would haunt him for days.

He knew he shouldn't care. After all, hadn't she rejected his love? But he *did* care. And he had thought that perhaps there was something growing between them again. It was tentative, and tainted with the hurt of the past, but it was there and he was falling under its spell again.

Had Charlotte's display ended it before it had a chance to begin? And did he even want to risk his heart all over again?

He didn't know the answers to these questions that seemed to spin never-ending through his mind. But right now, he wanted to speak to Caroline, to explain that Charlotte meant nothing to him. And, he thought with a grimace as he watched her pluck yet another glass from the table, to stop her from drinking herself into a stupor.

CHAPTER THIRTEEN

CAROLINE SHRUGGED OFF Rebecca's hand and drank deeply from her glass.

It was about time she started acting instead of just talking.

She had promised herself a season of scandal and all she had done was allow herself to fall more and more in love with Tom Crawdon.

Tom, who not thirty minutes ago had been locked in a scandalous embrace with a beautiful stranger. Oh, God.

Do not cry, Caroline. Do not let them see you cry.

"Caroline, do you not think—"

"Think? All I do is think! Well, dear sister, I have finally decided to do what you have been wanting me to do. Cause a stir and have a little fun. If Tom can do it, then so can I."

Rebecca frowned unhappily.

"Perhaps I was too quick to encourage you. This is not you, Caro."

"Well perhaps it should be."

"You've had enough to drink."

Caroline merely laughed and plucked her fourth glass.

Or was it fifth?

"I never realised how delicious champagne was you know. So bubbly," she giggled.

Already Caroline was feeling better about the whole nasty business with Tom. In fact, she was starting to forget what was so terrible to begin with.

The candles suddenly seemed brighter, the laughter louder. Why had she never drunk more of this before? It was truly marvellous stuff.

Lord Hadley chose that moment to seek her out.

"Good heavens, run," whispered Rebecca, "Hadley has spotted you."

Caroline looked up and favoured the approaching Hadley with a breath-taking smile, which caused him to stumble a little.

Poor man.

"G-good evening, my lady," he stuttered, unused to such a friendly reception.

"Lord Hadley, I am so very pleased to see you."

"Really?" he asked.

"Really?" Rebecca echoed.

Caroline tittered, which she had never done before, lightly tapping Hadley's arm with her fan.

"Of course," she answered flirtatiously, batting her lashes.

Rebecca watched in fascinated horror.

She was torn between concern and amusement. Caroline — proper, perfect Caroline — was well and truly in her cups.

Hadley for his part looked as though he might faint from the pleasure of having the undivided attention of a catch such as Lady Caroline.

"Will you do me the honour of dancing the next with me, Lady Caroline?"

"My dear Hadley, I thought you'd never ask," she answered lightly, throwing back the rest of her drink in one swallow and handing the flute to her bemused looking sisters.

Sisters? Why were there suddenly two of them?

Caroline staggered a little as the room tilted alarmingly. Thankfully though her arm was safely ensconced within Hadley's and so she did not fall straight out on her—

"Are you quite well, my lady?" Hadley's concerned voice interrupted Caroline's slightly fuzzy thoughts.

She hiccupped a little and grinned widely.

"I believe I'm better than I've ever been Hadley," she answered with what she hoped was a flirtatious wink.

Why is he looking more frightened than enamoured? she wondered, a little put out at his reaction.

The music for a cotillion started and Hadley moved to stand opposite her.

Caroline concentrated on staying upright and made sure to catch as many male eyes as possible to deliver surreptitious smiles and coy glances. If she was going to be a flirt, she wanted to do it right.

The music started and Caroline was about to take her opening steps when she heard an audible hiss behind her. Turning in confusion, she saw Rebecca anxiously waving and beckoning with an amused looking Edward standing beside her.

Caroline waved away Rebecca's interference and turned back to Hadley.

Heavens, this dance was never-ending, Caroline thought after only seconds. She was quite parched and was anxious to have some more of the delicious champagne on offer. Plus, Hadley was just as sleep-inducing as ever and she was beginning to think she should tell him so, for his sake as well as her own. He could never be expected to improve if he was oblivious to his faults.

And he was a terrible flirt. Looking scared instead of infatuated at her every smile. No, something would have to be done. The sooner she got rid of him, the sooner she could find someone more responsive to her efforts. And some more champagne.

Mercifully the dance ended and Hadley tried to escort Caroline to Rebecca and Edward at the side of the dance floor, but Caroline dragged him toward the refreshment table.

"Be a dear and fetch me some champagne, won't you?" she said, fanning herself profusely for it was stiflingly hot.

Hadley, who was becoming steadily more odious by the second, hesitated and began stuttering, "I am not quite sure, my lady, that you should—er—what I mean is, you seem quite—"

"Oh for heaven's sake." Caroline pushed past him and scooped up a glass of champagne. It was much warmer than her previous glasses had been and did not taste nearly as nice. But her throat was dry and she might as well have something. So she drank the contents in one giant gulp, grimacing as it hit her stomach. She did not remember the other glasses making her feel a little ill. She pressed a hand to her stomach and waited several moments for the nauseous sensation to pass.

It wasn't long before she felt somewhat better, however, and Caroline had something terribly important to say. The time had come to set this little man to rights!

"Viscount Hemley—"

"Hadley, my lady."

"Yes, yes. Hexley. I feel I must tell you that you are really quite an obn—"

"There you are. Come, the carriage is waiting."

Caroline spun around and immediately regretted it as her stomach roiled disturbingly.

Tom stood behind her, his face impassive, holding out a hand to her.

Had he run mad? Did he truly expect her to leave with him? Where was his chit? She almost laughed at his audacity to order her about but her stomach once again flipped alarmingly, so she judged it best to stay perfectly still and glare at him instead.

Tom watched worriedly as the colour drained from Caroline's face and her usually peachy skin turned slightly green.

Dear God, she wasn't going to cast up her accounts here in the ballroom was she?

The time had definitely come to remove her.

He'd been watching, torn between amusement and concern as she'd drunk more and more, and then staggered through the dance with Hadley.

Thankfully he was certain that only he, Edward, and Rebecca had been watching her so closely, and therefore her reputation wouldn't suffer for the spectacle. Until Hadley opened his sizeable mouth, of course.

He'd been too late to stop her dancing, reaching Rebecca's side just seconds after Caroline had waved away Rebecca's pleading gestures and thrown herself into the dance.

As he'd been making his way steadily towards her, he'd seen her leer at Hadley and wink comically at him. Hadley had looked like he had no clue what to do and Tom couldn't blame him. This was not the sort of behaviour Society had come to expect from the perfect Lady Caroline Carrington. She'd scared the poor devil out of his wits.

The dance had ended without incident, to Tom's relief, and he'd waited impatiently for Caroline's return, all the while ignoring the death stares from his tiny but formidable cousin through marriage.

But instead of making their way towards Rebecca, Caroline and Hadley marched in the opposite direction. Well, Caroline marched. Hadley was dragged. Rather ferociously. She was clearly stronger than she looked.

Tom muttered an expletive not too dissimilar to the one coming from Rebecca. Edward laughed. The cad.

"It isn't funny, Edward!" Rebecca had hissed angrily. "She

will regret this in the morning."

"I apologise, sweetheart. Do not distress yourself. I shall go and rescue Hadley from her clutches."

"Allow me."

At this request, Rebecca and Edward both turned their full attention to Tom and he had to fight the very real desire to stare at the ground and shuffle his feet just as he'd done as a lad when he was in trouble.

"I think not," Rebecca bit out crisply, and Tom was once again reminded quite forcibly of her older sister who could freeze a man with a single glare.

How odd, he thought distractedly, that Rebecca's handsomeness should be so famous and yet, in his eyes, could not hold a candle to the heart-breaking, ethereal beauty of her sister.

He turned to look again at Caroline, to make sure she wasn't doing anything too ridiculous, and was once more half amused, half horrified as he watched her barge past Hadley and throw back the contents of another glass of champagne.

His eyes widened in alarm at the sudden pallor of her cheeks. He recognised that look. He'd been wearing it for years. A sure sign of total overindulgence. And what usually followed was never pretty.

He knew that Rebecca was the best person to look after Caroline in her present condition. He knew that Caroline would be furious about the vulgar display with Charlotte, and perhaps a little jealous.

But whether she was foxed or not, he wanted to explain himself. Though God only knew why it should matter so much. He had his suspicions as to why her opinion of him was so important. But he did not want to examine them too closely. Nor did he want to question why Rebecca was so angry with him. Speculation of that kind led to hope and he had learned a harsh lesson the last time he had allowed himself to hope.

Either way, he intended to speak to her and he intended

to do it tonight.

"Rebecca," he said now, turning back to the younger sister to address her concerns before the older one did something irreparable, "Caroline's behaviour is sure to start drawing attention soon. If you leave now, who will be able to smooth over any gossip? Certainly not I."

Rebecca frowned at his words, true as they were. If just one person were to notice Caroline's behaviour and comment on it, it would spread like wildfire. And Hadley was sure to spread the news as soon as he recovered from his surreal ordeal.

Still, Rebecca was not about to let him whisk Caroline off. Especially in view of what Caroline had told her only tonight and what she'd witnessed between him and that horrid American.

"And you do not think the gossips will talk about Caroline leaving a ball with only you as company?"

"I dearly hope they do not notice. Not if I get her out quickly enough."

"And what is it you propose, Tom? A cosy little chat with you, Caroline, and that American b—"

"Sweetheart—" once again Edward's voice made a timely interruption— "let Tom take care of it tonight. You and I should concentrate on showing that nothing is amiss."

Tom looked across at Edward above Rebecca's head, which wasn't difficult since she fell quite short of both their shoulders. After a moment's glance, Tom gave a swift nod of thanks and moved to rescue Caroline. Or Hadley. He was not yet sure which.

As he approached them he was alarmed by the sound of Caroline's lilting voice, usually so soft and melodious, now harsh and very, very slurred, calling Hadley by anything other than his actual name, and sounding very much like she was building up to quite the set down.

Much as he'd like to see the irritating little lap dog sent

on his way, he knew that Caroline would be horrified in the cold light of day so he stepped in and said the first thing that came to mind.

"There you are. Come, the carriage is waiting."

He had no carriage waiting. And he was fairly certain that she would refuse to go anywhere with him. But he had to stop her from speaking!

And now, here she stood in front of him, turning greener by the second and swaying unsteadily.

Was it odd that, even then, he could barely control his desire to gather her into his arms?

Her instability was endearing and the icy flame of her anger, evident in those expressive eyes, was doing things to him that had no place in a public ballroom.

He took a step closer as she placed a delicate hand on her throat. He would pay good money to be that hand right about now.

"Are you alright?" he asked quietly, hoping she wouldn't screech at him like a fishwife and draw attention.

There was no screeching however. Just a look so bleak that it nearly brought him to his knees. He questioned why his appearance should cause such a look to taint her perfect face, wondered if he could possibly be right about what he was beginning to suspect.

But then she took a deep breath and pulled herself up to her full height. Which wasn't very high.

"Of course," she answered, slurred really, her eyes glassy and a little unfocused, "Why wouldn't I be?"

At her garbled speech, Tom supressed a grin. Oh, she would have a headache like the worse sort of drunkard come tomorrow.

"No reason," he answered, "but if you are ready to leave?"

"I am most certainly not ready to leave," she said indignantly, very nearly incoherent. "Hexley and I are just going to have some more champagne. Isn't that right?" She turned and directed her question to the empty space Hadley had scarpered from moments ago.

She turned back to Tom now, looking adorably confused.

"Wait, wasn't there somebody just there?"

"All right. That's enough. We're leaving."

Taking her elbow he pulled her gently from the refreshment table trying to forcibly remove the flute she was clutching from her hand. It was no use. Her grip was vicelike and he had no wish to draw attention to them. So he waited impatiently while she finished the contents then turned her towards the door.

He smiled and nodded along the way while Caroline hiccupped and stumbled against him.

He bit the inside of his cheek as she trod on his toe time and again but eventually, mercifully, they reached the foyer.

Tom sent a footman to fetch his carriage while Rebecca appeared beside him clutching Caroline's cloak.

"Now, Caro. Tom has agreed to escort you home. Edward and I will remain here so that everyone knows there is nothing out of place."

Caroline nodded her understanding as Rebecca tucked her into her cloak, for all the world like a mother hen, and once again Caroline looked so miserable that Tom wanted to grab her and protect her all over again.

He heard an audible sniff as Caroline's eyes welled with tears.

His cue to leave.

"I'll just check on that carriage," he said before he shot off down the steps.

His mind must be playing tricks on him. Or perhaps it was an unhealthy dose of wishful thinking; for he felt sure that he had heard Caroline, just before he disappeared from view, mumble something about loving him.

CHAPTER FOURTEEN

"DEAREST, DO NOT distress yourself. If you do not want to be alone with him I shall come with you and we will figure out another way to silence the speculators."

"I do want to be alone with him. That's the problem. He hates me. Truly. And I thought we were perhaps... Oh but what does it matter anyway? He's obviously gone and fallen in love with that girl, whoever she is. But, Rebecca, I love him."

Fat tears trailed down Caroline's face and she did nothing to stop them. She felt ill and suddenly tired. The cold air sweeping up the steps of the building was doing nothing to help her head. If anything, it was making it worse.

And now she'd be forced to ride home with him. In an enclosed space. Probably while he wittered on about that irritatingly beautiful girl he'd had climbing all over him. It was not to be borne.

"Caroline, I have no idea what happened between him and that creature but I would bet every penny of my dowry that Tom does not hate you."

Rebecca grasped Caroline in a tight hug which did very little to help Caroline's heaving stomach.

"Now listen carefully. You have drunk too much so you may feel less—er—inhibited than usual. You must *not* say anything about how you feel to Tom during the ride back home. Do you understand? I do not want you doing or saying anything that you will regret tomorrow."

Before Caroline could reply, Edward appeared from one direction, Tom from the other.

"The carriage awaits, my lady," said Tom warily, watching closely for more tears.

"Rebecca, Hadley's already talking, the little rat. Come. We must return. People are looking for us."

"I'll kill him if he damages her reputation," Tom muttered grimly.

"Best worry about your own, cousin. The gossip about you and Miss Noble is gathering speed too."

"Bloody hell. There's nothing between Charlotte and I, dammit."

"Watch your language!" admonished Rebecca sharply, which was ironic since she could out-swear the lot of them.

"A little rich, Rebecca," he shot back childishly.

"Stop squabbling, both of you," interjected Edward.

"Do not speak to me like that, Edward."

"Sorry, dear."

"You're apologising to her? She started it."

"Grow up, Tom."

"I think I'm going to be sick."

Caroline's weak mumble succeeded in bringing the extremely immature bickering to a close.

They all turned to her in alarm.

Rebecca immediately rushed to her side, holding her steady.

"I really think I should go with her," she said, worry etched on her face.

"I will take care of her, Rebecca," Tom insisted.

"You really are needed here, sweetheart," Edward

pointed out.

"Well I do not think she particularly wants to go with Tom right now."

"I am standing right here, you know."

They both ignored him.

"I am aware of that darling, but I do think it is for the best."

Caroline felt herself sway. She really did feel dreadfully ill. It was time to go. And at this point, she no longer cared who she went with. As long as she left.

She heard Tom mutter something and suddenly she felt herself lifted into his arms.

Gasping in surprise, her eyes collided with his. Blue on blue. Her own, she knew would be slightly unfocused since she was finding it difficult to see less than two of him. His, though. His caused her heart to gallop alarmingly. They blazed with a fire that, although she could not name it, made her feel like her whole body would be alight soon.

She felt the hard planes of his body as her own pressed against it. Felt the solid strength in his arms as they scooped her up against him.

Tom gazed at her for a moment before turning his attention to the now silent Rebecca and Edward.

"Goodnight" was all he said before he turned and walked down the steps and toward the waiting carriage.

Caroline spoke not a word as he placed her gently against the cushioned seat before taking his place opposite her.

What was there to say anyway? She had been stunned into silence. More than that, she did not trust her own voice. Her body had reacted quite violently to being so close to his and she was both excited and slightly alarmed by the sensation.

Also, still feeling more than a little sick, she was afraid to open her mouth at all for fear of what might happen.

Tom rapped on the carriage ceiling and they set off on a

slow trundle through the darkened London streets.

Tom watched Caroline closely for signs of sickness, all the while trying to get his hormones in check.

Picking her up had been a mistake. An exquisite, torturous, beautiful mistake.

But he had grown quite tired of his bickering with Rebecca and one look at Caroline's face, and her rather obvious swaying, had been proof that she needed to be removed.

He was frustrated that she was obviously in no fit state to hear his explanations about Charlotte at the moment. But he still wanted to be the one to see her home safely.

Otherwise, he'd spend the night worrying himself sick about her.

And, as foolish as it was, he found that any time spent with her was infinitely better than time spent away from her.

Which made him a prized idiot.

The feeling of her body, so light and supple and pressed so closely to his own, would haunt him for days. And nights. Especially nights.

The scent of her, still like a meadow in spring, tantalising and fresh. The impact of those icy eyes, glassy and unfocused as they were. The rosiness of her all too kissable lips. These things combined would serve to give him many a restless night.

He groaned aloud and let his head drop back against the plush velvet cushion behind him, closing his eyes. Being around her was going to turn him grey!

And tomorrow he was issuing the invitations to his house party at the estate in Essex.

Willingly throwing himself into her company for two weeks.

He was a glutton for punishment that much was clear.

"Tom." The whispered voice beside him caused him to jump out of his skin.

With a startled yelp he jumped from his seat and smacked his head on the roof of the carriage.

"What in the blazes?" he yelled as he frantically rubbed his head and sat down abruptly on the other side of the carriage.

During his morose silence, Caroline had deposited herself beside him. Now she was giggling like a schoolroom miss, wiping tears of mirth from her eyes.

"Good heavens, Tom. I did not take you to be so jumpy."

"I am when someone sneaks up on me," he answered sulkily.

"Terribly sorry, old chap," she said before bursting into peals of laughter once more.

It seemed the maudlin mood had passed.

Her nearness was affecting him more than he would care to admit. And, laughing or crying, she was showing emotion at least. He had loved her when he thought her coolly detached. Add humour, anger, fear, happiness, vulnerability, and a host of other emotions to the mix and he was in grave, grave danger of loving her more than he even knew he was capable of.

And that scared the wits out of him.

She had held that sort of power over him before and he had been left bruised and broken. He couldn't, wouldn't allow himself to feel it again. How could he take such a risk when he had barely survived the first time?

That didn't mean he wasn't lusting after her with every single breath that he took, however.

The giggling had mercifully ceased and Tom opened his eyes to find her scrutinising him with some intensity.

She was either in very deep thought or trying desperately hard to actually focus on his face. He had a feeling it was the latter.

"You will have the devil of a headache in the morning, my lady," he said wryly.

She shrugged her shoulders in total nonchalance. Because she had no idea what was coming, no doubt.

"What is all this 'my lady' nonsense? Can't you at least call me Caroline?" She paused for a moment, before continuing in a barely audible voice, "You used to."

Tom swallowed past the sudden lump in his throat. He didn't want her growing despondent again. That made him feel protective and caring. Things he wasn't strong enough to feel right now.

"Yes, I did," he answered. "And I shall continue to do so, if it pleases you."

Caroline beamed then and the breath caught in his throat. Dear God, she was utterly exquisite.

"It does please me. Shall I tell you what does *not* please me?" she continued.

Dammit.

He sighed.

"If you must."

She leaned forward, but way too much and he found himself having to grab her and push her back onto her seat.

"Thank you," she said piously as she faffed about fixing her gown, pulling the bodice and making him nearly expire on the spot.

"Where was I?" she demanded.

"I have no idea," he sighed.

"Oh, yes. I was telling you what I do not like. I do not like ghastly American girls hanging off you. I do not like seeing you engage in vulgar displays of—of—er—vulgarity in public." She was gathering steam now and the pitch of her voice was growing higher.

Tom winced slightly at the sound. But he had to admit that he felt rather smug at her obvious jealousy.

At least here was his chance to set her to rights about Charlotte.

"The 'ghastly American' has a name, Caroline. She is Miss Charlotte Noble. The daughter of an acquaintance and business associate."

Caroline sniffed which Tom took to mean that she was disinterested in the details.

He continued nonetheless.

"I agree that the display was rather vulgar but it was not of my doing. Charlotte has always been rather forward in her attentions. But she is harmless enough."

"Well perhaps you consider it harmless to cavort in the middle of a respectable ball, but I do not," she bit out waspishly.

"We were hardly cavorting, Caroline. She kissed me. I pushed her away. End of story."

She narrowed her eyes at him, as if trying to decide if he was lying or not. He suddenly found himself quite desperate for her to believe him.

"Hmm" was all the answer she gave before sitting back and sighing deeply.

"What is the matter, Caroline?"

"I did not like to see you with her."

His heart stopped. It was unfair, perhaps, to take advantage of a tongue loosened by alcohol.

He felt his body tighten and resolved to stop thinking about her tongue.

"And why is that?"

Unfair or not, he wanted to know.

"Because — well, because—" her cheeks flamed and his interest piqued— "she is not good enough for you."

Her statement was like being doused in freezing water. Always about standards and being good enough. Even when she was foxed.

"And why would you think that? She is the daughter of a

wealthy and successful gentleman. And I am not titled, as you know."

"What has a title to do with anything?" she practically shouted. She was very loud when she was drunk.

"You tell me!" he yelled back, his temper flaring. It was more than a little unfair that she should decide a title counted for nothing two years after he could have done with her having that attitude.

She blinked at him and swallowed hard, her eyes blazing with some fiery emotion before she once again sighed and dropped her head into her hands.

He didn't speak.

Finally, she raised her head and pierced him with a sorrowful gaze that plagued him.

"I do not think a title is as important as finding someone who makes you happy. And she—she is not good enough for you."

"You do not even know her." Why was he arguing when he had no interest in pursuing Charlotte Noble?

"I do not need to."

"I seem to remember you saying something about *me* not being good enough. Not even the grandson of a duke would do for you. Why should the rules suddenly change now?"

She flinched as if he had slapped her and he immediately regretted his harsh words. There was a time when he fantasised about speaking them to her. But seeing her upset now, he wished he could unsay them.

"I am aware of what I said," she answered now, her eyes filling once again with the dreaded tears. "And I bitterly regret every word I spoke then."

Tom's heart was hammering in his chest. What was she saying?

"But it does not signify. It is too late now, and I realise that. But not her, Tom. I could tell by her behaviour, by the whispers I heard about her. She does not see you. Really see you."

He frowned at this cryptic mark. More evidence of her inebriated state. She was not making sense.

"Her eyesight is perfectly fine to my knowledge," he answered dryly, annoyed with himself for attempting to get any sense out of a drunken female.

"I am not talking about her eyesight, for heaven's sake," she said in exasperation, as if he were the one talking gibberish.

"Forgive my confusion then, but just what are you talking about?"

She leaned forward again, this time grabbing his hands, though whether to keep herself from tipping over or because she genuinely wanted to he wasn't quite sure.

"I'm talking about *seeing* you, Tom," she said earnestly, "seeing how wonderful you are. How kind and witty, how handsome. How overwhelming."

It was garbled. But it was effective. It had rendered him speechless.

Finally, because he couldn't help himself, he answered, his voice hoarse with an emotion he refused to name.

"Why should she see all that, Caroline? When you didn't."

The look in her eyes was enough to break his heart all over again.

She swallowed hard before answering.

"I saw, Tom," she whispered so quietly that he had to lean even closer to hear. "I was just afraid to keep looking."

Well, what was he to say to that?

The silence stretched on. He had no clue what to say to break it. He wasn't even sure he wanted to.

He had suspected then that it was fear that had stopped her from giving her whole heart to him. But to hear her say it, well slur it. It played havoc with his mind and he was suddenly envious of her inebriated state. He could do with some of that himself right about now.

Well, what he really wanted was to crush her lips to his. To worship her mouth the way he'd been obsessing about almost daily for the past two years. But she was drunk; blast it all.

However, they couldn't sit here for the rest of the journey in complete silence. And yet, the moment seemed too special to ruin. The silence too magical to break.

"Tom." Caroline obviously had no such compunction. But her continued whispers led him to believe that she was as affected by the atmosphere as he.

He leaned closer still.

"Yes?"

"I feel—" She swallowed and Tom felt his heart rate increase.

"You feel what?"

He felt as tightly strung as a bow.

She leaned closer still and he felt surrounded by her.

"I feel—"

She looked straight into his eyes and it was as if he'd been struck by lightning.

"—sick."

And she proceeded to cast up her accounts all over the floor. And his shoes.

Well, he'd found a cure for his raging lust.

CHAPTER FIFTEEN

CAROLINE AWOKE FEELING like she'd fought ten rounds at Gentleman Jackson's pugilist club.

Sally had crept in some time ago and drawn the curtains. But at Caroline's agonised cry she had promptly shut them again.

The light had felt to Caroline like being stabbed through the eyes with a sword. In fact, she had come to think that being actually stabbed would be significantly less painful. She demanded that the curtains be drawn back again at once.

After Sally's sharp exit, Caroline had fallen back into a deep sleep.

Now, Sally had entered again and was fast becoming one of Caroline's least favourite people in the world.

"Sally, please. For pity's sake let me sleep. Or die. I genuinely believe these are to be my last moments on earth."

She couldn't be sure, since the task of lifting her head from the pillow seemed altogether too momentous to even attempt, but she thought she heard Sally's muffled laughter from across the room.

Her throat was parched. Her head more painful than she

could ever remember and the nausea of last night had not abated at all. In fact, it was well on its way to being worse.

"Oh, my lady. What are we going to do with you?"

"Kindly stop shouting, Sally."

"I haven't shouted, my lady."

"Well then. Whisper."

"Bailey, his grace's valet, has sent a concoction to help you. It doesn't look the nicest, to be sure. And it stinks something fierce. But he swears up and down that it will work."

Sally slammed the glass onto the table beside Caroline's head and Caroline winced as the noise rang through her ears.

Slowly, very slowly, she turned her head and looked aghast at the dull green liquid beside her.

"I am not drinking that," she rasped.

"Come now, my lady, I'm sure it doesn't taste as bad as it looks. Or smells."

With a sigh of defeat, Caroline attempted to sit up. A mistake! Her head swam, the room spun and she ended up making far more use of the chamber pot beside her bed than she would have liked.

Sally, being the trooper that she was, gave Caroline all the assistance she could — patting her back reassuringly, holding back her hair and giving words of comfort interspersed with the odd remonstration and lecture on the evils of over-imbibing.

"Spare me, Sally, please. I am well aware that I made a colossal mistake last night and shan't be doing so again. Why, I remember nothing! Poor Rebecca must have had a horrid time getting me home."

Caroline lay back against the pillows with a sigh and missed Sally's expression at her talk of Rebecca bringing her home. She knew there was perspiration on her face but could not lift a hand to even wipe her brow.

Sally stood frowning over her in concern before clapping

her hands together.

"Good Lord, woman. Keep the noise down. You sound like a marching army."

"Right, we must get you sorted out once and for all. You shall miss luncheon otherwise and her grace is anxious to see you."

"Luncheon? Whatever do you mean? What time is it?"

"Tis almost noon, my lady."

"Noon?" Caroline gasped.

In all her life she had never slept past eight in the morning.

"You did wake at the usual time, if you'll remember my lady. But you were in no fit state to get up. Still, it's of no matter. A late morning now and again never did anybody any harm. Why, there's ladies who would never rise *before* noon in their lives."

Sally bustled over to the window, drew back the curtains, and threw open the sash. She must have known that the light was killing Caroline. All these years, she'd been pure evil and Caroline had never known.

"Now, you drink that up while I ring for a bath for you. We shall have you feeling like yourself in no time. I'm not sure what to do yet about the green but we're sure to figure something out soon."

"What green?" Caroline asked. Her brain had not seen fit to engage itself just yet.

"Your skin, my lady. Tis green. Now, drink up."

Sally spoke quietly to the maid who had just entered, then shut the door once again turning in time to see Caroline heave herself up to a half sitting position and gingerly lift the horrid concoction to her lips.

Caroline took a tentative sip. Paused for a moment. Grimaced. And then made use of the chamber pot again.

But Sally showed no mercy and insisted that the potion be drunk.

By the time the maids had filled Caroline's bathtub, the contents of the glass had been emptied and to Caroline's great relief, had stayed contained in her stomach.

The room filled with the scent of lavender as the steam from her hot bath permeated the air. She stood shakily and made her way towards the tub, all the while feeling as though the floor were lifting to meet her.

This could not just be the effects of alcohol. Truly, she must be dying.

Lowering herself into the hot water, Caroline sighed in contentment. She hoped against hope that Bailey was right in his claims and that the vile liquid would work miracles soon.

And it did.

Thirty minutes later Caroline felt a lot better. Physically at least. Refreshed from the bath, she was delighted that her stomach had settled and her head pounded significantly less. And rather than feel nauseous, she found herself to be ravenous.

But with a clear head came remorse. And there was plenty of it. Good heavens would she ever live this down? She had no idea what had happened last night, but that in itself could not be a good thing. Being scandalous was a lot more difficult than Caroline had imagined. There was obviously a line between scandal and utter disgrace and she had an awful feeling that she had crossed it last night.

Though her memory was hazy, she had definite flashbacks of certain moments. Seeing Tom locked in an embrace with that beautiful girl being the foremost in her mind. And yet...

There was something else there. Something about Tom niggling at the corners of her mind. But her memories were fuzzy and her head hurt too much to try overly much to remember.

Regardless, she was sure to be the talk of London now, and in a wholly negative way. She wondered if Edward would ship her off back home to Ireland from whence her father would ship her to the bleak obscurity of the Cork countryside.

That prospect no longer seemed entirely terrible. In fact, it seemed preferable to facing anybody ever again. But face them she must.

Caroline felt herself well up at the thought and for a brief moment she allowed the tears to fall while she tried desperately to force her emotions back under her famous iron control. Thankfully by the time Sally re-entered to assist her, Caroline had managed to calm herself down.

Sally helped her to dress in an afternoon dress of palest blue muslin then fixed her hair into a simple style. Anything requiring more than a few pins was more than Caroline could face that day.

Her skin, which had indeed been rather green, was now back to a somewhat more human colour, though it appeared quite grey. There were dark circles under her eyes and her eyes themselves, instead of having their usual sparkle, looked dull and lifeless. In short, she looked as bad as she felt.

"How are you feeling now, my lady?" Sally asked gently, noticing the paleness of Caroline's skin.

"I no longer feel like I am at death's door so an improvement of sorts, I think."

"A good meal will do you the world of good, my lady."

"I am quite famished. But I am loathe to face Rebecca and Edward. What must they think of me? I still cannot remember much about last night. Sally, how could I have let myself behave in such a fashion? I've utterly disgraced myself. And my family. I am quite sure that I shall be shunned from all good society."

Caroline's eyes filled with tears again. Really, she had never been such an emotional creature but then, she had never gotten foxed in front of nearly every important member of the *Beau Monde* before.

"My lady, please do not overset yourself. It won't be as

bad as all that. You'll see. I'm sure his grace will have taken care of the nastier gossips and Mr. Crawdon—"

"What?" Caroline swung round to face Sally. "What about Mr. Crawdon?"

Caroline was astonished to see colour creep into Sally's already ruddy cheeks.

"Well, my lady it's just that—he—er, what I mean is, the gentleman—" here she paused again.

"Spit it out, Sally," said Caroline as a feeling of dread settled into the pit of her stomach. *Tom. Last night. In the carriage. Oh no. No, no, no.*

"Mr. Crawdon is the one who brought you home, my lady. You had fallen asleep by the time you arrived and he, well, he had to carry you."

Caroline groaned and dropped her head into her hands as memories, unmercifully vivid memories, assaulted her mind.

"He carried you all the way to your bedchamber."

Caroline gasped and her eyes flew to Sally's.

"What? But that is, he — what?" she spluttered.

"He wouldn't let anyone else touch you, my lady." Sally was wringing her hands now. "Said that he wanted to make sure for himself that you were settled. He was that worried, my lady."

"But, surely Edward—"

"His grace wasn't here."

Caroline stood up and began to pace in agitation.

"No. Of course he wasn't. I travelled alone with Mr. Crawdon, did I not?"

"You remember?"

"Yes," she mumbled miserably, "I remember."

"Oh, good." Sally was noticeably relieved that she no longer had to continue her painful recounting of the night before. "And do not worry about his shoes. If his valet is worth his salt, and I'm sure he is since Mr. Crawdon is rich as

Croesus, he will be sure to—"

"What about his shoes?" Caroline asked in confusion.

Sally stopped talking immediately.

But Caroline no longer needed an explanation as the memory hit her with the speed of a runaway stallion.

Her eyes widened in horror and her hands flew to her mouth.

"His shoes!" she whispered in terror, "I—I. Oh God."

Even Sally couldn't say anything to make this better.

And she had obviously decided to abandon ship, too.

With a gentle squeeze of Caroline's shoulders, Sally turned her towards the door of the bedchamber and pushed her outside.

It was time to face them.

Caroline walked slowly down the stairs, feeling like she was walking to the gallows.

There was nothing else for it. She must face Edward and Rebecca, find out exactly what she had done last night, and figure out how on earth to make it right.

As for Tom. Well, she wouldn't be seeing him for a very long time; she would make sure of that. In fact, never seeing him again seemed an excellent plan at the moment.

Coming to a stop outside the dining room, Caroline had to take several deep, calming breaths before entering. And even then, she knew her cheeks flamed scarlet.

Please, she prayed reverently, *please let it just be Rebecca in there.*

Taking one final deep breath, she squared her shoulders and entered the room.

"Ah, so you live."

Punishment. That must be it. Punishment for acting so abominably last night. For why else would the first person

who greeted her, a wide grin splitting his face, be Tom
Crawdon?

CHAPTER SIXTEEN

TOM KNEW THAT he was verging on the insane the second she walked in the room. Why? Because he felt better just being around her.

Even though he had every reason in the world not to.

It was lust. That was it. Lust and nothing more. It had to be.

Still, he had to stop himself from leaping from his chair and pulling her towards him when she walked in, frail and beautiful.

He had arrived a while back, intent on speaking to Edward and Rebecca, to find out what had happened after he'd left last night.

He had guessed, quite correctly, that Caroline would be nowhere in sight that morning.

When he'd arrived, Edward had taken him straight to the library where he promptly shut the door.

"How is she?" There was no preamble from Tom.

"Worried. But glad that Caroline was returned safely."

Tom frowned in confusion for a moment before swearing in frustration.

"You really think I'm asking about Rebecca? Good God man, do you manage to think of nothing else?"

Edward had the grace to look abashed, at least.

"I have no idea how she is," he answered, "since we haven't seen her. Her abigail, Sally, came to see Rebecca this morning and Rebecca said we weren't to disturb her. So we haven't."

Tom's frown returned. This time, though, he felt dreadfully worried.

"Do you not think you should go and check that she is well?"

"No, I do not. She was quite violently ill, as I understand it. Bailey had to send one of his magic potions. So I'm staying well away."

Tom got up from his chair to pace in agitation.

"But someone has been checking on her, yes?"

He could see the shrewd calculation on Edward's face but he cared not. He was far too worried to care about such things at that moment.

"Yes, Tom," Edward finally answered, "her maid spent the night with her and Rebecca has been checking hourly all morning."

Tom tried not to let his relief show on his face.

"Right. Well. Good. That's—that's good."

There was an awkward pause while Edward continued his speculative stare and Tom drew to a stop.

"So, what of last night?" Tom eventually broke the silence. "Did that little rodent Hadley cause much damage?"

Edward rose now too.

"No, not overly much. Rebecca and I did a lot of smoothing over. That is to say Rebecca smoothed things over with the ladies and I — well, I made sure he stopped spreading whatever it was he was spreading."

Tom grinned widely as he could well imagine the significantly smaller Hadley cowering before his redoubtable cousin.

"Still, I feel it would be a good idea for Caroline to lay low for a while. Give the tabbies a chance to sink their claws into some other *on dit*."

"Funnily enough, I think I have just the solution."

"You do?"

Tom nodded. "Come, let us find your lovely wife and we will discuss my plan."

They found Rebecca in the drawing room playing with a very happy Henry.

Edward plucked Henry from his mama's lap and swung him high into the air, eliciting squeals of delight from the baby, before settling him into the crook of his arm.

"I never thought I'd see the day, cousin," said Tom wryly, watching Edward coo over his son.

Edward merely grinned unrepentantly before rescuing his cravat from Henry's chubby clutches.

"Good morning, Rebecca." Tom went to kiss her lightly on the cheek. He assumed, hoped really, that their little spat from last night would be forgotten in light of greater concerns.

Rebecca's smile told him that it was.

"Thank you," she said as Tom took a seat across from her, "for taking care of my sister last night."

"It was my pleasure," Tom said softly. Now it was Rebecca's turn to gaze shrewdly at him.

They did a lot of that in this household. It was deuced uncomfortable.

"Tell me, Tom, how was Caroline last night?"

Tom thought back to Caroline's whispered declarations. Her confessions. And of course, the ruination of his carriage and boots, before responding calmly, "She was perfectly fine. Fell asleep before we reached the house and I had to carry her upstairs to her bedchamber but—"

"What?" Edward bellowed making them all jump and scaring the wits out of Henry.

"Blast it all, Edward. You nearly gave me a heart attack!" Tom yelled over the noise of Henry's wailing.

Rebecca moved to settle the baby and Edward turned to glare menacingly at Tom.

"What the hell were you doing in her bedchamber?" he growled.

Tom stared at him in astonishment. How ridiculous he was being! What did Edward think had happened between him and an unconscious woman?

"Since she had passed out, I was merely carrying her up the stairs so that her maid could see to her. I left as soon as I had deposited her on the bed. Fully clothed. Above the covers. Or would you rather I had dropped her in the hallway?"

Edward seemed to consider it.

"No," he eventually conceded, "no I wouldn't."

By this time, Henry was cooing happily again and the butler had arrived to announce lunch.

Rebecca excused herself to settle Henry for his nap before joining them again in just a short few moments.

Once they had retired to the dining room and seated themselves, Tom turned to Rebecca. "Tell me what happened after we left."

Rebecca sighed and rubbed her head gently. "It wasn't too bad, I suppose. Though I know Caroline will hate herself this morning. Hadley had managed to cause a few raised eyebrows but I think I managed well enough to silence the rumour mill. Then strangely enough, he stopped talking about it altogether. And left shortly after you."

Tom caught Edward's self-satisfied grin at this and could only assume the sudden silence had been a result of him scaring Hadley off.

More was the pity. Tom would have relished the opportunity to shut him up himself.

However, the important thing was that he'd been silenced and, with any luck, the whole thing would blow over with little or no consequences for Caroline.

"Edward thinks it best for us to keep quiet for a couple of weeks. Stay out of society for a while, though I do not want it to seem as though we are hiding."

"Ah, well I believe I have a solution."

"You do?"

"Indeed. I had held off on telling you until everything was ready, but I have acquired some property in Essex and I plan to hold a house party there."

"Oh how wonderful! That would be perfect. When do you plan to travel there?"

"I thought perhaps family could come as early as next week and then some friends and acquaintances could join us for a second week. I've met the local gentry. They seem pleasant enough so plenty of entertainment to be had. It will give me a chance to show off my new property and Caroline a chance to keep a low profile for a time."

"Yes, yes that is perfect Tom. I cannot wait to see it. Is it very big? What's it called?"

Tom smiled indulgently, feeling rather proud of Rebecca's obvious excitement.

He took great pleasure in telling her all about his new home, Woodview Hall. A sprawling red brick manor house built in the Palladian style that was all the rage a few years ago. It had belonged to a well-to-do earl whose son had squandered the family money before deciding that the European way of life was more suited to his desired lifestyle.

Rebecca was enchanted.

"Oh, it sounds just like the houses Caroline and I dreamed about as little girls," she sighed wistfully.

Tom tried not to let his reaction show. But hearing that Caroline would likely approve of the house caused him more happiness than he would have wished.

"None of my estates appeal to you then, sweetheart?" Edward asked with a raised brow.

"Everything about you appeals to me," Rebecca answered.

Tom sighed and averted his eyes from the smouldering looks between the two. Really, they were ridiculous.

"Anyway," he interrupted loudly, "I shall be travelling down in the next day or two and you are, of course, welcome to join me whenever it is convenient. It is really only a few hours ride so should not be too difficult for Henry."

"It sounds perfect. Just the thing that Caroline needs," said Rebecca excitedly before her eyes suddenly glinted with a mischievous light.

"You are inviting friends and acquaintances you say?"

"Yes," said Tom warily. She was up to something. She was always bloody up to something.

"Who?"

"I am not entirely sure yet."

"Perhaps I can suggest a few guests."

Tom looked to Edward for a clue as to what Rebecca might be concocting but he shrugged to indicate he was as in the dark as Tom.

"Who did you have in mind?"

"Oh," began Rebecca breezily, "just a few eligible gentlemen that might rouse Caroline's interest. She is, after all, on the lookout for a suitable husband. And if we drag her away mid-Season she will miss several opportunities. Of course, a house party where they can concentrate solely on her would be just the thing."

Tom felt his temper flare and clenched his fists tightly to try and reign in his emotions.

"Much as I'm sure your sister would appreciate having a parade of men fawning over her for a week or two, I do not particularly relish the idea of having strangers in my house," he said through gritted teeth.

"No, I don't suppose you would. But surely you must know some gentlemen who would suit Caroline?"

For God's sake. The woman didn't let up.

"I shall consider it when sending out invitations," he said now to shut her up.

The idea of handpicking potential suitors for Caroline was the outside of enough and he didn't want to think about it, much less talk about it anymore.

He did not need, he thought with murderous rage, visions of another man's arms around her soft, inviting body, another man's lips caressing hers, another man—

"Excellent. And if you do have trouble coming up with some suggestions I shall have plenty of my own," Rebecca said now with an iron stare.

So, his first thought of conveniently leaving all single gentlemen off his invitation list probably wouldn't work. Dammit.

"I shan't have any trouble," he muttered sulkily.

"Good."

Tom's retort was interrupted by the door opening slowly.

There was a brief pause before anyone entered and Tom felt the familiar prickling of his skin that told him it was Caroline.

Sure enough, seconds later she entered and damn near took his breath away.

Perhaps it was best that she had rejected him. If he were around her all the time he'd never breathe properly again.

Caroline looked as bad as he imagined she would. She was pale, except for two bright spots of red on her cheeks. She had dark circles under her eyes and those same eyes had none of their usual shine.

And yet she was still the most painfully beautiful woman he'd ever seen in his life.

Her eyes darted to his and then quickly away again. Ah. She remembered the shoes.

Only weeks ago he would have relished the idea of having something to use against her. To humiliate her. To sit back and enjoy while her family rang a peal over her head.

But now? Now the thoughts of her being embarrassed or upset were causing him almost physical pain. Which made him all kinds of an idiot, he supposed.

Nobody had spoken yet, so he did.

"Ah, so you live."

Her pale blue eyes, made bluer by the matching colour of her simple gown, darted back to his, then around the room like a frightened deer.

She was likely trying to figure out how much, if anything, Rebecca and Edward knew of what had transpired last night.

"Barely," she answered, her voice coarse.

He probably shouldn't laugh. She was clearly embarrassed and suffering greatly from the effects of a night of overindulgence.

But his mind suddenly conjured up images of last night — working herself up to deliver a set down to Hadley, forgetting Hadley's name for that matter, and although he hadn't exactly enjoyed the carriage ride home, the image of the prim and proper Lady Caroline Carrington acting like a drunken lush was more than a little amusing.

So, no, he shouldn't laugh. But laugh he did. And it wasn't long before Edward and then Rebecca joined him.

And the more they laughed, the funnier it seemed to get.

Well, at least it had livened Caroline up a bit. Because rather than look like a lifeless, frail doll, her colour was returning full force and her eyes were lit with the blue flame of her temper.

CHAPTER SEVENTEEN

CAROLINE'S STARED, FIRST in shock and then in anger as Tom, Edward, and then her own *sister* laughed hysterically at her misfortune.

It was not to be borne. She was suffering, for heaven's sake. And the fact that it was entirely self-inflicted was not something she wished to reflect on right now.

At least Edward and Rebecca were only laughing at her conduct at the dance.

Tom, however, was laughing at her utter humiliation that occurred *after* the damned dance. The swine!

"Well, I'm pleased to see you all in such high spirits at least. Do not mind me. I could be *dying* but do not let that stop you."

Her words, rather than bring the joviality to an abrupt stop like she had hoped, only served to send them all off into peals of laughter once again.

Childish. Utterly childish every last one of them.

Caroline stomped over and plopped into her seat then immediately regretted it as her head pounded in objection.

Her groan of pain had the effect that her lecture hadn't.

They stopped laughing at once.

Rebecca rounded the table and sat next to her, squeezing her hand.

"How are you feeling, dearest?" she asked with concern — said concern being ruined a little by the tears of laughter still in her eyes.

"Like I've been trampled by a horse," Caroline answered bitterly, "You?"

Rebecca chewed her lip in an obvious attempt to stop herself from laughing again.

Caroline couldn't believe they found anything amusing in this. Didn't they realise? She was ruined!

"Rebecca, how can you laugh at a time like this? Last night I—I—oh, I'm ruined!"

She dropped her head into her heads and closed her eyes against the onslaught of humiliation.

And there was still the little matter of her escapade with Tom in the carriage that she would have to address.

"You aren't ruined, Caro. Honestly. Edward and I made sure of it. And, with Tom's help, the whole thing will be forgotten about in a week or two."

At this glimmer of hope, Caroline raised her head.

"What do you mean?"

"Tom has decided to throw a house party and we are all invited. So we have a perfect excuse to disappear from London for a while without looking like we are running away from anything."

Caroline tried not to show her reaction to the idea of seeing Tom's home. Of staying there. There, where she might have been mistress of the household. But her heart fluttered at the thought and then thumped painfully when she remembered the image of Tom and that woman last night. Perhaps *she* would be the mistress of his home now. The thought did nothing to improve her mood.

Rebecca was still explaining, oblivious to Caroline's

turmoil.

"And Viscount Hadley—"

"The cad," interrupted Edward.

"Yes. Quite. Thank you, darling. Anyway, Viscount Hadley was doing his level best to tell all and sundry about your, erm, well about you. But he didn't get very far I can assure you."

"How did you manage to stop him though?"

"Well, your own reputation went a long way in helping. All I had to do was point out how unbelievable the idea of you doing anything improper was. The people he told tended to agree that he had grossly exaggerated. And then he just left."

"Really? I would have thought he would relish the idea of telling as many people as he could."

"I thought it was strange too. I do wonder what made him pipe down so quickly."

"I asked him to," said Edward, "nicely."

Both Caroline and Rebecca raised their eyebrows in disbelief.

"Nicely?"

"As nicely as he deserved," answered Edward mutinously.

"Well, thank you Edward."

Edward smiled kindly at her. "It was no trouble, my dear."

Caroline drew in a deep breath. Now was as good a time as any. "And thank you, Mr. Crawdon. For your assistance. And—" Caroline felt her cheeks burn with embarrassment but she must continue. Yet she could not bring herself to meet his eyes and so addressed her speech to the table in front of her. The table wouldn't judge her. It was a table. "I apologise, from the bottom of my heart for—for—"

"That's quite alright, Lady Caroline. I've been in much worse states myself, I can assure you."

"But your carriage—"

"Is very comfortable, I agree."

Caroline looked at him in confusion and then nearly swooned. Good heavens the man was beautiful. He looked like one of the Greek gods she had read about in her youth. Though his hair was nowhere near as light as her own it was still a beautiful shade of blond, like warm caramel. It caught the sun and glinted invitingly and made her itch to run her fingers through it. His eyes reminded her of the deepest blue of the sea, light and calm when he was happy, but sometimes stormy and deep when he was in turmoil. She had seen them both ways. And she adored them both ways.

And then there was the strength and hardness of his body, broad shoulders, lean—

"Caroline."

"Yes?" she shouted causing the questioning Rebecca to jump.

"Are you quite well? I've been trying to talk to you."

Caroline flushed again, grateful that nobody could see inside her head and the entirely inappropriate turn her thoughts had taken. What was wrong with her? She was facing the most serious scandal of her life and all she could think about was Tom.

Glancing up to catch his eye she was dismayed at the self-satisfied smirk he wore. Perhaps he couldn't know the direction of her thoughts. But he could obviously guess quite accurately.

Ignoring him, she turned back to her sister.

"I am sorry, Becca. What is it that you said?"

"I asked what you were going to say about Tom's carriage."

"Oh." *Oh.* "I—um—I"

"Lady Caroline was quite taken with the carriage and had asked that we take a turn in it this afternoon. Unfortunately, I am having a wheel repaired." Tom turned to look at her. "My apologies, my lady. But if you will still consent to ride out with me, I believe my curricle would be pleasant on such a warm day."

Caroline could have kissed him. Wanted, quite badly, to kiss him.

He had obviously kept secret her little accident in the carriage, had seamlessly covered any awkwardness, and was now giving her the chance to speak privately to him so that she could apologise properly. And ascertain just what had happened last night.

"Thank you, Mr. Crawdon. That would be quite lovely. No doubt the fresh air will do me the world of good," she added wryly.

Tom smiled, causing her heart to stutter, then he bid Rebecca and Edward a good day before leaving to ready his curricle.

As soon as he had left, Rebecca turned to Edward.

"Darling, be so kind as to leave me for a moment with my sister."

Edward, who had just settled down to make a start on his luncheon, looked longingly at his towering plate.

"But I'm hungry," he complained petulantly.

Rebecca's steely look was her only reply.

With a resigned sigh, Edward pushed back his chair and began to stomp out of the room, muttering under his breath all the while.

"Thank you, darling," Rebecca called after him, "I shall make it up to you."

At her words, Edward stopped and turned back to Rebecca. The look on his face made Caroline blush to the roots of her hair. She was quite sure that was not an appropriate way for a man to look at his wife in public.

"I look forward to it," he responded with a rakish wink before sweeping from the room, his demeanour much happier than it had been moments ago.

"And that, my dear sister, is how you get a man to do

exactly as you want."

Caroline laughed along with Rebecca and secretly wished with all her heart that one day she would have such power over a man. And not just any man — the man she had cast up her accounts all over last night.

Lovely.

"Anyway, the reason I wished to speak to you alone was to check if you are truly alright?"

Caroline looked down into Rebecca's concerned face. Was she all right? She scarcely knew what she was.

"Well," she answered as truthfully as she could, "I'd be infinitely better I'm sure if I had not tried to drown myself with champagne last night."

Rebecca grinned. "It was quite a spectacle. Seeing you act anything other than perfectly properly."

"Rebecca," Caroline swallowed nervously, "was I very bad?"

"No, of course not," said Rebecca dismissively. "You were enjoying yourself. That's all. And you were perhaps a little friendlier than usual. Oh, and you stumbled a bit during your dance with Hadley. But you weren't *very* bad. At least, not until we got outside but then it was just Edward and I. And Tom, obviously. But we didn't mind in the least!"

"Oh. Right. Well that doesn't sound *terrible.*"

"It wasn't terrible."

Caroline felt a flood of relief at Rebecca's words. And yet…

She could not put her finger on why exactly, but she felt decidedly uneasy about something to do with last night.

Obviously, being sick in front of, well *on* Tom wasn't exactly a shining moment of pride for her. But there was something else. Something that she could not quite remember but caused her to feel even more embarrassed. If only she could remember their conversation in the carriage. There had been conversation. She just wasn't exactly sure what it was.

"But last night, when we spoke in the powder room, you told me how you felt about Tom."

Caroline felt her cheeks flame at Rebecca's words.

"And that display between him and that awful Noble chit would be enough to overset anybody."

"You *know* her?" interrupted Caroline now.

"Not by choice, I assure you. And certainly as much as I'd like to. But yes. Tom introduced us last night."

Caroline felt a sinking feeling in the pit of her stomach. Tom had been introducing her to people last night? While she, Caroline, had been feeling utterly crushed.

Rebecca must have noticed Caroline's look of devastation, for she threw a comforting arm around her shoulders.

"Caro, she was simply awful. Rude and unbearably forward with Edward." Rebecca's eyes glinted ferociously with the memory. "But Tom assured us that he has no history with her past general acquaintance. And certainly no interest in her. And I believed him."

"Did you?" Caroline asked softly, hating how vulnerable she sounded but unable to help it.

"Yes," said Rebecca firmly, "I did. If I didn't, he would not have been sitting here today."

Caroline smiled at her sister's fierce loyalty.

But really, what difference did it make now? Whatever chance she had of showing Tom that she no longer cared about things like titles and positions in society, throwing up all over him was guaranteed to end any sort of attraction he felt towards her for good.

"It is not his fault that I feel the way I do, Rebecca. You cannot punish him for not feeling the same way."

"How can you be so sure that he doesn't?"

Well she wasn't going to divulge that. Thankfully, she was saved from answering by Edward coming back into the room.

"Caroline, Tom is waiting."

"Thank you, Edward. I shall return in time for afternoon calls."

"Oh, do not worry about that," said Rebecca, "if you're not here they'll leave quicker. Enjoy yourself."

Caroline quickly donned her straw bonnet with blue trim, her white spencer and white gloves and went out into the piercing sunlight to join Tom.

She felt nervous at the prospect of being alone with him again. At least this time she'd be conscious.

CHAPTER EIGHTEEN

TOM TRIED HIS best not to stare as Caroline stepped lightly down the steps towards his waiting curricle.

He was suddenly overcome with a vision of what it would be like if they had married. He would be at liberty to grab her and kiss her senseless whenever he wanted. And he always wanted to.

Instead he smiled and bowed over her hand before helping her into the curricle and then rushing around to the driver's side.

"I must say, you are the loveliest drunk I've ever encountered."

He could tell that she tried not to laugh but eventually, a bubble of mirth burst out.

"You are too kind," she countered dryly.

Tom noticed that she still wasn't quite meeting his eyes but he let it go for the moment, his attention mostly taken with steering his matching bays through the busy London streets.

It was not yet the fashionable hour to be driving so he assumed and hoped that Hyde Park would be relatively empty. He guessed that Caroline would not remember much if any of their conversation in the carriage last night. And fool that he was, he wanted to be sure that she knew there was no attachment between Charlotte and he.

As it turned out, he was right. The park was sparsely populated and even at that it was more littered with governesses and their charges than anyone else.

Tom slowed the horses to a leisurely pace before coming to complete stop underneath an overhanging willow. The tree offered some privacy without being outside the bounds of acceptability.

He turned to speak to her and was surprised to find her watching him closely.

"Are you well?" he asked rather alarmed. She wasn't blinking.

"Last night," she said without preamble, "before I—well, when I—"

"Caroline, truly it is forgotten. We need not speak of it again."

Her grateful smile made his heart soar. He would do anything to keep that smile on her face. His mind was busy conjuring up all the delicious ways he could go about it.

"Thank you," she said.

"Thank you," he replied making light of the situation that he knew must be painfully embarrassing for her. "It is not often I have a legitimate reason to carry a beautiful woman to her bedchamber."

Caroline's cheeks flamed at such forward talk. He looked forward to the set down he was about to receive. He remembered fondly the times that she would lecture everyone in sight on their manners and behaviour.

Now though, she seemed to ignore it altogether.

But her mind was definitely busy. Her poor gloves were being assaulted by her wringing hands.

"We spoke, did we not? In the carriage on the way home. Before—well, we spoke. And I'm afraid that I cannot remember what it was about exactly."

Ah. She was worried about what she'd said. There was no reason for her to be, really. What she had said had made him happier than he'd felt in two years, but equally sad for what they'd lost.

Tom wasn't sure he was ready to discuss it but Caroline was clearly anxious about it.

"Oh." He leaned back and spoke flippantly, deliberately acting nonchalant about it. "You regaled me with your opinion of Miss Noble mostly. You really did not like her, did you? Yet you do not know her at all. Strange that."

He was more than a little satisfied at the flash of fire in her eyes. Jealousy?

"Yes, well," she sniffed piously, "the girl ought to learn how to behave in public."

Tom bit back a grin.

"She should indeed. A perfect lady knows that in public one should drink excessive amounts of champagne, insult one's dancing partner whilst also forgetting his name, and—"

"Oh, stop, please. I am in an agony of embarrassment," Caroline protested but she was laughing too, as he had intended her to.

"I shall stop. Truly none but a select few noticed. And I shall own that kissing a man full on the lips in a crowded ballroom is infinitely worse."

Caroline's smile disappeared and a snarl replaced it.

Tom felt incredibly smug.

"Jealous, are we?"

Her mouth dropped open in shock and he almost groaned aloud at the slam of desire that shot through him. If he leaned forward just inches, he could take full advantage.

"Of course not," she replied. And he lost his opportunity.

"Why should I be jealous of a brazen little hussy that nobody has heard of?" she scoffed.

Tom was enjoying himself immensely.

"And she spoke so highly of you," he lamented.

"Well, Rebecca hated her. Simply hated her." Caroline felt sick at his championing the girl. He obviously cared deeply for her, whatever Rebecca thought. It was another depressing thought to heap onto the pile. Today, she decided, was not a very good one.

"Did she indeed?" he asked her now, watching her closely.

Caroline refused to back down.

"Yes," she said, warming to the subject. "Despised her, in fact. So I should think very carefully if I were you. If Rebecca hates her, I'm sure the dowager will too. And Edward. So it would be very awkward indeed if you were to marry her and have everyone hate—"

"What?" Tom's incredulous shout interrupted her rant. "Marry her? Where the hell did you get that idea?"

He seemed furious.

"Why, I just thought—I supposed that, well that you and she... That she was—I just...thought..." she trailed off quietly noticing that his rage seemed to be growing.

"I'm not bloody well marrying her."

"Watch your language!" Caroline bit out and Tom was reminded that he'd received the exact same scolding from her sister last night. Two shrews, the pair of them.

"Apologies," he said, far from sorry. "But you have been severely misinformed, if indeed you have been informed of such a thing?"

"Well, no. But I thought—"

"You think too much," he said now exasperated beyond compare. He turned to her and said, with as much sincerity as he could muster, "I am not marrying her. I do not intend to marry her. She is an acquaintance, the daughter of a business associate. That is all she ever has been. That is all she ever will be."

He watched the obvious relief flash across her face and

an imp of mischief awoke inside him.

"She doesn't *see* me, you understand."

He sat back and waited. At first she looked thoroughly confused at his words. Then slowly, as realisation dawned, her eyes grew wider and her skin paler.

"She—she doesn't see you?" she asked, licking her lips nervously which nearly snapped his tenuous control altogether.

"No," he confirmed with a smirk.

"Oh God," she moaned before dropping her head into her hands.

Caroline wished the ground would swallow her whole as the full conversation came flooding back.

She had confessed! Told him things she wasn't supposed to. Hadn't Rebecca warned her not to say anything? She vaguely remembered a warning of some description.

At least she had not told him that she still loved him with her very heart and soul. Had she? No. No, definitely not. She had been about to but then her stomach had chosen that moment to—well, she hadn't. That was the important thing.

"Come now," Tom's voice sounded laughingly beside her, "it is not so bad."

Caroline lifted her head to glare at him.

"Perhaps not. For you. You did not make a complete fool of yourself."

"Oh, I did," he said, quietly, "Just not last night."

The air seemed to crackle with tension after his words.

The breath clogged in Caroline's throat.

Would it always be like this? The most innocent of statements made huge by the implications of the past?

Probably. And there was no escaping it. They would never be able to escape their past. At least, Caroline wouldn't.

Not when she was so irrevocably in love with him. And grew more so every day.

And there was no escaping him. She was going to his house, for heaven's sake. Where everything belonged to him and would thus remind her of him. Remind her of how she had let him down. And how she would suffer for it for the rest of her life.

Tom did not know how to break this tension that cropped up between them, seemingly at every turn.

So he did what any man would do. He ignored it completely and hoped that it would go away.

"Come," he bellowed jovially, "let us walk."

Caroline at least seemed pleased about the distraction.

He climbed down from his high perch and moved round to assist her. Not bothering with the small ladder that the equipage came with, he reached up his arms to lift her down.

She hesitated for a moment before moving into them.

He lifted her and slowly, so slowly lowered her to her feet, relishing the feel of her soft body sliding against his unyielding one.

It was exquisite torture.

He noticed that her breathing was rather erratic by the time she landed on the hard ground.

There was no need for him to still have hold of her, yet he was loathe to let her go, his hands remaining fixed on her small waist.

Gradually, she raised her eyes to his and said, a little breathlessly, "Where shall we walk?"

That was it. Nothing scandalous. Nothing forward. Nothing suggestive.

Just a simple question. But it came from her lips, while he was holding her body closely to his own. And it was enough.

Enough to make him lose complete control.

He crushed her to him and covered her lips in one, swift movement. He was instantly lost. And judging from her tight grip around his neck and the soft moan that tore from her throat, he wasn't the only one.

CHAPTER NINETEEN

CAROLINE FELT AS if the whole universe had fallen away until it was just she and Tom and this unforgettable kiss.

She had not expected it, so distracted was she by the feel of his big hands spanning her waist, the masculine scent of him invading her surroundings, the press of the hardness of his body against hers.

But as soon as their eyes had met she'd felt the surge of attraction that was always lying just below the surface rise up and overpower her.

She'd tried to act normally, asking an innocent question. But it was almost like her question had been a catalyst for their mutual attraction to break free.

The second Tom's lips touched hers, her entire being cried out with joy, her mind, body and soul.

Her mind was in utter turmoil. She knew that there were problems between them. Questions they both needed to be answered. Things left unsaid.

But right then, in that moment, she cared not a jot for any of it. All that mattered was that he was kissing her and she never, ever wanted him to stop.

The sound of approaching horses had them springing apart in the next instance, however.

Tom's breathing seemed to be as heavy as her own.

He swore softly under his breath before taking her arm and tucking it into the crook of his own. Then he turned them both in the opposite direction of the approaching hooves and walked calmly out from behind the curricle.

Caroline allowed herself to be manoeuvred without speaking a word; still firmly under the spell his kiss had created.

"I do not think we were seen," Tom whispered, "since we were behind the curricle. Still, I apologise for behaving so recklessly."

At his words Caroline snapped out of the trancelike state she'd been in.

Dear Lord had she learned nothing from last night? Kissing a gentleman in Hyde Park in the middle of the day? Reckless did not even begin to describe it.

"Oh my goodness. What was I thinking? What were *we* thinking? If someone saw, we—"

"Caroline, do not distress yourself. We were not seen. I am quite sure of it. I should not have been so foolhardy."

Caroline tried to calm down, to reassure herself that he was right. More than that, she was trying desperately to recover from the effects of his kiss. Deep, even breaths and distraction that was the key.

"And you should not have been so utterly kissable."

For heaven's sake! How was a lady supposed to calm down when he said those sorts of things?

She stumbled a little at his words and Tom steadied her as a self-satisfied smirk broke out across his face.

The noise from the hooves got closer still and Tom led them just off the path to allow the riders to pass.

"Well, well. If it isn't Tommy and his blonde."

Caroline started and whipped round to see the infamous

Miss Noble and an older gentlemen smiling down at them.

Tom resisted the urge to swear long and loud as Charlotte and Fred Noble came to a stop beside them.

Already Charlotte had his hackles up with the way she had addressed Caroline. And today was not the day for a confrontation. Not when Caroline was feeling so delicate. And not when they'd just shared such an explosive kiss.

But he needn't have worried. He had momentarily forgotten that he was accompanied by the Ice Princess of the *ton*; though he knew from very personal experience that the name did her no justice at all.

He felt her stiffen and a quick glance showed that she had donned the expression that had quelled people far fiercer than Charlotte Noble.

"Miss Noble, Mr. Noble. How nice to see you both again." Tom was all politeness as he bowed. "Allow me to introduce Lady Caroline Carrington. Lady Caroline, one of my associates, Mr. Fred Noble and his daughter, Miss Charlotte Noble."

"How do you do?"

Tom almost shivered at the ice in her tone.

Fred Noble was as friendly as his daughter was aloof. He immediately dismounted and bowed graciously over Caroline's hand.

"A real pleasure, my lady. You are just as beautiful as Tommy here said you were."

Caroline's eyes darted to Tom's face.

"You are too kind, Mr. Noble," she demurred. "I had no idea that Mr. Crawdon would have talked about me while he was away."

Tom tried his hardest to communicate with Noble, using just his eyes that the man was to remain silent on this subject.

"He did nothing *but* talk about you for a month at least, Lady Caroline. And probably much longer than that."

So. He had no talent for communicating with just his eyes then.

"How interesting," was Caroline's only answer.

Tom noticed that her eyes strayed to Charlotte more than once. Charlotte, for her own part, stayed on her mount and refused to engage in the conversation or acknowledge them at all.

"How long do you stay in London, Freddie?" asked Tom hoping against hope that he would say until tomorrow.

"Oh, a couple more weeks I should imagine. Charlotte here wants to experience the famous London Season. I hope I can rely on you and you, Lady Caroline, to help ease her way."

Tom had been in some awkward situations in his lifetime but this felt excruciating.

How to tell his old friend that he would be unable to help because he was throwing a house party that he had no intentions of inviting said friend to?

Under normal circumstances he would, of course, invite Fred and Charlotte to come to Woodview Hall. But Charlotte was not to be trusted, and Caroline was clearly unhappy about his association with Charlotte. Then there was Rebecca who was very likely to cause bodily harm to Charlotte should she be forced to stay in the same house as her.

Not that it should matter to him what Caroline, they had no attachment to each other did they? Did they?

It was a mess and he was getting a headache that he was sure would rival Caroline's.

"We are actually leaving Town for a time, Freddie," Tom said, feeling like an ill-mannered cad. "I've recently acquired some property and I'm having a very small gathering for a week or so. Nothing formal…"

He trailed off uncertainly. This was deuced uncomfortable.

He noticed Caroline was watching him closely and he turned a desperate 'help me' look toward her.

She took a deep breath, which managed to distract him for a moment since it did rather interesting things to the bodice of her gown, before she turned back to Freddie with a charming smile that set the usually imperturbable American to blush.

"In fact, we were just discussing it before you came upon us Mr. Noble. I know that Mr. Crawdon is hopeful that you will be able to attend. No doubt that is why he was curious about when you would be leaving."

Tom gazed at her in surprised gratitude. She had just saved him from a terribly awkward situation and very possibly from ending a good friendship too. And in light of how she came to know about the Nobles, and Charlotte in particular, it was quite an act of kindness.

The Nobles' reactions were immediate. Freddie proclaimed his delight and looked forward to getting to know Caroline better. Charlotte, on hearing the news, scrambled off her horse and was immediately all sweetness and politeness.

She clung to Tom's arm while she rambled on about how excited she was, which was more than a little uncomfortable since Caroline's arm was still safely tucked into the crook of his other elbow. He felt her try to move away but refused to let her budge.

Charlotte would not allow him to get a word in edgeways so he settled for throwing Caroline a look of gratitude before returning his attention to removing Charlotte from his person.

He had seen the gleam in her eyes at the mention of the house party and he had no wish to encourage any ideas that she may be entertaining about him.

Finally, the Nobles remounted their horses and made their way further down the path. Charlotte hadn't once acknowledged Caroline and it set Tom's teeth on edge.

He would not have people disrespecting his—

His what? She wasn't *his* anything. The thought was depressingly accurate.

The Nobles had left a deafening silence in their wake.

Tom knew that he must thank her, and profusely, for saving him but somewhat surprisingly it was Caroline who broke the silence.

"I do hope you are not cross with me, for foisting two extra guests on you."

"Are you mad? You did me a great service. Certainly the house is big enough but I would not have had Charl— I mean Miss Noble there knowing that you felt in any way uncomfortable."

Caroline smiled a little cat-like smile, her eyes glinting with mischief.

"There is no need to worry on that score, Tom. I no longer have any concerns about you being caught in her web."

"Oh?" He turned her gently back in the direction they had come. "And why is that?"

"Because even if I hadn't noticed that your jaw clenches in irritation every time she addresses you, I'm not sure she'll survive an entire week without Rebecca murdering her."

They both laughed as they imagined the fireworks between Rebecca and Charlotte before Tom handed Caroline back into the curricle and they made their way slowly home.

Once back at the ducal townhouse, Tom came inside only long enough to take his leave.

Being the coward that he clearly was, he left it to Caroline to inform the others of their added guests.

"I shall travel into Essex tomorrow to make last minute preparations," he said with what seemed to Caroline to be a regretful look towards her. "But I hope it will not be too long before you can join me."

"I believe Rebecca plans on being there by Friday," Edward answered while Caroline concentrated on not throwing herself across the room at Tom.

Really, she must learn to control herself. But the smouldering glances he was sending her way were likely to make her go up in flames at any moment.

"Excellent news," Tom answered.

"Yes, well, she says that. But between her, Caroline, and my mother who is sure to insist on accompanying us, there is no way they shall be packed and ready to leave in three days' time. They're women, Tom," he explained as if telling a very small child something very, very simple.

Both Caroline and Rebecca objected hotly to his claim and Edward winked at Tom. Clearly, his plan to annoy them into getting ready in time had worked.

Tom could not help but admire his cousin's excellent manipulation skills.

Rebecca asked him to stay and dine with them and Caroline tried not to feel too disappointed when he refused.

She would see him in three days after all, it was just they had not even had the chance to talk properly since their scandalous kiss in the park and she wanted quite desperately to know his feelings on it.

Tom moved to kiss Rebecca on the cheek, ruffle Henry's mop of curls, and shake hands with Edward before finally stopping in front of her.

"Until Friday, my lady," he said in a gravelly voice that sent delightful shivers down her spine.

"Until Friday," she answered while he bent to kiss her hand.

She almost gasped aloud at the feel of his lips pressed against her skin. He squeezed her hand gently before reluctantly letting go and sweeping from the room.

Caroline felt instantly deflated.

Friday seemed a very long way away indeed.

CHAPTER TWENTY

THE HOUSE, AS PREDICTED by Edward, was in utter turmoil on Friday morning. So much so that Edward had decided to ride alongside the carriage rather than in it.

The dowager had arrived and announced that she wanted to travel with her grandson.

Caroline was delighted to see her. Having been staying with friends in Bath, the dowager had only arrived to Town the evening before and had therefore been unaware of the invitation to Woodview.

"But since my trunks were still packed, I saw no reason not to join you all today," she told them excitedly.

"I am delighted to see you," Caroline said truthfully.

"And I, you my dear."

They were a merry, if somewhat chaotic, party that finally set out from the Mayfair townhouse and onto the road that would lead them towards Tom's house.

Caroline was terribly anxious to see it, though in all honestly it would probably hurt her to do so.

She was more than a little confused by what was transpiring between her and Tom.

She knew that their kisses meant the world to her, because she loved him wholly and completely.

But she also knew that she had done irreparable damage to the love he had once felt for her. Was it merely lust he felt? Had he just taken advantage of the opportunity to kiss her?

The thoughts were both confusing and upsetting. But not nearly as upsetting as knowing that he was going to one day marry and the very halls she would walk this week would hold his wife. And then his children.

It was a painful thought and coupled with Rebecca's still very vocal objections to Charlotte Noble's presence, Caroline was worried she'd have another excruciating headache by the time they arrived.

Thankfully however, Henry settled down for a nap and conversation lowered to a whisper.

It was not enough to deter Rebecca, however. She continued her ranting, just at a quieter pace.

"I just cannot understand why you would take it upon yourself to invite that, that hussy into Tom's home," she berated Caroline for the hundredth time.

Caroline sighed and answered as patiently as she could.

"It was a terribly awkward situation, Rebecca. There really was no choice in the matter. I knew that To—" She stopped with a quick glance at the watchful dowager and continued more carefully, "that Mr. Crawdon would have wished to invite his old friend but was reluctant to do so because of his odious daughter. But it would have been more for our sakes than his own. And really, it is his house after all. Who are we to dictate who he should invite to stay in it?"

"So, this Miss Noble hasn't endeared herself to you then, Rebecca?" the dowager asked with a smile.

"No, she has not. She practically threw herself at Edward the other night and that was after her utterly awful display with Tom."

"What display?" the dowager asked curiously.

"She kissed him, on the mouth, in full view of every single guest at the ball the other night. Right in the middle of the ballroom," said Rebecca with feeling.

"And was this before or after she threw herself at Edward?"

"Before," said Rebecca, her teeth clenched.

"Well, she sounds as though she's made an impression at least."

"I once got covered in poison ivy. I was in agony for days. That has stuck with me for years. That is the sort of impression she's made."

The dowager laughed heartily at Rebecca's outrageous claim before turning to Caroline.

"And do you also dislike her, my dear?"

"I do not know her," Caroline answered perfectly composed.

And then, because she couldn't help herself, she added hotly, "But she seems dreadful and I do not know how anyone could help but dislike her."

"My, my," said the dowager, her eyebrows raised. "I wonder if I shall dislike her so much."

"You will," answered the sisters simultaneously.

The dowager merely smiled and said nothing. Could it be that history was repeating itself with her young nephew and the beautiful Caroline?

She would make sure to watch carefully.

Caroline had nodded off and was awakened by Rebecca's exclamation.

"Oh, we are here."

Turning to look out the window, Caroline's first thought was that she now understood where the property got its name.

On either side of them, past the tree-lined gravel

driveway and beyond the sprawling gardens, a lush green forest seemed to go on for miles. It was utterly enchanting.

"How beautiful," she whispered.

They had yet to see the house since the driveway seemed to bend a little to the right but it was mere moments before the building came into view.

Caroline gasped in delight and heard similar sounds of appreciation from her companions. Henry gurgled, oblivious to everything but his mama's hair, which he kept trying to pull from under her bonnet.

They had arrived in time to see the sun setting and it just so happened that it set behind the house lighting the whole structure in golden sunrays.

The house was itself was beautiful, the deep red brick seeming homey and welcoming, no easy task for such a huge building.

The Palladian style front gave it an imposing and regal air but it was not intimidating or soulless as a lot of great houses were.

As the carriage rolled to a stop the huge front door opened and there stood Tom, looking just as handsome as ever and entirely comfortable in such grand surroundings. He looked every inch the grandson of a duke.

Caroline longed to run to his arms but instead she sat and waited for the footman to place the steps at the door of the carriage.

Edward himself handed Rebecca out, taking Henry from her arms and kissing her gently.

"How was the carriage ride, my love?" he asked softly.

"Very pleasant indeed. Your son was extremely well-behaved."

"Well, he didn't get that trait from his mother," Edward answered playfully.

It was lovely to see the playful, loving communication between Edward and Rebecca, but Caroline wished they'd just get out of the way so she could see Tom. And then felt instantly guilty for her unkind thoughts.

Edward moved then to help his mother out just as Tom arrived beside their carriage.

"Hello Auntie," he leaned down to kiss the dowager on the cheek. She gripped his shoulders before he could straighten back up.

"I am so very, very proud of you Tom," she said, her eyes filling with tears, "This house is beautiful and I am so pleased to have you home."

Caroline watched the play of emotions on Tom's face and her heart ached for him. He never would have left were it not for her.

"Yes, well," he answered gruffly, "I am glad to be home. And I am very pleased you like the house. I hope you will spend many happy days here."

The dowager patted him on the cheek then turned toward the steps.

Tom stepped closer to the carriage until his large frame filled the doorway.

"And you, Caroline? What do you make of my humble abode?"

His eyes locked with hers, stormy and dark. They caused a flood of longing so strong that she clenched her fists against the onslaught.

"Hardly humble," she laughed, albeit a little breathlessly.

"But you like it?"

"I love it," she answered sincerely.

Without another word he held out his hand and Caroline was reminded vividly of the same action two years ago, on that fateful night when she'd said 'no.' When she should have shouted 'yes.'

She placed her hand in his and was struck by the fact that no matter how often he took her hand, the jolt of excitement was always the same. Would it always be that way? Probably.

Would she ever find it with another? Probably not.

Sighing wistfully she stepped down and surveyed the house once more. There was no point in entertaining such maudlin thoughts.

She had made her decision two years ago and had subsequently killed any love that Tom had felt for her.

It occurred to Caroline that he hadn't let go of her hand. And she hadn't asked him to.

It felt just as if it belonged there.

Tom was staring at her but Caroline was too distracted to notice. Her mind was whirling with possibility.

She had made no real effort to attract a man's attention. From the second he had stood in front of her all those weeks ago, Tom had her full attention.

And one or two disastrous attempts had ended her illustrious foray into scandal before it had properly begun.

In short, her well-laid plans for this Season had gone completely by the way side.

But what if…

No, thoughts of 'what if' were futile. Tom did not love her. And he very probably would never fully forgive her. But she was quite certain that he was attracted to her.

For her own part, Caroline had no interest in any other man but she was well aware that she would have to marry one.

She still wanted excitement in her life, memories of what used to be, before she settled for a husband she could never love.

So, what if Tom were the one to provide the memories? He would never be hers forever after. But could he be hers for the rest of the Season?

Quite suddenly, this house party became altogether more interesting than it had been up until now.

Tom watched the variety of emotions skim across Caroline's beautiful face. God, how he'd missed that face. Missed everything about her.

He'd been nervous all day, wondering what her reaction to his house would be. Hoping against hope that she would like it.

He'd been standing near the window of the drawing room for hours awaiting their arrival. Not that he'd admit that to anyone.

Whatever she was thinking had him completely intrigued. The play of emotions on her face had his attention almost as much as the feeling of her delicate hand still gripped in his hand.

She seemed to come to some sort of decision and the small smile of feminine satisfaction almost made his knees buckle.

How was he going to survive two weeks of such close proximity to her without begging her to be his?

Tom's thoughts skidded to a halt. What? Where had that come from? He didn't *want* to make her his, did he?

There was no way he could risk his heart again. No way in hell. No way could he let himself love her again.

Love — the most enchanting, soul-destroying, wonderful, and heart-breaking thing in the world. Gathering victims and creating havoc everywhere it went. For some, for the lucky few, it made the stars shine brighter and the world seem conquerable. For others, like him, it tore at the remnants of sanity and hope. Left him feeling more desolate than he ever thought possible, more frightened of the bleak and endless future than he could bear. She had done that. Her and only her. No one person should have that sort of enormous power over another. But she'd had. And he'd never recovered from it.

He'd been burned by that particular flame too badly once before. He wasn't about to risk his very soul again.

But he needed to learn to control this yearning for her.

This need that burned hotter every time she was around. He would just have to keep his distance. Yes, that was it. He'd stay away from her. Far, far away. Or at least as far as he could whilst under the same roof.

Caroline turned to him now and smiled invitingly. Was it wishful thinking or did she suddenly look altogether seductive?

"So, are you going to show me around?" She was practically purring, dammit. His blood heated instantaneously.

"Yes," he squeaked then swore silently at the adolescent sound. He cleared his throat and tried again. "Yes, of course. Shall we?" he placed her arm around his and moved to join the rest of the party who had taken it upon themselves to enter the house without him.

And he was glad that they did. Her close proximity was seeing to it that he was not fit to be viewed by anyone at present.

It was going to be a very long two weeks.

CHAPTER TWENTY-ONE

CAROLINE WAS MOMENTARILY distracted from her plans of seduction when she entered Tom's house. It was beautiful. Simply beautiful.

The entrance hall was dominated by a huge staircase above which hung a giant chandelier. It was very similar to her own house at Ranford, though the floor here was solely dark marble and Ranford was black and white. There was a giant mirror on one wall, which reflected the rays of the setting sun and helped to flood the area with light.

"Oh Tom, it truly is beautiful," cried Caroline.

"Yes, well I like it," he said humbly.

"Ah, there you are. Tom, I hope you do not mind but I took the liberty of ringing for tea, since you were taking your time reappearing." The dowager smiled with a twinkle in her eye.

Caroline immediately blushed and moved away from Tom.

"Of course I do not mind, Aunt," he said graciously, "No doubt you will have to act the hostess much more during the coming weeks."

"What you need, my dear, is a wife to run the place."

Caroline's heart thudded at this sentiment, which was foolish.

She felt Tom stiffen at the dowager's words.

"What do I need a wife for, when I have you and Rebecca telling me what to do?"

The dowager looked shocked at his question. Caroline hoped she looked disinterested.

It hurt. It shouldn't. But it did.

"Why Tom, how ridiculous. Of course you need a wife."

They had begun to make their way into the drawing room to the left of them and Caroline prayed that they would finish their conversation before entering it.

Whatever chance she had of hiding her reaction from Tom and the dowager, she had no hope of doing so with Rebecca.

"I should think that I am perfectly capable of deciding what I need." There was a hard edge to Tom's voice now.

The dowager either did not notice, or did not care.

"Well then you are wrong," she answered stoutly, "if you think that a man does not need a wife. Very wrong indeed. And what do you have this lovely, sprawling house for, if not to fill it with children?"

Do NOT blush Caroline told herself fiercely as she felt the heat rise in her cheeks.

"Now, see what you've done? You've embarrassed Lady Caroline. Cease your sermons," Tom told the dowager with mock sternness.

The dowager, for her own part, was immediately contrite.

"Oh I do apologise, my dear, for speaking in such a way in front of a single young lady. But this boy has been infuriating me for most of his life."

Her indulgent smile in the direction of her beloved nephew took the sting out of her words.

Caroline merely smiled and shook her head.

They did not know that the blush was not caused by embarrassment but by the visceral longing that shot through her at the thought of Tom's children. And the torturous pain of knowing she would not be their mother.

As soon as they entered the room Rebecca's sharp eyes took in Caroline's pained expression and Tom's rather stiff one.

"Caro, dearest," she called, "come sit with me. You must be longing for a refreshing cup of tea. And then I think we shall retire to freshen ourselves up. Shall we not, ladies?"

Caroline gratefully moved away from Tom's masculine presence. It was all she could do not to attack him where he stood when she was so close to him.

The gentlemen chose this as their cue to leave and the group agreed to meet back in the drawing room in an hour so they could have a quick tour of the house before dining.

"I fear I may have been a little forward in the presence of your sister, my dear," said the dowager, though she seemed less than contrite.

"Oh?"

"Yes, I spoke of Tom's having babies. Not entirely appropriate conversation for an unmarried woman but not too scandalous, I hope."

Caroline interjected before Rebecca could say something outrageous, or give away her secret love for Tom.

"Truly, your grace, do not concern yourself. I was not embarrassed at all. I am as aware as anyone that a man has to—" *Do not blush.* She blushed. "Has to make... I mean have children."

Now she knew her cheeks were scarlet.

"Yes, and Tom is no exception. Naturally I would never usually presume to mention such things in the hallway of his house. But I thought, given the parties present, it would be quite alright."

Caroline gaped in astonishment at the sometimes

eccentric dowager. Had she meant what Caroline thought she meant?

She glanced towards Rebecca and from the look of glee on her sister's face could only surmise that she had indeed meant that.

"Y-your grace," she stammered, "I would not have you believe that Mr. Crawdon and I — that me and Mr. Crawdon are — that is, we haven't, we *don't...*"

"Your grace." Tom's butler entered and bowed respectfully to Rebecca. He had just become Caroline's favourite person in the world. "Pardon me, your grace. The carriage with your maids has arrived."

"Excellent. Well, I think we are all anxious to change from our dusty carriage clothes," said Rebecca, standing and moving towards the door. "We shall talk in an hour or thereabouts."

It sounded like a threat. Caroline swallowed nervously and followed Rebecca to the door.

Henry had been taken off for a light meal by his nursemaid, so Rebecca would dress in record time and be banging down the door of her bedchamber in minutes, she guessed.

As it turned out, she was quite wrong. There was no sign of Rebecca or of anyone, save Sally and the young maid who was tasked with pressing Caroline's evening gown.

It had been more than an hour and Caroline had been ready for quite some time but still Rebecca did not come. Perhaps she had gone to see to Henry, though he was usually settled for the night by this time.

Well she couldn't sit here all evening and the party was probably waiting for her downstairs.

Sally had left her, declaring her as fit to be seen, so Caroline plucked up her light shawl, shook out her gown — a new one made by Madame for her — and gave herself one last critical look in the looking glass.

Caroline had been unsure about the colour at first but since it was Madame she had held her tongue. One did not argue with the formidable Frenchwoman who was well known for her delight in bodily removing insolent debutantes from her dress shop.

It was a light shade of rose. A colour Caroline would never have chosen, but she had to admit that Madame was truly a genius. The colour softened Caroline's sometimes slightly stern features. It brought out the rosy hue of her cheeks and contrasted beautifully with her pale hair.

A simple diamond on a thin gold chain and a matching set of diamond earrings were all the adornment she had.

Caroline knew, without conceit, that she looked rather well. And she needed to. If she were to seduce the man who had once loved her and whose heart she had once broken, the man she *still* loved, then she would need all the help she could get.

Being unsure about how to actually seduce anybody did not help. And she would certainly not be turning to alcohol for courage.

Giving herself a little nod of encouragement in the glass, she turned and made her way down the hallway to the stairs.

There was the very distinctive sound of giggling from Rebecca and Edward's closed door, followed by a masculine growl. So, that explained where Rebecca was. Caroline moved swiftly past trying to block out the noise. They always shared a room even though it was absolutely not considered appropriate by the *ton*.

Mercifully the dowager was on the other end of the long corridor and would not have to pass Rebecca and Edward's room to get downstairs. For heaven's sake, had they no control?

It mattered not a whit that she would love the opportunity to have the same lack of control with Tom.

Caroline had just reached the foot of the stairs when she

noticed the dowager's trusted maid leave the drawing room.

Strange.

The lady curtsied to Caroline then made her way back up the stairs.

Caroline assumed the dowager must have forgotten something upstairs. She entered the room and came to a stop.

Tom was standing, brandy in hand, staring intently into the fire as though it held the answers to all of life's questions.

He looked so deep in contemplation, so troubled, that Caroline felt a strong urge to both turn and leave him to his privacy, and rush to him to offer any sort of comfort.

If she was his and he hers, she would have no hesitation in going to him. As it was though, she felt awkward and nervous.

Which did not bode well for a seductress.

He was devastating; that was the problem. So handsome that her knees quite literally weakened when he smiled at her.

Perhaps she should go. Taking a step back, Caroline winced as the floorboard creaked beneath her slipper.

The noise grabbed his attention and he looked up, his gaze colliding with hers.

She couldn't leave now, even if she wanted to. She was held totally and utterly captive by that look.

CHAPTER TWENTY-TWO

Tom LOOKED UP to find Caroline standing in the doorway and she damn near took his breath away.

God help him. How was he supposed to survive being around her and not claiming her for his own in every conceivable way?

But he couldn't, because she didn't want him. That was the material point.

He had tried and failed. She had rejected him.

The pain of that rejection may have killed his pure, untarnished love for her. But it did nothing about the dark lust that plagued his every waking moment and every dream at night.

And the more time he spent with her, the more he feared the rejection had not killed every other feeling as he had once thought.

Every time there was some distance between them he was able to remind himself that they would never be together. He ran the gauntlet of pain, usually aided by far too much brandy, then pulled himself together again.

Only to see her and have it all fly out the window.

Just like now. Now, when she stood looking at him with those penetrating, wide eyes. That glorious golden hair that he wanted to see against his pillow. And that unrelentingly gorgeous body encased in the purest of silk.

Was she trying to kill him altogether?

He'd been thinking of her from the moment he and Edward had left the drawing room today. What she was thinking? How she was feeling? Whether he had run mad when he had thought she was looking seductively at him, as though she would welcome his attentions. And what her reaction was to that awkward, almost painful conversation with Aunt Catherine.

He'd meant what he'd said. He had no plans to marry. How could he? He would never trust another woman with his trampled heart. He'd barely even glanced at another woman since he'd met Caroline.

He didn't want to think about children, because every time he did he imagined them in her arms.

No, she had ruined any chance of marital bliss for him. And yet... saying so in front of her had been damned uncomfortable and had made him feel guilty which was just ridiculous.

Guilty for what? She had not wanted him. Not the other way around. He would never have said 'no'. To anything she wanted. He would have walked to the ends of the earth for her. But she hadn't wanted him to.

"Good evening, Caroline," he said because the silence was killing him.

Caroline smiled nervously and it was his undoing.

He swore softly.

"How can you be so heart-achingly beautiful?" he asked desperately.

He watched as her eyes widened at his words, her cheeks flushing, hopefully with pleasure.

"You are the first to arrive," he said, striving to be the

polite host when all he wanted to do was ravish her.

"Oh." She frowned in confusion. He found it adorable. *Get a hold of yourself, man.* "I saw her grace's maid, I assumed she had left something in her rooms."

"The journey tired my aunt out more than she realised, coupled with the long journey from Bath. She has chosen to keep to her room tonight and join us again in the morning. Her maid was sent to inform us."

"Oh," was all she said, again.

"But, er, Edward and Rebecca should be down momentarily." He felt like a nervous schoolboy being alone with her in the firelight. Was it hot in here? He longed to pull at his suddenly too tight cravat.

He watched in fascination as her cheeks flamed even brighter than before.

"I do not think they will be joining us for some time. They—uh, sounded distracted when I went by their door." This she told to the floor, refusing to meet his gaze.

Dear God, they were animals!

He wasn't jealous. It was just inappropriate, he thought piously.

"So, we are alone then," he commented for he truly did not know what else to say.

Her eyes snapped up from their perusal of the floorboards and he was surprised to see steely determination in them. Which was intriguing in itself, even without the healthy dose of nervousness so clearly evident.

"Yes, we are, aren't we?" she said, almost to herself.

"Er, yes?" he said it like a question, unsure as to whether she actually wanted an answer or not.

She walked towards him then. Well, marched more like. That glint of steel still flashing in her eyes.

He felt the mad urge to back up.

He didn't know if he felt excited or scared. He did know that he didn't want to step back into the fire and burn his a—

"Tom." She spoke then, but sternly as if he were in trouble.

"What?" he demanded, defensively. He hadn't bloody well done anything wrong.

"I'm not entirely sure how to do this."

"Right." *What?*

"So I'm just going to do it."

"Right," he repeated. Like an imbecile. "Er—do what?"

Caroline took a deep breath as if she were steeling herself for something momentous. Which she obviously had been for she suddenly lunged at him eliciting a *squeak* of fright that he wasn't exactly proud of, grabbing his neck in a vicelike grip, and bringing his lips into full contact with her own.

I cannot believe I did that, Caroline thought before all ability to think coherently left her.

Tom's arms wrapped around her in seconds, pulling her into full contact with the exquisite firmness of his body.

This, she thought hazily, must be as close to Heaven as one could get, only to realize in the very next instant that she was wrong. There was closer. Much closer.

Tom's mouth left hers and her feeling of momentary dissatisfaction was obliterated by the feel of his lips grazing her neck. She felt the tip of his tongue dart out to taste her and her legs finally buckled, making her grateful for his unyielding grip.

The sensations he was creating were completely overwhelming her. She was completely lost to him, totally under his spell.

She whispered his name reverently and was rewarded with a masculine growl that vibrated against her neck.

The sound of approaching footsteps invaded the bubble surrounding them and Tom leapt away from her so quickly that she staggered a little.

They looked at each other, both breathing rapidly, neither one able to put a name to what had just occurred. It was beyond a kiss. Beyond lust. For her, it was even beyond the love she had felt for him up until now.

It was as if her very soul had left her own body and planted itself firmly next to his. She didn't care. Didn't want it. All she wanted was him.

The footsteps turned out to belong to Edward and Rebecca and they arrived in the room looking decidedly dishevelled. Caroline wished they'd turn and leave again, which was very unkind.

But they had interrupted her first foray into seduction and it had been going so well. Very, very well.

"That was quick." Tom smirked at Edward.

"What?" shouted Edward, sounding immediately defensive.

Rebecca burst into a fit of giggles and Caroline had to bite her lip to stop from doing the same.

She looked up and caught Tom's gaze as he watched the action, his eyes darkening further still.

"So then, are we to have a tour of the house?" asked Rebecca cheerfully.

Tom shook his head a little as if to clear his mind and turned to Rebecca.

"Yes of course. I had thought that we wouldn't have time with you and Edward being busy. But as it turns out, we have ample time. We might even take time to stroll around the gardens."

"Not if I shoot you," threatened Edward.

Tom merely laughed and turned to Caroline.

"Shall we?" He held out a hand.

Her nerves were strung as tightly as a bow. Her heart had not yet stopped galloping and she knew that contact with any part of his body would only set it to racing faster still.

"Yes," she said quietly, stepping forward to take his hand.

She felt like she was answering more than just his simple question. And hoped that he was asking more too.

CHAPTER TWENTY-THREE

THE HOUSE WAS beautiful throughout. But Caroline could barely concentrate. Her mind was replaying the scene in the drawing room over and over and her body was remembering it even better than her mind.

Tom was giving them a very thorough guided tour, explaining the house's history and telling them all about his tenants and staff.

Under normal circumstances Caroline would have been riveted, desperate to learn every piece of his life that she could.

But her entire being was consumed with the memory of their kiss.

She felt as though she'd been possessed by temporary madness to have approached him that way. Not that she was in the least bit sorry for it.

As soon as he'd mentioned their being alone, it was like a sign. She had been wondering all day how she was supposed to go about seducing him. Had gone through a range of ideas from pretending to faint and fall into his arms to slipping laudanum into his drink, although she feared the second option would be something rather more sinister than seductive.

So she'd just taken the opportunity. Her nerves had made her a little abrupt, she could admit. But as soon as their lips had met, he hadn't seemed to mind.

Her lips curved at the memory. He was an excellent kisser. True, she had no basis of comparison since he was the only person she'd ever kissed. But she could not imagine anyone else being better at it.

"Keep smiling like that my dear, and we won't make it to dinner."

Caroline shivered at the whispered words and the feel of Tom's mouth so achingly close to her ear.

Her eyes darted to Rebecca and Edward who had wandered ahead of them in the long gallery they were currently walking. With some relief, she noticed they were too far away to hear his words.

"What can you have been thinking, hmm?" he asked, drawing them both to a stop.

Caroline turned slightly so that she was facing him. There was no sense in losing courage now.

"I was thinking about our kiss," she answered boldly.

His face registered shock before slipping into a wolfish smile that was altogether too much for her poor heart.

"Were you now?" His voice had dropped to a deep growl, sending shivers along her nerve endings. "And what, may I ask, were you thinking about it?"

He had been prowling towards her during his question and Caroline was surprised to find that she'd been backed into a small alcove, her back pressed against the cool wall.

They surely had only seconds before Rebecca and Edward noticed.

Caroline wasn't sure she had the nerve to answer him as boldly as she would like. After all, her impeccable behaviour had been present her whole life and it was hard to break the habit of a lifetime. On the other hand, now that she'd made the decision to seek all of her pleasure, her scandal, her excitement with him, shouldn't she at least make him privy to the information?

Grabbing her courage with both hands, Caroline looked him straight in the eye and said, "I was thinking about how wonderful it was, how I did not want it to stop. And how I want it to happen again."

Once again he looked utterly shocked and once again the shock gave way to a smile that weakened her knees.

"Funny, I was thinking the same thing."

And then he leaned forward, lowering his head towards her own.

Caroline's breath hitched in anticipation and she went up on her toes, eager to meet his mouth all the sooner.

She closed her eyes and felt...

Nothing.

In confusion, she opened her eyes again to find his own glittering with amusement and something else that was dangerous and delicious.

"But not here," he whispered making her almost whimper, "and not now."

"You swine!" Caroline snapped in frustration.

Tom's laughter echoed around the cavernous hall as he pulled her away from the wall and started to walk along the corridor again.

"Why Caroline, I think that's the first time I've ever heard to swear."

"And it probably shan't be the last," she retorted saucily.

He looked at her again, his brow creased.

"What has brought about this sudden change, I wonder? Do not mistake me. I like it. A lot," he said with a devilish grin, "It is just unexpected."

"Perhaps I've decided it is time to do what I want for a change, instead of what's expected of me."

He was silent for a moment and Caroline wondered

desperately what he was thinking.

"I rather like the sound of that," he said eventually though his voice sounded carefully controlled.

"I'm glad to hear it, since you feature quite prominently in my plan."

He stopped again.

"That sounds like a plan I would be very interested in."

At that moment, the butler arrived to inform them that dinner was ready.

"I want to hear more about this," Tom warned her as they turned back to dine.

"You will," she said with a self-satisfied smirk.

Finally, she was getting being scandalous just right. And with the only person she wanted to be scandalous with.

Tom tried to remain relaxed and nonchalant as they walked back to dinner, when it truth it was all he could do to stay on his feet.

He had no idea where this seductive, flirtatious Caroline had come from but he wanted to offer sincerest thanks to whomever had brought the change about.

Dear God, she had been driving him slowly mad before. Now, he felt as though he could not even breathe without her.

When she had kissed him in the drawing room he had thought, a little stupidly he could admit now, that he had actually died and was experiencing heaven.

Which granted, seemed like an overreaction but if he'd found her irresistible before, what was he supposed to do now that *she* was kissing *him*?

The entire time they'd been walking this damned corridor and he'd been prattling on about God only knew what, all he could think about was her kiss. He could not stop watching her, could not stop imagining her and what he would do if they were alone—

And then he'd almost come undone altogether at the sight of her secret, feline smile.

He hadn't been able to resist asking what was going on in her beautiful head. And her answer had been enough to make him want to pick her up and carry her straight to his bedchamber.

Which would probably cause a slight problem with Edward.

And now he had to sit through an excruciating dinner all the while trying to find some way to get her alone.

His mind raced as he took his seat at the table.

Should he fake an illness? But then he would have to leave her with Edward and Rebecca and hide in his room.

Perhaps he should lock Edward and Rebecca in their room and hide the key.

Or poison them, he thought desperately as Caroline smiled at Rebecca and leaned forward to speak softly to her.

No. Poison was definitely excessive.

"Tom." Edward's voice interrupted his rather alarming thoughts.

Tom cleared his throat nervously.

"Yes?"

"The ladies were retiring to the drawing room." Edward looked far too amused for Tom's liking.

"Yes, yes of course. Of course. Just—um—we will, we shall, if you—"

"So eloquent, Tom. We shall find our own way." Rebecca stood and offered a raised brow before turning to leave the room.

Tom paid scant attention. He was riveted by the sight of Caroline standing and moving away from the table. She moved like he imagined angels did, fluid and graceful.

Her skin glowed in the candlelight; her eyes sparkled like the diamonds she wore.

She smiled at him now as though she knew that she was the cause of his distraction, the minx.

"Gentlemen," she said, nodding her head a little as she turned and left to follow her sister.

And still he stared.

The sound of Edward's deep, rueful chuckle brought him back to his senses.

"What's funny?" he demanded defensively.

"Oh, just that look."

"What look?"

"The look that only a Carrington woman can put on your face."

He considered arguing. But really, what would be the point?

Edward was right.

So instead, Tom sighed and slumped back into his seat again.

"I need a drink."

"Yes," answered Edward sounding far too much like he was enjoying this. "I thought you might."

As soon as they were safely ensconced on the drawing room couch, Rebecca turned to Caroline with steely determination in her eyes.

"Right. Out with it."

"What?"

"Whatever is going on between you and Tom, I want to know all about it." Rebecca's excitement was as palpable as it was infectious and Caroline could not help grinning in response.

It would be quite beneficial to have Rebecca as her confidante and aide in this matter. For one thing, she had used up all her limited knowledge of seduction. And for another,

Rebecca would be the perfect person to help Caroline have some much needed alone time with Tom.

Caroline knew that there would be little or no chance of being alone with Tom once the rest of the guests arrived next week so it was now or never.

With a deep breath, Caroline looked Rebecca in the eye, and then lost her nerve.

How to explain to your younger sister that you were trying to seduce the man you had refused? Rebecca would think she had run mad.

But Caroline did need help. Quite desperately.

"I wanted to—well to, I mean I had thought to try to maybe, well at least attempt to—"

"Oh for heaven's sake, Caroline! Try to what?"

"Seduce him," Caroline burst out, her cheeks feeling as though they were on fire.

Rebecca's mouth dropped open in shock.

"Seduce him? Do you mean to, well to—you know?"

Caroline didn't know, being an innocent still. But she could guess.

"Rebecca!" she admonished, her cheeks redder still. "Of course not."

"You almost gave me a heart attack," Rebecca said now in relief, "Even I could not have approved of such a thing."

Caroline rolled her eyes at Rebecca's tendency to assume the most dramatic, before getting eagerly back to the subject at hand.

"I mean only to have some adventure. Perhaps a stolen kiss or two. You remember we spoke of my wanting to be scandalous? Well, I'm just not that type of girl. And I find I do not want to be, unless it's with him. It is not very bad to want to be with the man you love, is it? If even for a short while?"

Caroline did not know it but Rebecca's heart clenched painfully at Caroline's admittance, and at her tender and vulnerable expression.

"No, it is not very bad Caro. It is not bad at all," Rebecca said, "it is the most wonderful thing in the world. But it does not only have to be for a short while."

Caroline smiled sadly.

"I'm afraid it does, dearest. And I have come to terms with that, truly. Well, almost."

"But why—"

"Becca," Caroline interrupted her sister gently, "you must trust me when I say that there is little hope of Tom and I ever becoming attached to each other. You must accept that."

"No."

Well, she had always been the most stubborn of them.

Caroline sighed in frustration.

"You must," she repeated.

"No," Rebecca repeated mutinously. Well this was just ridiculous.

"Rebecca—" Caroline started firmly but Rebecca interrupted.

"Tell me why. The real reason, I mean. You were going to tell me, if you remember, before that—that—"

"Miss Noble," interjected Caroline softly before Rebecca could utter the word that was building.

"Yes. *Her*," she said now, making 'her' sound like quite the insult. "Before she attacked poor Tom, you were going to tell me what had happened."

It would be such a relief to unburden herself, Caroline thought. It would be so nice to be able to discuss with someone the deep, almost savage regret she felt whenever she thought about the past. And honestly, it would help in her future discussions with Rebecca. It was far too painful to have to keep convincing Rebecca that Tom could never love her.

"Tom will never love me because he loved me once. And I—I broke his heart."

CHAPTER TWENTY-FOUR

TOM HAD NEVER known a man to take so bloody long to finish a cheroot. Honestly, he could swear that Edward was doing it on purpose.

Tom had long since finished his own cigar and was now concentrating all his efforts on not dragging Edward out of the room by his feet.

Finally, *finally,* Edward took his last puff and put the damned thing out.

Tom made to stand from his chair when Edward sat back, propped his feet on the table and asked, "Shall we have another glass of port?"

"No!"

Perhaps roaring the word was a slight overreaction, Tom thought, as he watched Edward jump in fright and proceed to fall backwards off his chair.

"Hell and damnation, what is the matter with you?" bellowed Edward standing up and rubbing his—

"Remove your eyes from my sore spot," he said through clenched teeth, glowering at Tom.

Tom bit back a laugh and tried to look concerned.

"Are you well?"

"No, I'm bloody not well. I've aged a decade in the last twenty seconds. What are you shouting for anyway?"

"Nothing. It's just—well, the ladies have been alone for a long time and since I am the host I really feel that manners dictate that we join her. Them! I mean them."

Edward smirked at Tom's slip.

"I doubt you're thinking with your manners."

"Oh do shut up, Edward."

Edward merely grinned again. Which was most annoying.

"Luckily for you, I married the most beautiful woman in the world so I do not mind joining the ladies now," Edward said moving toward the door.

"Second most beautiful," muttered Tom.

"Did you say something?" asked Edward, stopping and turning.

"No. Not a thing."

Tom had learned to expect the unexpected from Rebecca, and in recent weeks, Caroline.

Even he was not prepared however, for what awaited them in the drawing room.

Crying women.

He hated the sight of crying women. Not as much as Edward, it seemed, since that man had actually turned to run and bumped into Tom.

"Coward," muttered Tom before turning to the ladies. "What on earth is the matter? What has happened?"

He addressed the question to Caroline, primarily because his gaze was always drawn to her and her alone.

And God how it hurt to see her cry.

Caroline blushed and looked down at the Persian carpet,

furiously wiping her eyes and trying to control herself.

He had only ever seen her cry in public twice before and both times it had been because of Rebecca's disappearance two years ago and her subsequent recovery from a nasty fall.

But since Rebecca was gripping Caroline's hands supportively, or so it seemed, he could only assume that the tears were for Caroline herself.

Caroline gave him a small, albeit watery, smile.

"Oh there is nothing amiss. I'm afraid my sister and I are feeling a little sensitive tonight."

Tom's heart was actually hurting more seeing her be brave.

"Caroline—" he came forward forgetting their audience— "if there is anything I can do to ease your upset, please tell me. I cannot bear to see you cry."

He'd said something wrong, obviously. Though he knew not what. For as soon as he spoke the words, Rebecca cried out and threw her head into her hands, crying even louder than before.

"What did I do?" Tom asked Edward in desperation.

Edward, who had yet to move from his position by the door, shrugged his shoulders most unhelpfully.

"Oh Tom." Rebecca looked up now and damned if he didn't feel guilty looking into her big, sad eyes even though he was quite sure he had nothing to feel guilty for. "You truly are a wonderful man."

Oh.

Well, that was good.

"Er, thank you?" he answered in confusion.

He felt nervous and sweaty. He really wished Rebecca would get control of herself. Although he enjoyed being complimented.

This had not been the evening he had in mind when speaking to Caroline earlier. He had hoped to perhaps convince her to take a turn around the gardens with him, maybe enjoy a nightcap after Edward and Rebecca had retired.

In truth, he would not have minded had the four of them been together all evening so long as he was with Caroline.

But now there were far too many emotions on display for his comfort and what he really wanted to do was run away until everyone was back to normal. And with dry eyes.

"Perhaps the day's travelling has taken its toll after all," he said regretfully, "I think an early night and a good sleep should put everyone to rights."

His interest was piqued by the glare Caroline shot at her snivelling sister at his words and Rebecca's apologetic glance in return.

What was going on with these females?

Nobody spoke for a moment. Caroline and Rebecca were clearly communicating through glares and shrugs, neither of them seeming particularly happy. Edward was still cowering by the door.

He needed a drink. Again.

"Fine," finally, Caroline broke the silence and stood, followed quickly by Rebecca. "Goodnight, Edward. Tom." With a nod to them both she turned and swept from the room.

Rebecca hurried after her without uttering a word.

Edward and Tom stared at each other in bafflement before Edward sighed and fixed Tom with a penetrating stare.

"I hope you realise what you're getting yourself in for," he said, shaking his head before turning and following the ladies from the room.

"Caroline, wait."

Caroline could hear Rebecca run lightly up the stairs behind her. She turned and glared at her smaller sister.

"Now look," Caroline whispered fiercely, "we've been sent to our rooms."

"Like naughty children, yes I'd noticed," answered Rebecca with a frown.

"It is your fault, you know."

"Yes, I know and I am sorry. Truly. Oh, but Caro it is such a tragedy," Rebecca said, her voice wobbling and her eyes filling again.

"Good heavens Rebecca, get a hold of yourself," scolded Caroline.

Her temper was frayed and, honestly, she was struggling enough with her own tears already. She could not bear it to see Rebecca's again.

"He loves you."

"Loved."

"Loves."

"Loved."

"Loves."

Caroline threw up her hands in frustration.

"I am not standing here having this ridiculous argument. You were supposed to help me seduce him. Not cry all over him."

"Well, there's plenty of time. Try not to fret so. All will be well."

"I did not want him to see me as a snivelling wreck."

"You cry beautifully," answered Rebecca stoutly. "Like an angel."

Caroline raised her brow at her sister's obvious and dramatic attempt at flattery.

"It is of no consequence. There's plenty of time for seduction."

"How so? He's terrified of me now."

"Do not fear, dear sister. First, all men are terrified of all women. And second, the man is already completely under your spell. You do not need seduction techniques. Your mere presence is seduction enough. What you need is time alone."

"But how? No doubt Edward will be vigilant in his care

of my virtue. Not to mention the dowager."

"You leave them to me. Just make sure to strike at every opportunity."

"Rebecca," Caroline laughed a little, "you talk as if we were on a battlefield."

"And so we are," said Rebecca, "and we are fighting for Tom's affections."

"I told you. He—"

"Yes, yes. I know what you said. He has no plans to marry. He will never love you again. We shall see. Now go to sleep."

Caroline sighed in resignation. There was very little point in arguing with Rebecca when she'd decided on something. Especially when the something she'd decided on happened to be Caroline's greatest wish.

CHAPTER TWENTY-FIVE

CAROLINE AWOKE THE next morning feeling refreshed and much more optimistic.

Last night had not exactly gone as planned, granted. But Rebecca was right; she had plenty of time.

For a moment, a tiny voice of reason popped into her head.

What happens after you've had your fun? How do you suppose to happily marry someone else if you allow yourself to get closer to the man you love?

Caroline pushed her doubts aside. She would worry about that when the time came.

Sally's entrance with Caroline's morning chocolate was enough to distract her from such maudlin thoughts.

"Good morning, Sally" Caroline chirped.

"Good morning, my lady." Sally set the chocolate down and held Caroline's robe open for Caroline to step into. "How did you sleep?"

"Wonderfully, thank you. Such a beautiful room," Caroline answered, her eyes taking in the décor of her beautifully appointed bedchamber.

There was a fine prospect of the driveway from the window that Sally was busy opening to allow the fresh morning air into the room. The room itself was dominated by the large four-poster bed that Caroline had just vacated. A writing desk in the same rosewood, a washstand, and a small chaise made up the rest of the furnishings. It was simply furnished but expensively so. The furniture was of the highest quality and the deep blue carpet was plush and soft underfoot.

The walls were painted the palest of blues making the room immediately refreshing without appearing cold.

It was very pleasant indeed and Caroline had felt immediately at home here. She could well imagine herself living here permanently, spending cosy evenings by the fire with Tom. Entertaining guests in the massive dining hall.

"—if that suits, my lady."

Caroline realised that Sally had been chattering about something while she had been miles away.

"I am sorry, Sally. I did not hear you."

Sally smiled indulgently.

"Daydreaming, my lady?"

"Something like that."

"I was just saying that her grace has suggested a morning ride around the estate. So I said I would get your habit ready if you wanted to wear the white muslin down to breakfast."

Caroline smiled in delight. A ride around the estate sounded wonderful. She was looking forward to seeing Tom's lands and meeting his tenants. And perhaps they would get a chance to converse together, if Rebecca kept Edward distracted. And she should have no trouble doing so, since she merely had to look at him for him to become distracted.

It was an enthusiastic Caroline therefore who made her way to breakfast a short while later, her hair pulled into a simple knot in anticipation of her newly acquired riding hat.

She was surprised to find that everyone else had arrived at breakfast before her.

"Good morning, my dear." The dowager was the first to greet her.

Caroline bid everyone a good morning then moved to sit beside Rebecca.

"Be sure to eat well, Caro, for we are to tour the estate this morning." Rebecca spoke as a waiting footman came forward to pour Caroline's coffee.

"Yes, I heard. I am so looking forward to it."

She looked up and caught Tom watching her closely, the look in his eyes smouldering. Immediately, an answering heat flamed up inside Caroline and settled into the pit of her stomach. Hurriedly, she glanced away.

Breakfast passed without incident and the young people began to depart to change for their ride. The dowager had plans to write to Caroline and Rebecca's mother, amongst other acquaintances, and waved them off with the assurance that she would be perfectly all right by herself and would see them all at luncheon.

Caroline entered her room to find Sally just laying out her riding habit. It was a new one purchased for her trip to London and Caroline could not wait to wear it.

The colour was a soft, dove grey outlined with black frogging. The jacket fit like a glove and fastened with black velvet buttons. The accompanying hat was the same grey material with a short veil and a small black feather, which curled slightly at the top.

It was a beautiful habit and showed off Caroline's slim figure to perfection.

"Ooh, my lady. How striking you look," breathed Sally.

Caroline smiled satisfactorily at her image in the looking glass.

Hopefully, Tom would be well pleased with what he saw.

He was. Or at least, the slack jawed expression and unholy gleam in his eye led her to believe he was. Her pulse sped up in response, as it always did.

"Tom, are you quite well?" she asked mischievously. She felt her nerves melt away in the face of his obvious appreciation. Flirting would be as easy as child's play.

Tom coughed once. Then twice. Then once more.

His eyes raked her head to toe before returning to land on her own and scorching her.

"Oh, I'm well," he said in a voice that sent her blood racing.

He stepped forward and Caroline's lips parted of their own volition. The man could control her body with a single glance.

"Ah, there you are."

Rebecca's voice sailed down from the top of the stairs making Caroline want to weep in frustration.

Rebecca was turning out to be more hindrance than help.

Glancing up, Caroline was surprised to see that Rebecca still wore the simple morning dress from earlier.

Ah. Perhaps she was here to help after all.

"Rebecca, shouldn't you be readying yourself for our ride?" Tom asked.

"Yes, about that," Rebecca said then stopped and gave a huge yawn, "I find that I am suddenly greatly fatigued. Would you mind terribly if I were to skip our outing?"

Caroline smiled up at her sister before quickly schooling her features to concern.

"Are you quite alright, dearest?" she asked now.

"Oh I shall be fine after a nap, no doubt. But please do not let me stop you. I should feel dreadful if you were to miss out."

Tom did not jump at the chance and Caroline worried that he did not want to be alone with her.

"Won't Edward be—" he started only to be interrupted.

"Won't Edward be what?" asked the duke, coming down

the hallway in his riding gear.

"Be staying here with me," jumped in Rebecca quickly. "I find I do not want to go out after all."

Edward frowned, looking between Tom and Caroline.

"Well they can't very well go without us."

Caroline tried not to look too disappointed, but really, she should have known. Edward was not likely to let her out of his sight, not when he knew that he was solely responsible for her.

But she had underestimated the manipulative powers of her sister.

Within seconds of Edward's comments Rebecca's expression became utterly crestfallen. Her eyes, which were always one of Edward's biggest weaknesses, became huge and sad. Even Caroline felt sorry for her.

"You do not wish to stay with me?" she asked in a small voice, her eyes brimming with unshed tears.

"I do," Edward practically yelled, sprinting up the stairs. "I do, sweetheart. But we can't let them go alone."

Rebecca said nothing, merely watched him with her big, brown eyes.

Edward groaned.

"Please do not look at me like that. Won't you come? For a little while?" he asked rather desperately.

"I do not want to go. I want to lay down."

Caroline wondered if Edward noticed the subtle shift in Rebecca's demeanour from sad little innocent to mischievous woman. Caroline certainly did. Poor Edward.

"Are you tired?" he asked now, suddenly all concern.

"Not particularly," she answered.

It took a second for her words to register. And when they did, Edward went from concerned to predatory in the blink of an eye.

"Well, what harm can come to Caroline on Tom's own estate? And really, there is nobody here to witness them. And even if they were, a morning ride through the countryside is hardly scandalous, is it?"

Rebecca smiled slightly and shook her head.

"Right, that's settled," said Edward brusquely. "You two enjoy yourselves," he shouted down the stairs as he turned Rebecca round and coaxed her up the stairs.

The silence he left behind was deafening.

Caroline all of a sudden felt self-conscious. What if he truly did not wish to go alone with her?

Perhaps she should refuse?

"Well, that was unexpected," she said though she had known from the first second what Rebecca was up to. "I suppose Edward is right. It really wouldn't be at all the thing if we were to go alone. Perhaps it is best if we leave it for another day."

"Like hell it is," Tom said roughly. "I haven't slept all night and won't do again until I hear this plan of yours. We're going."

He took her by the elbow and escorted her outside.

Caroline thrilled at his touch and obvious desire to know her plan. She only hoped that he desired to execute it too.

Once at the stables, Tom called the stable hand to bring out the horse he'd chosen for Caroline, as well as his own stallion, Brutus.

Caroline gasped in pleasure at the sight of her horse, a dappled grey mare with a beautiful white mane.

"Oh, she's beautiful," Caroline enthused, "what's her name?"

"Fortuna," answered Tom.

"Brutus and Fortuna. You are an admirer of Roman history?"

"All history really," answered Tom self-consciously.

"I am surprised. I did not imagine you to be very scholarly," Caroline answered and then immediately realised how insulting she must sound.

"Oh, dear. I did not mean that you lack intelligence. Of course you don't. You are terribly successful and I am sure that requires a vast amount of intelligence." She was rambling. A novice she may be, but she was quite sure that this was not the way to seduce somebody.

To her eternal relief, Tom just laughed.

"Caroline, do not distress yourself. I have worked hard to show people I am not the scholarly type."

"Why?"

He shrugged self-deprecatingly. "It seemed easier to be a rake, to act like a rake. Nobody expects anything of you then."

Caroline frowned at this cryptic remark but chose not to question him further, at least not yet.

The stable hand produced a box for her to stand on and moved to help her mount her horse. But Tom was there in an instant and rather than assist, he lifted her bodily from the ground and placed her gently in the saddle.

Caroline's heart raced at the feel of his hands on her waist.

"Thank you," she mumbled shyly, forgetting that she was supposed to be an alluring temptress.

Tom merely smiled and winked.

She nearly fell off her horse.

The morning was beautiful and perfect for riding. Fortuna was a steady, unexcitable horse and Caroline was able to handle her with ease.

Tom led them on a meandering journey through the fields and cottages of his tenants.

The estate was huge, much larger than Caroline had expected.

Several tenants and their families approached Tom and Caroline with deferential greetings and Caroline was pleased to see that Tom knew each of them by name, including their children with whom he was obviously a firm favourite.

As they rode, Tom told her about his time in America. She was most impressed by how well he had done in his business dealings. However, if he thought she was fooled into thinking he had led a life of innocence and purity, he was mistaken.

They came to a clearing by the river that ran through the estate. It was beautiful, with a weeping willow kissing the babbling water and the sun glinting off the surface of the river. Deciding it was a good time to rest the horses, they made their way toward it.

Tom jumped down and led his horse to the water, tethering him at a branch, then moved to Caroline. Without a word, he held his arms up and she leaned down to grasp his shoulders, delighted in the feel of his muscles bunching as he lifted her to the ground.

He lowered her slowly, as if relishing having her in his arms. Though perhaps that was just wishful thinking.

"So, this plan of yours," Tom said, and the glint in his eyes coupled with his firm hold on her waist was enough to shorten Caroline's breath dramatically.

Caroline did her utmost to appear aloof, alluring, and altogether sophisticated. Which was more than a little difficult since she couldn't even breathe around the man, let alone think.

"What of it?" she asked flirtatiously, though her voice was far squeakier than she would have liked.

"I think it's high time you let me in on it. Especially since I can think of nothing else. I'm intrigued," he finished, his eyes boring in to hers.

Alright, Caroline. This is it. Take a deep breath and tell him. And stop being distracted by how blue his eyes are and how wonderful he smells and—

"Caroline?" Tom prompted her.

"I have decided," she blurted out before he could distract her again, "that before I settle into my life as a boring Society wife, I should treat myself to a little fun."

His eyebrow rose, causing a lock of his dark blond hair to fall across his brow and Caroline resisted the urge to brush it back into place

"Your reputation from America has become quite the talk of the *ton*, and since I already know that you kiss very well—" here she felt her cheeks flame but carried on regardless— "I have decided that I would like to have that fun with you. If you are agreeable?"

Caroline took in a huge breath, her heart racing as if she had run a mile, and waited for his answer.

She watched the play of emotions across his face — surprise, what looked like anger, and then something she did not recognise before he once again became a total rakish predator.

This was what she had wanted.

Her skin heated in response to that smouldering look. Her knees weakened deliciously.

Tom stepped forward until their bodies were fused together. With one hand he cupped her chin and tilted her face up.

Caroline licked her lips nervously and saw his eyes darken in response.

He has not answered me, she thought distractedly before his lips dropped to claim her mouth in a searing kiss.

This was all the answer she needed.

His kiss consumed her from the first touch of his lips. She pressed against him, her hands tangling in his hair, knowing that she must seem like a total wanton but she could not bring herself to be sorry or even to care.

On and on it went until Caroline felt as though she had died and gone to heaven. Surely heaven itself would not feel so wonderful.

After what seemed like hours and mere seconds all at once, Tom pulled back and set her gently away from his body.

Caroline opened her eyes, knowing her own were probably glazed with passion and not caring a jot.

They gazed at each other for what seemed like an age.

Finally, he spoke.

"My answer," he said, his voice rich and deep, "is no."

Caroline felt as if she had been slapped.

She reared back in shock, the haze of desire doused as if she had been showered in icy water.

"What?" she sputtered. It made no sense. Not after that kiss.

Tom looked down at her, his expression a mask, his jaw clenched.

"I said, no."

CHAPTER TWENTY-SIX

TOM TURNED AWAY because he could not bear to see the look of hurt in her eyes.

But more than that, he did not think he had the strength to refuse her a second time.

Where he had found the strength to say 'no' in the first place, only God knew.

He had been completely taken aback at her bold request and was not ashamed to admit it had been incredibly flattering and had filled him with raging lust.

He could not help but kiss her.

"No?" she screeched. "Why the hell not?"

He nearly fell over hearing her swear. But he stood his ground.

Drawing himself up to his full height, he turned back around and uttered rather piously, "I am not a piece of meat, Caroline."

Her mouth dropped open at his set down but he ignored her and turned away to tend to Brutus.

He knew Caroline Carrington, knew how proper she was, knew how much pride she had. It would have taken a lot of courage and a very real desire for scandal to have said what she did.

And in the face of such boldness, which he found completely irresistible, he had kissed her.

He could no more have kept from kissing her than he could keep the sun from setting.

But what she was asking? It was madness, utter madness. And it was something that neither one of them would come away from unscathed.

When he had played along with her joke about plans, he had no idea what she was going to ask.

There had been a part of him that had thought, hoped even, that she was going to say—

Well, it mattered not. He had been foolish to entertain thoughts of the impossible.

He was a confirmed bachelor anyhow, wasn't he?

And that was the problem.

Caroline wanted a taste of scandal before she found herself someone appropriate. Someone like the men Rebecca had forced him to invite next week.

So Tom still wasn't good enough to be a husband.

And though he had told her that he had no intention of ever marrying again, it still hurt that she would not see him as worthy.

Then there was her reputation which she seemed not to care overly much about. But he did not want to see her hurt or to see her reputation stained in anyway.

That was why he had taken such pains to smooth over her night of drunkenness and that was why he would not agree to her crazy scheme.

If word got out amongst the *ton*, all of those men she deemed worthy would deem her to be unworthy.

All for the sake of a couple of weeks' mischief.

No, he would not be a party to her ruin. She would only come to regret it.

And Tom had lived with such overwhelming regret and pain for the last two years that he would never wish the same on anyone.

Especially someone he l— *cared for.*

A sound drew his attention and he turned to see Caroline trying to get herself back onto Fortuna.

No doubt she was trying to storm away. But since Fortuna was far too large for Caroline to be able to reach the stirrups alone, all she had managed to achieve was to be halfway up the horse, with one foot in the stirrup and the other dangling uselessly as her arms clearly did not have the strength to continue pulling.

"Er—what exactly are you doing?" he asked politely.

"Minding my own business," she snapped back, "you should try it."

Ah, she was still upset.

He didn't think he'd ever seen her in a rage before. It was most amusing.

"Let me help you," he tried again.

With a huff, she gave up on the frankly impossible task of mounting her horse alone.

She whipped round to face him, her face red from the exertion of scaling a horse, her eyes flashing fire.

"Oh, now you *want* to help?" she drawled sarcastically. "Well, no thank you. You have made your feelings on helping me perfectly clear."

Tom felt his temper rise to match her own.

"I cannot believe that you are angry with me for trying to preserve your reputation."

"Hang my reputation!" she shouted now.

"Hang it, indeed. You forget I know you Caroline, and I know that you may speak as if you do not care, but I was there the night you decided that your reputation was more important to you than anything else in the world, remember?"

His outburst brought an abrupt stop to her ranting and

there was a deadly silence between them both.

Had he thought that his words had taken the sting out of her mood? That she would apologise and say that he was right?

He watched as she bowed her golden head and he waited for her to lift it again, to see her eyes filled with contrition.

Lift her head she did, but her eyes were glinting with determination now. Not contrition.

He was immediately suspicious.

"I have told you before, I am well aware of what I did two years ago. And what it cost me."

His heart slammed at her words. Was she saying that she regretted it? That she felt she had lost him?

When all it would take was a word from her?

Before he could speak, however, she continued.

"I am prepared to live with the choices I have made. And live with them I will. I will become everything I thought I wanted to be and I will do so with good grace, as all ladies do."

She sounded now much more like the Caroline of old and he felt a certain relief at it. This new Caroline kept him constantly wrong-footed and it wasn't a feeling he liked.

"However," she continued, a hard edge to her voice now, "I am still absolutely determined to enjoy a little scandal before that happens. And if you won't help me I will find someone who will."

A rage such as Tom had rarely felt burst through him at her words. The thought of her kissing another man as she had been kissing him just moments before was enough to make him want to hit something.

"Like hell you will," he growled.

She raised a disdainful brow.

"And who will stop me?"

She was goading him. He knew it. He knew that he should not rise to it. Knew that she was probably calling his bluff.

And yet...

What if she were true to her word? What if she meant to give another man her smiles, her laughs, her kisses?

He'd be damned to hell before he allowed that to happen.

Looking her dead in the eye, he reached out and grabbed her to him.

Her eyes widened but rather than fear, they held unbridled passion and excitement. And it was his undoing.

"Me," he finally answered before once again crushing her lips beneath his own.

Caroline felt a burst of pride that her machinations had worked before her thoughts were flung every which way by the feel of his lips once again upon hers.

She had been so shocked when he had refused. So sure in his agreement that he had taken her completely by surprise.

The hurt had been swiftly followed by anger, anger at him for saying 'no' and anger at herself for putting herself into such a vulnerable position.

But she had been so sure of his attraction!

And then, a memory of a previous conversation with Rebecca had popped into her head.

Though Caroline had doubted it, Rebecca had told her there were a few sure-fire ways to get a man to do exactly as you wanted. Most of them, she refused to discuss with her unmarried sister. One of them however, had been to make him jealous. To make him believe that another man could fill his shoes.

Well, Caroline thought, she might as well try since she had nothing to lose. And though she had no intentions of or desire to kiss another man, Tom did not know that. Nor did he need to.

Surprisingly, it had worked. And now here he was, giving her exactly what she wanted.

This time Caroline was the one to end the kiss. Not that she wanted to. But she wanted to make sure he wasn't trying to trick her.

"So you will help me?" she asked him, watching closely for signs of trickery.

Tom sighed in resignation.

"If helping you means keeping some other bast— man's hands off you, and getting to do this, how can I refuse?"

Caroline smiled in triumph.

But rather than smile back, Tom frowned.

"I hope you realise what you're asking, Caroline. You are an innocent. I do not want you getting into something that is too much for you. And I do not want anyone finding out about this. If you do not care enough about your reputation, I do. And I will not see you throw it away on a whim because you—"

"Tom—" Caroline put her fingers to his lips and felt immediately the now familiar tug of attraction— "you worry too much. Who is there to know? I shall not tell and nor shall you. And besides, it is you. I trust you. I know that you will take excellent care of me and give me memories to last a lifetime."

She saw him frown again.

"Caroline," he spoke with tenderness now that tore at her heart. How she loved him! "When you marry, you will make beautiful memories with your husband. Those are the memories that will last a lifetime. Not two weeks in the country living on the edge of propriety a little."

Did any part of him know? Did he have any idea how much it hurt to hear him talk about her husband? To know that it would not be him? To know that she had no desire to make memories with anyone but him?

But now was not the time for such maudlin thoughts. She

had precious few days with him and she did not intend to waste them by bemoaning what she had done to herself.

She knew that she should agree with him but part of her, her insane heart most likely, could not bring itself to do so.

Confessing her love for him would put them both in a situation that neither would want to be in.

So instead, she smiled and said, "Tom, I know that the memories we create here at your beautiful home, for these wonderful days, will be the ones I treasure most for the rest of my life. I'm quite sure I shall have a pleasant life but I am equally sure I shan't ever be as happy as I am right now."

He said nothing in response. Not that she expected him to. Perhaps she had frightened him with her words. After all, he had made it abundantly clear that he was a confirmed bachelor and one who would never love. At least, not again.

But words were not necessary.

She had her agreement and that was what she'd wanted for today.

Silently, he helped her onto her horse and then mounted Brutus.

As they turned to leave the clearing, he reached out and stopped her with a hand on her shoulder.

Caroline looked at him enquiringly, and was stunned and touched when he leaned over and kissed her gently on the lips, just once, before pulling away.

"Whoever he is," he said softly and almost made her want to cry, "He'll be the luckiest man in the world."

CHAPTER TWENTY-SEVEN

THE NEXT FEW DAYS passed in a haze of pure and utter bliss for Caroline. Apart from one rather important detail, Tom was being the perfect gentleman.

Every day he found a way for them to be alone. Whether it was a walk in the gardens, a ride in the woods nearby, a trip to the village where he was obviously admired. A little too admired by some young ladies, in Caroline's opinion.

But he had not kissed her. Unless you counted the fleeting kisses to her hand, her cheek, even her nose for heaven's sake, as if she were a sister or matronly aunt rather than a desirable woman whom he had promised to scandalise.

She could not say that she did not love their time together, because she did. She got to know this new version of Tom. The one who had left for America and made a gargantuan fortune. The one who had been born to a cruel father. She wept as he told her the stories of his beatings and of the cruel words that had rained down upon his head. Then she had cried tears of joy as she heard of the dowager and Edward's father taking Tom under their own roof and raising him as their own as his father slowly drank himself to death.

It was a tragic start to be sure and Caroline wondered at the courage and determination of a boy who grew into a man, not adversely affected by his father's treatment but rather one of good humour, intelligence and kindness.

It had made her love him even more, which she had not even thought possible.

For her own part, she had felt able to open up to him about the pressures on her shoulders, her feelings of fear that she would not meet the expectations her family had of her, would not make them proud.

By unspoken consent, they did not speak of their own past together. They did not mention the night that ended what had blossomed between them.

They laughed together; they shared hopes, dreams, and fears.

And yet, he did not kiss her.

The day had come for the guests to start arriving.

Caroline was worried.

Although she had spent a wonderful week with Tom, their opportunities to be alone were sure to dwindle if not disappear entirely with the arrival of more guests. Guests who would be sure to notice should they spend time alone together and these people were not going to turn a blind eye the way Rebecca, Edward, and the dowager had been.

She had come down to breakfast that morning determined to speak to Tom to find out why he had distanced himself right when he had promised to do the exact opposite.

Upon entering the room, Caroline was surprised to see it filled with Tom, the dowager, Rebecca, Edward, and even Henry.

"Good morning, dearest," called Rebecca from her seat by Edward's side.

The dowager sat opposite with Henry on her knee, the picture of a doting grandmother.

But although Caroline greeted them all, her eyes were

inevitably drawn to Tom seated at the head of the table.

"Good morning, Caroline," he said softly, his words like a caress, his eyes filled with delight at seeing her.

But Caroline was too determined to learn why he was being so polite when she wanted passionate, friendly when she wanted fire, to allow herself to be side-tracked as usual.

Nodding politely she responded, "Good morning, Mr. Crawdon," and was well satisfied with the look of confusion that past over his features.

Rebecca too looked confused. Since she was privy to everything that had transpired between Caroline and Tom, Rebecca was sure to be just as surprised by her cool civility as Tom himself.

But until she spoke to him she would remain aloof.

She felt Tom try to catch her eye but she kept her face averted, concentrating instead on eating the toast she had picked from the sideboard.

"My apologies." Tom spoke, addressing the whole group. "I am going to be an absent host this morning. I have some business to attend to in the village. Nothing that should keep me too long so I hope to return this afternoon."

Caroline looked up at this and met his eyes, which had obviously been looking at only her for the duration of his speech.

"Oh, do not worry about a thing, dear" The dowager spoke while Caroline did her best to mask her disappointment. "We shall find plenty of things to amuse ourselves. In fact, I thought to pay a return visit to the vicar and his wife. They were such pleasant companions at dinner the other night. Ladies, would you care to join me?"

Rebecca snorted in a most unladylike fashion.

"No," she responded quickly, "oh they were nice enough but deadly dull. The man started talking about his nose hair for heaven's sake. I do not want a repeat of that, thank you very much."

The dowager smiled but was relentless.

"It is your duty, my dear, as duchess."

"What? Why?" she answered mutinously, "I'm not married to Tom, am I?"

The dowager laughed now, well used to Rebecca by now.

"No, you are not. But you are his family and good manners dictate that we pay a call. And were he married, I would be dragging his wife along, too." The dowager's eyes suddenly became calculating and Caroline inexplicably became nervous. "Speaking of which, Caroline, you will join us?"

Caroline jolted at the dowager's very obvious ploy, embarrassed by it, desperately wishing for it, and worried about Tom's reaction to it.

The cup that she had been lifting to her lips now dropped squarely into her lap.

Thankfully, the contents were no longer hot but she jumped up in shock, as did everyone else.

It was ridiculous, she thought distractedly as the room broke out in pandemonium, how one little cup could cause such chaos amongst five adults. Seven if you included the staff. And one baby.

Caroline had yelped, causing Henry to burst into noisy sobs, Rebecca was yelling at Caroline to see if she was all right. The dowager was doing the same. Edward had plucked Henry from the arms of his fretting grandmother and was trying to soothe him while calling for help.

How much help did he think she needed, for goodness' sake?

Tom had raced around the table and grabbed her, frantically wiping at her ruined gown with his napkin, worry etched on his face. It seemed as though he did care. Why then, the distance?

It was rather sweet actually. Noisy, but sweet.

"I'm fine, truly," Caroline was saying over the noise.

Nobody appeared to be listening however.

Thankfully, Sally came bustling into the room and had, in her own unique way, seated everyone back at the table, called the footmen to order and removed Caroline from the room to be changed.

They had only made it a couple steps up the grand staircase when—

"Caroline."

Caroline turned at the sound of Tom's deep voice.

"I shall just go and prepare another gown, my lady," said Sally before continuing up the stairs.

Tom walked forward until he stood at the foot of the staircase.

He was still taller, even though she stood two steps up, but their faces, their lips, were much closer than usual.

"You are truly not hurt?"

Caroline smiled at his obvious concern, her heart twisting painfully, wishing it stemmed from love and not just politeness.

"No, I am not hurt. Truly."

"Good."

He didn't say anything else so Caroline turned to leave but was stopped by his hand on her elbow.

"I—ah—I shall return as quickly as I can. From the village, I mean. I would not leave only, well it is necessary."

"That is quite alright. I am sure I shall be well occupied."

"Will you go to visit the vicar's wife?"

His question reminded her of the dowager's painfully obvious machinations.

She smiled ruefully.

"The dowager seems to want me to attend, does she not?"

Tom smiled in return, his eyes creasing as they had before, when he was not so hardened by their past.

"Yes, she did. Subtlety is not one of my aunt's fortes. I hope she did not make you uncomfortable."

"Oh no," Caroline answered flippantly, "I regularly pour coffee over myself. Helps to wake me up in the morning."

He laughed now and the sound made her heart sing.

He should laugh more.

He used to laugh all the time.

"Nevertheless, I will have a private word with her. Tell her, yet again, that she may give up on her hopes for me to marry. Selective hearing is another of her faults."

Caroline did her best not to let the pain show. This was not news to her. She knew their time together was limited. All the more reason why she wanted him to kiss her!

"Tom, I want—"

"Ah, there you are." Edward's booming voice interrupted them. "Tom, I thought to ride into the village with you, if you are agreeable?"

Tom's eyes never left Caroline's.

"That's fine, Edward," he said before pointedly ignoring him. "What were you going to say?" he asked softly.

Well she couldn't hardly blurt it out in front of Edward, could she?

"Never mind." She smiled. "It is of no great importance."

Well, that was a lie.

"Caroline—"

"So, I'll just go and get ready then, shall I?"

Swearing softly Tom turned round to fix Edward with what was no doubt a hard look.

"Yes. Why don't you?"

Edward grinned unrepentantly, either oblivious to or not caring about Tom and Caroline's desire to be alone.

Caroline watched for a moment as Tom and Edward engaged in some sort of very immature stare-off.

"Right, well I shall leave you two to it then," she said eventually, "I really must change my gown. Good day," she curtsied quickly then turned and rushed up the stairs, feeling both of their eyes on her back the entire way.

Tom watched Caroline go and could have happily punched his cousin in the jaw.

He watched her until she disappeared from view then turned to see Edward watching too, though their eyes had been watching two very different areas. And so they had better be.

"What the hell was that about?" grumbled Tom, without preamble.

"What?" asked Edward with feigned innocence.

Rather than reply, Tom just fixed him with a stare.

Finally, Edward relented.

"Did you really think I was going to let you follow her up the stairs? I have been lenient this past week, but that is the outside of enough, even for you."

Tom swore again, this time loudly.

"I wasn't following her up the bloody stairs, I just wanted to speak to her. And what do you mean 'even for me'?" he shouted feeling very affronted.

Edward shrugged, uncaring about Tom's obvious anger.

"Well, your reputation with women isn't exactly a secret, is it? You forget I was there when you were forming it."

Tom scoffed. "And you were a saint?"

Edward grinned again. "No, perhaps not. But I've never made any secret of the fact that I haven't so much as glanced at another woman since meeting Rebecca. Can you say the same thing?"

"Unfortunately, no. I cannot say Rebecca has blinded me to all other women."

"You know what I mean."

"Edward, what exactly is it that you have a problem with?"

Suddenly Edward dropped the easy-going manner and became serious.

"What happened between you two, well it must have hurt like the devil."

Tom tried to interrupt, not wanting to have this conversation now. Or ever, in fact.

But Edward held up a hand and continued on relentlessly.

"I can see that there are still feelings there, Tom. Anyone with eyes in their head could see it. But if your intentions aren't honourable, frankly, I don't want you near her."

Tom didn't know whether to laugh or cry. If his intentions weren't honourable? He hadn't touched her in days. All because he had no idea anymore what his intentions were.

He was clinging desperately to the idea of confirmed bachelorhood but it no longer seemed as appealing.

But then, the only wife he had ever wanted was the one who still planned to marry another.

His life was a damned disaster.

He knew he wanted her quite desperately. He also knew that the thoughts of touching her then casting her aside in a manner of days did not sit well with him.

So he was stuck.

Spending hours on end in her company, wanting her desperately, and feeling unable to do anything about it.

"So?"

Edward interrupted his thoughts.

"So what?"

"So, do you want to marry her? Or are you just stringing her along."

"You assume it's me doing the stringing?"

"Isn't it?"

Tom sighed and ran a hand through his hair.

"I don't even know anymore," he admitted.

Edward watched him silently for a moment before moving to grasp his shoulder.

"How about, when we get to the village, we have a

drink?"

"Make it about ten and you've got a deal."

CHAPTER TWENTY-EIGHT

"I'M TELLING YOU, Becca, it's not working. He hasn't tried to kiss me at all. At least, not in any way other than with brotherly affection. I have a brother. I don't need another one."

It was a pleasant morning and the sisters were seated on the veranda, enjoying the view of Tom's magnificent gardens.

Rebecca frowned in puzzlement.

"I just do not understand it. When he looks at you, I'm surprised the whole room doesn't catch fire it's so heated."

Caroline raised a doubtful brow.

"I believe that is your husband, Becca. It's positively inappropriate."

Rebecca grinned. "I know."

"Anyway, the point is I think that he has changed his mind. Or perhaps since spending time with me, he no longer wants me."

Caroline tried to keep her voice steady and matter-of-fact but she could not keep the hurt from showing.

"Caro—" Rebecca leaned forward now and gripped her hand— "I promise you, he wants you. Enough to give Edward a heart attack, in fact." She leaned closer still and looked

Caroline dead in the eye. "He loves you."

For one, brief, wonderful moment, Caroline's heart soared. But then reality hit.

"He doesn't, Rebecca. He did but I killed it. And I do not deserve it. Besides, you heard him. He is determined to never marry. So it is hopeless."

"Nonsense."

Both girls jumped at the sound of the dowager's voice behind them.

Caroline's cheeks burnt with embarrassment.

"It is never hopeless, child. Not as long as two people love each other enough."

To her horror, Caroline felt her eyes fill with tears.

"And when only one of them loves?"

The dowager did not answer at first, merely leaned forward and placed a motherly kiss on Caroline's head.

"When one of them loves it means the other is not quite ready to admit it yet. That is all."

And then she left Caroline to her thoughts, dragging a reluctant Rebecca with her.

Caroline was grateful that she did not have to join them at Mrs. Colson's. The vicar's wife was indeed a lovely woman, and Caroline would usually never dream of being so impolite, but she needed to be alone with her thoughts.

However, it had now been some hours and she could only assume that they had either gotten stuck with the very chatty Mrs. Colson or they had gone on to somewhere else.

Caroline was bored and decided to take yet another walk in the gardens.

Her stroll took her around to the front of the house and she was surprised to see the arrival of a lone rider to the front of the house.

Her brow creased in confusion. As far as she knew, Tom wasn't expecting his guests for another day or two.

Caroline's attention was further caught by the arrival of another two riders coming up the long driveway. She dearly hoped it was Tom to greet his guest.

Unsure as to whether she should greet the stranger or disappear until someone else arrived, she watched as he dismounted and made his way to the front door.

His gait was very familiar. So too was his dark hair.

Caroline stepped closer and then gasped in surprise.

It was Charles!

"Charles," she called and ran toward him.

Her brother turned at her shout, and he grinned as Caroline ran up the steps.

"Hello, Caro," he said in his deep voice before he pulled her into a hug that lifted her from her feet.

Charles had always towered over her and he made Rebecca look positively tiny.

"What are you doing here?" she asked, completely forgetting about the imminent arrival of the other riders in her excitement.

"I came to Town and was told by Edward's servants that you were all here. I was sure his cousin wouldn't mind if I paid a visit, since I came to see my family and my entire family is here."

Caroline smiled widely.

"No, I am sure he wouldn't mind, he is a very generous man."

Charles eyes, identical to Caroline's icy blue, narrowed slightly at her warm praise but he did not comment, instead pulling her toward him in another hug.

"You look very well, Caro. It seems England is agreeing with you."

Caroline made to answer but did not get the chance as she was suddenly pulled roughly from Charles' grip.

She looked up in confusion and was surprised and horrified to see Tom, looking murderous, push her gently away from Charles before throwing his fist and landing a fierce blow right onto Charles' cheek.

"Tom!" she screamed now, "what are you doing?"

"Getting this lecherous brute's paws off you," he snarled and made to move forward again.

"Stop it!" she screamed again, pulling out of his arm with all her might. "He's my brother."

Tom stopped mid-step and turned to look at her.

"Your brother?" he asked slowly, his breathing harsh.

"Yes, my brother!" she shouted back, furious with him.

"Ah, so it is. Hello Charles, nice to see you again."

Caroline's jaw dropped at Edward's nonchalance.

Charles grinned at Edward, seemingly as unfazed as the other man.

"Edward, nice to see you too," he said as the two men shook hands.

Caroline felt as though she had slipped into a surreal dream, or nightmare rather.

Charles turned back to face Tom and eyed him closely.

"You must be Tom Crawdon. Sorry to drop in unexpected, though it would appear I've had my comeuppance," he grinned ruefully, rubbing his cheek and extending his other hand.

"My apologies," said Tom now grasping Charles' offered hand, "I thought—"

"You thought some stranger was manhandling my sister. Believe me, I am well pleased to have someone take such good care of her. You must really care about your guests."

The two gentlemen shared a look that Caroline, still in a state of shock, did not even try to decipher.

Tom broke the brief silence.

"Please, come into the house and we will have someone look at your cheek."

"It's nothing that a glass of brandy won't fix," Charles said jovially.

The door had opened as this bizarre little exchange was going on and Edward stepped through, handing his hat to a waiting footman.

Both Tom and Charles turned back holding a hand out to Caroline then glancing at each other — Charles' face once again shrewd and questioning, Tom's trying and failing to look innocent.

Caroline stared at them both, completely overset by what had just occurred then shook her head and stomped into the house without either of their assistance.

She wished Rebecca and the dowager were here. She'd even take Mrs. Colson at this point.

In the space of a few moments, she'd seen Charles, watched as he was almost knocked clear out by Tom, and then listened to them bonding and talking about brandy of all things.

Her head began to ache. And in the midst of it all was the horrible realisation that now whatever chance she and Tom had of being together had been completely obliterated by the arrival of her overprotective big brother.

Tom led the way to his study feeling like he needed a drink just as badly as the viscount he had just punched.

Good God, he had been in some awkward positions in his time but this could safely be described as one of the worst.

He and Edward had finished up their respective business in a relatively short time and had headed straight to the village pub for an ale or two and to talk about Tom's predicament.

Tom had only been interested in the ale; Edward was the one pushing to talk about this blasted situation with Caroline.

"Why are you so insistent on talking about my feelings,

Edward? You used to be just as uninterested in that nonsense as I am."

Edward shrugged and said, "I'm married," as if it were self-explanatory.

"So then, what do you plan to do about her?" Edward carried on, unrepentant.

Tom swore quietly before he admitted, to his drink, not to Edward, that he had no idea.

"What would you do, if you were in my position, hmm? She's the only woman I ever loved, Edward. I moved to the other side of the world because of her, for God's sake. And still—"

Here he hesitated, unwilling to take that leap.

"Still what?"

He sighed and dropped his head into his hands.

"Still I'm not enough," he said hoarsely, as if the words were torn from his very soul.

"I'm confused," said Edward.

"Not the first time."

"I'm ignoring that. You say you're not enough yet she asked you to, well, to scandalise her." He grimaced. "I'm still not happy about that you know."

"Yes I know, you've said so. Several times. And I told you that nothing has happened."

"I believe you because I chose not to think of the alternative. But if she asked you, how can you think you're not enough?"

"I'm enough for a week or two." He laughed though there was no humour in it. "God I'm destined for a life not good enough. Not good enough for my father, not good enough for our grandfather, and not good enough for the woman who stole my heart."

Edward frowned in concern.

"Your father was a bastard," he stated now, matter-of-factly.

"You'll hear no arguments from me."

"And our grandfather did not particularly care for anyone."

"Except his heirs".

Edward could not argue the point.

"But Caroline, Tom. Are you really so blind that you cannot see how she feels?"

Tom refused to let himself hope, refused to let himself believe, and refused to show any weakness for her in front of Edward.

"Regardless of how you think she feels Edward, she has made it painfully obvious that she intends to marry a title. Even now, two years have passed and nothing has changed. She wants to marry a Peer and get on with her life and I will be stuck trying to fill a void that I know will never be filled."

"You underestimate her, Cousin." Edward was relentless.

"No I don't." Tom was starting to lose patience. "She said as much."

"So she did," said Edward calmly rising from his chair. "Just as you said you would never want to marry. You're both liars."

The ride home had been a quiet affair since Tom was wrapped up in his thoughts and Edward was wisely leaving him to it.

Should he risk it all then? Give her what she wanted and hope that it would be enough? Again?

He did not know if he had the strength to do it all again. To risk the pain once more.

No, it was best to leave things as they were, he had thought as they made their way up the driveway to the front of the house, it was best to keep his distance, enjoy her company but not get any closer.

That way, when he inevitably had to let her go, maybe it wouldn't hurt as much. He would see her with the man she chose, wish her well, and walk away.

This was a fine thought in theory. Unfortunately, that along with every other rational thought in his head, flew right away at the sight that awaited him on the steps of his house.

Caroline. In the arms of another man.

Without conscious thought, he urged Brutus to go faster, ignoring whatever it was that Edward was shouting at him.

His entire focus was on Caroline and the brute that was manhandling her.

She doesn't look as though she is in distress, his conscious spoke up. He ignored that too.

Charging up the steps, urged on by a savage jealousy at the look of happiness on her face, he pulled her from the man's grasp and landed him a facer, which connected with a satisfying *crack*.

Caroline had screeched at him but he'd had no desire to listen to her pleas for the man.

How could she do this to him? On the steps of his own damned house.

And then she'd screamed the words that had brought a brief second of relief, followed almost immediately by horror as realisation took hold.

He had just punched her brother.

And now that man was sure to be wondering why.

They had reached the study in silence and Tom immediately set to pouring generous measures of brandy for all three of them.

Caroline had stormed off to another part of the house and Tom had no doubt he was in for a stern lecture when they were next alone.

Of course, he frowned in displeasure, studying the deep amber liquid in his glass; they may never get a chance to be alone again, since her brother had arrived.

Speaking of which—

"I apologise, once again my lord, I had no idea who you were."

"Yes, that much is clear, or you wouldn't have hit me in a jealous rage."

Tom's head snapped up as he met the viscount's eyes. They were as blue as Caroline's though his hair and skin tone were darker, like Rebecca's. That penetrating look, however, that he shared with his blonde sister.

Tom's first instinct was to babble like a schoolboy and deny everything. But years of being a rakish man about town had thought him well — school your features into impassivity and talk yourself out of trouble.

"I felt duty bound to protect her, my lord. She is after all a guest under my roof. It would be remiss of me to see her in the arms of a man and not try to intervene."

"Yes it would," agreed Charles easily. "However intervention tends not to involve beating the man in question, so I think I shall trust my instincts on this one. Which brings us to an interesting point — just what is going on with you and my sister?"

His tone was easy enough, his manner all friendliness, but Tom heard the steel in the other man's voice.

He was not going to be fobbed off, that much was definite.

So now Tom had to decide how the hell he was going to explain what was happening between him and Caroline. An impossible task, since he didn't know himself.

"Honestly?" he said now, the brandy coupled with his earlier ale loosening his tongue somewhat, "I haven't a damned clue, my lord."

Charles Carrington, to Tom's surprise, leaned back and chuckled softly.

"I think it is safe to say that you are suffering rather badly. I also think, under the circumstances, you might as well call me Charles."

Tom swallowed hard but said nothing, waiting for the other man's lead in what was sure to be an uncomfortable conversation.

"So," Charles began, accepting another shot of smooth, amber liquid, "how long have you been in love with my sister?"

Tom, who had just taken a swallow of his own drink, choked and spluttered in alarm before finally being able to catch his breath.

He noticed, with some disgust, that Charles was completely unperturbed by Tom's near death experience. Even Edward hadn't rushed to help.

If Tom had been hoping that the choking would distract Charles from his question, he was sadly mistaken. Charles merely raised a brow, his expression disconcertingly like his sister's, and waited.

"What?" was Tom's only reply, which, he could admit, wasn't the wittiest.

"How long have you been in love with my sister?" Charles repeated calmly.

It was the calm that frightened Tom. He didn't trust it. After all, he knew Charles' sisters and had no reason to think that Charles would be any more predictable than the two shrews he was related to.

"I-I am not," mumbled Tom now, realising that he sounded like a naughty child and then realising that he felt like one.

"Why not?"

At this, Tom's eyes snapped up to meet the other man's. The same icy blue as Caroline's. The fact did nothing to improve Tom's mood.

"What?" he repeated like the dolt he suspected he was.

"Why not? What's wrong with her?"

"Nothing," he hit back immediately, thoroughly confused by this bizarre conversation.

Tom looked to Edward for support but Edward looked to be enjoying the exchange far too much to be any help.

"Of course, I know there are plenty of reasons why a man *wouldn't* be in love with her," Charles continued nonchalantly. "She is stuffy enough to bore a man to tears, I know. And though she's my sister and I love her, her personality is hardly worthy of comment, given that she doesn't exactly have one."

Tom felt his temper flare at Charles' continued insults. He was a God-awful brother and a complete idiot if he did not understand what a treasure his sister was. Unfortunately, he was also still talking.

"Growing up there were those amongst my friends who thought her quite pretty of course, but you must remember, rural Ireland is no place to see real beauty and sadly, her looks are not improving with age. Why, she—"

Tom stood so abruptly that his chair flew out behind him. His fists were clenched and he would love nothing more to land another blow on the viscount's other cheek. Several, in fact.

"Do not speak about your sister that way in my presence again," bit out Tom, uncaring of the fact that he was making his feelings about the lady more than a little obvious. "And you," he continued rounding on Edward, "how can you sit there and listen to this? How would you feel if it were Rebecca he so insulted?"

"Murderous," answered Edward now, a grin on his face, "because he would have been insulting the woman I love."

Edward's words hit Tom like a douse of icy water. His temper cooled and he immediately realised that he'd been baited. Turning slowly back to face Charles, he saw to his dismay that the other man was smiling knowingly and shaking his head.

"How not one, but two of Society's greatest catches could be so taken in by my irritating little sisters is beyond me," he said now, leaning forward to refill their glasses yet again. "But it seems that they have. We all know Edward was a damned fool waiting as long as he did to tell Rebecca about how he felt.

I wonder, are you any smarter than your cousin or is this idiocy a family trait?"

Tom made no answer save to throw himself back into his righted chair and down yet another glass of brandy. He would have to confront his feelings. And soon. Otherwise, he'd drink his cellars dry.

CHAPTER TWENTY-NINE

CAROLINE COULD HAVE wept with joy when she finally saw the dowager's carriage return.

She had been pacing the corridor outside Tom's study for the past twenty minutes.

There had been no sounds of punches, swords, or gunshots so she was feeling vaguely hopeful. In fact, all she heard was a low rumble of male voices, interspersed with a laugh or two.

Laughing was good. They wouldn't be laughing if they were killing each other, would they?

She rushed to open the door before even the footman got to it and skidded to a halt in front of Rebecca and the dowager.

"Caro, what on earth is the matter?"

"Charles is here. And Tom punched him. And now they're in the study and I have no idea what is going on," she said in a rush, breathing frantically.

"Charles is here? How wonderful!" was all the answer Rebecca gave.

Caroline stared at her in exasperation.

"Didn't you hear the rest of it?" she demanded. "Tom

punched him, Rebecca."

"I'm sure he's had worse," Rebecca answered, unfazed by the news. "None of us are deaf to the antics of our dear brother, Caroline. I'm surprised he hasn't been shot by a disgruntled husband or two by now. Frankly, if he got punched, he probably deserved it."

Caroline was well aware of Charles' reputation. If Tom was known as a rake, Charles was bordering on utterly debauched.

They all hoped that he was merely rebelling against the pressures on the shoulders of a young heir. Unfortunately, he seemed to have a knack for the type of rebellion that included drinking, gambling, and womanising. And since he was disgustingly handsome, or so they'd been told by more than one tearful debutante, it seemed he got away with far more than he should.

But that was hardly the point.

This time, he hadn't done anything except hug his own sister. And that was most definitely allowed.

"He didn't deserve it," Caroline argued, "he only arrived minutes before Tom and Edward. He was hugging me and next thing Tom had grabbed him and punched him."

"Ah, well that explains it," said the dowager, who had been listening avidly.

Caroline felt as though they'd all run mad.

"How can that possibly explain anything?" she almost shouted. Almost. Ladies didn't shout.

"Very easily, my dear. He was jealous. Imagine his surprise seeing you in the arms of a tall, and might I say devilishly handsome young man."

"Exactly, 'twas merely jealousy. Boys will be boys, Caroline. It's best not to try to understand it. I would wager they are now ensconced in the study and very probably halfway foxed."

Rebecca was right as it turned out. Though not quite

foxed, the gentlemen had certainly imbibed in a few glasses.

And to Caroline's relief and consternation, they seemed to be getting along famously.

After a brief knock, the dowager had entered followed by Rebecca and with Caroline cautiously bringing up the rear.

"Hello, trouble," Charles had called, standing and embracing his tiny sister.

"Charles, it is so good to see you. And with no bullet holes," answered Rebecca cheekily.

"I told you before, Becca, I have nine lives."

Charles turned then to execute a polite bow to the dowager.

"Your grace, I believe you are getting younger with time," he said smoothly.

The dowager giggled, actually giggled, and tapped him lightly on the arm.

"Do behave yourself, Charles," she admonished though her grin remained planted on her face.

Everyone seemed in fine spirits.

Caroline should have been relieved. But she felt furious, though she was unsure as to why.

Perhaps, she thought, it was because her relationship with Tom was certain to be at an end. And she hadn't even received a final kiss.

Or perhaps it was because she'd been aging decades in the hallway worrying about them all and they'd been in here joking and drinking and not giving a fig about her.

Or perhaps, and this was probably closer to the truth, perhaps it was because Charles had obviously decided that Tom held her in no particular regard and therefore deemed him safe.

The thought was utterly depressing.

"Well," she said now, sarcasm dripping from her every word, "don't you all look cosy. Never mind that I was left outside alone for hours wondering what was going on."

"Hardly hours, Caro," drawled Charles, "and would you rather we were at twenty paces?"

"Don't be ridiculous," she barked at him, too riled up to be placated.

Charles held up his hands in surrender.

"Good God, Caroline, if I didn't know better I'd say you're loosening up a little. I'd almost be tempted to say you're losing your temper."

Normally, or rather in the past, Caroline would have raised a contemptuous brow.

As it was, she was too highly strung, too disappointed, angry, frustrated, and a whole host of other emotions to even try to remain under control.

Charles wasn't the only person whose jaw dropped when Caroline swore at him, loudly too, and stomped from the room.

She left a stunned silence in her wake.

"Did she just—" Charles started then ground to a halt as words failed him.

Rebecca was laughing.

"Charles," she said taking his arm and leading him from the study, "I think you've just met the new Caroline."

CHAPTER THIRTY

THE NEXT FEW days were torturous for Caroline. Either Charles was being ridiculously overprotective or he was taking great amusement from her misery. Whichever it was, he had followed her like a shadow and she was heartily sick of it. And on the rare occasions that she managed to escape him, it was to find him planted next to Tom.

Whenever Tom suggested something, whether a morning ride or a trip to the village book shop, Charles found a way to invite himself along. Every. Single. Time. It was the outside of enough.

And what was worse today was the day that Tom's guests were due to arrive.

Caroline sat in the window of a small morning room and gazed out at the bright sunlight glinting off the verdant grass.

It pained her heart to know how much she loved it here. And it wasn't because it was so big, though big it was. Or so beautiful. It was because it was his. And she would love anything that belonged to him because it was a part of him.

And now it was all over. Charles had made sure to stick to her like a shadow; in fact she'd slipped in here when she knew he wasn't watching just to get some peace.

And in mere hours, the house would fill with Tom's guests, one of whom, Miss Noble, she knew wouldn't make for pleasant company.

She sighed and leaned her head against the cool windowpane, closing her eyes and wishing for the impossible.

The door creaked open and Caroline whirled around. As if her wishes had conjured him up, there he stood. And he was mercifully, beautifully alone.

"How did you manage to escape Charles?" she asked quietly, only half joking.

Tom grinned in response.

"I told him we were planning on riding to the river. I believe I last saw him rushing to the stables."

Caroline laughed softly and shook her head.

"I wonder why he has been so attentive to me," Caroline mused now, before adding dryly, "Probably because there are no light skirts to chase."

"I think it is me he is sticking to," answered Tom ruefully.

"I don't think you are his type."

"Funny! Think about it, Caroline. He's your brother. He's not going to leave you alone with a man like me. Nor should he."

"I'm not a child, Tom. There's no need for his constant watching."

"Of course there is. I don't blame him in the slightest." His deep blue eyes bored into hers. "If you were mine to protect, I would never let you out of my sight."

And all at once, as his words dropped into the air between them, the atmosphere of the room changed.

Caroline didn't speak, too afraid to break the spell that seemed to be captivating them both.

Tom stepped slowly, so slowly towards her and she stood to meet him.

He came to a stop right in front of her. Agonisingly close.

She would be able to touch him by just lifting a hand, kiss him by just leaning up. It was heaven and it was hell.

He reached out and brushed her cheek softly and Caroline had to close her eyes against the sheer force of her attraction.

Why could he not be hers? Forever, not just for a few days?

When she opened her eyes again he was staring at her and she thought, hoped, prayed that he would finally kiss her once again.

He leaned forward and pressed his lips gently against hers — once, twice, before finally, with a muffled oath, pulling her against him and devouring her.

"God, I missed this darling," he whispered against her lips.

"I missed it too," she gasped boldly. "It is what I've been yearning for."

He pulled back slightly, so he could look down into her face, his eyes roving her features.

"I wanted to keep my distance. So that it would be easier. But—"

"Well isn't this just the prettiest house you ever saw?"

The jarring voice from outside the door was enough to shatter the atmosphere into a million pieces.

Caroline felt the loss keenly as Tom took a slow and seemingly reluctant step away from her.

He smiled sadly at her.

"I should go and see to my guests. Miss Noble is not the most patient of creatures."

Caroline nodded, not trusting herself to speak.

Tom hesitated as if he wanted to say something but stopped himself and sighed.

"Will you join us in the drawing room?"

"Yes, of course," she answered clearing her throat past the sudden lump. "I shall come directly."

"Good, well I shall see you in a moment or two then."

He gazed at her for another second, then turned and walked out, closing the door softly behind him.

Strange how he was only going to the other room, she would see him but shortly. And yet, that had felt like goodbye.

Tom stood for a moment outside the morning room's door, trying to school his features into their usual, slightly insolent mask.

There was no denying it any longer. It was the most painfully tragic thing in the world. He loved, adored, worshipped her.

The only thing that had changed in all that time away from her was that his love had grown in depth and strength. And now? Now he felt that he could not even breathe without her.

So where did that leave him? Lost and desolate, that's where.

He wanted nothing more than to march back into that room and tell her he loved her. Beg her to reconsider him. Plead with her to see beyond a title and see a man so desperately in love with her that he would do anything, anything to make her his.

He knew her now, far more than he had two years ago.

He knew that she hadn't rejected him because she was mercenary or snobbish or wicked. She had felt the pressure of familial duty and had bowed to it.

Would she do any differently now? Could she?

He knew her father's health was still a source of great worry. He knew that she considered it her responsibility to carry out his wishes.

But would another man make her happy? He would certainly never try as hard to as Tom would.

He was sure that she felt something for him, but then, she had claimed to love him in the past and it hadn't been enough.

His heart would not be able to stand the rejection again. He knew it.

Was it better to love her from a distance?

God, this was excruciating.

Charlotte's high-pitched tone rang out once again through the cavernous house.

It was time he greeted his guests. More were sure to be arriving soon.

He thought, with a sickening lurch of his heart, of all the eligible gentlemen who were on their way to try to win the fair Caroline.

Bloody Rebecca! It was all her fault.

Well, he could only hope that Caroline wouldn't like any of them.

Then at least he'd have time to get away before she chose.

Because he knew now, just as surely as he knew that he would never sleep another night without having her in his dreams, that he would not, could not stay and see her marry.

He had thought he was strong enough to do it. Thought that he could settle into his life here, surround himself with family and be happy. He had thought that he'd moved on.

What a bloody idiot he'd been.

But it was asking far too much of himself.

No, he would have to leave again. His heart begged for it and his sanity demanded it.

He would leave.

And this time, he would stay away.

Caroline entered the drawing room having had a firm conversation with herself.

Yes, she had fantasised about running away and hiding

on the vast grounds somewhere but logically it would probably only result in a search and a pretty quick discovery.

No, she had to face the Nobles sooner or later and though later was infinitely preferable she had told Tom that she would come. And so she had.

The first thing she noticed was that Charlotte Noble looked as beautiful as ever. The second thing was that she was sitting far too close to Tom on the sofa.

At the sound of her entrance the occupants had stood to greet her. She exchanged pleasantries with Mr. Noble, who was as jolly and friendly as ever, and civil chitchat with Miss Noble who had, to Caroline's chagrin, kept hold of Tom's arm for the entirety of their exchange.

"Are you tired from your journey, Miss Noble?" she asked politely.

"Not terribly, Miss Carrington, it's not very far from London."

"I wonder that you need support then," Caroline responded, ignoring Charlotte's insubordinate refusal to use her title, her voice dripping sugar as she looked pointedly at Caroline's grip on Tom's arm.

The other woman's eyes flashed but her smile remained fixed, though a little strained.

"How odd that you should notice such an insignificant gesture," she laughed and the sound made Caroline want to slap her.

She hardly recognised herself. She never felt violent. Charles often said he did, though he was ridiculously laid back. And Rebecca's temper was legendary. But Caroline was usually so filled with composure, at least on the outside.

There was something about this woman however, and her territorial attitude to Tom, that really brought out the worst in Caroline.

Before Caroline could answer the dowager spoke up.

"Tom was going to take Mr. and Miss Noble on a quick

tour of the house, Caroline, before the other guests arrive."

Caroline's mind immediately flew to the other night when she and Tom had started — whatever it was they had started.

She found her eyes drawn to Tom at the dowager's words and her heart sped up as she caught his gaze. He was remembering too.

"Would you like to join us?" he asked softly.

Yes.

"No. Thank you." She gave no reason because she did not have one, other than not wanting to spend any more time than necessary in the company of Charlotte Noble. Especially when she was around Tom.

A sound by the door heralded the arrival of Charles and Rebecca. Edward had some urgent business to attend to and would join them later.

Caroline was childishly pleased to see that Rebecca greeted Miss Noble with icy civility rather than her usual warmth.

Tom used the opportunity of introductions to release Charlotte's hold on his arm.

"Lord Carrington, may I introduce Mr. Fred Noble and his daughter, Miss Charlotte Noble. Freddie, this is Viscount Carrington, Rebecca and Caroline's brother."

Caroline watched as Fred Noble bowed to Rebecca and Charles and watched closer as Charlotte Noble's eyes gleamed and raked over Charles, as if he were a piece of horsemeat at Tattersall's.

Charles, being the utter rake that he was, responded to Charlotte's appraisal with a broad grin and, when her father wasn't looking, a flirtatious wink.

For goodness' sake. They'd have to put him on a leash.

Caroline noticed that Rebecca was watching Charles' antics with Charlotte as well, her eyes narrowed.

Charles was most definitely in trouble now. And it

served him right.

"Tom was just going to take us on a tour of his house, my lord," Charlotte purred, *purred* up at Charles. "Would you care to join us?"

"I believe I would," drawled Charles before taking the young woman's arm and leading her from the room.

Caroline and Rebecca shared a look.

It was going to be a long week.

CHAPTER THIRTY-ONE

TOM FELT AS THOUGH he had been plunged into the fires of Hades itself as he dressed that evening for dinner.

He had heard word from some of his gentlemen friends. Their carriage had lost a wheel and they had sent a footman ahead to say that they would be late but were still arriving this evening.

In the meantime, he had to endure an afternoon of Charles' outrageous flirting with Charlotte, which did not bother him in the slightest and in fact made him feel extremely grateful to Charles, but he knew that Fred was starting to watch and that wasn't a situation he was looking forward to getting caught in the middle of.

Not only that, but Caroline had been avoiding him since their kiss in the morning room.

In fairness, it probably wasn't him, but the company he was keeping. There was certainly no affection between the ladies currently under his roof.

He loosened his cravat. It was like watching a pride of lionesses turn on each other.

The gentlemen had been scarpering all afternoon

avoiding getting caught in the crossfire of barbed comments and thinly veiled insults.

It was exhausting.

He pulled again at his suddenly too tight cravat and then sulked as his valet slapped his hand away and proceeded to retie it. Tighter, the swine.

He felt as though he were on a knife's edge.

The woman he loved, that he'd finally admitted he still loved, was avoiding him because a woman he barely liked wouldn't leave him the hell alone. Although, mercifully, Charles seemed to be doing an excellent job of keeping her occupied.

As if that wasn't bad enough, a carriage full of potential husbands for Caroline was on its way.

Never had he thought he'd be so uncomfortable in his own home.

His valet, after much fussing which always irritated Tom, deemed him presentable. Tom had learned not to criticise or comment on Philips' ministrations since he suspected the older man slowed down on purpose any time he did.

Tom made straight for his study where he intended to lock himself away until the dinner hour when he'd have to once again plaster on a smile, play the attentive host, and try not to throw himself at Caroline's feet and beg her to reconsider him.

And then, as if thinking about her had made her a reality, she was there. Gloriously, beautifully there, right in front of him.

He slowed to a stop.

She hadn't spotted him standing at the top of the stairs so he allowed himself the pleasure of just looking at her.

Her head was bowed; no doubt she was deep in thought. It was unlike her to appear from her room this early, usually she did not make an appearance until the exact time they were due downstairs.

He appreciated this punctuality. It gave him a chance to try and prepare himself for the impact of seeing her. It never worked. Every time, he was blown away all over again.

Tonight was no exception.

The colour of her dress was one of the boldest he had seen her in yet. The cerulean blue — and he only knew it was called that because he'd had to listen to his aunt rave about it earlier when the ladies had been discussing gowns — was beautifully bright against her soft, peaches and cream complexion. Her hair was a confection of twists and curls. He had no idea how she'd gone about getting it that way but it was stunning, interspersed with diamonds that glinted in the candlelight.

His eyes raked her and his entire body tightened at the image of her sinful curves, moulded as they were by the satin of her gown. It wasn't terribly low cut. But it was enough to make him thank God profusely for the gift of sight.

He could see the slightest outline of her legs as she walked towards him, fidgeting with her fan. It was enough to send his mind to places that Charles would surely shoot him for. Edward too, for that matter.

He realised, as he fought the urge to weep at the sight of her ethereal beauty, that she wasn't slowing down. She was going to barrel into him and though the contact would be welcome, he did not want her hurting herself.

So he called out softly, "Caroline."

Her eyes met his and for a moment, they lit with pure unadulterated joy. It made him want to declare himself then and there.

Hadn't he been about to do so this morning? Before his guests had arrived?

Would he have had the courage?

"Tom. You look very well," she said, her eyes raking over him, her tongue darting out to wet her lips.

He groaned at the sight. She was killing him. And it was

exquisite.

"Are you alright?" she asked in concern now, reaching up to touch his brow. "You seem as though you are in pain or sickness."

He laughed at the innocence.

"You have no idea," he responded and saw her frown in confusion.

But he figured it wasn't safe to elaborate so close to his bedchamber.

"I was just going to take a walk, perhaps along the gallery on the first floor," Caroline stuttered. "I am ready earlier than I expected and I find myself quite restless."

She was babbling. Was she nervous? If so, why? Interesting…

"Then I shall join you. I too am at a loose end."

He watched as she thought over his offer for a second and wished he knew what she was thinking.

But then she smiled and nodded.

"Very well," she said and turned to descend the steps.

Tom pulled her to a stop and turned her to face him, his hands firmly on her shoulders, the heat of her skin branding him.

"You look ravishing," he said simply and without preamble.

He watched, fascinated, as a soft blush bloomed in her cheeks.

"Oh, t-thank you. I felt that I should make an effort to look well for all your guests. The party will truly start now after all."

"You always look well. Better than well. In fact, you always look far too beautiful for my peace of mind."

He could tell that she was rendered speechless by this barrage of compliments so he took her arm and slowly started down the steps.

"And as for the party," he said softly, leaning close and

inhaling the fresh, light scent that was hers and hers alone, "it will not be nearly as enjoyable as it has been with just us."

Breathe, Caroline she reminded herself as they made their way down the stairs to the next landing.

She loved him so much it was starting to become unbearable.

She had been dreading the arrival of Charlotte Noble but had been both relieved and alarmed by that lady's obvious interest in Charles.

Relieved that she would not have to watch Charlotte flirt mercilessly with Tom. Alarmed because she knew what Charles was and she also knew that Charlotte was not the type of sister-in-law she wanted, should Fred Noble decide that Charles was getting too close to his daughter.

Caroline had been anxiously pacing her room for the last thirty minutes until even Sally got fed up and left her to it.

The truth was, as silly as she had been she had allowed herself to grow comfortable here, with nobody but Tom and her family. Had allowed herself to fantasise about living here with Tom, making a life together, raising children together.

Peacefully and quietly, away from the pressures and structures of a society that she no longer cared about.

In short, everything that she hadn't known she wanted and everything that she had given up two years ago.

And now the house was to be filled with people, most of whom she didn't know, possibly some of who would be here to snag a rich, well connected husband.

To hear Tom say that he didn't want it either caused her to hope when she had no right to.

They had reached the gallery, though Caroline wasn't overly interested, it was something to do to walk her anxiety out of her.

"Here we are," Tom said.

"Yes, wonderful."

She wished she'd said somewhere else. She didn't want to look at huge pictures of deceased strangers.

Tom sighed.

"Shall we go to the conservatory instead? We should be in time to see the sunset."

Caroline beamed.

"That would be wonderful."

He stared at her, as though unable to look away then leaned down and placed a soft kiss on her forehead.

Without another word he turned and led her from the gallery.

She wasn't sure why, but she felt like crying. Only this time, for the first time in her life, they were tears of joy.

The conservatory was blissfully quiet and peaceful. Still warm from the heat of the setting sun, it was pleasant to stand in, to inhale the heady scent of the flowers and plants that surrounded them.

They moved to the doors and stood watching the summer sun set slowly on the horizon. It was breathtakingly beautiful but Caroline barely saw it, so wrapped up was she in the man beside her.

It was there again, that tenuous something that always simmered between them. Something so wonderful it made her heart ache. Oh how she loved him and how her foolish heart believed he was starting to feel the same.

"It is beautiful," she sighed, unaware of the longing in her wistful tone.

"Yes, it is," he replied deeply but when she turned to look up at him he was watching her and only her.

In the distance, the door sounded and Caroline felt

desolate at the thought that this precious moment would end. Just like this morning, they were being interrupted by outside forces.

"We should return. Your guests have arrived," she said in a whisper, as though speaking louder would make their arrival and subsequent end to this, more real.

"We should," he answered though he did not move.

She looked back toward the dusk sky, stepping a little closer to the wall of glass that separated them and the manicured gardens.

"I shall miss this," she said now, the words torn from her heart, "I shall miss being alone with you."

It was rather bold but she no longer cared. It was the truth and it was high time she was honest with him about her feelings.

Caroline gasped as she felt him step behind her, his strong arms pulling her back against the hard lines of his body, his mouth dipping to whisper across her exposed neck.

"Not as much as I will, darling," he said, moving now to the sensitive spot behind her ear.

"But you did not even touch me, all those times alone, when you had the chance," she argued now though breathlessly.

She felt him sigh behind her as he stepped away. She almost cried out in despair at the loss of contact but suddenly found herself being spun toward him and gathered closely once more.

"I wanted to, more than I've ever wanted anything," he said, his eyes boring into her very soul, willing her to believe him.

"Then why?"

"Because if I started to kiss you, Caroline, I do not think I would be able to stop."

His words warmed her heart, her skin, her very blood.

Feeling a boldness born of love and sheer desperation,

she grasped his neck and pulled his head towards hers.

"I would not want you to stop," she said before their lips met.

And meet they did, in a kiss that branded itself onto her heart.

It felt like a fusion of their spirits, like a beginning of something life-altering. Something so wonderful she hardly dared to believe it.

They were on the precipice of a cliff. All it would take was for her to open her heart. To tell him how she felt and what she wanted.

"Tom—"

"Caroline—"

They spoke at the same time and laughed a little.

Strangely, she did not feel scared or nervous. All she felt was love and confidence that this time she could do it right. And have everything she had ever wanted.

"What did you want to say?" he asked softly, caressing her cheek.

"I—"

"There you are."

Caroline nearly swore at Charles' untimely interruption. Tom did swear. A lot.

"What are you doing, hiding away here? Your guests will be looking for you and dinner is fast approaching."

Although her brother remained his usual, friendly self, there was steel in his blue eyes as he took in the scene before him.

She and Tom had sprung apart as soon as they'd heard his voice but Caroline could not be sure how much Charles had seen.

They were spared any further questioning, thank goodness, by the arrival of Rebecca looking stunningly beautiful in an unusual bronze coloured gown.

"Caroline, there you are. Oh, my dear you look positively

enchanting," she bustled over and grasped her sister, turning back toward the door.

"Tom dear, do hurry up. Your guests have already gone straight to change for dinner. You men! I do not know how you manage to get ready for a dinner party in under five minutes but there you have it."

"Caroline," Tom called out to her but before she had the chance to turn around, Charles had clapped Tom on the shoulder, and from the sounds of it rather harder than necessary, and stopped him from following after her.

"Come Tom, let's have a drink before dinner."

It seemed her siblings were conspiring to keep her from Tom. But why?

As soon as the ladies were outside the conservatory and walking back toward the drawing room where the guests would congregate Caroline turned to Rebecca.

"What on earth was that about? Did you enlist Charles' help to keep Tom and me apart?"

"Not exactly," replied Rebecca, "Charles does not want you together any more than I do."

Caroline stopped and turned to stare at her sister.

"Why?"

"Because he is your brother and you are unmarried. You should not be alone in a conservatory. Besides, he knows Tom's reputation, since it is so similar to his own," she finished dryly.

"No, I meant why do you not want us together?"

"You know why. We spoke of this before. I was happy for you to have a little flirtation with him but I have not forgotten, even if you have, that if you do not find a husband and do so soon, you will end up leg shackled to that ancient creature, Lord Doncastle."

"But, Rebecca I think — I mean, I am not sure of course, but I hope that I shall be able to marry T—"

"And besides," Rebecca continued over her sister's protestations, "Tom has gone to all this trouble to gather up some suitable gentlemen for you. The least you can do is give them a chance."

Caroline felt as though all of the air left her body in one whoosh. It could not be true, could it?

While she was building up the courage to tell him that she loved him still and wanted a second chance, he was telling her that he was trying to marry her off?

"What do you mean?" she asked, her voice quivering, praying that she was mistaken in what Rebecca was telling her.

"That Tom has made sure to invite young, unattached, titled gentlemen. It was all put in place in London."

Rebecca saw Caroline's sudden change in pallor, saw the tears glistening in her eyes that she tried valiantly to hide.

"Caro, it does not mean that he doesn't care for you. He just—"

"He just doesn't love me. Or forgive me. Not enough to consider — well, never mind," she did her best to rally, to ignore the crushing pain coursing through her. "Come along, they shall be waiting."

"Caro—"

"Leave it, Rebecca," she said softly.

Why had she let herself believe? Hope? All this time, he'd been waiting for someone to come and take her off his hands.

CHAPTER THIRTY-TWO

TOM SPENT ALMOST the entire evening cursing himself, Rebecca, Charles, and anyone else he could think of straight to Hell.

If Charles hadn't interrupted them, would he have had the courage to confess his love? And what had she wanted to say? His heart told him that she loved him too, perhaps enough to fight for them this time. His head told him to stop being such a fool. Again.

But right now, he had a more pressing problem in the form of the gentlemen vying for her attention.

What the hell had he been thinking? Inviting men here who were going to fall in love with her?

Perhaps they wouldn't be interested, he thought desperately, then called himself all kinds of idiot.

Of course they would be interested. Who wouldn't be? She was magnificent.

Tom took another swig of his wine. At this point, he had stopped even trying to engage in the conversation that was surrounding him. Instead, he concentrated all his efforts on watching her and the baying hounds surrounding her, hunting for her attention.

It was maddening.

Looking over, he caught Edward's look of sympathy. What good was sympathy? Sympathy would not turn back time and prevent him from inviting them.

Tom looked down the table assessing his guests once more. This evening was a predominantly male party since all of his guests had not yet arrived. The rest would come tomorrow.

He had invited the vicar and his wife this evening thinking that at least the vicar's wife was another female to add to the party. Though he should not have bothered, since Edward only had eyes for Rebecca as always, Charlotte and Charles were bordering on inappropriate, and everyone else, including him, was hell bent on getting Caroline's attention.

When he and Charles had finally made it to the drawing room, one look at Caroline's pale face and hurt expression had confirmed his fears — she knew what he had done.

But she didn't know why. He had been forced to, against his will. It was Rebecca's fault.

And besides, he hadn't known then how utterly captivated by her he was going to become again. How little his pride and fear of rejection seemed to matter anymore when faced with the idea of losing her again.

Dinner was excruciating. For him anyway. He watched as Lord Deverill, an old school friend, ate her up with his eyes.

He listened as Lord Boxley, a man he knew from Whites, threw simpering compliments at her every two minutes.

It was nauseating. And she did not seem particularly happy about it.

And tomorrow would be worse, because tomorrow Hadley would arrive with his irritating sister and unattached female cousin and would either take up where he had left off, trying to win Caroline's affection, or would immediately tell everyone what had transpired the night Caroline had gotten drunk.

At the time it had seemed a good idea to invite him. Tom was still fairly confident that Edward had scared the wits out of the man enough that he would keep his mouth shut, and inviting him would hopefully flatter him enough not to want to cause any problems or upset to any of them.

If not, Tom would take great pleasure in shutting it for him. And of course, now Charles was here too, so he had no great concern that Hadley would try to get away with saying anything.

He felt the beginnings of a headache. She would not even look at him, for God's sake.

Mercifully, the meal had now come to an end so the ladies would retire to the drawing room and he would not have to endure the spectacle of grown men acting like lovesick puppies.

As the ladies traipsed out, Tom watched Caroline hoping to catch her eye. Right before she left, she looked at him as if she couldn't help it.

It was the briefest of glances but was filled with such pain that it caused *him* pain.

The footmen began to dole out port and cigars, which the gentlemen readily accepted.

Edward, who was sitting on Tom's right, leaned over and spoke quietly.

"You look like you are ready to punch someone. Or something. I take it this is to do with Caroline?"

Tom sighed then swore softly, running a hand through his hair in frustration.

"Why did I think I could survive this? What if she forms an attachment to one of these idiots? Right here, under my nose."

"It wasn't your fault. Believe me, nobody knows more than I that Rebecca is impossible to say 'no' to."

"Yes, well I should have."

"Why?"

Tom stared at him.

"What do you mean, why?"

"Why not have them here? Why not let her meet and fall in love with someone? It will be a damn sight better than being tied to that bumbling old man, Doncastle will it not?"

"Well, of course it will."

"Then why not sit back and hope that she falls in love with one of them?"

"Because."

"Because why?"

"Leave it, Edward."

"No. I'm interested. Why shouldn't she set her cap at one of them?"

"Because I love her, dammit," Tom burst out in a fierce whisper.

Edward leaned back in his chair and smiled.

"Yes," he drawled, "I know."

Tom groaned.

"What am I going to do? She won't talk to me now. Not when she thinks I've tried to marry her off."

"Surely she will be flattered by your help."

Tom thought back to their kisses, their half conversations as if they were both on the edge of admitting something wonderful.

"No," he said sadly, "if anything, she will feel betrayed."

"Then you must speak to her and explain yourself."

"Explain yourself to whom?" Charles had caught the tail end of their conversation and spoke up, drawing the attention of the rest of the gentlemen.

"It is nothing," Edward said quickly, "something to do with my mother." The lie fell easily from his mouth but Charles was clearly not fooled, if his sardonic expression was anything to go by.

"I thought you were speaking of my sister," he said

boldly.

He stared at Tom and Tom stared right back, refusing to look guilty. He had done nothing wrong. Except hurt her terribly and make her feel as though she had been betrayed by him, of course.

"Ah, your sister," slurred Boxley, who had obviously partaken of a lot of wine with dinner, "forgive me Carrington but she is quite extraordinarily beautiful."

Charles merely smiled and nodded but Tom felt his blood pressure increase instantaneously.

"Yes, quite so," this from Deverill who was so pompous Tom wondered why they were even friends. "A fine catch."

"She's not a fish," he said coldly.

Boxley laughed aloud.

"Of course not, old chap. Of course not. A fish indeed. No, no." Here his tone became lascivious and Tom had to clench his fists to keep from lashing out. "She is all woman, to be sure."

Tom noticed, in his peripheral vision, both Edward and Charles stiffen almost imperceptibly. Boxley was on dangerous ground.

"Of course, it must run in the family," he continued, oblivious to his precarious situation, "Your duchess is equally beautiful, your grace," he said to Edward now. "But since you snatched her up quick smart, we'll have to fight it out now for the other one."

Tom was going to kill him. And enjoy it. By the looks of things, he'd be fighting Charles to get to this stupid man first.

"And let's not forget the charms of the lovely Miss Noble," drawled Deverill. "Truly, Crawdon, you have done exceptionally well with the offerings at this party."

Freddie Noble spoke up now, though he seemed decidedly less bothered by the insolent young lords than the other gentlemen.

"Should we join the ladies?" he asked, before any punches

were thrown.

"Excellent idea," said Tom quickly, jumping up from his chair and practically running from the room. The sooner he could speak to Caroline the better he would feel.

As soon as the gentlemen entered the drawing room, his eyes scanned the ladies present. She wasn't here.

He looked toward Rebecca with a questioning frown. She looked utterly miserable.

"Where is she?" he asked without preamble.

"She—she had a sudden headache and has retired early, with her apologies."

He knew Rebecca didn't believe that, any more than he did.

"This is a disaster," he said miserably, slumping into the empty seat beside her.

Rebecca sighed and bit her lip, as if to stop herself from saying something.

Tom narrowed his eyes suspiciously.

"What?" he asked.

"What?" she repeated with wide-eyed innocence. Except he knew her so he wasn't fooled.

"What did you do?"

"Me?" she flared defensively.

"Yes, you. You look guilty. What did you do, or say or—or..." He trailed off to silence.

He was probably being unfair to Rebecca. She didn't have to do anything really did she? Wouldn't it be obvious to Caroline what had happened? Why these gentlemen were here?

No, he shouldn't blame her. He would apologise, be kind and—

"I told her you have handpicked gentlemen to marry her."

—and kill her.

"You did what?" he roared, which brought a sudden halt to the other conversations taking place in the room.

Edward marched over, his eyes stormy as he looked furiously between them.

"What the hell are you doing, shouting at Rebecca?" he hissed through clenched teeth.

"Calm down, Edward, it is quite alright," said Rebecca, rolling her eyes slightly. "Really there is no need for you to come charging over every time someone shouts at me. I'm always being shouted at, or at least I was in the past. It does not bother me in the slightest."

"Well it bothers me," he answered still looking at Tom. "I won't have anyone disrespecting my wife."

Tom bit back a curse of frustration and chose to ignore Edward completely. If the man thought his duchess was a delicate little flower, he was very much mistaken.

"Tom," Rebecca recalled his attention to her, "I told her, but not to cause any sort of distress. I had no idea that an arrangement existed between you."

She was watching him closely, her dark brown eyes so different from her sister's icy blue. Yet still having the ability to scare him when they looked so shrewdly at him.

"We're not, that is to say we, I–I–" Eventually he just sighed in defeat. "There is no arrangement."

"But you wish there was?"

She was relentless.

"Look, I just need to speak to her. To explain. I invited these blasted idiots here before—"

"Before what?"

He'd already told Edward he still loved her. What was he going to do? Tell the entire English countryside before he spoke to Caroline?

"Before she marries one of them and regrets it."

That would have to do for now.

But, he forgot, this was Rebecca.

"Why do you think she would regret it? They are perfectly respectable men, the type my father would definitely approve of."

Tom felt the last of his control slip.

Yes, her father would approve of their titles. But there wasn't a man in the world that would love her as much as he would.

He would run to the furthest reaches of the earth before he would watch her tie herself to someone so undeserving of her.

They didn't know her. Not the real her. They only knew the façade. Beautiful as it was. Nobody had ever thought to delve deeper.

But they didn't know that she had at least four different smiles. Didn't know that when she was excited or nervous, her breath hitched slightly. They didn't know she bit her lip to stop herself from laughing when she thought it was improper to do so.

They didn't know her heart. Her hopes, dreams, fears, and insecurities. He knew. Knew them all and he adored them because they were what made her who she was.

That was what she deserved. Not a meaningless title.

He hadn't fought hard enough two years ago. He saw that now. He had walked away because his pride had been hurt. But his pride could go to hell. He didn't want it. He just wanted her.

Yes, he would leave if she chose another. But not in anger. He would leave because he would not survive seeing her with another man.

He needed to fight. Both their futures depended on it.

CHAPTER THIRTY-THREE

"YOU CANNOT BE SERIOUS, Caro," Rebecca remonstrated, "you cannot hide in your room all week."

"I have no intentions of hiding in my room all week," Caroline assured her, "I just do not want to come down to breakfast."

Caroline had awoken that morning feeling tired and heart-sore. She had cried herself to sleep last night and was sure that her face was showing the effects of it this morning.

Her eyes felt puffy, her throat dry, and her head pounded.

Although it did not feel as bad as her recovery from over-indulgence of champagne, it wasn't far off.

When Sally had come in to coax her from bed, Caroline had refused and begged for a tray in her room.

The tray had arrived all right, but so too had her sister.

"Hiding from them won't make them go away, you know," Rebecca said stoutly.

Caroline sighed.

"Yes, Becca. I am aware of that."

Rebecca said nothing for a while, just gazed casually

round the room while Caroline sipped on her morning chocolate.

"He was terribly distraught, you know."

Rebecca was trying to draw Caroline in, to get her to show an interest. But she felt too raw to discuss anything now.

Besides, she didn't care enough to ask...

"Who was?" she asked quietly, wanting to kick herself.

"Tom, of course."

More silence.

"Why?" She was an utter fool.

"Because he fears he has upset you."

Caroline laughed, though there was very little humour in it.

"Why would he have upset me? By parading men in front of me so that I would marry and leave?"

Rebecca grasped Caroline's hand.

"It was I who told him to invite them, Caro. I made him do it."

"Why?"

"Because, because I thought it would make him jealous enough to act on his feelings for you. Or, if it didn't, I thought you might at least find someone you could like enough to marry."

Rebecca swallowed, her eyes filling with distressed tears.

"But all it's done is made you so miserable you're hiding away, and driven a wedge between the two of you. I'm sorry, Caro."

"You have nothing to be sorry for. You might have asked him to invite unattached gentlemen, but this is Tom Crawdon we are speaking of. He would not have asked them here if he hadn't wanted to."

Rebecca tried to interrupt but Caroline held up a hand.

"Becca, I haven't made any secret of how I feel about him, at least not to you. But—" here she drew a deep breath, not wanting to utter the next words but having no choice— "but it is high time I faced up to the reality of my situation. I had thought that perhaps Tom and I were — well, that he was starting to — but, regardless, the reality is no matter how much I love him, it is not reciprocated. If it were, he never would have done this. So I shall suffer the blow and carry on. But not today." She felt the tears pool in her eyes and could not make any attempt to stem them. "Today I just need to be allowed to cry and to grieve. Then I shall put the mask back on and accept my fate."

Rebecca leaned forward and brushed away Caroline's tears, failing to realise that she had her own coursing down her cheeks.

"I am so very sorry, dearest. You deserve the greatest of loves."

"I had it once, I think. That is why I wanted that week with Tom. I shall treasure the memories forever and they will help me to be content in life."

Caroline was pleased to see that Rebecca seemed somewhat comforted by her words. She had obviously done a good job of convincing her sister that she would recover from this. Now, if only she could convince herself…

The drawing room was stiflingly warm, or perhaps it just felt that way to Tom.

What had possessed him to think he was cut out for hosting house parties? He was hating every moment of it. Although, to be fair that could be because he could barely stand half the people in the room.

Hadley and his obnoxious sister had arrived along with their cousin some time ago and Tom was playing the dutiful host.

Thank God for Aunt Catherine, he thought, who was acting beautifully as his hostess.

Tom wished Caroline were here. Wished it with every fibre of his being.

He had not seen her since yesterday afternoon and he was constantly torn between worry for her and a desire to burst into her bedchamber and demand that she allow him to speak to her.

And he'd get away with it too, since Charles had disappeared suspiciously close to the same time that Charlotte had left the room.

Tom did not even want to know what was going on between the two.

Freddie had apparently become quite taken with Aunt Catherine for he seemed content to let his flirtatious daughter wander off alone whilst he remained here and conversed with the dowager.

Edward had gone for a ride while Rebecca sat with her sister.

He could go to her room. Rebecca would not be as horrified as some at the prospect and since she would remain in the room with them, he would be able to control himself. He thought.

His thoughts were suddenly interrupted by the screeching laugh of Theodora Hadley who was rather horrifyingly flirting with Lord Boxley in the corner.

She was truly a sight to behold. Her rotund frame was mercilessly stuffed into a gown of eye-wateringly bright puce, which clashed spectacularly with her bright red hair.

Theodora had always been something of an eccentric when it came to fashion and today was no exception. Society had long since gotten used to her penchant for bright colours and shunning the practice of pastels for debutantes.

Tom rarely noticed such things but even he could not miss the turban style headpiece with the alarmingly big feather sticking out the top, a feather which wobbled furiously with each nod of her head.

And when she laughed uproariously as she was wont to do, it actually hit her cousin in the face.

His ears still ringing from Lady Theodora's assault, Tom glanced at the cousin, a Miss Darthsire, so Hadley had informed him. Come to stay with the family from her own family home in Bath.

She was the exact opposite of Theodora — rail thin, mousy, bedecked in a beige gown that covered so much of her the collar was practically up to her mouth. She made no effort to converse save to answer the polite questions aimed specifically at her and she looked heartily disapproving of everything around her.

There was no way in hell these two were going to serve as a distraction from Caroline, though Boxley seemed to be enjoying the attention.

Rebecca entered at that moment and Lady Theodora almost fell over herself to greet her.

She had always been a real social climber.

"Your grace," she fawned in that ear-splitting squeak of hers, "how wonderful to see you and how beautiful you are. Oh, but where is your darling little boy? I long to see him."

Rebecca, to her credit, only mildly flinched at the sheer volume of the speech being bellowed at her.

She bid a polite hello to Hadley, Lady Theodora, and Miss Darthshire before answering. "Henry is with his aunt. Lady Caroline is still not feeling herself so she is taking a walk in the garden with the baby, hoping that some fresh air will be—"

She cut off mid-sentence as all of their eyes turned to Tom who had leapt from his chair and practically run from the room at Rebecca's words.

Rebecca sat down by the dowager and the two ladies shared a smile.

"He is becoming entirely too obvious," said the dowager with a smile.

"I'm glad of it," answered Rebecca, eyes still trained on the door, "one of them has to be."

Caroline breathed in Henry's baby scent as she kissed his curls and pointed out the various flowers they walked by.

He was heavy but she had chosen to carry him outside, craving his innocent nearness.

"Why can't all men be as uncomplicated as you?" she whispered to her gurgling nephew.

Henry smiled at her then smacked her round the chin with his chubby hand.

"It seems you're learning to be a Crawdon man already," she said wryly, "trick me with your smiles then hurt me."

"Is that really what you think?"

Caroline whipped round at the sound of Tom's voice behind her. Her heart hammered from the fright. How had he managed to sneak up on her on a gravel footpath for goodness sake?

"What do you mean?" she asked now, trying her hardest to remain coolly civil.

She had opened herself up to Tom, completely and utterly, and had ended up heartbroken and embarrassed that he had seen the real her. So she was desperately trying to put back together the pieces of the old Caroline — the one who was polite but never friendly, calm and never open.

Tom's eyes narrowed as she spoke, as though he was trying to work out what she was thinking.

Well, he would have a tough job because half the time she had no idea herself.

"You think I tricked you then hurt you?"

"I know you tricked me," she answered, her emotions bubbling to the surface, unaware of the icy fire that danced in her eyes. "And yes, you hurt me."

"Caroline," he took a step toward her and she immediately stepped back, which was ridiculous, she could acknowledge. What was he going to do when she was holding the baby, after all?

He stopped his advance and sighed, scrubbing a hand over his face.

He looks tired, thought Caroline then berated herself for noticing and for caring.

And to be fair, she had seen her reflection earlier when she had finally consented to get dressed and take some air, and her complexion was pale and drawn.

Though she had dressed with care, she still did not feel terribly attractive and she suddenly wished she had taken more care with her appearance. Her morning dress was pretty enough, a white muslin with a thin, sky blue stripe. Sally had pressed her blue pelisse to put over it. Caroline had barely noticed.

"I'm sorry," he said now, bringing her wandering thoughts back to him. "Those gentlemen — Rebecca said I should invite them to, to—"

He stopped and bowed his head, then cast his eyes to Heaven as if praying for words.

"When I agreed to have them here, I wasn't happy about it. In truth, I was damned miserable about it. But I did it because I know that you have to marry and I did not want—"

"Please don't," she said hoarsely, her voice cracking with pain.

He was going to try to break it to her gently, tell her yet again that he had no plans to marry. Had he noticed how much she loved him? Did it scare or worry him?

The thought that he knew, and that it bothered him or worse, made him pity her, was too much to bear. And she couldn't stand here and listen to him saying the words aloud.

She walked toward him and held Henry out to him, relieved that his arms automatically came out to take the baby.

"Please take him back to his mama. I fear my headache is returning. I need to rest."

Turning, she fled toward the house, hearing him call her but she did not stop.

I cannot keep thinking about him, she told herself sternly, *and I cannot allow myself to dwell on how good he looks with a babe in his arms.*

Caroline had no wish to return to locking herself away and so she turned toward the library guessing, and as it turned out correctly, that it would be empty at this time of day.

Breathing a sigh of relief, she sat and enjoyed the quiet. But it did not last long. The sound of giggles from outside the door drew her attention.

"You are truly wicked, my lord." The voice was undoubtedly that of Charlotte Noble.

Oh God, thought Caroline, please don't let her be talking to—

"Charles," the voice gasped now in mock outrage. Caroline would strangle him.

"Suppose we are seen?"

Caroline did not hear Charles' response, assuming that he whispered it.

But Charlotte's answering giggle sounded entirely too provocative to Caroline's ears.

She truly did not need to imagine what her own brother was up to; it turned her stomach.

Thankfully, they moved off down the corridor. For one horrifying moment, she thought they intended to come in here — and that was a spectacle she could go her whole life without seeing.

Still, it reminded her that no place was safe from prying eyes except her bedchamber, so with reluctance, she stood to leave.

Only to have her way blocked by Tom.

"We need to talk."

"Where is Henry?" she asked in alarm.

Tom rolled his eyes, which immediately rankled, and answered deadpan, "I left him in the garden of course."

Caroline arched a brow, not deigning his sarcasm worthy of a reply.

Eventually, he sighed and answered, "He's with Rebecca, just as you requested before running away."

"I did not run away," she answered hotly.

"Oh, no?" his eyebrow rose. She hated that eyebrow.

"I told you, I have a headache."

"No, what you have is a desire to avoid me. Why?"

"Why?" she screeched in disbelief. "You truly do not know? Perhaps I do not appreciate you lining up potential husbands for me, especially after we've—" she felt her cheeks heat and cut off abruptly, unable to talk about their kisses for fear of bursting into tears. Or begging him for more.

Instead, she shook her head and brushed past him. This time she was running away and she did not care.

Reaching the bedchamber, Caroline slammed the door and then leaned against it in relief. She was not strong enough to have that conversation with him.

Moving to the middle of the room, she gave a scream of fright as the door burst open and in he marched. To her bedroom.

"What in God's name are you doing?" she spluttered in shock. "Get out of here at once."

"No," he answered, his voice quiet but hard.

She would have thought him calm if it were not for the vein throbbing at his temple, and for the obvious clenching of his jaw.

"What do you mean, no?" she gasped in outrage.

"I mean I am not moving until we talk about this."

And just like that, the last shred of her control slipped.

"What exactly would you like to talk about? The way you

have brought men here to marry me so that you could be rid of me once and for all? The way you lied to me? Told me that you cared for me? Kissed me? While all the time you were planning to fob me off on one of your odious friends."

Her breath was heaving by the time she finished her rant.

And she hated herself for how much she wanted him to grab her in his arms and tell her that she was mistaken, that he wanted to marry her himself.

For a moment he did not react. Did not move. Did not even blink. And then, suddenly, as if her own anger had awakened his, he began to yell just as loudly as she had.

"Forgive me, my lady, but were you not the one who used me? You *told* me that you only wanted a week or so with me. You *told* me that you still intended to marry a title. How dare you stand there and accuse me of trickery and deceit. I'm the one who was fooled, Caroline. You fooled me two years ago and, idiot that I am, I almost fell for it again."

Caroline was shocked at his words, devastated as pain lanced through her. No, no, no. Didn't he understand she had only said those things to save her pride? He had said he would never marry.

"Tom—"

"Don't interrupt," he commanded and she stopped because he had never spoken to her that way and it surprised her into silence.

Tom advanced toward her.

"For two years I suffered sleepless nights and drunken depression. Torn between begging you to reconsider and trying to forget you in every way imaginable, most too scandalous for your innocent ears," he said disdainfully.

"Finally, finally I was able to function without needing you so desperately it felt as though my heart were being torn into a million pieces and what happens? You swoop in and get right under my skin again."

Caroline wanted him to stop; she was shaking under the

force of his anger, his pain. She wanted to fix it but she did not know how.

"Tom, please—"

"Do you think it was easy for me?" he continued, seemingly oblivious to the tears which now trailed down her cheeks. "Do you think I relished the idea of being your plaything for a couple of weeks until someone better came along?"

"You could have said no," she choked out.

It wasn't what she wanted to say. She wanted to tell him that she loved him, that she had only said it wasn't permanent because she had been so sure he did not want that. She wanted to tell him that he wasn't the only one suffering, but the words stuck in her throat.

He laughed harshly now, his face twisted by pain and anger.

"Do you know nothing?" he asked harshly. "I couldn't have said no, not even if my life depended on it. Because, damned fool that I am, I cannot refuse you anything you ask of me. Not even when it almost kills me to do it."

He turned and left. And she let him go.

Then she staggered to her bed and cried. Sobbed as though she was utterly broken. And so she was.

Perhaps she would not always feel like her heart was ripping in two.

Perhaps one day she would smile, instead of trying to. Laugh instead of pretending to. Experience joy with her whole heart, instead of with the shattered remnants of what her heart used to be.

But right now? Right now it felt like she would never smile or laugh again.

As for feeling joy? How could she, when he'd made her love him so much, she felt like she couldn't even breathe without him?

And he was walking away.

CHAPTER THIRTY-FOUR

THE NEXT FEW DAYS passed by mercifully uneventfully.

Caroline found the company of Lady Theodora and Miss Darthshire a little difficult on her ears and her intellect but it was far better than spending it with Charles, for example, who was so blindingly obvious in what he was up to with Miss Noble that Caroline fully expected Fred Noble to shoot him one of these days.

The Lords Boxley and Deverill had been irritatingly attentive to her so she had taken to organise so many activities for the ladies that her head fairly spun and her feet ached.

None of them were enjoying the constant stream of activities but Theodora was far too excited about the prospect of being close friends with the mighty Carringtons, and even better, the Duchess of Hartridge, that she never dared complain, not even once. And Rebecca and the dowager were always sure to greet each new activity with enthusiasm.

It served its purpose. For Caroline only had to see Tom at mealtimes and since the hierarchy dictated that they would never be seated together, the meals were not a big problem.

Yes, her heart still hurt every time he so much as entered

a room, but barring the very shortest conversations for the sake of image, she could avoid him and thus avoid bursting into tears at every available opportunity.

The evenings after dinner were trickier and Caroline found herself having to listen to a lot more of Hadley's tedious conversation than she would have liked.

She had sung herself hoarse the night before and even Caroline had had enough of Theodora Hadley's wailing assault on her ears. No, the ladies could not play and sing every night.

There was always a game of cards to play, of course, and she suddenly became an avid player.

Rebecca had urged her to give Boxley and Deverill a chance but honestly, she would rather listen to Hadley's wittering about Tattersall's and horseflesh than tolerate Deverill's self-inflated ego or Boxley's frankly lecherous conversation.

The end of the week arrived and along with it, the happy knowledge that the guests would depart the next day. The Nobles were heading straight to the docks in London so they could catch their ship home.

Although Caroline had grown fond of Freddie Noble, she would be happy to see the back of his daughter, especially in light of her assignations with Charles.

This evening, Tom was to host a farewell ball for his guests.

Caroline sat in her room and pondered the weeks ahead.

In two short weeks, the London Season would end. She had made no effort to find a husband and, she realised now, she would make no effort when they returned to Town.

The truth was that the idea of entering back into the fray of the marriage mart, especially in the last two weeks when mamas became more desperate and debutantes more scandalous, was completely unpalatable.

So too, of course, was the idea of marrying the practically mummified Lord Doncastle.

So she had no intentions of doing that either.

The familiar feelings of guilt and fear about her father's health swept through her but she pushed them down relentlessly.

Rebecca had married a duke and Charles would be the Earl of Ranford one day. Caroline should not be carrying the weight of pressure to marry well. Or at least, to marry a title.

Oh, she had lost her chance with Tom and, frankly, she knew now that she would never marry. But to tell her father that at the same time as coming home unattached and with a refusal for Lord Doncastle would probably be far too much for his heart to take.

Caroline sat and gazed at her reflection whilst in the background Sally was overseeing the filling of her bathtub.

How she had changed in these past few weeks.

There had been plenty of firsts for her — first brush with danger, though Tom had saved her. First brush with scandal when she had gotten completely foxed, though Tom had smoothed that over.

Tom, Tom, Tom. It seemed that her thoughts would not allow her to escape him anymore than her heart would.

The downstairs maids had finished filling the tub and the scent of roses permeated the air.

How she would have looked forward to this night, if things hadn't changed so much between her and Tom.

How she would have looked forward to him seeing her in her finery, to dancing in his arms, to strolling with him in the moonlight and, most of all, to feel his lips claiming her own, to feel his strong arms wrapping around her, making her feel as though she was the most treasured jewel in the world.

"My lady," Sally's voice interrupted Caroline's wistful

daydream, "let's get you ready."

Tom stood and gazed unseeing into the fire, nursing his brandy and cursing his fate. He was in a towering rage and was hanging onto his temper by sheer force of will.

Locked away in the study, he was taking a few moments' respite from the crowd of people invading his home. His aunt had insisted that this ball needed to be the event of the Season to make his mark and show everyone how well off he was. Little did she know that there was a very real chance he would soon be throwing it all away.

Caroline had been avoiding him since their last, brutal conversation. On the rare occasion that he did actually manage to speak to her, she had been coolly distant and it was driving him mad.

Did she really believe that she could go back to the Caroline of old and he would just accept it?

He was heartily sick of feeling so helpless about her. Of feeling so gut-wrenchingly guilty about the things he had said. But he refused to think that it was too late. He would insist that she speak to him tonight. He would declare himself once again, throw himself at her mercy. And if he suffered another rejection he would leave, like the coward he was. But at least he would know he had given it his best shot.

Caroline listened to the sounds of the hallway filling with people. Along with the guests who were staying, there were plenty of people arriving from London since it was only a few hours' drive away.

They'd been arriving all afternoon and would be staying

until tomorrow morning — some at the house, which was now filled to capacity, some at their own local estates or those of friends, and some at the village inn.

It was going to be a much larger affair than Caroline had expected, until she found out that the dowager had been given free reign over the event.

The lady, it seemed, was determined to show the *haute monde* that her nephew was a force to be reckoned with. His looks alone ensured that, thought Caroline, but the dowager was probably proud that Tom was becoming a respectable man and not the scandalous rake he had been up until now.

Caroline quite liked the scandalous rake in him. Not that her opinion mattered anymore.

A soft knock on the door signalled the arrival of Rebecca, resplendent in burgundy satin.

Edward and Tom had been dragged off to welcome the guests in the reception line beside the dowager.

Rebecca looked stunning. As always. Marriage certainly agreed with her. There was a constant happiness that just radiated from her, and it became almost tangible whenever she was in the same room as her husband and son.

Caroline was thrilled for her, but wished more than anything that she'd had the strength to give herself the same chance of happiness. The strength, in short, to have said 'yes'.

"Caro, you are breath taking," said Rebecca, standing back to admire Caroline as she stood and plucked up her fan and gloves.

Caroline was dressed in yet another of Madame Barrousse's confections. The colour was a light gold, only a few shades darker than her hair. The satin material of the gown was overlaid with the softest chiffon. Made in the nod to Grecian style that was all the rage at the moment, it fell from her shoulders to a soft, chiffon train. The highlight, for Caroline, was a jewel-studded band along the bodice.

It was dramatic and eye-catching. Everything one should

want in a ball gown.

Sally had threaded a golden ribbon through Caroline's hair, which was gathered in a pile of soft curls.

For her sixteenth birthday, Caroline's parents had gifted her an extremely unusual set of yellow sapphires. More gold in fact, than yellow, the necklace complemented the dress beautifully and the earrings added a touch of sparkle to Caroline's face.

A set of ivory evening gloves, along with a satin ivory fan completed the picture.

"I am very pleased with the dress," she responded modestly.

"The dress is beautiful," agreed Rebecca, "but only because you are wearing it."

Caroline smiled her thanks and moved toward the door.

Rebecca held out a hand and stopped her progress.

"Are you alright?" she asked softly.

Caroline had confessed all to Rebecca, the pain was just too much to keep to herself. It had almost killed her hiding it from everyone the last time and this was worse. Because this time she knew that she would not let fear rule her, but it was too late.

She nodded now, in answer to Rebecca's concern, not trusting herself to speak.

Even Rebecca had given up hope for them. As she had listened to what had transpired, her eyes had dulled and Caroline knew that Rebecca thought it was a hopeless case.

"I'm truly sorry, Caro," she had said, as she held her weeping sister, "I would have given anything to see you happily married to him."

"But you tried to keep us apart," Caroline protested.

"Only because I was sure it would force you together. He's a man, generally speaking I thought if you wanted them to do one thing, they would do the opposite."

She sounded genuinely confused and Caroline laughed in

spite of herself.

"I think there's just been too much damage," Caroline whispered.

And Rebecca hadn't answered, which was all the answer she'd needed.

Now they stood, waiting to go down and Caroline could do nothing but try to reassure Rebecca as best she could.

"Come along, Becca".

Rebecca looked as though she would have liked to argue but she merely clutched her sister's hand and walked from the room.

Tom had smiled and nodded at enough people to last him a lifetime.

"How many have you invited?" he whispered to his aunt.

"Just those who needed to be here. And everyone accepted," she answered smugly as if that were a great coup.

"Why wouldn't they?" he asked in confusion.

His aunt shrugged and answered in that brutally honest way of hers. "Because it's you. Even my ears have heard the stories, Tom. I was half afraid the mamas with any sense would keep their girls far away from you. But it seems your reputation is untouchable. Probably because you're ridiculously handsome," she finished candidly.

"You old flatterer," quipped Tom, earning him quite a hard smack on the arm.

"I am not old," the dowager bit out.

"My apologies, aunt," Tom answered with a grin. "So, have you bankrupted me?"

"As if that were possible. I believe that is another of your charms that has them all flocking here. Word of your success has been flying around London for quite some time. I knew it would draw them in."

"And tell me again why any of this is necessary."

"To cement your place in Society once and for all," she answered stoutly. "You are the grandson of a duke, Tom. It's about time some of your family's respectability rubbed off on you. Besides, look at how the ladies are admiring you."

Tom looked up to find a gaggle of them staring at him as though they wanted to gobble him up.

Was it him, or were debutantes much more shameless than they used to be?

And had that one just winked at him?

Good heavens.

He swallowed nervously and looked toward the staircase leading to the bedchambers. *To escape,* he thought longingly.

And then, he saw her.

His breath caught in his throat as the vision of Caroline appeared before him. God, she was too beautiful. It almost hurt to look at her. Dressed in gold, she made her way slowly down the stairs, her form outlined by the swirl of her gown with every step she took.

He felt as though he should not look directly at her. She looked like a Roman Goddess, golden, bright, and with an incredible power over mere mortals like him.

"Tom, are you listening?" his aunt admonished from beside him. But he could not even look at her, could not draw his eyes from Caroline.

"No," he answered truthfully, since he'd heard and seen nothing but Caroline since she had appeared.

The dowager followed his gaze and supressed a smile of satisfaction.

"My word, Caroline looks stunning this evening, does she not dear? Dear?" she coaxed as Tom continued to ignore her, his jaw so far open she was worried something would fly into it.

"Whatever you think is best, aunt," he stuttered, confirming that he had no idea what she was saying.

With a secret laugh to herself, she pushed him in the direction of Caroline.

"Go," she said gently, "Edward and I will finish receiving the guests. There aren't many left."

Tom wasted no time and ran off.

Edward, however, was not happy.

"What?" he spluttered. "How is that fair? Why does he get to go?" he whined like a petulant child.

"Do not whine, dear," said his mother calmly. "And don't sulk."

He sulked.

Muttering quite an impressive litany of profanities under his breath he turned again to his mother. "This isn't even my damned house. Why do I have to accept guests for him?"

"Do you remember, dearest, your engagement ball? Hmm? To my recollection you and Rebecca were neither on time nor in any fit state to receive anybody."

"That was different," he sulked some more.

"And why is that, pray?"

"Because we had just gotten engaged, mother. We couldn't stay away from each other."

His mother smiled serenely and looked over to where Tom was approaching Caroline.

"Exactly."

"My lady."

Caroline turned at the sound of Tom's voice, her body moving of its own volition, automatically taking a step closer so that she might be surrounded by his scent, his presence.

Her body was an idiot.

"Good evening, Tom," she responded politely, executing a perfectly lovely curtsy for the benefit of their various spectators.

"Would you do me the honour of dancing with me?" he asked, his eyes begging her to consent.

It was just like two years ago, Caroline thought now, watching his hand extend towards her.

Just like now, back then she had a decision to make — take his hand and give herself one final moment of bliss or turn away and face the future yet again without him. Heartbroken and alone.

Wouldn't it be easier to just keep avoiding him? Why make it harder for herself?

Yes it would be easier. But it wouldn't be anywhere near as wonderful.

So she took his hand. And they danced.

CHAPTER THIRTY-FIVE

TOM WAS SHAKING like a schoolboy. This was far, far too much like that fateful night two years ago.

She felt incredible in his arms — soft, inviting and like the most natural thing in the world.

He looked down at her and his breath caught again at her beauty. He would never get used to it. Even if he were lucky enough to spend every day of the rest of his life with her, he wouldn't get used to her.

Even when she was older, when her hair was sprinkled with grey, she would be the most beautiful thing in the world to him.

He pulled her closer to his body, filled with an overwhelming urge to run away with her. Away from the problems and confusion. Just the two of them somewhere where nobody could influence them.

He could feel her trembling too and guilt slashed through him. Was she nervous or excited? Or did she not want to be around him after the horrible things he'd said?

Suddenly, he was desperate to know, so without another word he turned and marched her toward the open doors, knowing but not caring that his erratic behaviour was drawing stares and gasps from the surrounding guests.

Once outside, she turned to face him in confusion.

"What are you—"

Her words were cut off by the sound of muffled laughter to their left.

Tom looked over in confusion. Wasn't it a little early for the dandies to be trying to tempt young debutantes?

"Oh for heaven's sake," muttered Caroline beside him.

"What?" he asked in confusion.

"You don't recognise the voices?"

"No, should I?"

"Well since they are guests under your roof then I would say yes, you should. That, Tom, is my irascible brother and your esteemed friend, Miss Noble."

He'd never heard the word 'esteemed' sound like an insult before, but it sure as hell sounded like one now.

"What should we do?" he asked, completely side tracked for the moment by the horrifying idea of seeing Charles' seduction technique.

Caroline took in his nervous demeanour and rolled her eyes.

"I shall deal with it," she said in a tone that reminded him of the proper Caroline of old, and put the fear of God into him. And he wasn't even the one in trouble.

Caroline stepped closer to the noise. If the rustling potted tree on the balcony was anything to go by, that was where Charles had chosen to, well, best not to think about it really.

Tom leaned back against the balustrade and prepared to enjoy himself. Seeing Charles being told off like a naughty schoolboy would be most entertaining.

"Charles."

Tom winced at the icy tone.

"A word, if you please."

The rustling stopped abruptly.

And then, Charles stepped sheepishly out from behind the tree.

"Evening, Caroline," he said merrily. "Lovely night, is it not?"

Tom didn't hear a response from her but, based on the fall of Charles' smile coupled with his pulling at the cravat wound round his neck, he could only guess that Caroline's expression was doing the talking for her. And it wasn't happy.

"Miss Noble?" she called out, all calm politeness. He wondered if Charlotte would be lulled into a false sense of security.

After a long moment, that lady stepped out from the behind the tree too.

"G-good evening, Lady Caroline."

It seemed, shockingly, that Charlotte was embarrassed by her behaviour. Or perhaps scared of the consequences.

Caroline stood with her arms crossed, her back rigid. And Tom had to wonder at his sanity since he found it quite attractive.

Which made him want her to get the lecture out of the way so that he could get back to making up for the upset of the last few days and trying his damnedest to get her to marry him.

"It appears you two have an announcement to make."

Charles looked horrified, Charlotte suddenly calculating.

Tom laughed.

"Don't be absurd," Charles finally spluttered. "It's just a bit of fun, Caro."

Charlotte's eyes narrowed as her head whipped round to glare up at Charles.

Tom had the sudden urge to shout, "Run, man. Run." But he didn't. He stayed where he was, enjoying the show.

"A bit of fun?" Charlotte screeched now.

Charles coughed a few times, pulled some more at his cravat, uttered a couple of profanities for good measure before finally shrugging his shoulders in the timeless tradition of rakes who knew a slap was coming and had resigned themselves to it.

"Well, yes. You are leaving tomorrow, my dear. But I shall remember our time together fondly."

And there it was. The slap.

It resonated in the night air with a rather loud *crack*.

Tom winced in sympathy. He'd been at the receiving end of many such slaps and they always hurt like the devil.

Charles began to protest but Caroline held up a hand and silenced him.

Then she turned to Miss Noble.

"I trust you have learned, Miss Noble, not to trust every word that leaves the mouth of such a creature as my brother. A handsome lord he may be, but he is all too aware of it. I am glad you slapped him. No doubt it was deserved. But I should think long and hard about who you disappear behind trees with in the future."

Charlotte coloured but nodded her head briefly, then with a look of outrage on her face, turned and swept back inside the ballroom.

The silence she left behind was deafening.

"Well," started Charles, suddenly once again in the best of moods, "that was a close call. It seems the chit was getting ideas. My thanks, Caroline. I—"

"Consider yourself lucky, Charles—" Caroline's icy tone brought an abrupt halt to Charles' speech— "that it was I who discovered you and not Mr. Noble or you would have been caught in the parson's trap before you knew what was happening. And do not," she continued her tone become even colder, "think that I did this to help you. Your cavorting is disgraceful and the way you treat women utterly shameful. Count your blessings Charles. I would rather save your sorry hide than have Charlotte Noble as a sister, and that is the only reason I did not march her father out here with me."

Tom waited in total silence, wondering what Charles' reaction to such a set down would be.

He imagined their children, his and Caroline's, looking as abashed as Charles did now, should their mother catch them getting into trouble.

It was an enjoyable thought indeed.

Charles however, bounced back from his sombre mood in record time.

With a grin, he gave his sister a light pat on the shoulder.

"I'll be good in the future, Caro. You have my word."

At that moment a loud laugh caught their attention and Charles' eyes swept the form of a young lady whose laugh it was that had grabbed their attention.

"In the distant future," he amended with a wink before sauntering inside, determination in his eyes.

Caroline threw up her arms in frustration.

"He'll never change," she said in exasperation.

"He will one day," Tom said softly coming forward to grasp her shoulders, "when the right woman comes along, he'll change whatever she wants him to if it means he can be with her."

CHAPTER THIRTY-SIX

TOM'S WORDS CHANGED the atmosphere the second they were muttered.

All of the things left unsaid were suddenly clamouring for attention.

Caroline thought back to their awful fight, her subsequent avoidance of him.

Of course, he could have been talking about Charles alone but the way he held her, the way he stared into her eyes, his own deep blue eyes staring into hers, made her think there was more to it.

But was he saying she was the right woman, worth changing for? Or that she wasn't?

For the entirety of their dance, in fact since the moment he'd left her bedchamber on that horrid night, she had been wondering at his words.

He'd been so angry, his pain still so raw, and it killed her. She felt such guilt that he'd been hurt by her proposition and such regret that she had not explained herself to him, told him that he was wrong, so wrong, that she only asked for two weeks because she dared not dream of any more time with him.

Caroline had been so sure that she had no chances left with Tom. But then he'd said he would never refuse her anything, *could* never refuse her anything. So did that mean he still cared?

It was exhausting, this confusion. And she was heartily sick of it.

"Caroline."

She looked up at the sound of his voice, from her unnecessarily deep contemplation of his cravat. It might not be as beautiful as his eyes but it had less of a thought-scattering effect on her. And she could not afford for her thoughts to scatter anymore or she may just end up in Bedlam.

"Y-yes?" she croaked.

Tom took a deep breath and then suddenly grinned in that crooked, carefree way of old. It made her heart sing. How she loved that smile.

"What are you thinking of? Does my cravat hold any special fascination for you?"

She let out a breathless little laugh.

"No. I just—"

"You are just afraid to look at me. Why?"

"Am I not looking at you now?"

"*Touché*," he acknowledged and hit her with a brief smile. Then he looked serious again and repeated his question, his voice dropping to a soft growl, "What are you thinking?"

Caroline shook her head trying to clear it of the hundreds of fractured thoughts swirling around in there.

What was she thinking? She had no idea.

"I'm not sure," she answered honestly. "I am thinking, I suppose, of the hurt I have caused you. Both two years ago and then again, recently. I never wanted to hurt you, Tom." She felt her eyes fill with tears. "In fact, I want to do quite the opposite. I want more than anything in the world to make you happy, but I cannot seem to do so."

Caroline was too afraid to look at him now, too afraid of his reaction to what she had said.

She pulled herself gently from his grasp and went to stand at the balustrade, looking out unseeing into the night.

"You think you do not make me happy?" he asked now from his position behind her.

Caroline shook her head at his question, still not turning to face him.

"I know I do not," she answered quietly. "The other night—"

"The other night I was a damned cad," he said bluntly moving to stand beside her, to look out at the garden too. That got her attention.

"No, Tom. You were right to berate me. I never meant for you to think that I only wanted to—to use you. I did not think of it in those terms."

"What terms did you think of it in?" he asked in curiosity.

And so, once again Caroline faced a decision. Tell him the truth about her feelings or walk away for good.

It was now or never. Never seemed more attractive. But now meant that she could finally fight for what she wanted.

So she turned to look him square in the eye.

"I thought of it as a chance for me to experience real happiness, for probably the last time in my life."

Tom's eyes lit with a blazing fire at her words.

"Do you mean that?" he asked hoarsely.

"Of course I mean it," she answered with a cry. He still did not trust her feelings and who could blame him, really? "I am well aware of how much I hurt you, Tom, and it kills me. And I thought, because you are so determined to remain a bachelor, that perhaps you would not mind — I, I didn't realise it would be so difficult for you and—"

She was rambling, Caroline knew, but she could not seem to stop herself.

Thankfully, Tom stopped her by taking her shoulders

gently in his large hands, effectively rendering her speechless.

"I did not mind, darling," he said softly. "I only minded that it was temporary."

Caroline's eyes widened. Was he saying that he wanted—

"And those men," he continued though she was finding it difficult to concentrate on anything but the feel of his skin against her own, the spicy scent that was uniquely his surrounding her. "I would have sooner torn my eyes out than see you chose one of them for a husband. Rebecca made me do it."

Caroline could not help but laugh at his petulant tone.

He immediately grinned in response then took on an expression of mock severity.

"You think it funny that I was bullied by your sister into driving myself insane with jealousy?"

"You were jealous?"

"Caroline, I get jealous when those men breathe the same air as you," he answered matter-of-factly. "Of course I was jealous at the thought of you marrying one of them."

"Well, you needn't worry," she answered a soft glow of happiness beginning in the pit of her stomach. She dared not hope for too much just yet, but this was fast becoming the most wonderful conversation of her life. "I have no intention of marrying any of them. Or anyone else."

"You mean you have decided to sacrifice yourself to Doncastle?" he sounded horrified.

"No," she answered seriously, "I have decided to do what I want, for the first time in my life. I have decided to remain single."

The silence was screaming with everything that remained unsaid between them.

"You do not want to marry? Have children?"

Caroline gulped. Now or never.

"Yes, I do. But only with the man I love."

He didn't say anything. She expected him to. But he

didn't.

"Does your father know? About your decision not to marry a Peer? Unless, unless the man you love is titled?"

Caroline was unsure as to whether he was being cautious or he really didn't know that it was him. That she still loved him. Always had. Always would.

"No, my father doesn't know. It was a decision I only made recently."

Tom nodded but remained silent.

"And the man I love — he doesn't have a title, he has something much more important."

"Oh? And what's that?"

She stepped closer, so that her body pressed against his.

"He has my heart."

Tom felt the impact of her words, right down to his toes.

Could it really be that she was saying what he'd always wanted her to? That she was willing to risk her father's disapproval, society's disapproval? For him?

"So, if you love this man," he said though how he was managing to form a coherent sentence with her delectable body crushed so closely to his, he had no idea. "Why do you say you will not marry?"

Caroline was looking up at him, boldly, beautifully. But he saw the vulnerability in her eyes. He saw how difficult it was for her. It was damned difficult for him too.

"He is a confirmed bachelor," she whispered now, sounding wistful.

"How confirmed?"

"As to that, I cannot say. I only know that he does not want to marry. He did once. But the girl — well, she was too foolish, too scared to accept his offer."

"And she regrets this?"

"Every second of every day."

"What if he were to decide he wanted to marry? Yet her family still did not approve?"

There was a brief pause and Tom realised that he could not breathe. Had she been so caught up in whatever was happening between them that she forgot momentarily all the reasons she had said no? Was she remembering now that her family's approval was of utmost importance?

"Then they would have to get used to it. Or she would walk away from them forever," Caroline answered finally and Tom felt almost weak with relief.

Their lips still hadn't touched, yet Tom felt that this moment was more intimate than any other they'd shared.

"Caroline—"

"Tom."

Edward's voice sounded behind them and Tom did not even try to hide his frustration, turning to shout profanities at Edward.

Edward, for his part, looked completely unfazed by Tom's obvious anger.

"You're upset. I understand. However, I think you need to come inside."

"This is rather important, Edward."

"As is this, cousin."

"I can promise you it is nowhere near as important as you leaving us alone. Now."

Edward sighed and stepped closer.

"Your American guests are causing something of a scene. And since it involves Charles too, I thought you might want to put a stop to it and smooth things over."

Caroline rushed forward at the mention of Charles' name.

"What happened?"

"A disgruntled woman, a notorious rake who upset her, and a father with a fondness for shot guns. Apparently."

Caroline gasped and made to run inside but Tom

grabbed her arm to stop her.

"I will fix this," he assured her, his stomach clenching at the worry in her eyes.

They'd been so close. But now, obviously, her focus was on her idiotic brother.

She nodded once and her eyes were filled with questions that he desperately wanted to answer.

"Tomorrow," he said softly.

Then she smiled, beamed really. And it was like the sun coming out after two years of the bleakest of days.

"Tomorrow," she repeated.

It couldn't come quick enough.

Tom sighed as he finally put his feet up on his desk and loosened his cravat.

It had taken a lot of tact, patience, and heavy reliance on their friendship to keep Fred Noble from shooting Charles, or demanding a marriage.

Charles, for his own part seemed less than concerned. Tom tried to tell him that being an earl, or a future one rather, did not hold much sway with disgruntled American fathers.

Between them both, Tom and Edward managed to take the arguing men along with Charlotte into Tom's study while the dowager, Rebecca, and Caroline had worked like social butterflies ensuring that those who noticed were assured that it was nothing to talk about and those who didn't notice remained oblivious.

By the time he'd sent Fred to his room with the assurance that Charles had not damaged his daughter irrevocably and gotten Charlotte to admit that she had grossly exaggerated the story she'd carried to her father, it was well past three in the morning.

The guests who were leaving after the ball had already

left and the rest had retired for the night.

Tom had hoped that he would get a chance to speak to Caroline before she went upstairs but was unsurprised to find that she had long since retired to her bedchamber.

He had been so busy trying to sort out things between Fred and Charles that he hadn't had a chance to think of their conversation in the garden. But he was thinking of it now. Could it be that he was truly on the cusp of having everything he had ever wanted?

He thought of her now, wondered if she was sleeping, sure that he himself would get no sleep.

Tomorrow, he would go to Charles, a more sober Charles, and state his intentions. With Caroline's father still in Ireland, Charles was the person he should speak to. If he had to, he would travel to Ranford Hall in Ireland and speak to her father himself. But Caroline was so sure that she did not care whether her family approved or not and he believed her. Still, he would not have her hurt for anything in the world. So he would do his utmost to convince the aging earl that he, Tom Crawford, was the best choice of husband for his daughter.

Downing the last of his brandy, he stood and made his way quietly to his room. At the top of the staircase he turned toward her bedchamber, fighting the overwhelming urge to knock, to see if she was awake.

With a sigh he turned and went to his own instead.

There would be plenty of nights alone with her when they married.

The thought did nothing to alleviate the aching want strumming through his veins. But it was enough to keep a smile on his face for the rest of the night.

CHAPTER THIRTY-SEVEN

THE NEXT MORNING dawned bright and crisp and Caroline nearly threw herself from her bed.

Surprisingly, she had slept well, dreaming of Tom and the life they would share.

Of course, he had not said that he wanted to offer for her again, but surely that is where they were headed?

In fact, if it hadn't been for Charles' wandering hands and Charlotte Noble's penchant for lying, she might be engaged to Tom right now.

The thought caused her heart to skitter happily.

Engaged to Tom. She could not keep the smile from her face.

Sally came in with Caroline's chocolate then and Caroline drank it in record time, telling Sally to pull the first gown from the wardrobe for her to wear.

"Dear me, my lady," said Sally, smiling at Caroline's obvious giddiness, "what has you so up in the boughs?"

"Just looking forward to enjoying the beautiful day, Sally," said Caroline. She did not want to blurt out anything foolish, not before she spoke properly to Tom. Which she wanted to do. Now.

Sally, thank heavens, sensed the urgency and so took little time in helping Caroline into a simple pale lemon morning dress and pinning her hair into a simple style with a lemon ribbon as its only decoration.

Caroline was ready and making her way downstairs in less than fifteen minutes, a far cry from her usual ablutions.

Upon entering the breakfast room she was disappointed to see that it was occupied only by Hadley, who was among those staying at the house, Rebecca, and the dowager.

Tom and Edward were nowhere to be seen.

Caroline bid them all a good morning, ignoring the pang of disappointment in her breast. He may yet come. After all it was early and she had no idea how long he had stayed up sorting out the ghastly situation with Charles and Mr. Noble.

"Lady Caroline," Hadley said as soon as she sat, "might I say you look simply exquisite this morning. Like the finest china doll."

Caroline paused with her cup halfway to her lips, shocked by the rather over the top compliment.

Rebecca's unladylike snort coming from beside her didn't help.

"Er — thank you, Lord Hadley. That is, um, very kind."

Dear lord, he was a pompous creature.

"I wondered, if you would be so kind as to consent to a ride with me, after luncheon perhaps?"

Caroline looked to Rebecca in horror. The last thing she wanted to do was spend time with Hadley alone. For one thing, his company was beyond odious and he made her vastly uncomfortable. For another, his poverty and subsequent desperation for an alliance with a rich family was now common knowledge and Caroline had absolutely no intentions of being his wife. Or his bank.

Besides, she rather hoped that she and Tom would be spending time together this afternoon.

Rebecca was quick to pick up on Caroline's silent plea.

"A ride sounds wonderful, Hadley. I'm sure we would all enjoy it. After luncheon you say?"

Hadley's face was a picture in comical disappointment but he rallied quickly enough.

Bowing to the ladies, he stood from the table and said, "Until our ride, then. I have some pressing business. Some life-changing business." This with what could only be described as a leer in Caroline's direction, before sweeping from the room and leaving them in silence.

"What an odd little man," said the dowager eventually.

The sisters laughed in agreement.

"Shouldn't he be leaving?" asked Caroline.

"Yes, of course he should. Edward said he mentioned something about pressing business last night too, how odd. Who could he possibly have pressing business with now?"

Caroline shrugged and then put the thought from her mind. Hadley did not matter. Even their ride this afternoon did not matter. Caroline was quite sure Tom could be convinced to join them.

Her mouth broke out into an unstoppable smile.

"What has you so happy?" asked Rebecca shrewdly.

"Nothing. Just—just looking forward to our ride," answered Caroline, knowing that nobody believed her but not really caring either.

Tom did not come to breakfast, and Caroline had lingered long enough. Rebecca invited her to go to the nursery with her and the dowager; they were going to spend the morning with Henry.

But Caroline was too excited and nervous to spend time with anyone other than Tom at the moment.

She thanked them but said that she would rather walk in the gardens.

Making her way outside, she kept an eye out for Tom but he was nowhere to be seen. Supressing her disappointment, she struck out across the formal lawns to the meadow beyond. A nice, long walk to help straighten her thoughts would be just the thing.

Charles staggered down to breakfast later than most, he was sure. His head was pounding as a result of last night's excesses. Still, he had no bullet holes in him and the Nobles had left for London and their boat back to America at first light. So all in all, a successful night.

He was looking forward to a hearty breakfast and was daydreaming about hot, strong coffee when he was suddenly accosted in the hallway.

"Carrington."

Charles yelped as a hand touched his shoulder.

"What in the damned hell are you doing?" he roared at Hadley, who it turned out belonged to the hand.

"Forgive me, I—I did not mean to startle you. I have a, um, pressing matter that I would speak with you about."

"Right, well. Can it wait until after breakfast?" asked Charles, not knowing or particularly caring what Hadley could possibly want to discuss with him.

"Well, no. Not really. That is to say, I would prefer it to be now."

Charles made no real effort to bite back the curse of annoyance, but he relented nonetheless.

"Will it take long?" he asked as he preceded Hadley to Tom's library.

"No, I shouldn't think so," said Hadley smugly.

What the hell was this about?

Upon entering the room, Charles turned toward Hadley and folded his arms, waiting for the other man to speak up.

Hadley suddenly seemed nervous. And was he sweating?

"Your sister is, I mean I wanted to—I would—"

"Oh spit it out, man," Charles interrupted Hadley's bumbling.

"Right. Yes. Yes, right. I will."

Charles merely raised a brow and waited.

"My lord," Hadley, if possible, sounded even more pompous than usual, "you are aware, I am sure, of my excellent lineage and connections."

Charles wasn't but thought it best not to interrupt.

"And I know that an esteemed family such as your own would appreciate an alliance with another esteemed family."

Charles knew that such things were rather important to his father, though he himself couldn't give two hoots. So he nodded, wishing the smaller man would get on with it.

"The thing is, my lord. I wanted to speak to you about Lady Caroline..."

Tom finally made it down the stairs having spent the morning rummaging through things that he hadn't even looked at in years.

His mother had died when he was a child and his father had never been very forthcoming with information about her.

Aunt Catherine had told him stories of his mother — a soft, gentle woman, beautiful and kind. Aunt Catherine left out the part about her being mercilessly bullied by his tyrannical father, but Tom had read between the lines.

He didn't miss her, since he did not really remember her. But he missed having a mother he supposed, though Aunt Catherine had always loved him like a son.

Before his death, Tom's father had given him a box of things belonging to his mother. Nothing of great importance — letters, some drawings, some jewellery. But one thing in particular had been very important. Her ring.

A ring that had belonged to Tom's grandmother and

which would have been passed down to a daughter, had there ever been one. But since there'd only been Tom, he got it.

It was beautiful — a delicate band of gold, which held a brilliant sapphire surrounded by tiny diamonds.

Tom had not seen it in two years. Not since the last time he'd held it on his way to speak to Caroline. Much like now.

Now, though, he was sure that it would be on her finger soon.

He could not stop the happy grin that spread out on his face.

It would look beautiful on her delicate hand. And then finally everyone would know, she was his.

He was on his way to the breakfast room, hoping that he wouldn't be too late to meet her when he was interrupted by the sudden appearance of a pleased looking Hadley and a bored looking Charles coming from the library.

Hadley bid him a quick 'good morning' before hurrying off mumbling something about his sister.

Tom turned to look enquiringly at Charles.

"What was that about?" he asked Charles, "because I know even you would not have seduced Theodora Hadley."

"Good God, no," answered Charles with a dramatic shudder. "No, believe it or not, Caroline has just caught herself a husband."

Tom felt the blood leave his face, felt the colour drain.

"What do you mean?" he asked, as calmly as he could.

"Hadley's just asked for her hand, hasn't he?"

"But have you spoken to Caroline?"

"Well, no. But Hadley seemed quite sure that she would say yes, so I can only assume he's spoken to her about it. And he did say they talked this morning and that she had consented to spend the afternoon with him so..." he trailed off with a casual shrug, not realising that he was making Tom angrier by the second.

"He told you that?" he ground out now, clenching his jaw

against the torturous pain of Charles' casual words.

"Yes, seemed very well pleased with himself. I admit I don't particularly like the man. But he will be an earl someday and you know Caro, she's always wanted to marry well."

"I had thought that was less important to her nowadays."

"Well, to tell the truth I do not know if it is or not. Maybe, when faced with the prospect of being a countess it was just too good an opportunity to pass up."

His words were like a blow to Tom's heart. How? How could he have gotten it so wrong again?

She had been given the opportunity of a title and had once again sacrificed him, and her own happiness, for the sake of it.

He had believed her when she had said she loved him. He still believed her. But then, he had believed her back then. It just hadn't been enough. And it seemed as though it still wasn't.

The sun was higher in the sky now and its heat was beating down upon Caroline as she meandered through the gardens. She had spent much longer than she had intended in the meadow, sitting by the river and daydreaming happily about the life she and Tom would have here.

She imagined the family coming to spend holidays, imagined Henry growing up and running around the halls, hopefully with a cousin or two trailing behind him. Perhaps even, if a miracle occurred, Charles would settle down and bring a wife to stay.

It would be blissful and the sooner she saw Tom, the sooner they could make plans.

Caroline was unsure as to how her parents would react. She thought her mother would be well pleased, and her father too, if a little disappointed that she wouldn't have a title.

But a title meant nothing to her and she could not understand why she had ever thought it had.

When she arrived back to the house and glanced at the long case clock in the hallway, Caroline was shocked to see how late it was. She had been gone for hours. It was past noon already. Dashing upstairs to change into her habit, for she was quite sure that everyone else would be ready to leave after a light meal, she changed once again in record time and was headed downstairs in a matter of minutes, dressed now in her grey habit.

Caroline hurried toward the drawing room, hoping to find Tom at last and make sure he knew to accompany them on their ride this afternoon. She had no intention of going without him.

Upon entering the drawing room however, she was greeted by Theodora, Miss Darthshire, Hadley, who was looking at Caroline far too lasciviously for her taste, and a very confused looking Rebecca. But no Tom, she noted to her disappointment.

"Caro," Rebecca stood as soon as Caroline entered the room. "I must speak with you immediately."

Caroline frowned at Rebecca's tone. She sounded distressed and Caroline felt a prickling of fear.

"Of course, Becca."

They turned to leave the room but Hadley stood and addressed them.

"If you please, my ladies, I—ah—I had hoped to speak to Lady Caroline myself on a matter of some urgency."

Caroline felt her jaw drop in surprise at his words.

She could be in no doubt as to what he was angling for, neither could anyone else for that matter. Theodora looked positively ecstatic and Rebecca even more distressed than before.

Caroline darted a startled glance at Rebecca.

"I'm afraid this is rather more pressing, Lord Hadley,"

said Rebecca in a tone that brooked no argument. Then without another word, marched Caroline from the room.

Caroline was in such a state of shock about Hadley's suspected intentions that she did not even realise where Rebecca was taking them until they stepped into Tom's study.

Caroline looked around in surprise.

"Becca, I am sure we should not be here. If Tom—"

"Tom's not here, Caroline."

Edward's voice sounded from behind Tom's desk, his face drawn and worried.

Charles stood by the window with much the same expression and, Caroline noticed with a stab of fear, the dowager was sitting on the chaise, sniffling and holding a handkerchief to her face.

"What do you mean he's not here?" she asked now, her voice shaking, "Where is he?"

"Halfway to London, I would imagine, based on the speed he tore out of here," said Edward with, strangely, a dark look at Charles.

Charles noticed it too for he glowered right back.

What on earth was going on here?

"London? Why? Why would he go to London and why would he leave without saying goodbye? Has something happened? Does he have urgent business there?"

She looked to Rebecca who was looking more distressed by the second.

Caroline laughed to ease the strange tension in the room. She felt sick with fear but did not know why.

"This is a strange morning indeed," she said struggling to keep her tone light, "Why I fear I've almost been proposed to one minute and the next I'm being dragged in here and told that Tom has gone off for the day."

"Not for the day," said Edward and his gentle tone scared her even more. "He's gone to catch the boat that is leaving for the Americas."

Caroline felt the room tilt alarmingly as Edward's words sank in.

"What? No. No, that can't be. He and I—we, we talked last night and he was going to—I mean, he did not say the words exactly but we were going to..." she trailed off in the face of her family's sympathetic looks.

This could not be happening. It simply couldn't. Last night they'd said, well, they hadn't said they loved each other but surely they would have? He would have?

Suddenly feeling weary, she moved to sit in the chair opposite Edward.

"Why?" she asked in a whisper, no longer trusting her voice to stay strong.

"Because, well because he said he could not be made a fool of twice. I did not know what he was talking about, I only came upon him when he was saddling Brutus."

"Wait, he only took Brutus? Then surely he cannot mean to go, without packing? Without sorting out his affairs?"

"He still owns his house in America, Caroline," Edward explained gently, "and he has left hasty instructions for the estate steward. It does not seem as though he intends to come back soon. His valet is to follow with his trunks."

Caroline stood again, too agitated to just sit and hear this.

How could he have left her? Was it revenge? Did he truly hate her for her rejection two years ago? Was this a punishment?

"I do not understand," she said now, her voice thick with tears.

"It's my fault, Caro." Charles came forward and stood in front of her, looking guilty and miserable. "Hadley came to me this morning to ask me for your hand."

"You did not say yes, Charles?" she asked horrified.

Charles looked sheepish.

"Er, I may have done. But I did not know that you and Tom were—well, Edward explained after he threatened to shoot me. That happens a lot around here," he said.

"Charles," both Rebecca and Caroline shouted at him to get his mind back to where it needed to be.

"Yes, well, anyway. He asked. I said he had permission to ask you. But you know I would not have insisted you marry that snivelling little—"

"Charles!"

"Alright, alright. Well, he asked. I said yes. Then I happened upon Tom and mentioned it casually. Next thing I know, he's racing off to London and all the females are crying and Edward looks fit to kill me."

"That's because you're an idiot," blasted Rebecca.

"And how was I to know? Nobody tells me anything," came the heated retort.

"Perhaps we would, if you were sober long enough."

"For God's sake, Rebecca," Charles yelled.

"Watch yourself," Edward interrupted quietly, but there was steel in his tone.

Caroline was in a state of complete, shocked devastation.

Letting their bickering wash over her, she stared out into the beautiful summer's day. The sun that had seemed so pleasant now seemed too bright. The birdsong that had sounded so wonderful before now seemed to mock her in its happiness. She would never feel happiness again.

Unless…

"How far is London from here?" she asked of nobody in particular.

"About three or four hours riding. More in a coach. Why?" asked Charles suspiciously.

Caroline did not want to tell them about the plan that was forming in her head. They would surely try to stop her.

So she shrugged slightly and said, in her most desolate voice, "I just wondered if I had come back sooner, would I have seen him before he went."

As she had hoped, she got the information she was after.

"He left about an hour ago, Caro. And in such a towering rage that I do not think anything would have stopped him."

Caroline nodded her head to show that she was listening, but her brain was whirring furiously.

Was she going to let history repeat itself? Stand idly by while the man she loved walked out of her life?

She turned to Edward, her eyes serious, her tone firm.

"Does he think that I wanted to marry Lord Hadley?"

Edward stared right back, as if trying to figure out what was going on in her mind.

"He was barely coherent, but yes. That's the gist of it. I tried to stop him of course but—"

"Never mind," she interrupted quickly, not wanting to waste any more time talking.

Then she swung round to Charles.

"Charles, I—I am worried that Lord Hadley will think, I mean I would rather he did not have the opportunity to ask me for my hand. I do not want to be alone with him."

She wasn't afraid of Lord Hadley, since he was more irritating than dangerous, but he would like to keep Charles and Hadley out of her way for a while.

"Don't worry, Caro," said Charles at once, obviously keen to make up for his colossal mistake. "I will speak to him. He won't be asking you anything."

Caroline smiled her thanks.

Rebecca came forward then and caught her arm.

"Are you well?" she asked with no little concern.

"No," Caroline answered truthfully, "but I will be."

She turned to leave the room and Rebecca stopped her at once.

"Where are you going?"

"I just want some time alone." Then, because she wasn't sure that Rebecca would leave her, she leaned forward and whispered, "Do take care of the dowager, Becca. She seems most distraught."

Rebecca glanced back at the older woman.

"Yes, she had hoped—" She stopped on seeing Caroline's stricken expression. "Yes, well. Never mind. I shall look after her."

Caroline nodded then without another word, walked silently from the room.

"Should I go after her?" she heard Rebecca ask worriedly.

"Perhaps, sweetheart, we should leave her be."

Caroline silently thanked Edward and made her way swiftly to her room. There was no time to lose.

CHAPTER THIRTY-EIGHT

SNEAKING OUT OF the house was harder than Caroline had thought. She was surprised, upon reaching her bedchamber, to find Sally there.

"Sally, are you alright?" she asked immediately. Her abigail was never here during the day, at least not that Caroline knew of.

"Oh, yes my lady. I just, I heard the news about Mr. Crawdon having left and I, well I wanted to make sure that you were well."

Caroline smiled gratefully at her friend of many years. But she really could do without her being here at this particular time.

"Actually, now that you say it I think I feel a bit of a headache coming upon me. Perhaps a lavender soaked cloth and some tea?"

Sally jumped up looking relieved at having something to do to help and rushed from the room.

As soon as she was gone, Caroline took some money and stuffed it in a reticule then snatched up the hat matching her habit and sneaked from the room.

She knew that Sally would not take long. She also knew that Rebecca would not leave her all afternoon so she was unsure as to how much time was available to her.

Tiptoeing down the stairs, she slipped past the main rooms and out into the blessedly empty conservatory, then round the house and to the stables without having been detected.

Once there, she called out to Jimmy, the stable lad whom she had gotten to know over the last couple of weeks.

"Ah, Jimmy. Be a dear and saddle up Fortuna will you?"

Jimmy looked undecided and Caroline felt her stomach drop. *Please, do not let my plan be foiled now.*

"Is there a problem?" she asked as calmly as she could.

"No, miss. I mean, my lady. It's just, should you be going out alone?"

He was sweet to care. Caroline knew that. So she shouldn't feel irritated by his concern.

"Oh, there is a party of us. I just thought to get a bit of a head start. Only in the gardens, of course. I would not go far unattended." Caroline gave him a blinding smile and noticed his cheeks turn scarlet.

"Very good, my lady," he stuttered. "If you are sure."

"I am quite sure, Jimmy," she answered confidently acting as though she had all the time in the world.

It did not take long for Fortuna to be brought out, saddled up and ready to go. Caroline stood on the mounting block and pulled herself into the saddle with ease. She and Fortuna had gotten to know each other very well over her stay and Caroline would be relying on their camaraderie to get Fortuna to London in record time.

Caroline stayed on the normal track for a few moments, until she was sure that Jimmy had stopped watching and gone back to the stables, then as soon as she felt the coast was clear she set off for the road.

Of course, they would discover she was gone soon

enough and it would not take much to figure out where to. But that did not concern her right now. What concerned her was finding Tom and telling him, once and for all, that she loved him.

The journey was more arduous than Caroline had supposed it to be and some hours into it, she began to worry about the folly of her plan.

It was all well and good galloping off with these grand notions of romance but practicalities had a habit of getting in the way of grand notions and it wasn't long before Caroline began to think of all the things that could go wrong with her journey.

For one thing, she did not know for sure where Tom was headed. For all she knew, he could decide to go to his home in London before going to the docks.

For another, once she was seen in London, galloping about alone, her reputation would be in absolute shreds. Nobody would accept her anywhere and she would bring disgrace to her family's name, as well as Edward's.

And what if she could not find him? What if, by the time she got there, he had already left? What then?

Caroline began to feel decidedly panicky. She had never ridden so far alone before. She was frightened and, since the road was quite rough in parts, she was bloody sore too.

Plus, the sky was starting to darken ominously.

Caroline was seriously tempted to turn back. But, she had been travelling for some hours now and was, in fact, closer to London than she was to Essex.

And besides, if she were to turn back, what would she be turning back to? A life of emptiness, of never experiencing the joy of love and being loved?

She had lived that life for too long. And Tom deserved

better. Deserved to know that Caroline loved him, that he hadn't been let down again.

So, with renewed steel in her spine, Caroline continued on the road to London and prayed that she was not too late.

The sounds, sights and smells of London's docks would haunt her forever, Caroline thought some hours later as she lead Fortuna cautiously toward the harbour.

This was no place for a lady.

She had often heard it said and now she understood why.

The closer she got to the harbour, the stronger was the smell. It was the stench of fish and of uncleanliness.

Everywhere she looked, men leered at her in a way that she had never experienced, and hostile looking women, who wore a lifetime of drudgery on their faces, made their unacceptance clear.

Caroline was afraid. Truly afraid.

The darkening sky was starting to empty and soon there would be a tumult of rain and nowhere to shelter from it.

She could, she thought desperately now, hide out in one of the taverns, but they really weren't establishments she would like to enter. For one thing, most of them were filled with raucous and extremely ungentlemanly sailors. For another, she was afraid of getting caught up in one of the brawls that seemed to break out for no obvious reason.

She was beginning to regret her impetuous decision. She was lost, alone and had nobody to turn to for help.

Of course, there would be people of her own class milling around the transatlantic ship but she had no idea where to go or even what time the sailing was. If she'd missed it already then she truly had no idea what she would do.

The rain began to come down in earnest now and Caroline stood in the middle of the muddy, dirty street and felt like crying.

This was not how she had intended things to go. She should be back in Essex, with Tom, celebrating their engagement with her family.

Caroline looked around and saw, to her terror, that she was garnering more and more attention. And none of it good.

Perhaps she should turn around and leave, she thought desperately. Her heart was pounding and she noticed that she had caught the attention of a group of dirty looking men who had stumbled out of a building to her left. She did not think it was a tavern. No, based on the women who were milling outside and even leaning out of the windows, it was the type of building that Caroline had never wanted to see.

She swallowed her tears of fright as the men began to call out to her.

"Ain't this a pretty one?"

"And what's a fancy thing like you doin' alone in a place like this?" they called as they approached slowly.

Oh, God, I do not know what to do, thought Caroline frantically.

Perhaps she should run? But where to?

Her breathing became shallow as she panicked in earnest. It would not do to faint yet she felt dizzier by the second.

Suddenly, her arm was grabbed and she screamed in fright.

"My lady." She looked down into the startlingly green eyes of a very beautiful young woman. "My lady," the girl repeated, "come, it is not safe here, for either of us."

Caroline had no idea who this girl was, or if she could trust her. It was entirely possible that she was being led away to be robbed. Or worse.

But something told her that this young woman was just as scared as she, and that she clearly did not belong here either.

"Come," she urged Caroline again. So Caroline pulled on

Fortuna's reins and followed the girl quickly back up the street.

They came to a sort of square, in the better part of the port, Caroline supposed, though it was still a less than salubrious place.

Caroline's companion slowed to a stop. The rain was beating heavily on them both and Caroline noticed the young girl carried two trunks with her.

"Who are you?" she asked without preamble.

This was fast become a total nightmare.

"My name is Julia, my lady. Julia Channing."

"Lady Caroline Carrington," answered Caroline.

The girl looked to be about Caroline's own age and her manner of dress and speaking indicated that she was highborn. Or at the very least upper middle class. So what was she doing here alone?

"Are you with someone?" Caroline asked now and noticed a flash of emotion across Miss Channing's face before she schooled her features into impassivity.

"I—no, my lady. I am quite alone."

"Well, where are you going?" asked Caroline, amazed to think that there were two young ladies wandering around London by themselves. It simply wasn't done.

"I have no idea," Miss Channing laughed, though it sounded a little hysterical. "I had thought to catch a ship but it seems that the passenger boats are not sailing for a few hours yet so I am rather stuck. Are—are you travelling too, my lady?"

"No," said Caroline, shouting to be heard over the torrential rain. At least it had cleared the streets somewhat and she felt slightly safer. "No, I came to look for someone but I have no idea where to start."

Caroline felt a little better about her hopeless situation, knowing that she was not entirely alone. And she trusted Miss Channing. The girl was shockingly beautiful but seemed sweet and she had helped Caroline, after all.

"Perhaps—perhaps we should leave here. My family's townhouse is in Mayfair, though I do not know if my brother opened it before coming to Essex." She knew she was talking of things that Miss Channing would not understand but she was cold and frightened and worried that she had lost Tom for good. "If not, we could always go to my sister's. She is not there but the staff know me. I do not think it would benefit either of us to stay here for much longer."

Miss Channing looked shocked at Caroline's offer, but relieved too.

"Yes, perhaps that is best."

They turned to go, Caroline trying not to cry about missing her chance to see Tom. If the boats weren't sailing until later, she could go back to Mayfair and get some of Edward's footmen to accompany her on her search. That was sure to be safer and more efficient.

Caroline was brought up short to realise that, as they'd been speaking, the men who had been shouting at her further down the street had stealthily surrounded them. They were stuck.

Tom lowered his glass and shook his head at the bartender's silent offer of another. He'd had quite enough.

How idiotic he'd been to come tearing off to London. His boat did not leave for hours, which left him far too much time to nurse his heartache.

It had happened again. He called himself every kind of damned idiot.

Two years of trying to forget her totally wasted. And what was more, he knew now that he would never forget her. She was unforgettable. She was his heart, his soul, his whole world.

He had been sure, so sure, of her love for him. But then, he'd never told her that he'd loved her. Never said the words. But surely she had known?

He thought back to last night. It seemed like a hundred years ago. She had wanted him, he was sure of it.

So how could everything have changed so much? Perhaps she was still as much a coward as she had been before. Perhaps the love of a title was still stronger than her love for him.

God, if he could buy a kingdom for her he would. He could probably afford it too.

Tom shook his head. Sitting in a tavern in the docks for hours on end would not help, much as it was tempting to forget the whole world right now. He would be better off returning home and coming back in a few hours.

Slowly, wearily, he made his way to the door, ignoring the various invitations being thrown his way by the light skirts who liked to frequent places like this.

He pushed open the door and was surprised by the downpour. So much for sunny summer days. Well, the weather befitted his mood.

He was about to walk round and collect Brutus when he noticed a group of men, and he could not accuse them of being gentlemen in any way, surrounding what looked like two lone women.

From his quick glance, the women looked like they did not belong here. He wondered if they were in some sort of trouble.

Blast it all. He would have to help. His conscience would not let him do otherwise.

So he made his way over to the group, sizing them up and noticing with some satisfaction that they were extremely unsteady on their feet. That should make it easier should things turn nasty.

Tom was about to call out, when suddenly the air left his

lungs. Two of the men parted a little and he got a clear view of the women. He had no idea who the shorter red-head was, but whoever she was, she was standing with Caroline.

Caroline was whispering furiously to Miss Channing, urging her not to panic.

"We shall wait for them to part a little, and then we shall run. Do you understand?" she asked urgently.

Miss Channing could only whimper in fright but she nodded her head.

The men were swaying unsteadily and Caroline hoped that would make it more difficult for them to follow.

Her habit was soaking wet and heavy. Caroline thought back to Rebecca's ordeal when she had been kidnapped by the awful man who had been psychotically obsessed with her. It had rained then too, she remembered Rebecca telling her. And it hadn't stopped Rebecca from escaping, so it would not stop Caroline either.

She noticed suddenly that one of the men stumbled, meaning that there was a break in the circle.

Shouting "run" she dashed towards it, only to slam into something solid. Before she could fall back, two strong arms snapped out and caught her.

Caroline looked up, preparing to scream, and found herself looking into the most beautiful eyes in the world.

"Tom," she gasped before throwing her arms around him and sobbing into his neck.

Tom had no idea what was going on, but he had no time to try to figure it out. The young girl who had accompanied

Caroline was standing unaccompanied and he could see their group of admirers trying to figure out whether she was with Tom or not.

Caroline still clung to him, her body trembling, so he moved her gently to one side then reached out an arm and pulled the young lady toward him.

"Stay close," he muttered to her and she nodded her consent, though she looked as shaken as Caroline.

What on earth was going on here?

"Are those yours or Caroline's trunks Miss?"

"Channing. My name is Julia Channing. And yes they are, mine that is. Mister?"

Tom smiled at the young lady's spirit.

"Crawdon," he answered easily. "If you'll excuse me."

Removing Caroline gently from his side, but not before dropping a kiss on her head, because he couldn't help himself, he walked over to the gentlemen, still surrounding the lady's trunks.

"Be careful," he heard Caroline whimper. He turned back to wink at her, before returning to the men in front of him.

He walked straight through them and picked up the lady's trunks, staying alert for any sign of danger.

"They both belong to you?" asked one of the men in a slur that could hardly be described as English.

Tom gritted his teeth but gave no answer as he plucked up one trunk then another and turned to walk back toward the ladies.

He deposited the trunks at their feet, placed Fortuna's reins firmly in Caroline's hands, then turned back to the men.

He did not want any trouble, not in front of Caroline, so he said nothing, just gave a speaking glance before turning away.

He needed to get the ladies out of here.

"They can't both be his..." The conversation went on behind him and he did his utmost to ignore it.

"Well one of 'em is."

"My money's on the blonde. See the way he looked at her?"

"Can you blame him?"

A raucous laugh and Tom felt his blood begin to boil.

He should just leave it. Walk away.

"No, I can't. If she was my bit of skirt I'd take—"

He didn't get to finish as Tom's fist slammed into his mouth. Probably not the best idea he'd ever had. But the bastard had it coming.

Thankfully, the rest of the drunken men decided they didn't want any trouble and quickly scarpered away.

Tom walked back to Caroline and waited until her eyes connected with his gaze.

"Now—" His calm tone belied his inner fury. Had she any idea how much danger she was in walking around here with only another young woman for company? When he thought of what could have happened to her, the fear was unlike anything he'd ever felt. "Do you want to tell me what the hell you're doing here by yourself?"

Caroline was in such a state of shock, fear, and relief that Tom was here that she could not string a sentence together.

But there was so much, so much that she wanted to say.

He was furious. That much was clear from the flash of fire in his blue eyes, though his voice remained calm. Too calm.

"I-I c-came to f-find you." She tried to speak, truly she did. But her teeth were chattering and the wet was soaking into her skin.

Tom bit out a curse then looked around as if trying to figure out what to do.

"Alright," he said after a moment's silence, "Come with

me."

They set off at a slow pace, and how strange they must have looked.

Caroline had ridden Fortuna to exhaustion so Tom left her with the reins while he plucked up Miss Channing's cases and they made their way toward where Brutus was tethered.

Tom had arranged for Brutus to be picked up later by a footman but he would be home now before someone even left to pick up the horse.

So now he had two horses, two hysterical females, two heavy trunks and no idea what to do with any of them. *Marvellous.*

CHAPTER THIRTY-NINE

TOM PACED ANXIOUSLY in the study of his townhouse while he waited for Mrs. Smith, his housekeeper, to see to his unexpected guests.

He had dispatched a footman as soon as they had returned with a note to his estate in Essex informing them that Caroline was, bizarrely, here.

The journey back to the house had been interesting to say the least. They had walked past several unsavoury characters until Tom could hail a hackney into which he'd deposited the ladies and the cases, before mounting Brutus and leading Fortuna beside him.

It had been a slow progress but at least Caroline was out of the rain now.

Tom had been worried sick that she would catch her death but Mrs. Smith was an extremely capable woman and he knew that she was in safe hands.

He also knew that he had no women's clothes here so sent someone round to Edward's. A strange request to be sure, but in his note he had asked that two of Caroline's or Rebecca's gowns be sent round.

Tom did not know if they would fit or not but the ladies had to wear something and he could not very well lend them some of his clothes.

He groaned aloud at the vision of Caroline in his shirt. Now was not the time.

His head was reeling. What the hell had happened that Caroline had turned up alone in the middle of the London docks? And where were the people who were supposed to be looking after her?

The answer came soon enough.

Just as he was pouring himself a much-needed drink, the front door had been thumped loud enough to shake the house.

He heard the footman scramble to open it but Tom did not need to guess who it was.

Before he had a chance to stand, his study door burst open heralding the arrival of Edward, Rebecca, Aunt Catherine, and Charles. They scrambled into the room, nearly falling over themselves.

"What the hell is going on here? Why is Caroline here alone?" bellowed Charles.

Tom immediately jumped to his feet.

"Funny, Charles. I was about to ask you the same thing."

"Boys, please," Rebecca spoke calmly, "let's not start drawing pistols just yet."

"How did you know she was here anyway?" Tom demanded, still furious at the lot of them for letting Caroline slip away so easily.

"Let me ring for tea and I shall explain."

"I do not want tea," Tom answered mutinously then, taking a look at Rebecca's expression, he swore under his breath and rang for it all the same.

Caroline sighed in contentment as the hot water soaked

into her shivering bones. For a while there she had thought that she would never get warm again.

She could not believe her luck in Tom finding her, just when all seemed lost.

And now she was here, in his house.

She knew that as soon as news got out of this, and it always did in London, she would be utterly ruined. Yet she could not bring herself to care.

No, all she cared about was the fact that she was here with Tom and she was not going to leave until she told him how she felt.

Caroline soaked until the water began to cool and then reluctantly stepped out, allowing herself to be assisted by one of Tom's downstairs maids.

She was sitting wrapped in a fluffy blanket drying her hair by the fire when a knock sounded on the door.

Mrs. Smith, the kindly housekeeper, had said that Tom was arranging gowns for her and Miss Channing. She had no idea how, nor did she care; she was just anxious to see him and tell him what a silly mix up all this marriage nonsense had been.

Calling, 'come in' Caroline turned back to the fire to continue drying her hair. It was almost done, with just a few damp strands left.

"Caro."

Caroline nearly yelped at the familiar voice.

Rebecca stood in the doorway, clutching a bundle of material that Caroline guessed to be clothes.

"Becca, what on earth are you doing here?"

"Oh, dearest, we were so worried," said Rebecca coming forward and dumping the bundle on the bed before clutching Caroline to her in a brief hug. "Are you alright?"

Caroline was too shocked by Rebecca's presence to answer for a moment.

"Y-yes I'm fine. But, how are you here?"

"Well, I came to check on you in your room and Sally said you had disappeared. We searched the house and then the stables and finally Jimmy confessed that you had tricked him and taken Fortuna. At first we thought it was just for a ride but then, why would you lie about that? Charles guessed that you must have headed straight to London. And it looks as though he was right."

There was a brief pause before Rebecca burst into speech again.

"Oh Caroline, how could you be so foolish? What a risk you took. Anything could have happened to you. You could have been killed or—or worse."

Caroline wondered if she should ask what could be worse than being murdered but Rebecca wasn't finished.

"And as for your reputation, well you can kiss that goodbye. Who knows who saw you riding through the streets of London? And then to come here and send for a dress. I mean, really. What can you have been thinking?"

Caroline listened to Rebecca's lecture and was suddenly struck with how much their roles had reserved. Only two short years ago they'd had similar conversations only it had been Rebecca sitting meekly while Caroline delivered a sermon.

She could not help it. She burst into peals of laughter.

"How can you possibly think this is funny?" asked Rebecca sternly.

"I do not. Truly, Becca. I am sorry for worrying you. But does it not strike you as a little humorous that I should be sitting here with you ringing a peal over my head about behaviour and propriety?"

Rebecca tried to remain stern faced but eventually laughed along with Caroline.

"Be that as it may, it is still a very serious situation. I do not know what we are going to do. Hadley was of course there for the uproar and since Charles told him in no uncertain terms that he was not welcome to pay his addresses to you, I am afraid London will be filled with news of your disgrace."

"I am sorry," Caroline said now sincerely. "I know that yours and Edward's names will be dragged through the mud because of me."

"Oh I do not care about that," said Rebecca stoutly. "Nobody will be brave enough to say it to our faces and Edward's reputation is impeccable enough that we could withstand anything. And Charles thought that perhaps with Tom leaving, the scandal might die down soon enough. Especially if there's a new one soon, which I'm quite certain Charles could orchestrate, given his talent for it."

"Tom is not leaving."

Rebecca looked confused.

"Oh. Isn't that why he came here? To leave?"

"Yes, but he's not."

"Did he tell you he was staying?"

"No."

Rebecca gazed at Caroline in some astonishment before frowning and touching her forehead.

"Have you caught a fever?"

Caroline stood and brushed Rebecca's hand away.

"I'm perfectly fine, Rebecca. Did you bring those clothes?"

"What? Oh, yes. We had just arrived home and were preparing to send out search parties when a note came requesting clothes. So we all came rushing round."

"Right," Caroline answered distractedly, pulling the clothes on haphazardly.

Rebecca stood to help with the buttons and then was left standing in shock as Caroline rushed from the room, her hair flying out behind her.

Tom, Charles, and Edward had finished with the

recriminations and were settling down to discuss how to do damage control when the study door flew open signalling the arrival of Caroline with Rebecca fast on her heels.

Aunt Catherine had gone to attend to Tom's surprise guest, Miss Channing, and had not yet returned.

He felt his mouth open at the vision Caroline presented.

Rebecca had obviously brought one of Caroline's own gowns for it fit her like a glove, the light blue muslin skimming her slender frame. She had obviously put it on in a rush for she did not have that well put-together air that usually surrounded her.

But what really grabbed his attention was her hair.

Tumbling loosely around her shoulders, it was like a curtain of golden silk. How many times had he dreamed of it like this? Framing her face and flowing down her back like a river of purest sunshine?

He had to physically stop himself from grabbing her and burying his face in all its glory.

She looked stunningly beautiful, her cheeks heightened by anger or excitement, her rosy lips parted, and that hair. Dear God how could he leave her? And yet, how could he stay?

"You're not leaving," she said as if she could read his mind.

"What?" he asked in confusion.

"You're not leaving," she repeated firmly.

"I—" he stopped because, in truth, he had no idea what to say.

He looked to Rebecca for some clue as to what was going on but Rebecca merely shrugged. She clearly had no idea either.

"Is she sick?" he asked Rebecca.

"I'm standing right here. And no I am not."

"Right."

He had no idea what to say and clearly, neither did

anyone else as they all watched with avid interest.

Caroline marched over to him.

"How could you do this to me?" she asked, her tone accusatory.

"Do what?" he asked affronted because really it was she who had done something to him. At least, that was what he had thought until Charles had explained what had happened with Hadley.

Tom felt massively relieved but more than a little foolish that he'd almost gotten on a boat to New York in a fit of temper. In hindsight, it seemed a little overdramatic. In his defence though, his heart had been completely shattered.

"How could you leave? I thought—"

He stood now and moved to stand in front of her, in the middle of the room.

"You thought what?" he asked, his eyes piercing her own.

Would she be brave enough to say it? In front of everyone?

He watched as her eyes danced round the room, as her tongue darted out to wet her lips and very nearly gave him a heart attack in the process.

"I thought you loved me," she said huskily now and her vulnerability tore at his heart.

Of course he loved her. But he was terrified. He had believed, so easily, that nothing had changed. Did he deserve her? Did he trust her?

She had never said that she loved him.

But Caroline wasn't finished.

"I hoped that you loved me. That you would ask me to be your wife." Her eyes filled with tears and he moved to take her in his arms but she moved back and shook her head slightly.

And then he understood.

She wanted to do this alone, wanted to prove to him that she meant what she had said. That she was going to be brave this time, in a way that she hadn't been two years ago.

"I want to be your wife," she said now boldly, clearly.

From the corner of his eye, Tom noticed that Aunt Catherine and Caroline's beautiful companion had silently entered the room.

Caroline, it seemed, had not noticed at all.

"I want to be your wife because—because I love you. I have always loved you and I will never love anyone but you. And I meant what I said. I will only marry the man I love. If—" she swallowed nervously and the action nearly brought Tom to his knees.

She was being so brave. His brave, beautiful Caroline.

"If he will consent to have me."

He didn't know what to say. His heart was filled with words of love but none of them seemed enough.

So he answered her in the way he knew always worked for them.

He grabbed her, pulled her close and gave her an earth-shattering kiss.

Caroline felt light-headed as the impact of what she'd done registered within her. She had declared herself in full view of them all, after she had ridden alone to London to chase after a man.

Her father would kill her.

But all rational thought was fast leaving her body as Tom's mouth worked its magic again. She never wanted it to stop. But stop it did and all too soon.

Tom held her away from him and when Caroline reluctantly opened her eyes, they were met with his glowing with the power of his love. The sight made her heart catch in her throat.

"If I will consent to have you?" he said, hoarsely but reverently. "Caroline, I haven't wanted anything but you since the first time I met you when you marched straight into my heart and captured it."

Caroline beamed at his words. To hear him say it, it was the most beautiful thing in the world.

"I do not just love you. Love is not a strong enough word for what I feel. I'm consumed by you, mind, body, and soul. I am yours. I always have been."

Caroline felt a tear trickle down her cheek but it was a tear of exquisite happiness.

"Marry me," he said now and to her shock, produced a beautiful sapphire ring.

"I've been waiting two years to give you this," he said shyly before slipping it onto her finger.

It fit as though it had been made for her.

"Be my wife."

Caroline smiled and wound her arms round his neck.

"I thought you'd never ask. Again."

EPILOGUE

NEITHER CAROLINE NOR Tom wanted to wait overly long to be married so Tom applied for a special licence and, thankfully, got one.

There was only time then for the banns to be read before the day came, four weeks later.

Caroline would have been married at home, of course, but her parents had assured her that they were ready to sample the delights of London again and were happy to make the journey to see her wed.

Her father had appeared even older and weaker since she had last seen him and Caroline felt the familiar stab of guilt.

Had she weakened him by not doing as he wished?

Her answer came during one fine autumn morning while she and her father sat in their townhouse.

"Papa, do you like him? Are you happy? I know it is not what you wanted but—"

Her father had held up a hand to silence her.

"What I wanted," he said, his voice weakened by the strenuous journey, "was for my little girl to be happy and well settled. Caroline, if I had known you had fallen in love with a man as excellent as our Tom, I would have been delighted."

Caroline had grasped his hand tightly.

"Truly?" she whispered.

Papa had patted her hand and smiled kindly.

"Of course. Caroline, I have only ever wanted your happiness. And that of your sister and brother. Tom is a wonderful man and I know you will be well looked after."

Caroline had felt her heart soar and a massive weight lifted from her shoulders. All that worry, all those years wasted for nothing. It was a sobering thought but rather than dwell on what she had missed, she focused on all the wonderful years that lay ahead.

And now, here she stood, resplendent in ivory silk, waiting for her father to walk her down the aisle and give her to the man she loved.

"We're leaving," Tom growled in her ear, sending delicious shivers down her spine, an hour later as they stood amongst the guests at their wedding breakfast.

"No, we are not," she answered back, though she could not keep the longing from her eyes.

"If you look at me like that again, we won't even make it home," he warned.

Caroline shivered. Perhaps they had been here long enough.

"How long have we been here?" she asked in a whisper, smiling at the guests milling around her parents' townhouse.

Tom checked his pocket watch then swore softly.

"Fifteen minutes," he answered.

Caroline laughed.

"It would cause a scandal if we were to leave so soon."

"And you've had enough scandal?" asked Tom regretfully.

"Oh," she answered with a mischievous wink, "I wouldn't say that."

He gave her a wolfish smile that turned her knees to water.

"Minx," he whispered in her ear before sweeping her from the room, bidding the swiftest goodbye in history to their respective families and tearing out the door to his waiting carriage.

Nobody heard from them for days.

Julia Channing stood a little awkwardly to the side of the crowded room, trying desperately to blend in.

She did not think that anyone would recognise her. But she did not want to take the risk.

"You know, if you move back any further you'll hit the wall."

Her breath caught as the silky tones of Charles Carrington's voice slid over her skin.

Julia was almost afraid to meet his eyes, knowing that she would feel the impact of them like a jolt to the heart.

"G-good day, my lord," she said breathlessly, curtsying and hoping he would move on.

No such luck.

"I never did get a chance to thank you properly," he said.

Julia frowned in confusion.

"For what, my lord?"

"Well, when that slithery little snake Hadley rushed back to London to destroy Caroline's reputation, you really stepped up and saved her hide, in a manner of speaking."

Julia had tentatively suggested, during the crisis talks that followed Mr. Crawdon's truly romantic proposal, that they put it around that she had been travelling as Caroline's companion.

Nobody knew where she had come from, so they had concocted a plan — the dowager was to say that she had hired Julia as her companion, and she had consented to travel with Caroline to London from Essex, where she lived.

It wasn't true, but then who was to know that?

And it had suited Julia in the end. After all, when she had left her father's house in the middle of the night with nothing but a small valise and a bagful of coins, she hadn't any plan in mind. Any thoughts of the future. Merely thoughts of escape.

She had been at the docks hoping to get on a boat, but she did not really know where she would go. Her aunt in France was sure to send her straight back to Papa and she had no other family.

She had no idea what she was going to do with her life and in helping the new Mrs. Crawdon, Julia had managed to secure a position for herself.

The dowager insisted that Julia become her companion for at least six months to lend credence to their story. And since Julia had made plans as far as escaping and not much else, the companionship was an ideal solution.

That was, of course, unless someone recognised her. But she did not think they would. Her father was a baron of very little importance when compared to the leading ladies and gentlemen of the *haute monde* assembled in this room. No, the Channings were decidedly below the attention of most here. And hopefully the dowager would only move in such vaulted circles, for Julia knew that she would be recognised instantly by her father's peers, perhaps even her father himself would come looking for her. Him or the horrifying Lord Larsden...

Julia wasn't sure which was worse.

She realised the ridiculously handsome viscount was awaiting a response.

"It suited me well, my lord. Besides, Lady Caroline, I mean, Mrs. Crawdon is a good person. She did not deserve to have her reputation tarnished."

"But surely you could not have meant to be a companion?" Charles asked incredulously.

Julia felt her hackles rise.

"And why would you think that, my lord?" she asked still politely, though now with iron in her tone.

Charles noticed it and grinned. She was a sassy little thing. And with the type of looks that men went mad for; it was a heady combination.

"Just that you do not look like a usual companion, Miss Channing."

"I don't?" she asked in adorable innocence.

"No," he answered, his eyes raking over her and his blood heating instantaneously, "you are far, far too beautiful."

Julia felt shocked at his compliment and, to her surprise, her skin began to heat beneath his scrutiny.

Having been hiding all day, Julia had had the benefit of hearing what the gossips had to say about the handsome viscount. It was none of it very flattering, though the younger ladies sounded more enthralled than horrified.

Still, the result was that she knew his character and she would do well to remember that.

"Thank you," she answered primly. But rather than put him off, her rigid answer seemed only to amuse him.

"Oh, Miss Channing, I do so look forward to getting to know you better," he said with a rakish wink before moving off to another part of the room.

She tried not to watch him. He towered over most of the other men in the room, his walk languid and graceful, like that of a panther.

He had danger stamped all over him and Julia would do well to heed that.

He turned then and caught her watching him, his icy blue eyes boring into her green ones.

Julia's heart raced in response.

This viscount was going to be trouble. Why then, did she

feel only excitement and not fear?

About the Author

Nadine Millard is a writer hailing from Dublin, Ireland. Although she'll write anything that pops into her head, her heart belongs to Regency Romance.

When she's not immersing herself in the 1800s, she's spending time with her husband, her three children, and her very spoiled Samoyed. She can usually be found either writing or reading and drinking way too much coffee.

BLUE TULIP

PUBLISHING

Printed in Great Britain
by Amazon.co.uk, Ltd.,
Marston Gate.